Praise for the Rogues' Dynasty series from *New York Times* and *USA Today* bestseller Amelia Grey

"Bewitching, beguiling, and unbelievably funny…absolutely enchanting and addictive."

—*Fresh Fiction*

"Deliciously sensual…storyteller extraordinaire Amelia Grey grabs you by the heart, draws you in, and does not let go."

—*Romance Junkies*

"Exemplifies the very essence of what a romance novel should be…superbly written."

—*Love Romance Passion*

"What a sinfully delicious read…completely beguiling and never misses a beat."

—*Book Junkie*

"A captivating mix of discreet intrigue and potent passion."

—*Booklist*

"The writing is fantastic, the plot thickens as the story progresses, and the characters are absolutely wonderful."

—*Long and Short Reviews*

Also by Amelia Grey

Dear Readers,

I hope you enjoy Race and Susannah's story as much as I enjoyed writing it.

While doing research for another book, I came across a scrap of information about the Talbot pearls and knew I wanted to write a story that included the famous necklace. History tells us that it was five strands of perfectly matched pearls, with each strand measuring thirty-two inches in length.

Finding out what actually became of the pearls proved harder than I thought. I found very little written about them, and they weren't found on any museum's list. My information has led me to believe that the pearls were eventually pawned or sold by family members after Lord Talbot's death.

All quotes from Lord Chesterfield at the start of each chapter are taken verbatim from his letters. However, throughout the book I attributed quotes to him he didn't say. I do this for entertainment, not to give credit where it isn't due.

I would like to thank organist extraordinaire Tommy Watts for help with the music terminology I used in this book and Susan Broadwater for help with researching the Talbot pearls.

I love to hear from readers. Please visit my website at ameliagrey.com or email me at ameliagrey@comcast.net.

Happy Reading,
Amelia Grey

ONLY A Duchess WOULD DARE

AMELIA GREY

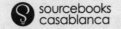

sourcebooks casablanca

Published by Sourcebooks Casablanca, an imprint of Sourcebooks
P.O. Box 4410, Naperville, Illinois 60567-4410
(630) 961-3900
sourcebooks.com

Originally published as *A Marquis to Marry* in 2009 in the United States
of America by Sourcebooks Casablanca, an imprint of Sourcebooks.

Printed and bound in Canada.
MBP 10 9 8 7 6 5 4 3 2 1

To my husband, Floyd, who is an unending source of encouragement by helping me in ways he never suspects.

One

My Dearest Grandson Alexander,

I am confident you will agree with these wise words from Lord Chesterfield: "At all events, a man had better talk too much to women, than too little."

Your loving Grandmother,
Lady Elder

ALEXANDER MITCHELL, THE FOURTH MARQUIS OF Raceworth, stared at the cards in his hands but his mind was on the surprisingly bold albeit beautiful Miss Maryann Mayflower. She sat beside him, slowly rubbing her foot up and down his leg. It was her second Season, and the talk around the clubs was that she would do anything to make a match before it ended.

That rumor gave Race pause, even though the invitation she issued under the table was tempting. He never minded a tryst in the garden from a willing miss, but he wasn't interested in getting caught in parson's mousetrap.

For the past three years, Race had held an afternoon card party in his garden during the Season. Only this year, the coveted outdoor event had to be moved inside because of a hellish rainstorm. The social gathering was so well attended he had to move the furniture out of his drawing room and the dining room and place it in other areas of the house so that he could accommodate the more than three dozen guests who had come to play whist, cribbage, and speculation.

"Excuse me, your lordship."

Race looked up at his housekeeper. "Yes, Mrs. Frost?"

"Could I have a word with you in private?"

The stocky-built woman was well-trained. She wouldn't interrupt him unless it was something important. "Of course, I'll be right with you."

He looked at the players at his table. There was the comely blonde who wasn't letting a little thing like a housekeeper standing so closely keep her from seducing him with her foot. The other lady at the table was the quite charming and unattached widow, Mrs. Constance Pepperfield, and the other gentleman of the foursome was his cousin Morgan, the ninth Earl of Morgandale.

Race laid his cards face down on the white linen-covered table. "Excuse me, ladies, Morgan. I have to bow out of this hand. As you know, this is the problem with being the host of a party."

"Must you?" Miss Mayflower asked, pouting.

"I'm afraid so," Race assured her pleasantly and moved his leg away from hers. "It seems that duty is calling me. Morgan, can I depend on you to charm the ladies while I'm away?"

"More than happy."

"Good. Ladies, I'll return shortly," Race said with a smile.

He then rose and went in search of Mrs. Frost. He found her in the vestibule, closing the front door.

"You needed to see me?"

"Yes, my lord," she said with a grimace on her plump face. "I'm sorry to disturb you, but I knew you would want to know that the Dowager Duchess of Blooming is here to see you."

Race's brows drew together. He didn't like surprises. "A dowager duchess to see me?"

"That's what the lady said."

Race started clicking off in his mind all the dowager duchesses he could remember and couldn't think of a reason any one them would come to see him. "I wonder what has brought her to my door."

"I have no idea, my lord."

Unlike his cousin Blake, the ninth Duke of Blakewell, who was notorious for forgetting appointments, Race knew every entry on his social calendar. He certainly would have remembered it if a dowager duchess had requested to call on him. But what was he going to do? He couldn't see her this afternoon. His house was stuffed with people chatting noisily around card tables.

"Where is Her Grace now?" Race asked Mrs. Frost.

"In her carriage. I didn't speak to her. The duchess sent her companion to the door to say she would appreciate a few minutes of your time, if you would be so kind." Mrs. Frost's eyes widened. "I told her you had a party going on. The companion apologized for the interruption and said Her Grace was content to wait in her coach until you are available to speak to her."

"That's odd," Race mumbled more to himself than to his housekeeper.

"It was a quick win for me after you left," Morgan said, walking up to Race. "Those two ladies don't know much about card games. I gave them both a cup of punch and told them I would check in with you to see if you wanted us to wait for you or find another partner. What's going on?"

Race stepped away from Mrs. Frost and in a low voice said, "I don't really know. The Dowager Duchess of Blooming is here to see me."

His cousin's blue eyes narrowed. "Good Lord, who is she?"

"The devil if I know." Race brushed his light brown hair away from his forehead and studied over her name, drawing a blank. "There are at least a dozen dukes, if not more. I'm not acquainted with all of them. And I certainly don't know how many dowagers there are."

"The area of Blooming is up near the Northern Coast," Morgan offered. "That must be the reason we're not familiar with the name."

"It would seem so, but I haven't a clue why the dowager would be here to see me."

"Maybe she was a friend of our grandmother's and wants to converse with you about her."

"Damnation, Morgan, I can't do that now with a house full of lively guests to entertain. She's come without an appointment and says she's willing to wait until I'm available to see her."

Morgan grinned. "And I can see you are on the verge of telling her just where she can wait."

Race smiled mischievously. "Tempted? Yes."

"But you won't. Our grandmother would roll over in her grave that you would even think of treating an older, titled or not, lady any way other than if she were a queen."

"Don't remind me," he grumbled, all good humor vanishing from his face. "Why wouldn't Her Grace do the proper thing and leave, and then later make an appointment to see me?"

"It tells me she wants to do more than just converse about our grandmother. Is there any chance she's here because you seduced one of her maids, or worse, one of her granddaughters?"

Race glared at his cousin but stayed silent.

"Blast it, Race, whoever it is you've taken to your bed, I suggest you turn on that charm you are so famous for and make amends right now. It's better to win her over upfront. She'll go easier on you if you have to ask her forgiveness later."

"Bloody hell, Morgan. I don't even know who she is, so how can I know if I've seduced someone she's related to?"

"Are you in any other kind of trouble that I don't know about?"

"No," Race stated, cocksure.

"Hmm," Morgan said and then added, "It's too bad Blake and Henrietta missed the party. With his being a duke, they would know exactly what is and what isn't acceptable in a situation like this."

"Why the devil isn't our cousin here? What's he doing today, anyway?" Race asked in an annoyed tone.

"He married Henrietta two weeks ago." An amused

twinkle danced in Morgan's bright blue eyes. "You figure out what he's doing on a rainy Sunday afternoon."

Race uttered a curse under his breath. "Oh, right."

"Where is Gibby? He's been around long enough he should know what to do."

"I don't know what he's up to. I received a short note from him earlier today saying he couldn't make it."

"So what are you going to do about the duchess? She's waiting to speak to you and you can't just leave her in her carriage. That's an outrage."

As much as Race didn't want to concede to Morgan or the dowager, his grandmother had raised him and his cousins to respect women. As inconvenient as it was now, he couldn't change his nature. And he had to admit that the woman had piqued his interest. While he'd had his share of unannounced females appear at his door, none of them had been old or titled.

"You know I'll do the proper thing," Race finally admitted.

He called to Mrs. Frost, who had remained silently by the front door. "Go out to the carriage and inform Her Grace that I insist she come in and join the party. If she refuses, which I expect she will, have some of the servants move enough furniture out of the music room to make a comfortable place for her to sit down. See to it that she is served tea and some of Cook's plum tarts, and tell her I'll make time to see her."

Race turned to Morgan and grinned. "Satisfied?"

"I am, but she'll probably think you've treated her atrociously. You know how fretful dowagers get when they feel they haven't been pampered and treated as if they were queens. She will probably tell everyone what a scoundrel you are." Morgan chuckled lightly. "And if she does that, you will be the talk of the ton after this little escapade."

"Most certainly," Race agreed. "No doubt it will give the scandal sheets a week's worth of articles if anyone finds out I've not rushed to do her bidding."

"Or more, and the gossipmongers will love you for it. A titillating story makes them money. And look on the bright side of this."

"Is there one?"

"Of course. This could encourage other ladies to arrive at your door unannounced."

"I don't see any harm in that as long as they are younger than a dowager."

Morgan clapped Race on the back, and they laughed as they rejoined the party.

Several games of cards and at least two glasses of wine later, Race was enjoying another good hand of cards at a table with two delightful young ladies and their father, when Morgan tapped him on the shoulder.

Race looked up at his cousin and frowned.

Morgan leaned down and whispered, "Have you met with the mysterious duchess?"

"Not yet," Race said, glancing down at the amazingly good hand he had been dealt. "I was giving her time to have a cup of tea."

Morgan cleared his throat and whispered, "She's been in the music room over an hour. I think her cup might be empty by now."

That got Race's attention. "Has it been that long?"

Morgan nodded. "She's probably fuming by now."

Race downed the remaining wine in his glass, and with a grimace asked his cousin, "Do you mind taking over this hand for me? Some problems just won't go away without a little push."

Once again, Race excused himself from the game and headed for his music room. Upon entering, he saw a prim-looking gray-haired woman dressed in black, sitting in a side chair with mountains of furniture piled up behind her.

Race stopped in front of her, bowed, and then took her hand and kissed it. "Your Grace, you should have joined us. I take it you aren't fond of cards, but I trust my servants have made every effort to keep you comfortable."

"Please, my lord, I am Mrs. Princeton." The tall woman rose and backed away from him while she curtsied. "May I present the Dowager Duchess of Blooming."

The woman pointed to a much younger lady who stood by the window, staring at him with an amused expression on her lovely face. Race's heart skipped a beat. The dowager was not an old, unattractive lady. She was a stunning beauty.

She walked toward him with a slow, confident stroll, stopping a respectable distance away. "You know, I've heard that about you," she said.

His stomach did a slow roll. "What's that?"

"That you can charm a leopard out of its spots and a nun out of her virtue."

Race raised one brow. "You shouldn't believe everything you read in the gossip pages."

"In your case, I think they may be right."

Race let his gaze slowly peruse her. He appreciated the fact that she looked him over as closely as he looked at her.

She had the prettiest eyes he'd ever seen. They were a light shade of green, large and expressive. She wore a forest-green traveling dress banded at the high waist by a black velvet ribbon. Her shiny, dark-brown hair was swept up to the top of her head with soft, wispy curls framing her face.

"Then tell me, Your Grace, are you a leopard or a nun?"

Mrs. Princeton gasped.

Race cleared his throat. For a moment, he'd forgotten the other woman was in the room.

The dowager quickly hid her grin behind her hand, not answering his question at first, but finally saying, "I can see you are surprised by my age, as most are," the duchess continued. "My husband died a short time after we married. His son from his first wife is now the Duke of Blooming, and he and his duchess reside at Chapel Glade in Blooming. I live nearby at Chapel Gate."

Her words brought to mind the vague memory of a young lady who married an older, reclusive duke because of an indiscretion. Could she be that lady?

"I see," he said. "I have to admit that you have caught me at a busy time, Your Grace, and I feel at a complete disadvantage."

"I'm sure that's not a place you often find yourself."

"To say the least."

Suddenly, that same amused smile played at her beautifully shaped lips again, and it irritated the hell out of him. So much for his and Morgan's thinking she'd be horrified at being left alone to sip her tea for the better part of an hour.

"Do you mind if we speak alone?" she asked.

She was full of surprises.

"No, of course not. I'm more than willing if you are sure you are comfortable with that."

"Your Grace?" the duchess's companion said, moving to stand closer to her. "Are you sure you want me to leave the room?"

"I am. The rain has stopped. Perhaps you could take a short walk in the garden."

"Yes, Your Grace." The woman's spine stiffened, and her shoulders lifted as she turned and marched out of the room.

The duchess turned back to him and smiled again. Race's heart fluttered so fast he felt thunderstruck. What the devil was that feeling all about? And why was he so sensitive to every move she made?

She was the most intriguing woman he'd ever met. And it had nothing to do with her being a duchess. Because of his cousin Blake, Race had been around dukes and duchesses all his life, and he wasn't awed by them as were most of the people in Polite Society. Her Grace's beauty was very appealing, but that wasn't what unnerved him, either. He often had the pleasure of spending time with beautiful women.

She unsettled him because of her poise, her self-confidence, her regal manner. She was simply alluring, and when he looked at her, he was completely enthralled. His fingers itched to touch her. He had never met anyone so captivating. Everything about her told him that with her, he had met his match.

"I believe I owe you an apology for arriving at your home unannounced."

"Why do I get the feeling you don't apologize often, Duchess?"

He saw a brief look of admiration flash in her eyes.

"I'm sorry that in my eagerness to speak to you I rushed right past my good sense as if I had none. I should have written and asked for an appointment to see you."

"That's difficult to dispute. I admit to being a little astonished that you didn't."

A soft smile lifted just one corner of her lips. "Only a little?"

She was teasing him. *All right, it surprised him a damned lot!*

The duchess was controlling their conversation, and he seldom let that happen with anyone other than his two cousins. She was too confident, too beautiful, and too desirable.

His gaze focused fully on hers, and in a more relaxed tone he said, "Tell me what I can do for you, Your Grace."

"I'm here because you possess something that belongs to my family, and I want it back now."

Race went still. That proclamation raised the hair on the back of his neck. He couldn't have been more shocked if she had suddenly slapped him.

What kind of accusation was that? You have something that belongs to my family, and I want it.

What astonishing nerve she had.

Race grinned, and then he laughed. She was truly an amazingly strong-willed lady who had no problem speaking her mind. He appreciated the courage he sensed in her, but he couldn't let her get away with being so brash.

His laughter caused the first crack in her overconfident demeanor. She bristled noticeably. It made him feel damned good to finally see her rattled.

"I'm sorry for laughing, Your Grace."

She lifted her chin a notch to counter his arrogance. "No, you aren't." Her voice was taut and steady. There was a determined set to her lips and genuineness in her eyes that gave him a moment's pause, but only a moment.

"All right, I'm not. I must admit you have amused me greatly."

Her stance changed from relaxed to rigid. She didn't care for what he said any more than he had liked what she had said. "I wasn't aware I had the capability to be so humorous, my lord," she said.

"Then allow me to enlighten you."

A couple of steps took him close enough to her that he could have touched her if he'd lifted his hands. He caught the scent of freshly washed hair and lightly perfumed skin. His body reacted strongly to her feminine draw.

He expected her to move away from him, but she stood her ground without flinching, and that impressed him all the more. He heard her labored breathing and for a moment he watched the rise and fall of her chest. She was so fascinating he found it difficult to concentrate on the matter at hand.

Yet he couldn't let her accusation that he had something that belonged to her family go unchallenged. That went against his easygoing nature.

His gaze swept up and down her face before settling on her gorgeous green eyes. Her breaths evened out, and he said, "First, you are certainly bold to walk in here and make such a claim. Second, I'm amused that you were so blunt. If you truly thought I had something that belonged to you, there are nicer ways to say it than 'It's mine and I want it back.' And third, Duchess, I don't have anything that belongs to your family. And even if I did have something of yours, I wouldn't turn it over to you simply because you demanded it."

He bent his head closer so that his nose almost touched hers. Only a couple of inches separated their mouths. The fragrant scent of mint tea lingered in the air. With great effort, he resisted the impulse to press his lips against hers and feel their softness.

In a husky voice he said, "And finally, Your Grace, just who the hell do you think you are to imply that I have stolen anything from your family?"

A light blush tinted her cheeks, but she didn't shrink from his nearness. Rather than his forward advancement intimidating her, she relaxed a little. Just enough to hint that he might have caused her a flash of compunction before she summoned an inner strength to carry her forward.

Her face remained dangerously close to his, but her courage didn't waver. "Your points are well-taken, and perhaps I should apologize once again. It wasn't my intention for you to feel I was accusing you of stealing anything from my family. I assure you that is not the case. I merely said you have it in your possession."

He heard sincerity in her voice, and that gave him some measure of assurance that she wasn't a madwoman or just trying to trick him. Whoever came up with this scheme had her convinced she spoke the truth.

"What is it that you think I have?"

Her eyes sparkled and softened. "Oh, I know you have them. The Talbot pearls."

Race's mouth tightened as his eyes narrowed. His grandmother, Lady Elder, had left him the priceless and coveted necklace in her will. Five perfectly matched strands of pearls, each strand measuring thirty-two inches.

His gaze scanned her face once again, looking for deception. "My grandmother's necklace?"

"*My* grandmother's pearls," she insisted.

Her courage was impressive, her beauty undeniable, but her assertion was troubling. Her bold gaze stayed locked on his. He appreciated the fact she looked him in the eyes and didn't cower under his nearness. She obviously wasn't lying. She actually believed what she was saying.

"Your audacity is almost as priceless as the pearls, but stand in line. You are the fourth person this month to approach me about the pearls. Though I admit none have come forward with as creative a claim as you."

Concern flared in her dark-lashed eyes. "What do you mean?" She reached down and picked up some folded sheets of paper from the table beside her and extended them to him. "I have with me documents proving the necklace belongs to my family."

Race didn't offer to take the folded sheets of aged parchment from her. "Interestingly enough, the gentlemen who have come before you are not as clever as you. They are not claiming ownership of the pearls. They are offering to buy them."

Her brow furrowed, and alarm etched across her face as she took a hesitant step toward him. "Who are these men?"

For the first time, Race sensed anger inside her, and it was seductive. Desire for her filled him once again. He wanted to pull her into his arms, crush her against his chest, and feel her soft, pliant lips beneath his in an eager kiss. He wanted to take her to his bed and unleash the passion he sensed inside her. That thought brought him up short.

He returned his thoughts to the matter at hand and said, "The first person to approach me was Mr. Albert Smith, a one-armed antiquities dealer, who wants them for an unnamed buyer. Does that unnamed person happen to be you, Duchess?"

She scoffed. "Absolutely not. I would never pay for what already rightfully belongs to my family."

"Then perhaps you are acquainted with Mr. Harold Winston. He is employed by the Prince himself. It seems that Prinny has long had his sights on the Talbot pearls. He wants to add the collar to His Majesty's Crown Jewels."

"That's absurd. The Crown already has more pearls, diamonds, and gems than all other countries put together, including Rome and the Catholic Church."

"Ah, then that leaves only the mysterious buccaneer, Captain Spyglass, who recently sailed into London on his extravagant ship, the *Golden Pearl*." Race tilted his head in puzzled consideration as his gaze settled on her green eyes once again. "I'm told he has mesmerized most of the ladies in Town. Perhaps you have formed an alliance with him?"

"I have read about the man, but know this, my lord, I have formed no alliance with anyone. Moreover, from what I have heard, Captain Spyglass is nothing but an unrepentant pirate."

"So some say," Race admitted.

"What does he want with the pearls?"

"No doubt to add to his vast collection. I'm told he's been acquiring pearls from all over the world and garnering quite the collection, from what I understand."

"Why is he buying pearls?"

Race bent his head closer to hers, and once again, she didn't flinch. He had to admit that most everything about her impressed him. She was too intelligent, too sensual, and too confident for her own good.

He eyed her skeptically as he whispered, "Are you sure you don't know, Duchess?"

"I can tell you only the truth. I have never met nor have I ever had dealings with Captain Spyglass or any of these men you speak of. These documents prove the Talbot pearls belonged to my grandmother. They were stolen from her more than twenty-five years ago."

He refused the papers yet again. He didn't know if he should believe her about any of the men in question. Though in truth it hardly mattered. He didn't know what kind of madcap scheme she had mulling in that pretty head of hers or why she had brought it to his door, but he wasn't interested.

"I see no significance to your having documents. They can be easily forged to look old or authentic. But know this, Your Grace, there is no way I'm selling the pearls to a one-armed antiquities dealer, a pirate, or the Crown. And I'm sure as hell not going to be bluffed out of them by a beautiful duchess."

Two

My Dearest Grandson Alexander,

What do you think about these wise words from Lord Chesterfield? "Take care never to seem dark and mysterious; which is not only a very un-amiable character, but a very suspicious one, too; if you seem mysterious with others, they will be really so with you, and you will know nothing."

Your loving Grandmother,
Lady Elder

SUSANNAH BROOKEFIELD, THE DOWAGER DUCHESS OF Blooming, had met her match, and he was standing before her, his nose to hers, in all his handsomeness. He was no ordinary man. Everything about him spoke of power, privilege, and wealth. The Marquis of Raceworth was just as she had imagined him: tall, self-confident, pleasing to look at, and terribly spoiled.

Not that she could really hold any of those things against him. Titled men were used to getting their way, but then she had to admit that so were most titled women, herself included, though she didn't used to be so headstrong. Sometimes fate caught you unaware and startled you, as happened to her almost a dozen years ago.

Her gaze slowly rose past his clean-shaven chin to lips

that were so masculine and so very close to her own that her heartbeat fluttered. She held her breath for a moment before looking into the most intriguing brownish-green eyes she had ever seen.

Susannah had long ago come to terms with her blemished reputation, and she hardly thought about it anymore. It was easy to forget the past when living in the quiet countryside, but here in London, where it happened, those old feelings of weakness and ridicule threatened to descend on her again. She would not let that occur. She would do what she must for her mother, but she would not fall victim to another charming, magnificent-looking man who set her heart to fluttering.

From somewhere deep inside herself, she found the strength to step away from Lord Raceworth and put a little distance between them before she asked, "Do you really think I would be here and subject myself to your scurrilous scrutiny if I was not certain the necklace belongs to my family?"

He gave her an indolent appraisal with his questioning gaze. She stood perfectly still, not saying a word as he studied her once again. She felt no guilt or shame when his gaze lingered for a few seconds on the swell of her breasts before returning to meet her stern stare once more.

"I don't know, Your Grace, because I don't know you. I have no idea what you are, or what you are not, capable of."

Susannah hoped neither of them would have to ever find out. But so much for thinking this man would quietly read the documents, understand that he had stolen property, and calmly return it to her with no fuss or controversy. She could see now that she had been too innocent and had expected too much from this powerful man who looked at her with such intense feeling in his eyes. She hadn't anticipated his strong attitude, though in retrospect she should have, considering his title. He obviously wasn't used to anyone taking him to task.

By the tightness around his mouth, she sensed he was growing weary of their conversation, but how could she give up so easily?

She took a deep breath and asked, "Do you mind telling me how your grandmother came to be in possession of the pearls?"

He took an unfriendly step toward her, once again closing the distance she had put between them. A quickening feeling she didn't quite understand started low in her abdomen and moved quickly to her breasts. She had to deny his strong appeal and remember the reason she was at his house. Her only interest in him was the pearls.

Not even the furrow on his brow could mar the attractiveness of his high cheekbones, well-defined lips, and his narrow, high-bridged nose. He stood straight, commanding, and powerful-looking. Thick light-brown hair was cropped short over his ears but fell longer and straight at his nape. And even with his elaborately-tied neckcloth and impeccably tailored coat, he somehow managed to look casually sophisticated.

"I don't feel it's necessary to assert my claim on them, and since I have no such inclination, I'll refrain and

simply say once again I do not intend to give up ownership of the necklace."

His condescension knew no bounds, but she wouldn't
let him intimidate her with his strength. She must fortify
herself with thoughts of her mother's wan face and dull
eyes, asking her to go to London, find the collar of pearls,
and return them to the family.

Susannah gripped her hands together behind her
back, hoping the marquis wouldn't notice the tension
inside her. Coming to London and approaching him
about the pearls was not something she had wanted to
do. For years, she had fiercely detested London Society
with its rigid rules and endless penchant for gossip. The
city held nothing for her but heart-wrenching memories
she had buried long ago. She had hoped never to return
and resurrect them.

"It's come to mind," the marquis said, "that maybe
you are mixing the Talbot pearls with the Countess of
Shrewsbury's. Both were extremely rare necklaces, and
I believe the countess had possession of both of them at
one time."

She glared at him and then gave him a humorless
smile. "I'm sure you don't really think that I don't know
the difference between the two necklaces."

He lifted one eyebrow again. "There was reason for
hope."

"I am familiar with the countess's pearls, my lord.
Her ropes consisted of five strands of perfectly matched
pearls as well, but I believe her ropes were much longer
than the Talbot pearls. And she bought them for herself,

one pearl at a time, as I believe those who have preserved her account books have authenticated. Last I heard, it was assumed that one of her daughters pawned her pearls for twenty-thousand pounds after her death, and they have not been seen since."

"You do know your pearls," he said with no real appreciation in his tone for her knowledge of the subject.

"Obviously, so do you."

For some reason, Susannah couldn't let this man get away with his unwavering arrogance. Not yet. Before leaving, she had to try one more time to get him to look at her proof. She would have to use a different approach, though. Obviously, something as simple as the plain truth and facts were not going to win him over. Perhaps she had been too bold and too outspoken in how she first broached the issue.

Trying to be more affable, she renewed her self-confidence with a deep breath and said, "I believe your grandmother, Lady Elder, left Valleydale to your cousin, the Earl of Morgandale. It borders the Morgandale lands, is that correct?"

A suspicious expression narrowed his eyes once again, and he shifted his stance. His black, fine wool coat stretched perfectly over his broad shoulders and chest. His sky-blue waistcoat with its gold-colored buttons fit seamlessly over a flat stomach and enhanced his slim hips. She didn't know why she noticed everything about him.

"That's right," he said cautiously.

"I had occasion to visit her at Valleydale shortly after my marriage."

He continued to eye her warily. His brow furrowed. "You met my grandmother?"

"Yes. Lady Elder was quite famous for her house parties."

"My grandmother was famous for many reasons."

Keeping her tone casual and her body relaxed, Susannah said, "Perhaps she was most noted for her long-standing friendship with Lord Chesterfield."

His expression softened, and he gave her a genuine smile. For some reason, it pleased her that he enjoyed talking about his grandmother. Susannah felt a little hope rising inside her that she might have found a chink in his armor. She had to be careful and not overplay her hand.

"No doubt she regaled you with many stories about the pompous man. She worshiped him and considered him the grand master of teaching a man how to be a gentleman."

"When I was with her, there was no doubt she was fond of Lord Chesterfield. She quoted him often. It was clear she missed him after his death."

"You don't know the half of it, Duchess," he said on a whispery breath.

"It is because of her that I am so familiar with Lord Chesterfield's letters to his son."

Lord Raceworth's expression turned quizzical. "You read them?"

She nodded. "Most of them, I believe. Though my thoughts are that if his son had still been living when they were first published, the poor man would be horrified to know that everything his father had written to him all those many years was available for anyone to read."

The marquis folded his arms across his chest and appeared to be studying her once again. "I agree concerning the son, but I think Lord Chesterfield would be pleased to know he lives beyond the grave through his egotistical, posturing letters to his son."

Susannah smiled at him and realized how wonderful it was to converse with him when they were on a neutral subject. In this composed atmosphere, she found him utterly charming. She considered it a good sign that the marquis was continuing to talk to her and had not yet dismissed her from his home.

"Your other cousin, the Duke of Blakewell, recently married. I read in the *Times* that his duchess is a lovely young lady, new to London, I believe."

The marquis stepped closer to her again. His head dipped lower, bringing his lips almost to the point of touching hers.

A tempting, roguish grin lifted the corners of his lips. Her breathing became shallow, and her heart thudded wildly in her chest as he whispered, "All true, Your Grace, but telling me how much you know about my grandmother and my cousins and even Lord Chesterfield and his letters does not tell me anything about you."

If possible, Susannah planned to keep it that way, but looking at him now she knew it wouldn't be easy. His brownish-green eyes turned dark and dreamy. Susannah's stomach tightened. Somehow, she must fight her immense attraction to him.

Perhaps this was the time to leave. He probably wanted time to look into this matter about the pearls for himself. She had no doubt that he would inquire about her before they met again. And they would meet again. Something told her he was not a man to let a claim such as hers hang in the air unresolved for too long.

She had learned a lot in the years since her husband had died. Other than independence, the main thing she had mastered was when to back away from an argument and return another day, refreshed.

Susannah stepped away from the marquis and turned to the chair where Mrs. Princeton had been sitting among the stacked furniture and picked up her bonnet, cape, gloves, and the documents.

"I've kept you too long from your guests, and there is no more for me to say today except to tell you that I've leased a house not far from here."

He cast a curious glance her way. "Really?"

"Yes, number 12 Woodlawn."

Disbelief lit his eyes. He pointed toward the back window with his thumb and said, "The next street over?"

"Yes, in fact my house is directly behind yours." She paused and took in a moment of pleasure at the surprised look on his face.

It was sheer luck that of all the houses for lease in Mayfair, one of them was directly behind Lord Raceworth's town house. At first she had declined even to consider the house, as she had no desire to be anywhere near the man who held what her mother desperately wanted. In the end, she had decided there might be some advantages to being so close to him and had decided to lease the house.

"My guess is there are less than a hundred yards of gardens and a thick row of tall yew between our two houses," Susannah continued. "When you change your mind and decide you want to look over the documents I have, you'll know where to find me."

He almost smiled. "So you think I'm going to change my mind?"

"There's always reason to hope," she said, echoing one of his earlier statements.

The sudden sparkle in his eyes let her know he knew what she was doing.

She gave him a single nod, started to walk away, but suddenly stopped and said, "If for some reason you should decide you want to sell the pearls to one of these three men you mentioned, would you notify me before you call on the gentlemen?"

He stared at her for a long moment, taking stock of the sudden change in her position. "What happened to the lady who said she would never pay for what rightly belonged to her family?"

"My lord, have no doubt that she is standing right in front of you," she argued. "However, I would pay for the collar before I would see it fall into the hands of someone like Captain Spyglass, the antiquities dealer you mentioned, or the prince."

The marquis looked at her from guarded eyes. "I'll give you that much. I will notify you first if I ever have any intention to get rid of the pearls, but, Duchess, don't count on that happening."

She glanced down at the papers in her hands and

then quickly back up to the marquis. "I must ask before I leave, have you no natural curiosity about what these documents say?"

"None whatsoever, but I do have an interest in you."

She gave herself time for his words to register, and then she smiled. "Ah, now I remember why I've stayed away from London the past twelve years."

"Has it been that long since you've been here?"

"Almost to the day."

"I have a vague memory of a young lady marrying an older duke shortly after the Season began. That was probably about twelve years ago. Was that you?"

"Possibly. I married and immediately went to Chapel Glade in Blooming. I've not kept up with the comings and goings of London Society until recently."

"When you heard that I have the Talbot pearls."

"Yes. My mother read about them in the newsprint."

"I remember when the gossip pages decided everyone should know what my grandmother left to me. But tell me, you say your husband died shortly after you married him?"

He was turning the conversation back to her again, but she didn't really mind. "We were together a little more than a year before he passed away of fever."

"I'm sorry."

"It was a long time ago, my lord. No condolences are necessary."

"Something tells me you want to avoid more questions about yourself."

And he had left no doubt he wanted to ask more.

People always did when they saw how young she was for a dowager duchess, but she had told him enough.

"You seem more than willing to talk about me but not the pearls. Why is that?"

"Quite frankly, Your Grace, you are a lot more intriguing than five strands of pearls, but something tells me you aren't about to fill in the answers to any of the questions running around in my head."

For some ridiculous reason, it thrilled her that he was full of curiosity about her. Perhaps it was good that he was. Maybe she could hold his interest until he became reasonable and decided to look at her documents.

"Thank you for making time for me. I'll let you get back to your guests. Don't worry about seeing me out. I'll find Mrs. Princeton and be on my way."

Head held high, she walked past him, assuming all had been said, but when she reached the door she heard, "Your Grace?"

She stopped. Her heart hammered in her chest. Her stomach quaked. Maybe he would look at her papers after all. She exhaled slowly and turned back to him.

"Yes, my lord?"

He gave her a knowing smile. "It was a pleasure meeting you."

Her body went rigid. That's all?

It was a pleasure meeting her?

He knew she expected more from him than that when he called her name and stopped her. Was he amusing himself with her again?

"Likewise," she said.

His brownish-green eyes twinkled as he said, "You know, you never told me whether you were a leopard or a nun. Should I feel safe knowing you are now living in my neighborhood, or should I feel threatened?"

Susannah held her breath for a moment and weighed her answer carefully before saying, "Perhaps I am both, my lord, and perhaps you should feel both."

The marquis gave her an easy, generous smile. It was so engaging, it took her breath away. Oh, goodness, she didn't want to be smitten by him. Fate couldn't be that cruel to her again to let her fall for another handsome scoundrel.

"Good day, my lord," Susannah said and walked out to find Mrs. Princeton.

———

Race watched the duchess walk out of the music room in a swish of green skirts. He laughed under his breath and then whispered to himself, "What a lady."

She had enough courage to back any man, including himself, into a corner and make him happy she'd put him there. When had he ever been so intrigued, so fascinated by a woman? How long had it been since he'd been instantly attracted to a woman, as he was to the duchess? He wanted to know more about her. He wanted to see her again, and she knew it. Was that why she was being so evasive? She wasn't going to tell him everything about herself at one time. She wanted him to dig a little, as she had about him, and find out about her on his own. But why? Was it as simple as wanting him to be drawn to the mystery surrounding her? If so, it had worked.

Surely she knew it challenged him, but maybe she didn't know that he had never met a challenge he didn't accept and win.

He was still pondering her pronouncement that his grandmother's pearls belonged to her family. But what surprised him more than that was the intensity with which she appealed to him. He hadn't been that instantly attracted to a woman in years. He had seriously considered kissing her when their faces were so close he felt her minty breath on his cheek.

Why hadn't he kissed her? It wasn't as if she was an innocent miss who'd never been kissed. She'd been married. Had she had lovers in these past eleven years? Did she have one now? His gut tightened, and he pushed that kind of thought from his mind. Even if she did have a lover, he was aching to get her beneath him on a soft bed.

What kind of bewitching hold did she have on him?

"Race, I saw Her Grace pass by the drawing room on her way to the front door," Morgan said, sauntering into the music room. "She wasn't with you very long. What did she want?"

Race had to shake his head to clear his mind of his wayward imagination. "She wants the Talbot pearls."

"Grandmother's necklace? Just like the men who have been to see you recently?"

Race nodded.

"How much did she offer you for the pearls? I'd guess a lot more than Mr. Winston or Mr. Smith wanted to pay. The pirate offered you the most, right?"

"She made no offer," Race answered, still deep in thought over the fascinating woman.

Morgan flashed Race a bewildering glance. "Nothing? That doesn't make sense."

"She says the necklace was stolen from her family more than twenty-five years ago, and she wants me to give it back."

Morgan's eyes widened. "What bloody nerve," he exclaimed. "I hope you told her where she could go, and that place is a damned lot hotter than her fancy carriage in the heat of summer."

"Not exactly."

"Well, you should have." Morgan paused. "You look pensive. What are you thinking?"

"Do you know where our grandmother got the pearls?"

Morgan rubbed his chin and studied over the question. "No, can't say I do. There was never a reason to ask. She seldom wore them."

"That is what I'm thinking, too. I can remember her wearing them only at private dinner parties in her home."

"I think you may be right about that. I haven't thought about the pearls in years. Not until her will was read and they were left to you. Why do you ask? Did the duchess accuse Grandmother of stealing them?"

Race quickly shook his head. "She didn't go that far, but she did ask me how Grandmother obtained possession of them."

"I'm sure one of her four husbands must have given them to her," Morgan offered.

"Probably."

"Or, knowing our grandmother, she could have bought them from someone for herself."

"That's very likely, too. We both know how she had a penchant for going after any anything she wanted."

"Maybe Gibby will know for sure," Morgan suggested. "Ask him."

"I will."

"Have you heard again from any of the men who wanted to buy the necklace?"

"I hope I made it clear that I didn't want to hear from them again," Race said firmly.

"Any chance you think the duchess is working with one of them?"

Race shrugged. "It crossed my mind, and I questioned her about that. She denies any knowledge of them. She seems very believable to me about that, but I can't say anything for certain."

Morgan seemed to study over their conversation thoughtfully. "Maybe there is something about the pearls you don't know."

"Like what?" Race asked.

Morgan blinked slowly, and then his eyes narrowed. "I don't know. Maybe they were stolen. There has to be an underlying reason for the sudden interest in the necklace. It's just too coincidental that four people have come to you in the past month, wanting the pearls."

"I agree that it's unusual. How about the fact the pearls are old, extremely rare, and there are probably more than six hundred pearls on the five strands? The duchess said she wasn't aware of where the pearls were until it was written in the *Times* that they were left to me. Mr. Winston said the same. I remember that somehow it was leaked to the scandal sheets that you were left Valleydale and I was given the pearls."

"I remember when that happened. So you are thinking that nobody but our family, and maybe a few friends, knew Grandmother had the necklace until a few weeks ago?"

"That we know of."

Morgan sidestepped some furniture and walked over to the window. He pushed the floral-printed drapery panel aside. "I see the duchess walking to her carriage."

Race saw the desire for Her Grace in his cousin's eyes, and he was struck with sudden jealousy. That took him aback. He'd never objected to one of his cousins vying for the same young miss, lady, or mistress as he. He often welcomed it just for the challenge. But somehow with this woman, Race felt differently about that.

Morgan turned back to him. "Who is her companion?"

Why was Morgan asking about the older woman?

"I think her name is Mrs. Princeton. Why?"

"She must be widowed if she's a companion."

"I have no idea, Morgan. I wasn't exactly interested in the woman."

"I don't see why not. She's absolutely stunning. Perhaps I'll find out more about Mrs. Princeton while you find out about the duchess."

Suddenly it dawned on Race that Morgan was making the same mistake he had, thinking the older woman was the duchess and the younger her companion.

Race laughed. "You have it wrong, as I did in the beginning. The Dowager Duchess of Bloomfield is the younger, beautiful lady. Her companion is the older, gray-haired woman, Mrs. Princeton."

Morgan glanced back at him and grinned as he let the drapery panel fall back to its rightful place. "You blackguard, you can't fool me."

"I'm not trying to, Cousin. The younger lady is the dowager duchess. She was very vague about her past, and I didn't press her, but do you remember something about a young miss being hastily married off to an older, reclusive duke about twelve years ago?"

Morgan's brow furrowed deeply. "I'm not bringing anything to mind. Why? Did that happen to her? Was she caught dallying with a blade and then forced to marry someone else?"

"Possibly, I really don't know her story, yet."

Morgan pushed a small table and two chairs aside to get to a sideboard that held a crystal decanter of brandy. He poured a splash into two glasses, and giving one to Race, he quipped, "You intend to find out for sure, don't you?"

Race clicked his glass against Morgan's. "Of course," he answered, leaving out the fact Her Grace all but challenged him to do it.

Morgan smiled ruefully. "I see she has intrigued you."

Race shrugged and sipped his brandy. It was more than just her beauty that drew Race, but he wasn't about to admit anything.

"Perhaps I should go see her and tell her I'm the only one who can talk you into giving her the pearls."

Race stiffened. Cousin or not, he would not have Morgan near her.

Without fear or humor, Race said, "Don't even consider paying her a visit."

Morgan searched Race's face with his cool blue gaze. Race remained firm. He didn't want to fight his cousin about this, but he would if he had to.

"All right, all right," Morgan relented, lifting his hands in surrender. "I agree she is all yours."

Race relaxed. Morgan was smart enough to know that with this woman, Race didn't want any competition.

"So tell me, what proof did she offer to back up her claim about the pearls?"

"Some documents."

"What did they say?"

"I never looked at them."

Admiration shone in his cousin's eyes, yet he asked, "Was that wise?"

"What do you think?"

Morgan grinned as he leaned against a side table. "I think it gives you reason to see her again, if you decide that's what you want to do."

"And I might decide to look at the documents because…?" Race asked.

"Because she has fascinated you beyond your wildest dreams, and it's been a long time since a woman has caught your interest with such astounding zeal."

Race gave a short laugh and then took a long sip of the brandy. He wasn't surprised that it didn't take long for Morgan to see right through him.

"Is there anything you would like me to do? I could talk to Gibby or make some inquiries for you?"

"I want to take care of this myself."

"Understood. But keep in mind it might be wise to find out more about her before you get much further along in this intrigue. There must be a reason for all this sudden interest in the pearls."

"Instinct tells me it is only greed and lust."

Morgan laughed at Race's assessment. "Probably. I would think Blake knows the current Duke of Blooming, so Blake might have some information on her, as well. You should at least find out if she's actually who she says she is and not just someone out to create mischief."

Race shrugged. "I'm not sure I want to go that fast. I might take my time and first hear most of the story from her. And then I'll go to Gib and to Blake to see if what they have to say about her agrees with what she says."

"If that's the case, I'll leave it all to you." Morgan drained his glass and then clapped Race on the back. "Let's go back to the party and not think any more today about a beautiful duchess or strands of pearls."

"I'm with you on that," Race said, walking with Morgan back into the drawing room that was filled with fetching young ladies eager to impress the marquis and the earl with their beauty and card-playing skills.

But Race's mind had room for only one lady: the intriguing duchess.

Three

My Dearest Alexander,

I cannot improve upon these words from Lord Chesterfield: "Pray remember to part with all your friends, acquaintances, and mistresses, if you have any, in such a manner as may make them not only willing but impatient to see you again."

Your loving Grandmother,
Lady Elder

SUSANNAH SAT AT THE SMALL DESK IN HER BEDROOM of the leased home, reading over the letter she'd just written to her mother. Several false starts lay crumpled on the floor beside her. She knew her mother would be impatiently waiting to hear that Susannah had made contact with the gentleman who had the pearls. That had happened three days ago, but every time she had attempted to write her mother since then, words had failed her.

At last, she'd been able to complete the letter. Though she didn't tell her mother everything about the marquis, Susannah felt comfortable telling her mother that Lord Raceworth was easily the most handsome and the most arrogant man she had ever met. She could have added that he was also the most infuriating, stubborn, and confusing man she had ever met, too. Instead, she ended by reassuring her mother that she would obtain the pearls, but it might take longer than she had expected.

Susannah had worded the letter as carefully as possible, not wanting her mother to worry more than she already was. After a lifetime of excellent health, her mother had suddenly taken to her bed and seldom came downstairs any more.

As her mind drifted back to the intriguing marquis, Susannah leaned back in her chair. No, he wasn't confusing. It was Susannah who was confused by the feelings he'd stirred inside her when she had looked at him and when he'd looked at her. She'd been bemused by how fast her heart beat, how shallow her breath became, and how hot curls of desire had tightened her abdomen and skittered across her breast when he was so close their noses almost touched.

At one point when she was with him, she had thought he was going to kiss her and for one madcap moment she had wanted him to. Thank God he hadn't, and she had avoided that mistake. She had been so taken with him that day she probably would have let him. What a disaster that would have been.

Susannah squeezed her eyes shut for an instant as she tried to force that dizzying memory from her thoughts. She obviously wasn't on his mind. It had been three days since she had met the marquis and she hadn't heard one word from him, but that hadn't kept her from thinking about him. And she had thought for sure she would have heard something from him by now.

She was trying hard not to be attracted to the man, but so far she hadn't had much success. Maybe she thought about him so often simply because he hadn't behaved in the way she had expected.

But too, it was more than that.

The marquis had unleashed an assortment of perplexing sensations in her as well as a muddle of emotions that she had wanted to keep hidden in her past. He was a fascinating man. A desirable man. That should be reason enough for her to find a way to banish him from her thoughts. She wanted to have contact with him only concerning the pearls.

Most of the gentlemen who had approached her since her husband's death, wanting to win her favor, were in such awe of her being a duchess that she had no interest in them whatsoever. Susannah had vowed to keep it that way, much to Mrs. Princeton's chagrin, but one visit with Lord Raceworth and already her resolve was weakening.

Susannah sighed and picked up the letter to her mother and read it again. Satisfied that she had worded it to give the best possible scenario for what would surely prove to be a major uphill battle, Susannah folded the two pieces of vellum and laid them aside.

She glanced around the room that would be her bedchamber for the next few weeks. Early afternoon sunlight streamed through the parted draperies of windows that flanked each side of the simple, spool-turned bed. A sky-blue brocade slipper chair, cozy for curling up and reading during the long evenings, stood in one corner, while her many books were stacked neatly on a bookshelf beside it. The dressing table with its lovely aged-lace skirt and dainty oval mirror was old but serviceable. Over the mantel hung a painting of a beautiful brown-haired little girl, laughing happily as a spaniel puppy licked her chin. The one large piece of furniture in the room was the wardrobe, but big as it was it hadn't held all the clothing her maid had packed for her.

The house wasn't spacious or extravagant in furnishings, and the grounds and garden were in sad, neglected shape. But the value of this property was not in what it afforded but where it was located. The worth in this house was that only a tall hedge of yew and less than a hundred yards of gardens separated her from Lord Raceworth's house and the pearls her mother desired.

Susannah could easily have afforded a much more elaborate place to live. Not only had her father been very mindful of her future in arranging the marriage contracts to her advantage, her husband had been very generous to her in his will. Even her husband's son was kind to her, and she had not wanted for anything since her husband's death.

While in the hectic city of London, Susannah would miss daily visits with her mother and the quiet life they lived in Chapel Gate. She had little desire to become involved in the busy Society life of the Season. She would stay occupied with needlework and reading. She would also look into the possibility of leasing a pianoforte so she could play in the afternoons as twilight descended on the neighborhood.

But right now, Susannah was daydreaming about a handsome gentleman and wondering why she had agreed to come to London and see this error made right. She had suggested to her mother that their solicitor approach the marquis about the pearls. But her mother had insisted Susannah do it, and she had agreed because she loved her mother and wanted to please her. After Susannah's father had died, her mother came to live with her. Madeline Parker had been a tremendous source of comfort and company for her these many years. It was the least Susannah could do for her.

Susannah closed her eyes again and envisioned herself back at Chapel Gate with its grand view of lush gardens dotted with hidden nooks, beautiful waterfalls, impressive fountains, and natural vistas. Suddenly, Lord Raceworth was walking beside her as they stepped on cobblestone walkways and threaded their way through a field of sky-blue flowers. They were laughing and holding hands. His face bent closer and closer to hers until...

A knock at her open door brought Susannah out of her daydreaming. She glanced up to see Mrs. Princeton standing in the doorway.

Clearing her throat and her mind of such fanciful notions, Susannah said, "Yes?"

"I'm sorry to disturb you, Duchess, but the Marquis of Raceworth is below stairs in the vestibule. He asked me to give you this."

A rush of excitement filled Susannah's chest and it tightened. He'd come just when she was beginning to think she would have to make the next move. Afraid even to speculate on what the note might say, she rose and quickly took the folded paper, and turning away from Mrs. Princeton she opened it. Written in bold black lettering were the words:

> Duchess,
>   I want you to join me for a ride in Hyde Park. If you are otherwise presently entertained, I shall wait in my carriage until you are available to join me.
>   Race

Susannah gasped in surprise as a new appreciation for the marquis filled her with a sudden, eager anticipation.

She turned and looked at her companion. "What nerve that man has," she exclaimed in a whispered voice, letting the note flutter to the top of her desk.

"What's the matter?" Mrs. Princeton asked, her soft brown eyes rounding in concern.

Susannah took a deep, steadying breath, her mind whirling with possibilities. "That man is unbelievably brash."

"What did he say to you, Your Grace? Has he been horribly rude to you?"

"No, no, Mrs. Princeton, nothing like that. In a most informal manner, the marquis has invited me to go for a ride in Hyde Park with him. No, not invited," Susannah amended, "it's more an order."

Mrs. Princeton's expression relaxed from concern to almost a smile. "I don't see that as being brash, Your Grace. It's perfectly acceptable for a gentleman to ask a lady to go for a ride in the park with him."

"Of course it is," Susannah said, trying to tamp down the thrills of joy filling her. "It's not what he says but how he says it that puts me in a dither. He writes that he understands if I am busy at the moment. He is happy to sit in his carriage and wait until I'm available to go with him."

The skin around Mrs. Princeton's eyes crinkled and she laughed softly. But seeing the annoyed expression on Susannah's face at her mirth, she quickly composed herself.

"I'm sorry, Your Grace, I didn't mean to be disrespectful."

Susannah smiled. "Don't be ridiculous, Mrs. Princeton. I know exactly why you find humor in his note. He is treating me exactly the way I treated him a few days ago. I would laugh, too, if I weren't so provoked by it. I can see that he has decided to play my game and annoy me. And I'm quite sure he thinks he will win in the end."

The older woman, whom Susannah sometimes treated more like an older sister than a paid companion the past ten years, faced her once more. "Thank you, Your Grace. As you know, I do worry sometimes that I overstep my place."

"And you know you have no reason to censor your words when you talk to me. Sometimes I need your perspective, whether or not I solicit it, want it, or use it."

"In that case, I will tell you that I think it is a splendid idea that he wants to take you for a ride in the park, and I think you should go."

Susannah pursed her lips for a moment and looked at Mrs. Princeton. "Are you thinking of trying to be a matchmaker once again?"

Mrs. Princeton lifted her sharp chin and sniffed. "Absolutely not. You have chided me too many times on that account, and I have promised never to do it again."

"Good," Susannah said, but wasn't sure she believed the woman who had once told her that her greatest sorrow in life was that after her husband died, she never remarried and had children.

Relief washed over Mrs. Princeton's face, and she asked, "Do you think his invitation means that he is ready to look at the documents you have?"

Susannah folded her arms across her chest and drummed her fingers on her arms. "I seriously doubt it. I think he simply wants to let me know that he can play my game as well as I can. The problem is that this is truly not a game with me. The pearls rightfully belong to my mother, and I'm determined not to leave London without them. Unfortunately, rather than simply enlightening Lord Raceworth to the truth as I had hoped, I only amused him."

"I'm sure that is not the case," Mrs. Princeton argued as she brushed aside a tight curl of hair that kept falling across her forehead.

"I'm sure it is," Susannah corrected her. "I should have known that in London the title dowager duchess would not carry the enormous prestige and intimidation it does in smaller villages like Chapel Glade. I miscalculated that point, and I'm going to have to rethink some things."

"In that case, a ride in the park with him will not be so bad."

That's the problem. It wouldn't be bad at all.

"But you know I didn't come to London to be drawn into Polite Society with all its rigid rules and fierce machinations. I have done that and have no desire to get caught up in it again."

Mrs. Princeton rubbed the palms of her hands down the sides of her black dress. "It's just a ride in Hyde Park, Your Grace."

"In any other town or village, perhaps. Not so in London. It is more than that. The park is a place where the elite of Society gather to praise themselves and ridicule everyone else. Polite Society and the ton are nothing but organized madness."

"And you must live on the fringe of that madness for a time, but don't fret, Your Grace. I believe in the end you will convince Lord Raceworth to do the right thing by your family and return the pearls."

Susannah remained quiet and thoughtful, letting her companion's words sink in.

"Does your silence mean I should tell the marquis you are unavailable and ask him to make an appointment to come back at another time?"

Those fluttery butterfly feelings started in her chest again. Why did just the possibility of seeing him thrill her so?

Susannah looked at her companion and smiled. "Absolutely not. I'm going to look at this as an opportunity to have Lord Raceworth examine the documents I have. I shall take them with me."

She walked over to one of the windows flanking the bed and looked out. From the second floor window, she could see the entire back of the marquis's house and his expertly tended lawn. She must have stared at his house a hundred times since she had moved in a week ago. Occasionally, she had been tempted to sneak over in the late afternoon and smell the delicate petals of the fabulous pink roses that were the masterpiece of his exceptional garden, but of course she hadn't dared invade his privacy.

The grounds of her leased house were in great need of care, with weeds, flowers, and shrubs growing haphazardly wild. Perhaps she would hire someone to make them lovely for her, and yes, she would get a pianoforte, even if she had to buy one. Playing music at the end of the day had always soothed her, even during her most difficult times. Since it appeared she could be in London for quite some time, she might as well make the house and grounds as pleasing as possible.

Lord Raceworth had asked her for a ride in the park, and she would go, but only because her mother was ill and wanting to reclaim the Talbot pearls for the family before she died. Susannah must keep that uppermost in her mind and forget that thrill of anticipation that curled low in her abdomen.

Feeling more confident, she turned back to Mrs. Princeton. "I realize now that I was naive to think the marquis would simply look at the documents, authenticate them, and give me the pearls so I can be on my way."

Mrs. Princeton agreed with a nod and said, "So what are you going to do, Your Grace?"

"Whatever I have to," Susannah answered. "I realize now that mother asked me to do this, I should have insisted that our solicitor handle it. No doubt the marquis wouldn't be playing games with a man. He would have accepted the documents to read, examined them carefully, and made an intelligent decision."

"You can still turn this over to a solicitor, can't you?"

Could she?

No matter her frustration, Susannah had found pleasure in sparring with the marquis. He was charming and challenging, and for the first time since she was eighteen, she was drawn to a man. She had enjoyed matching wits with him. She hadn't wanted to be captivated by him, but she was. She hated like Hades to admit that to herself, and she would never admit it to anyone else.

"He would probably respect a man more than a woman," she said to Mrs. Princeton.

"That is probable."

"But no one can argue our rightful claim to the pearls as efficiently as I can because I'm more passionate about having them returned to my family."

Mrs. Princeton nodded. "You are your best ally."

"I will accept his invitation and go for a ride in the park with him."

Mrs. Princeton folded her hands together in front of her. Looking quite satisfied, she said, "I suppose you will, but there is one other good thing about this, Your Grace."

"I can't think what that might be."

"Lord Raceworth is a handsome man and not an old or ugly one."

Susannah laughed. "You are right about that, Mrs. Princeton, but I'm not so sure that is a good thing for me."

"Of course it is. You are still a young and beautiful

woman. You need to be interested in a dashing young man like the marquis. You need to remarry and have children."

"This is not a conversation I want to have with you today, Mrs. Princeton."

She took a step back and said, "My apologies, Your Grace."

"Accepted. Now go tell Lord Raceworth that I will be down in an hour. Make sure you give him a cup of tea with a sprig of mint in it, and whatever kind of tart or sweet cake you have in the kitchen."

"An hour, Your Grace?" her companion questioned.

"Yes. He will understand that it's the same amount of time he kept me waiting when I was at his house and in far less generous surroundings. If he's going to play my game, he is going to find out that he must use my rules."

Four

AS SOON AS SUSANNAH'S COMPANION WAS GONE, SHE took a deep breath and plopped onto the chair at her desk. She was annoyed yet relieved. She was pleased Lord Raceworth had finally come but rather frustrated that she must bow to his wishes for a ride in the park.

Susannah had to do something other than be anxious while she waited until time to meet the marquis, so she changed into a pale pink dress with a sensible bodice, trimmed with delicate white lace at the neckline and high waist. She fastened a delicately styled ruby necklace around her throat and added matching earrings. She reworked the chignon at her nape and rubbed lavender-scented lotion on her hands and face.

When the hour was up, she squared her shoulders, lifted her chin, and took in a deep breath before entering the small, sparsely decorated sitting room. The marquis rose from his chair and bowed. Her breath caught in her throat and she went still.

He was too handsome for words with his rakish long hair and impeccable dress. If possible, the over-the-knee Hessian boots he wore made him look all the more powerful, more roguish, and more handsome than when she'd first seen him in more formal attire. She couldn't keep the dizzying beat of her heart from pounding.

She quietly cleared her throat and said, "My lord, this is a surprise."

His eyebrows drew together while a half grin lifted one corner of his mouth. Cautiously, he said, "Is it really? I thought you issued an invitation for me to stop by for a visit."

She willed herself to relax and be natural, even though his charming manner didn't make that easy. All of her senses were on high alert.

Calmly clasping her hands in front of her, she said, "I issued an invitation for you to stop by and view the documents I have, showing my family's ownership of the Talbot pearls, not to invite me for a ride in the park."

He faked a frown as his generous lips curved into another slight grin. "Ah, I must have misunderstood. I didn't remember there was a qualifier attached to your invitation. But it is a beautiful afternoon, and my carriage is outside, complete with a basket filled with wine, cheese, and curried apples. What do you say?"

Her resistance melted like spring snowflakes in the April sun. "I say what lady can resist curried apples? I'll get my cape and parasol, and of course the very important documents in case you decide you would like to review them while we are out."

"Fair enough."

The marquis followed her to the vestibule where Mrs. Princeton was waiting with Susannah's outdoor things, including a pink velvet drawstring reticule with several sheets of rolled papers sticking out of the top. At the carriage, Lord Raceworth took hold of her gloved hand and helped her step up and into the curricle. His grip was firm, masculine, and a tingle of something wonderful radiated throughout her body.

She made herself comfortable on the far side of the seat and neatly arranged the skirts of her dress while he climbed up beside her.

She popped open her dainty parasol, which was trimmed with pale pink flowers and ribbons to match her dress. Years ago, she learned that the parasol was good not only for keeping the sun off her face, but she could easily lower it from one side to the other so that it would be impossible for anyone to see her face when she passed by. She had no plans to do that today. She had no idea if anyone would remember her fall from grace twelve years ago. She had been gone so long that it was probably foolish of her to think anyone would recognize her at all, or that they would point a finger of shame at her if they did.

Susannah had told herself for years that she could no longer be hurt by Polite Society, and that was still the case. She had paid her debt to the unforgiving upper class by marrying the duke.

The marquis was right. It was a beautiful day, and she was delighted to be out of the house and in his company. Spring had been long in coming to England this year, but it had finally arrived. The wide expanse of blue sky didn't have a cloud in sight. The air had lost its chill, and there was a clean and fragrant scent to the breeze. The trees and shrubs had fresh green leaves covering their branches. Signs of spring were everywhere, and all indications were that winter had disappeared.

Lord Raceworth picked up the ribbons and released the brake handle. He clicked the ribbons on the horses' rumps, and the two bays took off with a jerk, jingle, and a clank of harness. Rather than guiding the horses along at a brisk pace, he had them walking along the streets of Mayfair as if they had all day to dally rather than only half an afternoon.

As they rode along, Susannah remembered the last time she traversed the streets of London in an open carriage. She was with the man she loved, and at the time thought he loved her. Suddenly she shivered.

"Are you all right?" Lord Raceworth asked.

Susannah looked over at the marquis, and somehow she knew he was nothing like Lord Martin Downings. She smiled at Lord Raceworth and confidently said, "Yes, I'm fine."

And she was. She hadn't intended for it to happen when she came to London, but just the same she was doing more than just trying to recover the pearls for her mother. She was exorcizing some old ghosts that had haunted her for years. It had taken time, but she had finally forgiven herself for being young and foolish. She was ready to forget the past, forget the last time she was in London. She was no longer a young miss with a tender heart.

"You're very quiet," he said after they had ridden in silence for a while.

She looked at him from underneath the parasol. "So are you."

"Me?" He threw her a questioning glance. "I thought I was being considerate. I got the impression you wanted to be alone with your thoughts."

"I was simply enjoying the afternoon ride."

"You know, for a few moments back there at your house, I thought the dour Mrs. Princeton was going to come with us."

A smile came easily to her lips. "Really?"

"It crossed my mind when I saw her waiting by the door like a Roman guard with your cape and gloves in her hands."

Susannah laughed and felt herself completely relax. She said, "She is entirely harmless. Don't let her intimidate you."

A grunt that sounded very much like a swear word passed his tempting lips. "The day will not come that I let her discourage me," he said.

Chuckling, Susannah said, "Would it have been so terrible if I had intended my companion to come with us?"

"No, but…" He paused and grinned. "I would have taken it to mean that you were afraid to be alone with me."

She stared at him with an easy smile, enjoying their playful conversation. "I am not an innocent miss who has never been alone with a man before, my lord. Why would I be afraid to be with you in an open carriage?"

He shrugged lightly and said, "Because I can tell that you don't want to be attracted to me, but you are."

Susannah protested with a soft laugh. "Why am I not surprised to learn that you think so highly of yourself?"

"Because you knew my grandmother, and you've read Lord Chesterfield's letters. But I spoke the truth, and you know it. And I know you can see that I am definitely attracted to you, too."

This engaging man beside her was entirely too perceptive, but she wasn't willing to let him know that. "I don't believe I know anything of the sort, my lord."

"Be modest if it pleases you to do so," he teased her. "It makes you even more beautiful. But know this, Duchess, before we leave the park this afternoon, I will make sure you have no doubts about just how attracted I am to you."

Anticipation rippled through her, and she looked away from him. He had obviously seen way too much in her eyes already. By the saints, what was she going to do about the marquis?

Traffic was thick and slow as they approached the entrance to the park. The marquis queued with the other carriages waiting to enter the park through the west gate. Their curricle fell in line behind a fancy closed carriage that was driven by a handsome, liveried driver and drawn by a matching set of chestnut-colored horses.

The warm, sunny day had the park bustling with activity. The grassy areas were packed with distinctively dressed gentlemen and elegantly fashioned ladies. Some of the people wishing to see and be seen strolled the vast grounds with their children and dogs, while others were on horseback or rode in the open carriages.

Lord Raceworth stopped the curricle and threw the ribbons to a groom. When he reached back to help Susannah down from the carriage, she hesitated. She couldn't help feeling odd. She swallowed her trepidation and took Race's hand. As he held her firmly while she stepped down, she felt his warmth even through her gloves.

"Why the hesitation?" he asked as he let go of her and reached back into the carriage for the food basket. "You said you weren't afraid to be alone with me."

This time he wasn't smiling. There was real curiosity in his features. Did she owe him an explanation?

Susannah inhaled a deep breath of the spring air and slowly released it. "I'm not. It's just that it's been a long time since I've been to Hyde Park, since I've strolled beside a man. I'm simply adjusting to this very different life than I've lived for the past few years."

"Understood."

They fell into a slow walk, she holding her parasol and her reticule with the documents sticking out of it, and Lord Raceworth carrying the food basket.

"You said your husband has been gone for years. Why haven't you been back to London for a visit?"

"There has been no reason to return until now. My husband was very generous and left me a charming cottage called Chapel Gate, which is on the lands of Chapel Glade, and a more than adequate allowance to see to my needs. When my father died five years ago, my mother came to live with me, so my life has been full. I've been quite happy there, and I've not needed anything London has to offer."

"Do you still attend the kind of grand house parties that my grandmother used to give?"

"No, not since my husband died, and we didn't attend very many while he was living. Though he was a kind man, he was very careful about whom he socialized with, and your grandmother was one of the few. He thought highly of her."

"That doesn't surprise me. I've always known that many men adored Lady Elder, but not a one of them more than Gibby."

"Gibby?"

"Sir Randolph Gibson is a good friend of mine, and he was my grandmother's dearest friend for many years. He claims that she is the only woman he ever loved."

"I remember my husband once told me that a lady who could outlive four husbands had his respect and his compassion."

Lord Raceworth laughed, a gentle, genuine sound that sent shivers of awareness throughout Susannah's body. Just looking at him made her feel warm and good inside. He was right. She was very attracted to him, but she didn't intend to do anything about the way he made her feel. Her only goal must be to obtain the pearls for her mother.

"As I get older, I find that the more I learn about my grandmother the more respect I have for who she was and all that she accomplished. She was an exceptional lady in many ways, but there were numerous times in my life that I wished she had never met Lord Chesterfield."

"Why is that? He was a brilliant man."

Lord Raceworth let out a half laugh, half grunt. "You think so?"

"Yes. I told you I read his letters to his son. I considered him a very wise and humorous man. He had the most wonderful way with words."

The marquis shrugged and then tipped his hat to a couple they passed. "Maybe one of the reasons I and my cousins detest the man is because from the time we were seventeen, at which time my grandmother considered us men, until her death not much more than a year ago my cousins and I received a letter from her at the beginning of every month without fail."

"Truly? How wonderful that she took the time to stay in touch with you. And every month? I'm impressed."

"Don't be. The only thing her letters ever contained was, as she would call it, more wise words from Lord Chesterfield, and then she would quote something from the irritatingly pompous man like: 'Always look people in the face when you speak to them; not doing it is thought to imply conscious guilt; besides that you lose the advantage of observing by their countenances what impression your discourse makes upon them. In order to know people's real sentiments, I trust much more to my eyes than to my ears, for they can say whatever they have a mind I should hear, but they can seldom help looking what they have no intention that I should know.'"

Susannah's gaze settled on his as they walked. "I believe that to be true, and it sounds like very good advice to me. You are being unkind to your grandmother and Lord Chesterfield. Many gentlemen today still heed his advice."

He countered, "You and my grandmother must have gotten along very well together."

Susannah tried not to laugh but couldn't help herself. "We did. But, truly, were Lord Chesterfield's quotes the only thing she ever wrote to you?"

"Month after month after month." He tipped his hat again and said "Good afternoon" to another couple they passed. "There was never anything about how she was doing, what she was doing, what or how we were doing, only quotes from that ingratiating old man that we should heed lest we fail to become the gentlemen she wanted us to be."

"Still, she must have loved you very much to write to you every month without fail."

"I suppose she did, in her own way. So, tell me, what is your given name, or should I continue to call you Duchess and Your Grace?" he asked as they continued their stroll through the park.

Surprise lighted in her eyes. "You mean you didn't ask anyone my name or look at old copies of newsprint to find out anything about me?"

"There was no need. I'm a patient man. I can wait until you are ready to tell me."

"Hmm. I assumed you would try to find out everything you could about me since I was last in London."

"I hope you aren't too disappointed."

"No, not disappointed, but I am astonished. Perhaps I should realize I'm not as intriguing as I thought I was."

He lightly touched her upper arm to stop her, and she turned to face him. "Not so, Duchess. You are the most intriguing lady I have ever met. But I want to hear about you from you. Not from anyone else."

His gaze fluttered sensually down her face. His words elated her. He was a patient man.

"Why is that?"

"Only you know the real story. Anyone else would just tell me what they have heard that someone else heard from someone else. I don't care anything about hearing gossip."

Susannah looked away, suddenly feeling shy, suddenly wishing he didn't have to know the truth.

"Your Grace," he said softly.

She exhaled heavily and looked back into his lovely brownish-green eyes. "Mine is not a pretty story, my lord, so I think it is best kept where it is. I had forgotten that a man's curiosity is not as great as a woman's."

"All right," he said, and they started walking again.

Susannah didn't know if she was grateful or disappointed he didn't press her to say more. She remained silent for a few moments and collected her thoughts before saying, "When I heard you had the Talbot pearls,

I wanted to learn all that I could about you, and in doing so I learned a lot about your cousins as well. It seems that one of you makes Lord Truefitt's Society's Daily Column almost every day."

"It's not something we strive for, I assure you. But at least now I've found out a little something about you."

"What's that?"

"You admit to reading the gossip pages. I'm told they are habit-forming."

"Only recently have I read them, my lord. My mother read about the pearls in Lord Truefitt's Society's Daily Column and discovered you had them. She asked me to come to London and get them for her. The attic at Chapel Glade is full of old newsprint. I asked the Duke of Blooming if I might spend time going through the copies, reading about you and your cousins as well as many other people."

"See, that is the reason I will not read gossip of the past about you or ask others about you. Not much of what you read in the scandal sheets is true."

"So you don't believe in the old adage that 'where there is smoke there is fire'?"

"Of course not. It sounds like something Lord Chesterfield would have said, and I've already told you what I think about him."

When she saw sincerity in his eyes, his smile, suddenly her past indiscretion that had all the gossipmongers chattering for weeks didn't seem so bad.

"I believe you."

"Good. Besides, how could I read about you? I don't even know your name."

Susannah lowered her parasol to her shoulder and lifted her face to the warm sunshine and said, "Sometimes I forget I have a name other than Duchess or Your Grace."

"But you do have one."

She darted a curious glance his way. "Of course."

He changed the food basket to his other hand and moved to walk a little closer to her. "You're not going to tell me what it is, are you?"

She stifled the urge to smile. "My name is listed in the documents I have with me." She lifted her arm, showing him her drawstring reticule dangling from her wrist, papers sticking out of the top of it.

He laughed. "You are very clever, Duchess. I am not ready to look at the documents."

Why did her heart seem to dance in her chest every time he looked at her? Of all the gentlemen in London, why did she have to be tempted by the one man who had the pearls?

"I am a patient lady," she told him, echoing one of his statements. "I can wait. Let me know when you are."

"Look," Race said, pointing in the distance. "A crowd is gathered over there. Do you want to see what is going on, or should we look for a place under one of the trees to spread the blanket and enjoy our fare?"

She smiled eagerly. "Oh, by all means, let's go see what has caught everyone's attention."

"All right, but first, might I ask a favor?"

"Of course."

His eyes turned serious. "Since you know my name, will you call me Race?"

She would love nothing better, but should she?

Already he was filling her dreams at night and her thoughts during the days.

"Perhaps it wouldn't be wise for me to be that familiar with you, my lord."

She saw what looked like disappointment flash in his eyes, but he quickly hid it by saying, "All right, Your Grace, we'll continue to play by your rules. Let's go see what has enthralled this crowd."

Susannah knew she had put a sudden damper on their lovely afternoon, but Lord Raceworth was already too charming for her own good. Somehow she had to keep him at a distance, and formality might give her an edge. For a time, anyway. If she allowed herself to become too entangled with him, she might be reluctant to deny his tempting appeal and to fight for the pearls when the time came.

She watched as Lord Raceworth scanned the crowd.

He lightly touched the small of her back, but the warmth of his hand spread all over her.

"Come this way. I see Gibby, Sir Randolph Gibson whom I mentioned earlier. I'm sure he will know what's happening."

They walked up to a dapper older gentleman with a head of beautiful silver hair and lively brown eyes. "Gibby, what's going on here?"

"Afternoon, Race," the tall gentleman said as his gaze quickly fell on Susannah. He swept off his hat and bowed.

Race immediately made the introductions.

"It's my pleasure to meet you, Your Grace. I don't believe we have met before, but I remember your husband. The duke was a fine gentleman. I guess it's been a while since he passed."

Susannah gave him a grateful smile. Her husband was seldom mentioned by anyone anymore, including his son. She instantly liked the friendly, robust man. "It's been ten years, and yes, he was a fine man. Thank you for remembering him with kind words, Sir Randolph."

"And how is his son the Duke of Blooming and his family doing?"

"All are well. The duke plans to come to London next year for the Season."

"Is that right? I remember his father never liked the city much. Stayed away from it like the plague."

"His son is somewhat like him," Susannah agreed. "The duke's eldest daughter will be presented at court and make her debut next year, so her father will be here for that. She's excited to come and see London."

"Tell him I'll look forward to seeing him while he's here. It's been a long time."

"I'll be pleased to remember you to him when I return."

"Will that be soon?" Race asked, thrusting himself back into the conversation.

Susannah turned to him. "That hasn't been established yet. I've not made any final plans and won't until I accomplish what I came here to do."

"Keep in mind, Duchess, that I am in no hurry to look at the papers you brought with you."

She gave him a confident smile. "I know that well."

The marquis nodded to her and then turned to Sir

Randolph. "What is going on here? Why have so many people gathered?"

"I'm not sure if it's a fair that is coming to Town or simply a small carnival, but I'm told there will be a man arriving soon who will climb into that cage with a tiger. Everyone's waiting to see if it happens."

Susannah looked at the empty cage that had been placed on a platform. "That sounds very dangerous to me."

"I'm sure it is," Sir Randolph agreed.

"Why would he do something like that?" Susannah asked.

"It's how the performers make their living," Race said. "They will travel to a town, set up a small camp, and do free shows for a few people. They are taking a chance that the audience will be amazed and go back to their homes and businesses and talk about what they saw, which will make other people want to see it. Of course, when others come, they will have to pay money to watch the man get in the cage with the tiger."

"A clever way to build excitement and anticipation," Susannah admitted.

"Yes," Gibby said. "They'll stay in one location until the crowds stop coming, and then they will pack up their tents and shows and move on to another town and start all over again."

Lord Raceworth turned to Susannah and asked, "Do you want to stay and watch this, or should we find a quiet place to sit?"

"If the man is going to be courageous enough to get in a cage with a tiger, he must need money. I'd rather come back and pay to see him do it."

Race smiled at her. "I like your reasoning, Duchess, and I agree with you. We'll come back another time to see him. Gibby, we're going to find a place to sit and have refreshments. Want to join us?"

"There you are, you blasted scoundrel and seducer of innocent ladies," someone shouted above the chatter of the crowd. "Ha! Now I've caught you. You will pay for what you did to my sister."

Susannah, the marquis, Sir Randolph, and several other people in the small crowd all turned to see who had shouted.

Susannah's blood ran cold, and her eyes rounded in alarm. It looked as if the irate man was pointing his finger directly at Lord Raceworth.

The marquis went still. From what she had read, she knew him to be a rake of the highest order, but to be vilified in the park like this, with ladies and children looking on, went beyond the pale.

She threw a questioning glance toward him. His gaze caught hers. His stunned expression asked that she reserve judgment until they found out what this man was talking about.

Without hesitating, Susannah instinctively moved closer to the marquis.

Five

Dearest Alexander,

I was reading through some of Lord Chesterfield's old letters yesterday and found this shining gem from one of his early posts. "The strong mind distinguishes, not only between the useful and the useless, but likewise between the useful and the curious. He applies himself intensely to the former; he only amuses himself with the latter."

Your loving Grandmother,
Lady Elder

RACE HAD NEVER BEEN SO CAUGHT OFF GUARD THAT he was speechless, until now. He felt Susannah's protective step toward him and Gibby's, too, but the last thing he wanted was for them to witness this stranger's outrageous behavior. What the devil was this man thinking to make such a claim in front of more than two dozen people?

He didn't know this short, rotund, and very angry man staring at him, accusing him of being a seducer of innocent ladies, but that was about to change.

Through the years, Race had tempted many young ladies into giving him forbidden kisses in dark gardens at parties and balls, and in his younger years he had tempted a few of them into letting him share their bed, as well. This was the first time he had ever been accused in public of such risqué behavior.

As of late, the younger ladies had lost their appeal, which was evidenced by Miss Mayflower just a few days ago. More than once she had tried to corner him at his card party, but he'd avoided her each time. Recently, he'd much rather spend a leisurely evening in bed with his mistress than chasing after insipid ladies who were too young to know what they were doing.

The first thing he had to do was safeguard the duchess from this ill-mannered oaf. Race slowly set the food basket down at his feet and calmly stepped in front of Her Grace, shielding her.

"Sir, as you undoubtedly know, I am the Marquis of Raceworth. Identify yourself."

"I know who you are, my lord." The older, balding man bowed quickly. "I am Mr. Steven Prattle. I am here to defend my sister's honor."

Race felt the duchess move from behind him to his side. He tried to step in front of her again, but she took hold of the crook of his arm and held firm, releasing him only when he stopped trying to shield her from the man.

Gibby remained at his other side. They were both making it clear that no matter this man's claims, they were supporting him whether he liked it or not. And while their defense made him feel damn good, it was not comfortable to find himself in the middle of this situation. He didn't like being called out in public, and he was incensed it had happened in front of the duchess, not to mention at least two dozen other people who were inching closer to them with every second that passed.

Race didn't recognize the man's name, and he couldn't remember a young lady named Prattle, either. He searched his memory for what incident this could be about. What the hell had he done to a young lady whose name he didn't recognize? The sun that earlier had been warm and inviting suddenly seemed scorching hot. He felt as if someone was pulling on his neckcloth, choking him.

"And well you should look after your sister," Race said calmly, even though his insides were shaking with anger at this man's ill manners, "but this is not the place to do it. This matter should be handled in private, not in a public park."

The man walked closer but still kept a reasonable distance. "I went to his house, but he wasn't there."

His house? That didn't make sense. Unless…

Race's eyes narrowed. "Are you talking to me, sir?" Race asked.

The man's bloodshot eyes bulged with rage, and his heavy cheeks shook. "Of course I'm talking to you! But he is the man I want to talk to! That man standing beside you, Sir Randolph Gibson."

This time it was clear the man pointed to Gibby, not Race.

Gibby?

Race felt as if a fist slammed into his stomach, and he jerked toward his elderly friend.

"Me?" Gib said and pointed to his chest with his

thumb. He threw a questioning glare to Race, to the small crowd that had now gathered around them, and then back to Mr. Prattle again. "You are accusing me of compromising an innocent young lady, sir?"

"I am," he thundered. "And it's not that she's that young anymore, but she is innocent."

It was one thing for the man to accuse Race of a vile act—he could easily defend himself—but accusing Gibby was a whole different matter. Race wouldn't let the man get away with that. Everyone in London knew Gibby was a man of impeccable honor.

Race turned to his friend and in a low voice said, "Gib, do you know what he's talking about?"

The old man shrugged his shoulders and held up his hands as if to say *I have no idea what this man is talking about*, and Race didn't really want to find out here in the park with more than two dozen pairs of eyes and ears crowding even closer to listen.

Sweat beaded on Prattle's upper lip and trickled down his neck to his collar. Clearly he was fighting angry. His clothing and speech indicated he was a man of some means, but obviously he was deep in his cups and had forgotten civility. Surely, even his sister would not want him announcing this kind of information in public. Race considered it an insult to her that her brother was doing this.

Race took a deep breath. "Mr. Prattle, I must insist that we move out of the park and finish this conversation at a more private location. We will meet you wherever you wish."

"No, I'm not going anywhere," he shouted and pointed

his finger at Gibby again. "He compromised my sister, and I'm calling him out. I'm challenging him to a duel."

Race swore under his breath. The duchess and half the crowd gasped loudly before everything went deathly quiet.

Gibby's shoulders flew back, and his chest puffed out proudly. "I accept!"

Race swore again and mumbled, "Be quiet, Gib," before his gaze darted toward the duchess.

Her Grace looked concerned but not horrified, so he took that as a sign she was holding up under this unsavory situation, but he would have given anything for her not to have witnessed this. Gibby might have stolen a few kisses from a lady or two in his time, but damnation, men his age didn't go around accosting ladies.

"There will be no duel, Prattle," Race said firmly. "I have no doubt we can clear up this matter quickly if you will just be reasonable about this and exit the park."

The man completely ignored Race and said, "Penelope was crying by the time we got home from Lord Tinkerton's party last night. I asked her what was wrong, but she was too distraught to talk about it. This morning she admitted to me that Sir Randolph had accosted her on the portico of Lord Tinkerton's home and forced her to do things she didn't want to do."

Gibby took a step forward, putting him closer to the man than Race wanted. "I remember meeting your sister on the portico last night, but as a gentleman, that's all I'm prepared to say."

"Ah ha!" the man yelled with such fury he almost

popped the buttons on his waistcoat. "He admits it! Choose your weapons."

Race stepped in front of Gibby this time, shielding him from the enraged brother. "Nobody's choosing weapons, Prattle. He didn't admit to accosting your sister. I insist we move to a more private place to finish this discussion." Race turned to Gibby, who didn't look in the least concerned about this man's accusation. "I know you didn't do this, Gib, but this is not the place to defend yourself. Let's go."

"He can't go until he chooses his weapons. I've challenged him to a duel, and now he must respond."

"Gibby, don't say anything else," Race warned in a stern but low voice. "I will handle this."

"Choose your weapons!" Prattle yelled again and started toward Gibby. Two men from the crowd grabbed his arms and held him back as he struggled to get free.

"All right." Gibby shoved his two clenched fists in the air. "These!"

Race was almost as angry with Gibby as he was with Prattle. "Gib, you are making this worse. You can't reason with this man. He's lost control of himself, and he needs to leave the park and calm down. Then we'll discuss this privately with him."

"What do you mean?" Prattle asked, blinking uncontrollably. "Is your choice swords or pistols?"

Gibby brushed Race aside and shook his balled hands at Prattle again. "I mean fists. My weapon of choice is my fists."

The man struggled to get loose from his captors once

again. His eyes were wild, and his coat was half torn off his arms. "You are insane. We'll use pistols."

Gibby pulled on the tail of his coat and squared his shoulders, seeming unperturbed by this turn of events. "I might be old, but I'm not stupid. I don't see well enough anymore to shoot a pistol and hit anything, especially you. Fists it will be."

"Stop this, Gibby," Race said with anger in his voice. "There will be no duel or fight of any kind going on in this park or anywhere else."

"Well, then we'll use swords," the deranged man said as spittle flew from his wet lips.

"I haven't picked up a sword in years," Gibby argued calmly. "You told me to choose my weapons, and all these people heard you." Gibby waved his hand at the crowd that had not only grown larger but had moved in closer. "You can't take that choice away from me just because you don't like my preference. We'll have a pugilism match."

"We will not!" the man yelled. More spittle flew from his mouth as he tried once more to break free from his captors. "It's not my fault that you can't see to shoot a pistol or that you haven't picked up a sword in years. We've got to be gentlemen about this and use a gentleman's weapon."

"It's gentlemanly to bare-knuckle fight. The prince himself enjoys going to matches. I'll invite him." Gibby looked at the crowd, smiled, and waved to them. "And we'll invite all these nice people, too."

Someone in the crowd yelled the word "Fight!" and suddenly everyone was shouting "Fight! Fight!"

This was lunacy, but Race didn't know what to do, short of picking up Gib and throwing him over his shoulder and walking out of the park with him. He was powerless to stop Gibby, Prattle, or the crowd that was now part of this mayhem.

"I don't know how to fight with my fists," Prattle yelled in a hoarse voice to the crowd, and he seemed to go weak in the arms of the men who held him.

"Then you shouldn't have given me my choice of weapons. That's your fault. Not mine."

Race held up his hands and said, "Stop this madness, both of you, before I call the magistrate and have you thrown in prison. Do I have to remind you two that dueling is against the law?"

"Pugilism isn't," Gibby said with an innocent grin.

That's when Race realized why Gibby wasn't more upset about this outrage against his character. He was loving the attention he was getting.

Race felt tight as a new drum, but the old man was having the time of his life. Race should just walk away and leave the old codger to clean up his own mess. But Race couldn't do that. He had too much respect for Gibby to leave him on his own.

"I don't know how to box," Prattle said again in a desperate, high-pitched voice.

"In that case, I'll go easy on you and make it fair. I'll give you a month to train." Gibby turned to the crowd and with a wide smile on his face said, "What do you say, ladies and gentlemen? Do you think I should meet Mr. Prattle here in the park one month from today at midday?"

"Yes!" the crowd roared.

"Then it's settled. All of you are invited, and bring all your friends, too."

The crowd erupted with more cheers and chants of "Fight! Fight!"

Race felt like he was watching a madcap play at the Lyceum. He'd never felt so helpless.

He looked over at the duchess, who was moving closer to Gibby. "Sir Randolph," she said, "you are not helping yourself in this matter. Perhaps you should listen to Lord Raceworth. He has the best plan to help you with this unfortunate turn of events."

Gibby smiled and tipped his hat to her. "I can't stop it, Your Grace. The man challenged me and I have to accept. My honor demands I fight him."

Race moved to stand between Gibby and Prattle, and in a low voice sternly asked, "Did you do anything to his sister?"

"I've said all I'm going to say on the subject," he said and then set his lips in a firm line.

Race exhaled slowly. He looked at the fellows holding Prattle and said, "Will you men see that Mr. Prattle gets home?"

"Yes, my lord," the men said in unison, and they walked off with Prattle still muttering that he wanted to use pistols.

Gibby smiled and waved to the jubilant crowd as they dispersed.

"You can't be serious about any of this, Gib. Prattle looks to be at least ten years younger than you."

Gibby looked from the duchess to Race. "How old do you think I am?"

"I don't know," Race muttered. "Mid-seventies, I guess?"

"Oh, he cannot be that old, Lord Raceworth," the duchess said. "See how strong and fit he is. And he hasn't even started to lose his hair yet."

"What does it matter? My only point is that he is too old to box with anyone."

Gibby smiled at Her Grace. "You're right, Duchess. I'm not as old as he thinks." He then turned to Race and frowned. "I'm sixty-six, and by the looks of him, I'd say Prattle isn't much younger. The problem is that you don't think I can beat him, do you?"

"Of course I do." Race swept his hat off his head and ran a hand through his hair. "I mean, no, because I don't want you to even try."

The duchess smiled affectionately at Gibby and said, "Sir Randolph, you look much younger than sixty-six."

He grinned. "Thank you, Your Grace."

"Now you're the one not helping, Duchess," Race said in an exasperated voice.

"Oh, sorry."

She gave him a sheepish smile, and Race felt his heart trip. Damn, she was beautiful. Her parasol had dropped to the back of her shoulders. A gentle breeze danced through curls free of her bonnet. There was wonder in her eyes. Sunshine fell across her beautiful face in a way that made him want to pull her to him and kiss her. Even with all the folly happening around him, he wanted to taste her lips and feel the weight of her breasts in his hands.

He shook his head and half laughed to himself. The desire he was feeling right now wasn't appropriate for where they were, so he willed his mind back to the matter at hand.

"What are we doing talking about age? Blast it, Gib, all that matters is that you are too old to be fighting anyone."

"You are worrying too much about this, Race. I'm going to be fine."

Race sighed. "I'm going to take the duchess home, and then I'm going to see what I can do to stop this madness before it goes any further. There will be no duel with fists or anything else if I have anything to say about this."

"You don't." Gib turned and tipped his hat to the duchess once again and said, "Nice meeting you, Your Grace. If you're still in Town, you are invited to the boxing match, too."

With those parting words, Gibby turned and walked off, with several men crowding around him.

"He is a very strong man," the duchess said.

"Gibby doesn't like for anyone to challenge his honor."

"A true gentleman."

"No, a crowd pleaser," Race corrected. "He loves attention, and he knows that either I or one of my cousins will somehow get him out of this."

Race picked up the food basket, and they started walking back the way they had come but at a much faster pace than before.

"I'm sorry, but we are going to have to postpone our refreshments for another time. I need to find my cousins."

She gave him an understanding smile. "No need to apologize. I'm in complete agreement that you need to see to this matter quickly."

"I know you came with me only because of the curried apples," he teased, wanting to lighten the heavy mood that had settled over him.

Susannah looked at him with sparkling eyes. "I did say that, didn't I?"

He nodded. "I'll leave the basket with you."

"May I make a different suggestion?"

He gave her a quizzical look. "Of course."

"When we get to the entrance of the park, why don't you hail a cab to take me home? That way, you can get about your duties and do what you must for Sir Randolph."

He was incredulous. "Absolutely not. I wouldn't think of doing such a thing."

"I suggest it only because I know you are deeply troubled about your friend and you are in a hurry to help him. I saw your frustration because neither man would listen to reason."

Damn frustrating.

"Duchess," Race said, "I would never take a lady to a park and not see her home. You live only a street over from mine. It will take no extra time to see you to your house."

"All right, but you said you needed to find your cousins. Do they live near you?"

"Close by, but let me show you how I will do that," he said as they made it back to his curricle.

He took the reins from the groom as he tossed the basket onto the floor of the carriage. He asked the groom, "Are you free to run an errand for me, lad?"

"Yes, my lord."

"Good. I need you to find the Duke of Blakewell and the Earl of Morgandale. Try their homes first and then the clubs. White's first, then Harbor Lights, and then the Rusty Nail. When you find them, tell them to come to Raceworth's immediately. Can you remember that?"

"Yes, my lord," the young man said again.

Race reached into his pocket and pulled out some coins and gave them to the youngster. "Take these. There will be more waiting for you at my back door if the earl and duke get there within the hour."

"Yes, sir!" the young man said happily and ran away, his feet kicking up dust from the ground as he flew.

Race quickly helped the duchess into the carriage and jumped in beside her. "I'm going to push the horses. Will that bother you?"

The duchess snapped her parasol shut and placed it between them. She grabbed hold of the armrest on the side of the cushion. "Not at all. I'm ready whenever you are."

Race clicked the ribbons on the horses' rumps, and they took off with a jolt and a shimmy of rattling harness. Race let the horses run as they flew past pedestrians, carriages, and horses that were plodding along, enraging them all with his reckless driving. People yelled at them, and several dogs barked and chased the carriage as they left the park and pulled out into the busy street.

Race took his eyes off the road in front of him long enough to throw a quick glance at the duchess. She was smiling. His heartbeat sped up. She was enjoying their wild ride. The wind whipped at a few strands of her dark brown hair and feathered it across her beautiful face. He couldn't help but notice the papers sticking out of the reticule hanging from her wrist.

"I'm sorry there won't be time for me to look at your documents."

She smiled at him. "You weren't going to look at them anyway, were you?"

"I'm beginning to think I may have to if I want to find out your name."

One of the carriage wheels hit a hole and almost bounced both of them out of the seat. They looked at each other and laughed, but Race didn't slow the horses.

"Are you all right?" he asked as the curricle bumped along at a mad-dash clip.

"I'm enjoying the excitement," she exclaimed. "Keep going."

Race liked the duchess more and more. He was sure if he'd had any other young lady with him today she would be screaming or fainting from fear.

Race wouldn't be so careless if he wasn't sure he could handle the horses as they darted around the slower traffic. He and his cousins had been racing curricles since they were boys. And they still loved to do it when they were out at Morgan's Valleydale estate.

Within minutes, he'd pulled the bays up short in front of her house. He set the brake on the curricle and hopped down. He reached for the duchess, grabbed her by the waist, giving her a twirl around before setting her feet on the ground. He didn't know what madness came over him, but he bent down and kissed her soundly, quickly, on her soft lips and stepped back.

Her green eyes rounded and she gasped. At last he'd done something that left her speechless.

He smiled. "Thank you for going to the park with me, Your Grace."

"You kissed me," she whispered. "In bright daylight."

"Yes, I did. I promised you would know just how attracted I am to you."

Fear replaced shock on her face. "Someone might have seen you." Her gaze darted from side to side to see if anyone was standing in the street, watching them.

"No one saw me. I checked to see if anyone was nearby as I swung you around." He reached back into the carriage and grabbed the food basket. "Get used to it, Duchess. I'm sure I'll kiss you again." He handed her the basket, tipped his hat to her, and climbed back into the carriage.

"Race," the duchess said and rushed up to the side of the carriage as he picked up the ribbons and released the brake handle.

She looked up at him with bright eyes and rose-tinted lips. Race's stomach flipped.

"Susannah," she said and then stepped away from the carriage. "My name is Susannah."

The rush of hot, heady desire raced through him, and

he smiled as he drank in her beauty. He flicked the ribbons on the horses' rumps, and the carriage took off at breakneck speed.

Six

RACE STRODE THROUGH HIS FRONT DOOR, FLINGING off his cape and throwing his hat and gloves onto a side table.

"Mrs. Frost," he called as he walked down the corridor to the drawing room.

He entered, taking off his coat and tossing it across a chair that sat by the window. As he untied his neckcloth and loosened his tight collar, Mrs. Frost appeared in the doorway, looking alarmed.

"Yes, my lord?" she asked, twisting the hem of her apron with her short, stubby fingers.

He hadn't meant to frighten the woman, but he had to admit he had seldom stormed into the house the way he had moments ago.

"I'm expecting my cousins shortly. Don't stand on ceremony. Show them in here immediately when they arrive."

"Yes, my lord."

He picked up his coat and rummaged in the pocket. Pulling out some coins, he said, "If they get here within the hour, a lad will arrive at the back door. Give him these, and thank him for the good job." He dropped the money into her palm.

"Yes, my lord. Will there be anything else?"

"That's all for now."

Mrs. Frost turned away, and Race went to the window and looked out. As the duchess came to mind, a peaceful calm settled over him. So Susannah was her name. A lovely name for a beautiful, confident lady. He couldn't see her house from this window. He would need to go into his book room at the back of his house for that. Somehow just knowing she was not far from his back door pleased him immensely.

He smiled and then chuckled to himself. All it took to get her to tell him her name was a quick albeit possessive kiss on the street. That had been risky. Downright foolish, in fact, especially if she had been ruined years ago, as he suspected. But he hadn't been able to stop himself.

He had wanted to kiss her since he first saw her walking toward him in his crowded music room. After Gibby's foolhardy stunt and their wild ride through Town, Race's inhibitions were down, and his senses were acutely aware of his surroundings. He'd kissed her without forethought. He was glad he had, and now he couldn't wait to kiss her again. But next time he wanted to linger over the kiss and take time to taste her sweetness. He wanted to hold her close and feel the warmth of her pliable body in his arms.

She was surprised he had kissed her, but she wasn't angry. That pleased him.

There was something exciting about her, something intriguing and elusive. Because she withheld her past from him, it made him want to know everything about her. And he wanted to know it from her, not past copies of scandal sheets or anyone's faded memory of that time. Not that he thought her past would change how he felt about her. It wouldn't. He was much more interested in the present.

Did it matter that she wanted his grandmother's pearls? Not one damn bit. He had no intentions of giving them up, no matter what her documents said.

And all that aside, he wanted her. That was as plain and simple as night and day. She wasn't indifferent to him, either. He was sure of that. He'd sensed passion in her that afternoon in his home when he had stood so close to her he felt her minty breath caress his lips.

He wasn't being foolhardy. He realized there was still the possibility she was working with Captain Spyglass, Winston, Smith, or possibly some other person in order to obtain the necklace. So why was he so attracted to her that he risked kissing her on the street? Because she enchanted him. Because she was so different from the usual London lady that caught his fancy.

The priceless Talbot pearls were rare and had a long history. No one had collars made like that anymore. He really wasn't surprised so many people wanted them. But the pearls would remain safely tucked away in his safe hidden behind some books on his bookshelf.

Race stared out at the side lawn of his immaculately kept grounds. Even the vegetable and herb gardens were tended to perfection. Race liked order in his life, and Susannah was disturbing that, but in a way that was exhilarating. Even now he should be concentrating on Gibby and his problem, but instead Race was remembering a warm, firm kiss on soft, sweet lips, and astonishment sparkling in cool green eyes.

"Race, what the devil is going on?" Morgan said, walking into the drawing room with his usual swagger. "I was at home when some lad showed up and said for me to come to your house right away."

"Good, you're here. Sit down." Race turned away from the window and walked over to the mahogany sideboard that was inlaid with ivory swirls, and poured a splash of claret into two glasses.

"All right," Morgan said and seated himself in a large upholstered chair. "I don't like that pensive look on your face. What's going on?"

Race walked over and handed him a glass. "I don't think you're going to like what I have to tell you."

A wrinkle formed between Morgan's eyes. "That sounds ominous. There's nothing wrong with Blake, is there?"

"No, it's Gibby."

Morgan leaned forward. "Is he hurt?"

"Not yet." Race took a drink from his glass. The deep red wine went down hard and settled like a rock in his stomach. Race was frustrated that he hadn't been able to stop the insanity in the park. "He's been challenged to a duel, and he intends to fight."

Morgan jumped up from the chair, wine sloshing out of his glass over his hand, to stand toe-to-toe with Race. "Damnation, Race, you had better be lying to me or pulling a prank, but either way this is no way to amuse yourself."

Morgan was an inch or two taller than Race, but Race still managed to look him square in the eyes and hold his ground. "I assure you, Cousin, I'm not doing either one."

"This is lunacy. He is too old to duel, not to mention it's been against the law for years."

"I know all that and told him so, but he insists he's going to go through with it."

"This is unbelievable. Why didn't you tell him he couldn't do that and put an immediate end to this?"

Race's frown deepened. "There is one small problem you seem to be overlooking, Morgan. Gib is a grown man. Besides, didn't it cross your mind that I might have already told him that, as well as every other reason I could think of to insist this fight will not take place?"

"One of you had better be dead or dying," Blake said, striding into Race's drawing room with a grimace on his face. "But no, you both look healthy as horses to me, so why was I told to get over here for an urgent matter? I was already in my carriage, about to take my new bride for a ride in the park, when a ragamuffin showed up and told me I had to get over here in half a shake."

"It's urgent all right," Race said, walking over to the sideboard.

"Damned urgent," Morgan agreed and took a long drink from his glass.

"All right," Blake said, his concerned gaze darting from one cousin to the other. "In that case, one of you best speak up quickly and tell me what's going on."

"It's Gibby," Race said. "I was in the park less than half an hour ago and while I was there, a man named Steven Prattle approached Gibby and challenged him to a duel."

"What the devil?" Blake said.

Race handed Blake a glass of the dark red wine and said, "It's true."

"You were there and heard the challenge?" Blake asked with an incredulous expression on his face.

"Every blasted word."

"Well, why in the hell didn't you stop him?"

If only he knew.

Race was getting tired of the accusations, but losing his temper with his cousins wouldn't help solve this problem.

A tired half chuckle escaped Race's lips. "Give me some credit, Blake. It's not as if I wasn't trying like the devil himself to stop the whole thing. Do you think I want to see Gibby having a boxing match at his age?"

"Boxing?" Morgan asked.

Blake edged closer to Race. "With bare-knuckle fists?"

"Yes," Race admitted. "As farfetched as it sounds, the man gave Gib his choice of weapons, and the old dandy chose his fists."

"You can't fight a duel by pugilism," Morgan exclaimed. "That's outrageous. What kind of tomfoolery are you asking us to believe, Race?"

"The cold, hard facts, Morgan," Race said, raising his voice, too.

"All right, calm down both of you," Blake said. "Just start at the beginning, Race. What were you and Gibby doing when he was challenged?"

"Having a conversation. I was there with the duchess, and I saw Gibby with a group of people who were waiting to see a man crawl into a cage with a tiger."

Morgan's gaze zeroed in on Race's face. "You were there with the duchess?"

"Yes," Race said innocently. "I took her for a ride in the park."

"What duchess?" Blake asked, his gaze sweeping from one cousin to the other.

"That's right," Morgan said with a sudden twinkle in his eyes. "You didn't meet her, did you?" Morgan turned to Race. "And you haven't mentioned her to Blake?"

"It's been only three days since I met her," Race said, unable to hide his annoyance at being hammered with questions about Susannah and Gibby. "I haven't seen Blake until now. He's married, remember? He's not attending the parties as often or visiting the clubs at night as he used to."

Confusion wrinkled Blake's brow and screwed up his lips before he asked, "What duchess are you two talking about, and what were you doing in the park with her?"

"Obviously, he was courting her, but what he was courting her for I don't know."

"Morgan," Race said in a warning voice.

"Duchesses are usually married to a duke. What kind of trouble are you getting yourself into?" Blake asked.

"She's the Dowager Duchess of Blooming. Ever heard of her?"

"I can speak for myself, Morgan."

Morgan gave him a dry smile. "Of course, my apologies, Race."

"I've met the Duke of Blooming a couple of times," Blake said. "I can't say I know him well. He seldom comes to London. Why were you with his mother?"

Morgan chuckled deep in his throat.

Race shook his head in exasperation.

Blake's eyes narrowed suddenly, and he said, "No, wait, if I remember correctly, the dowager duchess isn't his mother. She is his father's second wife, or maybe she was the third wife, but I was told she was much younger than he was. I don't think I've ever met her."

"Probably not," Race said.

"Take my word for it," Morgan added. "You would have remembered if you'd met her. She is as beautiful as Henrietta but not quite as young. I'd say she's about our age, thirtyish, wouldn't you, Race?"

Morgan was being impossible. "Yes. And if you had met her, it would have probably been somewhere other than here. This is her first visit to London in twelve years."

"That long? Sounds like she is as reclusive as her husband when he was alive. You were in the park with a beautiful woman, and Gibby was challenged to a duel? What else has been going on since I married that I don't know about? I can't believe you two have been keeping all this news from me."

"It's not as if we wanted to or intended to, Blake. It's just that you aren't as accessible as you used to be."

"I live less than a mile from the both of you, and I damn well expect that one of you will stop by once in a while and fill me in on what's happening in my own family."

"Can we please get back to Gibby and the fight?" Race asked in an irritable voice. "The challenge happened less than an hour ago, so it's not as though days have passed concerning Gibby. Right now, his situation is more important than the duchess or your hurt feelings."

Blake growled. "My feelings aren't hurt. I'm angry I was left out."

"I agree that we do need to discuss Gibby," Morgan added. "But there's one more thing about the duchess that Blake needs to know before we quit the subject. She wants Race to hand over our grandmother's pearls to her."

"What?" Blake asked, clearly taken aback by this news.

"Yes," Morgan continued. "She says they were stolen from her family and wants Blake to give them back."

"What gall! Would you two blackguards not keep things like this from me ever again? Even if I am married, I still want to know what is happening."

Race suddenly felt as though he was back in the park again. He wasn't having any better luck keeping control of the conversation with these two than he had with Gibby and Prattle.

"All right, you've made that clear already, Blake. Morgan, you've said enough. Now, would both of you please sit down so we can get back to Gibby? The duchess and the pearls can wait."

Grumbling to themselves, his cousins took the two upholstered wing chairs that flanked a small circular table, and Race sat in the middle of the flower-printed settee facing them.

"I'll make this simple for you. Mr. Steven Prattle's sister, Penelope, accused Gibby of compromising her at Lord Tinkerton's party last night."

"Gibby?" Blake exclaimed. "No way in hell. That didn't happen, I'm sure of it, but start at the beginning and tell us everything."

Race briefly filled them in on all that happened in the park, leaving out only the part about his kissing the duchess when he took her home. Contrary to what his cousins thought, he did not have to tell everything.

"And you couldn't persuade Gibby to give up this preposterous idea of a boxing match?"

Race drained his wine glass and placed it on the rosewood table in front of him. "No. I think Prattle might have been convinced to forget this idea if I could have persuaded Gibby, but Gib had whipped the crowd into a frenzy to get them on his side. They were with him all the way, shouting 'fight' at him over and over again. You can't imagine what it was like."

"What in the devil made Gib want to box the man like a bruiser?" Blake asked, shaking his head.

"Who knows what goes through that strange mind of

his? It's clear we have to figure out a way to get Gibby out of this and let him save face, too."

"Usually the only way that is done is by marrying the lady in question," Morgan offered.

"Do either of you know of her?" Blake asked.

"I'm thinking she's one of the spinsters who usually sit around the dance floor at the Great Hall," Morgan said. "Seems she's rather tall and buxom and maybe about fifty years old. Do either of you think Gibby wants to marry her?"

Race was the first to answer. "I wouldn't think so. He certainly never made an indication he wanted to marry anyone. You both know that he's always maintained that the only woman he has ever loved or wanted to marry was our grandmother."

"I agree," Blake said. "What exactly did he have to say for himself?"

Race sighed. "He didn't say anything other than he had been on the portico with Prattle's sister."

"I bet Prattle loved hearing that."

"You can't even imagine the rage the man was in," Race said. "I thought his eyes were going to pop out of his head and his buttons burst off his waistcoat. If two bystanders hadn't grabbed Prattle and held him back, he would have attacked Gibby right then and there."

"All right, one thing he can do is marry the woman," Blake offered, "but we all agree he probably doesn't want to do that, especially if he didn't compromise her."

All three men nodded.

"He can go through with the fight, and we can hope he won't get hurt," Morgan offered.

"No," Race and Blake said in unison.

"We have to do something," Morgan reasoned. "I don't want to see Gibby boxing a man either, even if they are close to the same age, but bare-knuckle fighting probably wouldn't kill him the way a sword or pistol could if Prattle decided to do something stupid."

"I agree, but that seems as distasteful as getting caught in parson's mousetrap," Blake said.

"We all know that Miss Prattle could have made this whole thing up in hopes Gibby would be forced to marry her."

Race nodded. "That's very possible."

"All right, I suggest we offer them a reasonable sum of money," Morgan said. "The brother and his sister. It's the quickest, safest, and easiest way to settle the matter."

"I agree," Race said. "None of us believe Gibby would have intentionally compromised the woman, but if for some reason she felt he crossed the line while he was on the portico with her, then she will at least be compensated for whatever injury she feels he caused."

"It's a good idea only if Gibby, Prattle, and his sister go for it," Blake injected. "Do either of you know the man well enough to approach him?"

Morgan and Race shook their heads.

"I thought as much," Blake said. "The plan sounds good to me. And, Race, I believe it's your turn to take care of Gib."

"Oh no, not me," Race complained.

"Yes, you. I just finished getting him out of that ridiculous balloon venture he was tangled up in a few weeks ago, and Morgan recently got his money back for him from that blasted time machine invention he was so crazy about a few months ago."

Race had a sinking feeling in his stomach. Somehow he had known they would leave it up to him to handle this.

"All right, I'll see if I can get Gibby to agree to us talking to Prattle."

"If he agrees, and they take the offer, we need say no more about this," Blake offered.

"There might be a few disgruntled people who wanted to see a fight, but soon a new scandal will come along and everyone will forget about this one."

Morgan finished off his drink. "There are always new scandals on the horizon."

"Now tell me more about the duchess," Blake said.

Race tensed. He didn't want to talk about her. He wanted to keep her all to himself. He couldn't ever remember feeling that way about any other woman. He didn't know why she was different; he knew only that she was and he didn't want to discuss Susannah with them.

"It's a fascinating story," Morgan began when Race didn't speak up immediately. He rose and walked over to the sideboard. "She arrived unannounced at Race's card party, which you missed by the way."

"Sorry about missing that, Race. We had good intentions of coming. It would have been Henrietta's first card party, but we, ah—she—I mean…"

"You're forgiven," Race said with a laugh, getting Blake out of the corner into which he'd backed himself.

"So you invited her to your card party? How did you

know she was in Town? And what's this about her claiming Grandmother's pearls belong to her family?"

"That's part of the irony of this entire story," Morgan said, speaking for Race once again. "Race didn't invite her. He had never even heard of her until she arrived at his door and demanded to see him."

"It wasn't a demand," Race countered.

"I distinctly remember you thought so at the time."

"Morgan, that's enough," Race muttered.

"Oh, quite right," he said sarcastically. "I keep forgetting it's your story to tell. I'll just end my part of it by saying I can't believe she's been hiding up in Blooming all these years, unless of course she had a very good reason to stay there."

Race threw imaginary daggers at Morgan's chest.

"So you took her to the park today," Blake said. "My, my, things are moving fast, but tell me more about her claim. I knew you had some unsavory men asking about the pearls. By the way, I saw that fop Captain Spyglass last night. He was at the Great Hall, dancing with every young lady whose mother would let him near her daughter."

Morgan grunted. "I can't figure out why any of them would. It's all over London that he obtained his wealth by pirating ships."

"But not proven," Race added.

"It must be the secrecy that surrounds him that intrigues the ladies," Morgan said, picking up the claret decanter. "I suppose that's why people invite him to their parties. For some damned reason, they think it adds an element of danger and mystery to their lives to be associated with a man who might very well be a real pirate."

"And all it really adds is an unsavory character into their lives," Blake inserted.

The cousins laughed.

"So tell me more about why the dowager thinks our grandmother's pearls belong to her family."

"She says they were stolen more than twenty-five years ago," Morgan said.

"Morgan, do you mind if I tell this story?"

"No, please do," he said innocently. "You tell it. I'll pour myself another glass of wine."

Race had said all he was going to say about Susannah or the pearls. "There's nothing more to tell."

"That means she is as secretive about her past as is Captain Spyglass," Morgan said, "but Race decided he didn't want to know about it from anyone but her. However, I would like to know anything you can tell me, Blake."

Race started toward Morgan and then stopped. "Blast it, Morgan, would you just get your wine and be quiet."

"Easy, Race," Blake said, holding up his hand to stop Race. "I would tell either of you anything I knew. I simply don't know anything about her, but that said, it wouldn't take me long to find out."

"No," Race said firmly. "I'm quite capable of finding out anything about her I want to know. And just so you know, Morgan, Gibby met her this afternoon. He knew her husband well."

"Hmm. So did you talk to him about her?"

"Prattle showed up before much was said."

"I'm just going to say one last thing," Morgan said as he recapped the wine decanter.

"Don't," Race and Blake said at the same time.

Morgan laughed and then said, "Race is going to have a quite good time getting to know this beautiful lady and getting to the bottom of why she thinks the pearls belong to her family."

"Why didn't you just ask her?" Blake asked, looking confused.

Morgan sat back down in his chair and sipped his wine. "That would be too easy. Once he knows that, the intrigue surrounding her will be gone, and he fancies the idea of not knowing."

"Go to hell, Morgan."

Morgan laughed. "Be glad to when the time comes, but for now I'm having too much fun on earth."

"With a dowager duchess in Town, I'm sure Henrietta will want to invite her to tea. It's the proper thing for her to do."

"By all means," Race said with a confident smile and relaxed into the settee.

He wasn't worried about Susannah meeting Blake's wife, the Duchess of Blakewell. He had the feeling Henrietta wouldn't get any more information out of the duchess than he had.

Seven

My Grandson Alexander,

I was reading one of Lord Chesterfield's letters today and found this extraordinary quote from him. Read this with interest: "He who flatters women most, pleases them best; and they are most in love with him, who they think is the most in love with them. No adulation is too strong for them, no assiduity too great, no simulation of passion too gross; as, on the other hand, the least word or action that can possibly be construed into a slight or contempt is unpardonable and never forgotten."

Your loving Grandmother,
Lady Elder

SUSANNAH AND MRS. PRINCETON WALKED THROUGH the front door, laughing.

"I really can't believe the judgment of that French dressmaker we talked to earlier today," Susannah said as she took off her black cape. "It did not take me very long to decide that she will not be designing anything for me."

Mrs. Princeton set her packages on the floor beside her and began taking off her outdoor clothing. "Some ladies go for the more extreme styles of diaphanous fabrics for evening and wide stripes for day."

"Hmm, and very vivid colors, too, but they are not for me. I prefer simple lines, pastel shades, and basic fabrics. Thankfully, I didn't have to choose a dressmaker today. I can interview more modistes later in the week. However, I am very pleased about my purchase of the pianoforte," Susannah said with a smile, untying the ribbons on her straw bonnet. "I can hardly wait for it to be delivered tomorrow."

"I didn't want to say anything in front of the shop-keeper, but what will you do with it when we leave? Do you plan to have someone take it to Chapel Gate for you?"

Susannah laid her gloves and reticule on the side table. "Of course not. Why would I, when I have one there? I will leave it here for the owners of this house so others can enjoy it, or," she added thoughtfully, "perhaps I can find a small church here in London that is in need of a used pianoforte and donate it to them. That might be a nice thing to do, don't you think?"

"Very nice," Mrs. Princeton agreed, brushing her wiry gray hair away from her eyes.

"What is important to me right now is that it will give me comfort and pleasure to play in the afternoons. And since the owner of this house has not seen fit to keep a gardener employed on a regular schedule, I think I will look into the possibility of hiring someone."

"I would be happy to see to that for you."

"Thank you. It appears I'm going to be staying in London longer than I originally thought," she said more to herself than to her companion. "So I might as well make this house as pleasing and comfortable as possible."

"Oh, my, look at this," Mrs. Princeton said, thumbing through the calling cards that lay on a silver plate on the vestibule table. She looked up at Susannah with a sparkle in her eyes. "You have become popular since we left the house today. You had several callers while we were out. And look, more invitations have arrived. Isn't that wonderful?"

Susannah pursed her lips and frowned. "I don't consider that wonderful. You know I was hoping to stay out of the public eye while here."

Mrs. Princeton chuckled lightly. "How could you do that when you have now been seen in Hyde Park with one of the most popular, most handsome, and most eligible gentlemen in all of London? The marquis was the perfect gentleman for you to be seen with. He is not seen as a gambler or a fortune hunter."

"What did I tell you about trying to be a matchmaker?" Susannah said with more merriment than she was feeling.

"Not to."

"That's right. The eligibility of a gentleman does not matter to me. I am not here to find a husband."

Mrs. Princeton sighed. "More's the pity," she mumbled under her breath and then quickly added, "I see the *Times* has been delivered, too. It's been two days since you were with the marquis. Do you think perhaps you should look at it and see if you are mentioned in Lord Truefitt's Society's Daily Column today?" Mrs. Princeton held out the newsprint for her.

"Do I really want to know the answer to that?"

"Up to you, of course," Mrs. Princeton said, the twinkle returning to her eyes.

Susannah took the *Times*, folded it, and tucked it under her arm without answering her companion. She would decide later if she would read it.

"You have four calling cards, all from ladies, it seems. Obviously someone recognized you when you were in the park a couple of days ago."

"Perhaps. Also, the marquis or Sir Randolph could have mentioned to someone that I am in Town. And you were right when you said it would be almost impossible not to have been noticed after what happened with Sir Randolph in the park. That in itself was enough to set tongues to wagging for months."

"From what you told me about it, I wish I had been there. It all sounded so bizarre."

Susannah headed toward the drawing room with Mrs. Princeton following her. "In a way, it was. The marquis is certain of Sir Randolph's innocence and I don't doubt him, but I couldn't help feeling sorry for Miss Prattle. Her brother truly did her a disservice in confronting Sir Randolph in public."

"I'm sure she hopes she will never have to show her face in public again."

"That would be my guess, too," Susannah said thoughtfully, having some knowledge of what the woman must be going through.

"It looks as though you also had two notes delivered while we were out. They are probably invitations. Should I open them for you?"

"Let me see." Susannah stepped closer to Mrs. Princeton.

"Look here, one is obviously from an ill-mannered boor. It is addressed simply to Susannah. That is shameful. Who would dare be so informal to a duchess?"

Race?

"Should we just throw it away without opening it?"

Susannah's chest tightened. "No, of course not. I will see who it's from."

Mrs. Princeton gave her the letters. The first one was properly addressed to her as the Dowager Duchess of Blooming, as her title demanded, and the second a bold, black script that simply said Susannah.

It had to be from the marquis.

Not wanting Mrs. Princeton to think she was eager, Susannah slowly opened the formal invitation first and scanned the words. "It's from the Duchess of Blakewell. She's inviting me for tea tomorrow afternoon."

Mrs. Princeton smiled. "The wife of Lord Raceworth's cousin, how very nice of her."

"And expected. No doubt Lord Raceworth told his cousin, the duke, and his duchess that I am in London, and now she feels obliged to invite me for tea."

"And well she should. Would you like me to put this on your calendar and send her a message that you will be delighted to attend?"

"No, thank you, Mrs. Princeton, I won't be going."

Mrs. Princeton's bushy gray eyebrows rose. "Oh. I don't understand. A duchess has asked you for tea. It's only polite to accept."

Susannah felt no regrets about declining. She hadn't come to London to once again become embroiled in Society with its strict rules. "She will understand that since I've so recently arrived in Town, I'm not accepting many invitations right now. Make the decline very nice, and be sure to thank her for her kind offer."

"Yes, Your Grace."

Clearly her companion was disappointed by Susannah's answer, but she said nothing else. Susannah stepped away from Mrs. Princeton and willed her fingers not to tremble with expectancy as she carefully unfolded the second note. It read:

> *I want to see you.*
>
> *Race*

That was all? He was incredibly presumptuous and brazen, and for some reason she couldn't fathom, it thrilled her.

I want to see you. Not when, not how, not where, not what for. But he wanted to see her. For some silly reason, her hopes soared.

Suddenly Susannah smiled and then laughed softly.

"What is it, Your Grace?" Mrs. Princeton asked anxiously, taking a step closer to her. "Is it anything you can share?"

Susannah stepped back and folded the paper. She recognized the gleam in the woman's eyes. Mrs. Princeton wanted it to be from a gentleman.

"Only that this is not an invitation, and you do not

need to write an answer for me. I think I will go up to my room and rest before dinner is served." She took in a deep, satisfying breath.

Mrs. Princeton's soft brown eyes twinkled, and Susannah knew she hadn't fooled the woman for an instant. Susannah was sure her companion assumed the note was from Race.

"Would you have Cook bring me up a cup of tea?"

"Right away, Your Grace."

Susannah climbed the stairs with a spring to her steps. She held up the hem of her dress with one hand and the note from Lord Raceworth to her chest with the other. She hurried into her room and closed the door behind her. She walked over to the window, dropping the newsprint on her bedside table as she passed, and looked out at the marquis's grounds and the back of his house. She didn't understand it but she felt close to him when she looked at his home. Getting that note from him made her feel like a young, carefree miss again, and that was a heavenly feeling.

The window was open, and Susannah inhaled deeply and took in the fresh scent of the late afternoon. It had rained earlier in the day, but now it was gloriously beautiful. The sky was clear and bright, littered with patches of wispy white clouds that appeared as thin as gossamer, slowly sailing across the blue. The gentle breeze that wafted across her cheeks was almost warm. Sunshine had already dried the rain off the grass, shrubs, and flowers in Lord Raceworth's magnificent garden, leaving them washed clean to show their vibrant spring colors.

Susannah closed her eyes and remembered Race's kiss for the hundredth time. The touch of his lips against hers had been firm, possessive, and inviting, but oh so brief. She had tingled on the top of her head, low in her stomach, and even in her toes. An eager wanting for more sizzled deep inside her.

His kiss earlier in the week had surprised her, thrilled her, and troubled her. What was she to do? She didn't want to be enamored of him, which was not in her plans, but she was. He seemed to make it easy for her to like him, enjoy him. He had been so handsome when he came to her house a couple of days ago in such a cavalier fashion. He'd told her he would prove to her just how attracted he was to her, and he had by giving her that quick kiss on the street where anyone who happened to be passing by could have seen him.

That kiss and now this unconventional and quite scandalous note proved he cared nothing for her title and not much about Society's rules, either. That fascinated her.

All he had written was that he wanted to see her. Just the thought of that made her tremble with expectancy, and she didn't want to lose that feeling.

Foolish as it was, she wanted to see him again, too.

Desperately.

But why?

The last time she had felt this way about a handsome young man, he had broken her heart. Race had already made it clear she was going to have to fight him every step of the way for her grandmother's necklace. How could she afford to get any more entranced with him than she already was?

Susannah was a widow, not an innocent. She knew what a man's touch felt like—one man she had thought she loved and one she hadn't.

It pained her to admit, even to herself, that she hadn't loved her husband. She would have liked to. She had respected him immensely. He was good to her and had never said a sharp word to her. But there was never any passion between them.

Now after twelve years, there was once again a man who had caught her eye, a man who created yearnings inside her too powerful to deny. Was she strong enough to enjoy the marquis's unconventional attention and fight him for the pearls at the same time?

Susannah pored over his note again. She felt the stirrings of desire low in her abdomen. He was a clever man. He purposely wanted to leave her questioning what his note really meant. Did he want her to respond to him in some way? It hardly mattered if he did. She wouldn't. Race was obviously a master at seduction, because he had made progress where no other man had in a dozen years.

Should she deny herself his attention and go back to her celibate life in Chapel Gate? Live with the memory that she had wanted to spend time with him, laugh with him, kiss him, touch him, but didn't? Or would she go back home and live with the memories that she had wanted all those things, and the marquis had fulfilled her every desire and more?

Susannah looked at his house again and remembered the reason she was in London. The Talbot pearls. She had to come up with another plan to get them, since it was obvious he had no interest in or intention of looking at the records from her family that detailed the purchase of the pearls and their theft.

She'd had some hope of his looking at the documents as long as he didn't know her name. As she continued to stare at the back of his house, she laughed to herself. But no, she ruined that chance. One little kiss, and she had blabbed her name as quickly as if she'd been a school girl hoping to get praises for learning her lesson.

Susannah believed the marquis to be a good man, an honest man, and loyal to a fault, as evidenced by how he stood up for Sir Randolph in the park. If she could just get him to look at the documents, she was sure he would see they were not falsified. She had to believe he wouldn't want to keep the pearls once he was convinced they had been stolen from her family.

A thought struck her. Maybe that was why he wouldn't look at her evidence. If he did, and he believed it to be true, his honor would demand that he must turn them over to her. She could go only on the way she would feel if their roles were reversed. She would never want to keep anything that had been stolen from another person, no matter the monetary or sentimental value of the item.

Perhaps now was the time for her to contact a solicitor and have him contact Race or his solicitor about the documents. That was an idea that had merit, but her mother had been convinced Susannah could handle it by herself.

Susannah was beginning to doubt that. If Race's solicitor was convinced of their authenticity, perhaps he could assure Race of the validity of her family's ownership.

She half laughed again and turned away from the window. It was amazing how easily and quickly she'd come to think of him as Race. Why had his note simply said "I want to see you" with no specific time or date? No doubt his only motive was to keep her guessing about his interest in her. And if that's what he'd wanted, it had worked.

With a smile on her lips, she walked over to her dressing table and opened her jewelry case and carefully tucked the note from Race under one of the velvet folds.

He probably wouldn't be happy if she had someone contact his solicitor, but she wouldn't spend any time worrying about that. As desirable as he was, she wanted him to know that when it came to the pearls, she meant business and she wasn't about to give up.

Susannah turned away from the window, and her gaze lighted on the newsprint. She picked it up and turned to the page with Lord Truefitt's column. She scanned the article and found what she was looking for. Lord Truefitt was eager to learn the identity of the lovely lady who was seen in Hyde Park with the dashing Marquis of Raceworth.

Susannah smiled. London Society hadn't changed one bit in the twelve years she'd been gone.

Race strode through the front door of the Harbor Lights Club, taking off his cloak. He handed off his hat and gloves to a servant and headed straight for the taproom, nodding to some gentlemen he knew along the way but not stopping to chat. Gibby had never shown up at Race's house after the debacle in the park with Prattle, and now two days later, Race was still having a devil of a time finding the man.

Race had been to his house twice, the clubs, and searched several of the parties the past two nights, trying to locate him, but the whipster always seemed to be one step ahead of him. Race hadn't made it home until almost dawn and had ended up sleeping longer than he'd intended.

Already this afternoon, Race had checked Gibby's home, White's, and the Rusty Nail. Now, here he was at Harbor Lights again at the end of the day. If Gib wasn't inside, Race wouldn't know where else to look. He stopped at the entrance of the taproom and saw the old fellow sitting at his favorite table by the window, an empty plate in front of him. A slice of late afternoon sunshine fell across his face, heightening his ruddy cheeks.

Just looking at him enjoying the sights outside the window curbed Race's annoyance at having to search for him. Maybe Gibby didn't try to get himself into one mishap after another, but it sure seemed that way sometimes, and it had especially seemed that way with Prattle and the pugilism match. This had to be the most outrageous of all the things with which he had become involved over the years.

Taking a deep breath, Race walked over and pulled

out the chair opposite Gibby and sat down without bothering to speak.

"You don't look so well, Race. Something wrong?"

Race harrumphed, leaned back, and folded his arms across his chest. "Don't act as if you are blameless in the reason behind my ill temper."

"All right, I won't," he offered innocently, searching Race's face as if he didn't understand his attitude.

Race uncrossed his arms and leaned forward. "I'm worried about you. Damnation, Gib, you had me dreaming that you were getting pummeled by a rotund, balding man named Prattle while his spinster sister stood by and laughed. So you're damned right something is wrong with me."

"Hell's bells, Race." Gibby laughed good-naturedly. "I didn't know you were given to nightmares. You need something to put you in a better disposition. What are you drinking?"

"Something strong," he muttered, trying to hold on to his annoyance, but with Gibby, that was a hard thing to do. He was just so damned likable.

Race looked down and saw a glass in front of Gibby that looked like it had milk in it. It must be some new concoction the club had come up with. "What are you drinking?"

"Milk."

Race couldn't think of any drink that would be good in milk except a very sweet, very strong liqueur. Given his bad humor, that would work for him.

"I'll have whatever it is you are drinking."

Gibby motioned to the server, pointed to his glass, and then held up two fingers.

"Now, tell me why you didn't inform me the Duchess of Blooming was after your grandmother's pearls? I thought you two were just out for an afternoon stroll."

Race was taken aback by Gibby's terse question. And was that anger he saw in Gib's dark brown eyes?

"We were just out for a stroll until we met you, and I couldn't very well introduce her to you as the duchess who wants my inheritance from Grandmother, now could I?"

"No, but you could have told me about her when you told Morgan and Blake. Why am I always the last one to know what goes on in this family?"

Race felt his own ire rise again. "What I'd like to know is why everyone in this family is suddenly feeling left out if they don't know everything about my affairs before I know it?"

"Well, I do feel left out," Gib said. "I don't like being the last one to know what is going on with you three guardian fools."

Something told Race this conversation was going the same route as when Blake found out he hadn't been told about the duchess and her quest for Lady Elder's pearls. Race hadn't come to talk about that. He wanted to discuss Gibby's outrageous stunt in Hyde Park.

"Listen, Gib," Race said, trying to stay calm. "I'm not any more concerned about the duchess than I was about Prinny's representative, the one-armed antiquities dealer, or that arrogant buccaneer who's trying to worm his way into every titled man's home in London. In fact,

I'm probably not as worried about her as I should be about the other three."

Gibby's eyes narrowed. "You know that all three of the men who want the pearls are still in London, don't you? Four, if you count Her Grace."

"I know Spyglass and Winston are inserting themselves into Society, and I know the antiquities dealer has a shop on the other side of Town," Race said, refusing to acknowledge Gibby's remark about Susannah.

"Spyglass is attending every party he gets invited to, and Winston is making his presence known at the parties and in all the clubs."

"That's not surprising about either one of them. With Prinny's backing, Winston can go wherever he wants. And I've heard rumors Spyglass intends to host his own party before the Season ends."

"I've heard that about Spyglass, too. Everyone wants to get in good with the prince, and every young lady wants to say she's danced with a handsome buccaneer. Smith is another story. He doesn't have the heritage to ease his way into Polite Society, but he's been seen at a few places in the Hells recently."

"That's probably where he belongs."

The men's presence in London didn't worry Race, but he was beginning to get tired of being pursued because of the necklace. It was true that the pearls would be worth a fortune in any market, but that's not where their value lay as far as Race was concerned. The pearls were his grandmother's most prized possession, and she had left them to him. He wasn't about to give them up to anyone.

"Gib, do you know where or how our grandmother got the pearls?"

"Sure I do. I don't think there was much about your grandmother's life I didn't know."

Race waited, and when the old man didn't say more, Race sighed and said, "Do you mind telling me where?"

"Not at all. Her second husband, Sir Walter Hennessey, gave them to her shortly after they married."

Race thought on that a moment and frowned. "Are you sure it wasn't Lord Elder?"

"Of course I'm sure. She already had them when she married the earl."

"The pearls would have been very costly, even twenty-five years ago. Did she question how Sir Walter could have afforded such an extraordinary necklace for her?"

"Probably not," Gibby said. "I don't think she cared how he got them. I know of only one other thing that ever made your grandmother as happy as receiving those pearls."

"What was that?"

Gibby leaned back in his chair and smiled. "When she became Lady Elder. She wanted to have a title attached to her name more than she wanted to live."

Race smiled, too. "I do remember that. After she married the earl, she always signed her letters to us as 'Your loving Grandmother, Lady Elder.'"

Gibby leaned back in his chair and laughed lightly as a faraway look glistened in his eyes. The man never changed. Gibby's countenance always softened whenever he talked about Lady Elder.

"Yes, I remember. She didn't even want me to call her by her name anymore. I had to call her Lady Elder."

"She certainly was an unusual woman. What else can you tell me about the pearls?"

"Nothing, I suppose. Why?"

"When I was talking to Morgan and Blake, we couldn't help but wonder about them. It just seems odd that four different people are suddenly after the necklace."

Gibby tilted his chair on its two back legs and said, "My thoughts would be because not many people knew where the Talbot pearls were until it was written in Society's Daily Column that they were left to you by your grandmother."

Hearing Gibby confirm what he and his cousins had considered brought Race up short. Cautiously he asked, "Tell me, did you ever know of Grandmother wearing the necklace outside private dinner parties in her home?"

Gibby seemed to study on that. "Not that I can remember, but she might have. Keep in mind, the pearls were irreplaceable. I can't say for sure, and it's only a guess, but she must have worn them when she was married to the earl and they attended Court." Gibby ran a hand through his thick silver hair. "It's never a good thing to let everyone know what valuables you have in your possession."

"True," Race said, turning pensive.

"Are you sure you're not worried about these people who want the pearls?"

Race shook his head as the server put two glasses on the table between them. "They are safe."

Race picked up his glass and took a big swallow. He

screwed up his face and wiped his lips with the back of his hand. "Blast it, Gib, what is this stuff?"

"Milk. I told you I was drinking milk."

"I know, but I thought there must have been some kind of sweet liqueur in it."

"It is plain milk," he said with a cunning smile.

Race looked closely at Gibby. The old man looked fine, yet Race asked, "Are you sick?"

Gibby leaned back in his chair again and puffed out his chest. His lips tightened together for a moment. "No, I'm not sick. I'm in fine shape. Why?"

"Why do you think?" Race said, exasperated. "Bloody hell, you're drinking milk, for mercy's sake."

"Of course I am. I'm in training."

Race stuck a finger down his collar, trying to loosen it. The muscles in his neck and shoulder had begun to ache. Gibby could heat his blood to boiling. "In training? What the hell does that mean?"

"It means I'm not drinking anything but water and milk. I'm not eating anything but fish, vegetables, and fruit. I'm not taking my carriage. I'm walking everywhere I go until after my fight with Prattle."

"I've never heard of such a thing. Not drinking ale or wine, and walking everywhere? That's insane, Gib. You've lost your mind, and you're taking this too far."

Gibby placed both his hands on the table and leaned forward. "All the winning pugilists train, Race. I'm good-sized for a man my age, but did you notice that Prattle is built like a tree trunk?"

Race swore under his breath. "Yes, I did happen to

notice that, Gib. Why do you think I'm trying to stop you from meeting him in Hyde Park a month from now?"

Gibby waved his hand as if brushing away Race's comment. "It's less than a month now. You just want to mind my business. That's all you and your cousins ever do."

"It's full time employment, and somebody needs to. You aren't doing a very good job of it."

"Don't worry about me, Race. I can beat Prattle once I get in shape. I'm sure of it. And I would like to hear that one of my favorite people in the whole world had some confidence in me about this."

How could he let Gibby know he and his cousins were worried about him and didn't want him to take the chance of getting hurt? The old man was just too stubborn to admit he had made a mistake in encouraging Prattle.

"Let me tell you what I do have for you—an answer. I discussed this with Blake and Morgan a couple of days ago. We want you to give us permission to offer Prattle and his sister money to end this farce."

Gibby threw his shoulders back and bowed up his chest. His eyebrows wrinkled together, and his lips pursed into a sneer. "That's an insult."

"Not if money is what Prattle was after in the first place."

"I'm not talking about Prattle," Gibby exclaimed. "I don't care what he wants or doesn't want. It's an insult to me. My honor is at stake here."

"So is your life."

"What kind of life would I have without my honor?"

Race softened. "Gib, we don't believe for a moment you did anything to his sister, and I don't want you fighting and possibly getting hurt over something that didn't happen."

"You don't know what did or didn't happen, because I'm not talking."

"You don't have to. We know you. We know you are an honorable man and would never push a lady into something she didn't want."

"It's unforgivable what her brother did to her by his blathering in the park, but I can't change that. I can only answer his challenge," the old man said, shaking his head.

"We can do what Prattle didn't do and settle this quietly."

"No, I've given my word now. Besides, every gentleman, no matter his station in life, loves a good, fair fight."

"Not when one of the bruisers is a member of Polite Society," Race argued.

"Tell that to Figg, Broughton, Jackson, Mendoza, and all the other great pugilists who have been welcomed by the ton. Even that sap Lord Byron enjoys a good match and writes about them. He has been known to go a few practice rounds at one of the fight clubs in Town."

"Most of us have, Gib, but it's always been in private, not public," Race emphasized. "Besides, we use gloves in practice. You'll be expected to bare-knuckle it. Look, my job was to talk you into letting me offer them money. If they don't take it, we'll go from there."

Gibby leaned forward. "Do you realize there are already hundreds of wagers at every club and gaming hell in London about this match, and I've heard betting has spread to outlying towns?"

"I've been to White's and the Rusty Nail, looking for you. I know the furor this has caused."

"And I can't believe you want to take this away from me. You tell your weak-kneed cousins I'm going through with this, Race. And I'm going to win."

Gibby picked up his glass and drained it. Race's stomach tightened. Gibby's hands were red and chafed. His knuckles were swollen, too. No doubt he was in the process of toughening his hands with some harsh concoction like all prize fighters used.

"I'll finish this for you," Gibby said and reached over and pulled Race's glass toward him. "Now tell me, what can I get you to drink?"

Eight

My Dearest Grandson Alexander,

I hope you will remember these sobering words from Lord Chesterfield. Take heed, dear one, he is seldom wrong about anything and never wrong about a man. "That great wit, which you so partially allow me, may create many admirers; but, take my word for it, it makes few friends."

Your loving Grandmother,
Lady Elder

RACE WAS IN A QUANDARY AND FILLED WITH frustration as he entered his house late in the afternoon. He'd had a frustrating and unsuccessful meeting with Gibby at the Harbor Lights Club a couple of days ago, and he'd just come from another long, heated discussion with his cousins. He was beginning to feel as if he was going in two different directions at the same time. Gibby had been absolutely giddy with excitement over his duel—if this travesty could be called that. And Blake and Morgan still thought Race should talk to Prattle and find an amenable way to settle his accusation against Gib, even though the old man was dead set against him doing it.

Race really had no idea how Prattle would take an

offer of money, if in the end he decided to approach him. Except for Gibby's objection, there certainly wasn't anything out of line about doing it. Through the ages, men, and maybe a few ladies too, had been saved from marriages they didn't want by the exchange of money, lands, or making other suitable arrangements with the offended parties. But this sort of thing usually happened with young ladies and randy blades, not people the ages of Gibby and Miss Prattle.

Blast Gibby's rotten soul. What was a man in his sixties doing training for a bare-knuckle fist fight and drinking milk? Gib was too damned old to be a pugilist.

Race strode into his book room and straight over to his sideboard and poured himself a glass of wine. He took a sip of the velvety liquid as he loosened his neckcloth. The stiff collar had been choking him all day. He walked toward his desk and stopped midstride. Was that music he heard? He looked over at the open window. The brown and gold wide-striped draperies were parted, and the alluring melody drifted inside.

The sound was coming from a pianoforte, but was it a composition of Bach, Mozart, or some other composer? He listened to the soft engaging theme for a few seconds.

He half laughed as he took another sip of the wine. Hell, why hadn't his grandmother insisted they learn more about music and less about Lord Chesterfield and his bloody blubbering about how to be a man?

Race walked over to the window and looked out over his grounds and realized that the music came from Susannah's house. Was it her, Mrs. Princeton, or someone else playing? He stood there for a few moments, looking at her house and listening to the strains of the score.

Finally, he pulled a chair over to the window, sat down and propped his feet on the windowsill, and let the soothing, lyrical notes float in and relax him as he enjoyed his drink. He felt the tightness leave his eyes, mouth, and shoulders. The stress of the past couple of days, brought on by his conversations with his cousins and Gibby, seemed to ebb out of his body. His neck and shoulders loosened up, and he melted more comfortably into the chair and thought about Susannah. He liked that she was unconventional. She created an excitement inside him whenever she was near.

Race had sent Susannah an informal note four or five days ago, saying that he wanted to see her, but as of yet he hadn't had the time to call on her. He supposed he should have been more decorous when he wrote to her. After all, she was a dowager duchess and deserved the most circumspect protocol, but to him she was simply a beautiful, desirable woman named Susannah. He wanted to put aside her title, and his, and simply enjoy her. He didn't really know why yet, but she enchanted him.

He wanted to see her again.

Today.

Right now.

What would she do if he went to her door and asked her to go to the park with him again, or to a party or the opera? Vauxhall Gardens was open. She might enjoy walking around the gardens with him and watching the fireworks. Or they could walk right here in his own gardens.

He really didn't care what they did. All he knew was that he wanted to look into her sparkling green eyes and kiss her again. But this time he wanted to kiss her properly, in private. He didn't want a quick peck on the lips while standing on a street. He wanted a long, leisurely kiss so he could drink in her essence. He wanted to pull her close and feel her warmth against him and lose himself in the softness of her tempting, womanly body.

Suddenly, without real thought about exactly what he was going to do, Race set his glass down on his desk and headed for his rear door. The only clear thing he knew he wanted to do was to establish who was playing the pianoforte.

Afternoon mist lay gray and gloomy in the air when he stepped outside. A gentle breeze blew a strand of hair across his face, and he quickly brushed it behind his ear as he hurried down the steps that led to his back grounds.

People often commented that he had one of the largest and loveliest formal gardens in Mayfair, but he had seldom walked through it. He never had the time for such niceties. But today as he stomped on the stone pathway, he noticed that it was indeed beautiful. The foliage in his garden was a lush, deep shade of green. No doubt from the drenching spring rains that had plagued London for months. All of the roses in the beds were different shades of pink, but the various kinds of flowers that dotted the landscape seemed to be of every color imaginable.

The formal knot garden had been laid out to form an intricate pattern, with shrubs trimmed in different sizes and shapes. Obviously his gardener had a sharp eye for detail. And the large waterfall fountain that stood in the middle of the garden was expansive and flowing with water.

When he reached the end of his property, he was perplexed for a few seconds. He stood in front of a seven-foot yew hedge that had made a solid fence, separating his grounds from Susannah's, and whispered, "Bloody hell."

His gardener was obviously worth the money Race paid him. The man had made it impossible to pass through or around the thick yew wall that completely surrounded his garden on three sides. What the devil was he going to do now?

But Race was not of a mind to be stopped by a tall green shrub. He strode back to his gardener's supply room, picked up a hatchet, and returned to the green mountain hedge, knowing what he had planned was not going to be easy with the small hand-held ax. He mathematically studied the corner where two ends met, and then carefully started chopping and hacking a hole at the bottom of the yew big enough for him to squeeze through.

It wasn't an easy task, and it took him quite a while, but after he finished, he stepped back and looked at his handiwork of the closely cropped hedge. He was satisfied that it would be difficult for him to crawl through but not impossible. He looked around at the clippings that were scattered all around his feet. His gardener was not going to be a happy man when he found the mess the next day.

After forcing himself through the hole, Race stood and brushed small bits of the shrub from his coat as best he could. He straightened his neckcloth as he traipsed through Susannah's property. He couldn't help but notice, after passing through his own well-tended gardens, that the grounds surrounding Susannah's house had been sadly neglected. He supposed that was to be expected when the place hadn't been lived in for at least a year.

The music grew louder as he approached the rear of the house, and he realized the sounds came from the right. He finger-combed his hair and cautiously walked around the house until he saw a slate pathway that led to a side door. A window was nearby, so he quietly eased up to it and peeked inside.

He saw Susannah sitting at the pianoforte, her back to him. His breath quickened, and his loins thickened at the sight of her. She sat on a cushioned bench. Her spine was straight, the nape of her slender neck accented by a stray curl of hair that had escaped her chignon. He admired the gentle slope of her softly rounded shoulders. It stimulated him to watch the way her nimble fingers danced across the ivories while her hands and shapely arms moved gracefully.

She was in a small room that held only the pianoforte, two upholstered side chairs with matching pillows in them, and a summer-blue settee with a brocade footstool in front of it. There was no one else present in the room that he could see.

He stood there watching her, listening and thinking how lovely, how romantic she looked.

The tempo of the music had him wanting to take Susannah's hand and dance a waltz with her. Dances like the quadrille were fast and fun, but a man never got to actually feel the frame of a woman in his arms with those dances.

Race had been taught better than to spy on anyone, but he couldn't take his eyes off her. Although he was only looking at her back, he could see from the way her body moved and swayed with each note, she was intense and derived much pleasure from playing. And he found great pleasure watching her and listening to the lovely music. His desire for her grew, unrelenting and tense.

Race moved closer to the windowpane. He reached up to shield his eyes with his hand so he could see better, when the gold family-crest ring he wore hit the glass. It sounded like a pistol shot.

Susannah jerked around, and their eyes met. Race jumped back, stumbled, and almost fell. She rose and put her hand over her mouth. He could see she was laughing at him by the glint in her eyes and the way her shoulders shook with each breath.

He deserved it, peeking in her window like a common thug.

He shrugged and gave her a guilty smile. She motioned for him to go to the right where the door was located.

Race felt more than a little naughty, getting caught watching her through the window, but he didn't care because he wanted to see her.

"My lord," she said, stepping out onto the slate-covered landing. "By the saints in heaven, what is a fine upstanding gentleman like you doing lurking around my house and peeking through my window?"

He liked the twinkle in her eyes and the teasing smile on her beautiful, shapely lips. In fact, there wasn't anything about her he didn't like.

"Pardon me, Duchess, but I was listening to you play."

"And watching me, too?"

He raised his eyebrows but didn't admit to that.

"That is not a very polite thing for a marquis to do, is it?"

She moved closer to him and reached up to his neckcloth as if to touch him. A shiver of anticipation and excitement surged through him. She lowered her hand and held up a piece of yew for him to see.

"Why is your coat littered with these?" She brushed more of them away with her fingertips. "You didn't come through your garden to get here, did you?"

He nodded. "And it wasn't easy."

She laughed softly, making Race want to pick her up and swing her around.

"I can see that by the twigs in your hair. You could have come to the front door and knocked like a proper gentleman."

One side of his mouth lifted in a half grin as he brushed a hand through his hair. "What fun would that have been?"

"Probably none."

"My thoughts exactly."

They both laughed, and Race was suddenly glad that he had cut a hole in the hedge and crawled through. When she looked at him like that, he would crawl through hell to get to her.

"I must admit that my being here is simple. I heard lovely music and I came to find its source. I didn't know if it would be you playing, Mrs. Princeton, or someone else. That is all there is to it." He stepped closer to her; his gaze swept down her face and then back up to her eyes. "All the years I've lived here, I've never heard music before."

"Perhaps that's because the pianoforte is new to the house. I bought it a few days ago."

"You are very good."

She smiled shyly and looked away for a moment. "Thank you. My life at Chapel Gate is very quiet, and I've had much time to practice over the years. You don't have to stand outside to listen. Come inside and I will play for you."

"Are you sure? I really didn't want to be a bother if you are practicing," he said, knowing that couldn't be further from the truth. He didn't mind disturbing her at all.

"You are not bothering me."

She turned away to go back inside, but he caught her by the wrist, letting his hand slide down to cup her fingers. Just the feel of her hand in his made him desire to make her fully his.

He held her and said, "Wait."

She turned to him and looked down at his hand on hers. For some ridiculous reason, touching her made him feel very protective of her.

"What I would really like to know is what parties you will be attending tonight. I want to meet you there so I can dance with you."

She lifted her shoulders slightly, rested her green gaze

on his eyes, and said, "I've received some invitations the past couple of days, but I haven't planned to attend any of the parties or balls. I did not come to London to enjoy myself. I have only one mission in mind."

She tried to pull her hand free of his, but he gently held her firm. He stepped closer to her. "I'm not going to go away, Susannah."

"Why do you want me to go to a party so you can dance with me? You don't know anything about me or my past, because you haven't bothered to inquire."

Race took in what she'd said. "Do you think I have no interest in you because I haven't tried to find out about your past? Nothing could be further from the truth. I haven't wanted to delve into your past because it's not important to me, Susannah. And how can I get to know more about you if I can't persuade you to spend a little time with me?" Race brought her hand up to his lips and kissed the back of her palm.

She sighed as he allowed her to pull her hand free of his. "You are a difficult man, my lord."

"And contrary to the way I behave most of the time, I stand by my statement that I am a patient man." He gave her a teasing smile. "So, now can I sit for a while and listen to you play?"

"Mrs. Princeton isn't here right now, but Cook, the housekeeper, and my maid are here, so I suppose it is acceptable for you to come inside." She headed for the door. "May I offer you some tea?"

"Just music." He smiled at her again and wondered if she knew that right now he wanted to pick her up in his arms, take her upstairs to her room, lay her on her bed, and make slow, sweet love to her.

Susannah had had very few opportunities to play the pianoforte for anyone other than her mother and any staff who might happen to hear her practice, but she wasn't in the least nervous about playing for the marquis. She knew she was very good.

"Sit where you like," she said.

She watched him sit down in the middle of the settee and prop one of his booted feet on the opposite leg. He was divinely handsome in his crisp white shirt, red waist-coat, and black jacket littered with tiny bits of shrub. She enjoyed simply looking at him.

Susannah needed no written music, and that was good because she didn't have any with her. But what should she play for him? Should she ask if he had a favorite? No, what if he asked for a song she didn't know how to play? That might prove embarrassing.

Her fingers splayed onto the ivories, and she felt Race's hot gaze on her face. Suddenly, she started playing the sprightly melody of Bach's "Invention."

About halfway through the piece, she glanced up at Race. He was watching her with admiration and desire in his eyes. It pleased her to know her talent gave him enjoyment.

She looked back down at the ivories, but what she wanted to look at was Race's seductive eyes. She wanted to tell him she was charmed and flattered that he had come over, that he wanted to hear her play, that he was pursuing her.

He must know how difficult it was for her to resist

him. His smile, his manner, and even his roguish reputation captivated her, intrigued her, and seduced her.

She took in a deep, languid breath as she finished Bach's score and went immediately into a Beethoven Sonata. As she played, she kept thinking about Race. What was she going to do about him? If she accepted invitations and attended the exclusive parties in London, would she be opening herself up to the kind of shame and ridicule she experienced before she married the Duke of Blooming? Did Society ever truly forget about indiscretions, she wondered? Would being with the charming marquis be worth the risk of heartache again? She didn't know the answer to any of those questions.

When the music was over, she rose, moved from behind the pianoforte, and curtseyed.

Race rose and clapped. "Bravo, Duchess, bravo." He took both her hands firmly, warmly in his, kissing first one and then the other. "These hands are magical when you're playing."

She smiled and laughed lightly. "You are such a flatterer."

With the backs of his fingers, he skimmed down her cheek and brushed aside a wispy strand of hair. "I have been, but not this time. I'm telling the truth. Thank you for playing for me. I had a hell of a—pardon me, I had a trying day, and listening to you play soothes me."

"I'm glad."

Bending his head, he gently brushed his lips across hers. The kiss was so gentle and brief that if she tried, she could probably convince herself it never happened.

Yet her heart rate told a different story. It was beating out of control.

She gazed into his eyes, her heart hoping he'd kiss her again because she knew she wouldn't resist him.

He gently tugged on her hands, and she went willingly into his strong, waiting arms. They tightened around her and snuggled her against his chest. He lowered his head again, and instinctively her lips parted, her mouth opened, and his tongue slipped inside with a warm, slow, easy thrust. The kiss was long, generous, and eager. Short, choppy breaths mingled with long, whispery sighs.

He lifted his head barely an inch from hers and said, "I've wanted to kiss you like this since I first saw you standing so poised and so proper in my house, telling me I could charm a nun out of her chemise."

Susannah laughed. "You know I never said such an outrageous thing."

"Oh, right," he teased. "You asked me to guess if you were a tiger or a nun."

He was simply too charming for words. "You know it was a leopard, and I never asked you to guess anything about me," she said with a smile. "You are a devilish rogue who has twisted my words beyond recognition. You have forgotten what I said."

His eyes turned serious as he held her close. "No, I haven't forgotten one thing about you. But what I remember most about that afternoon was that our attraction to each other was instant and mutual. We both felt it."

A quickening started in the depths of her abdomen

and shuddered all the way up to her breasts and lingered there before moving on to her throat, tightening it.

"I'm not denying that," she whispered.

His eyes searched her face. "What do you suggest we do about it?"

"Accept it?" she questioned.

His lips crooked into a captivating grin. "Perfect answer."

His head bent toward hers again. Susannah knew what they were doing was not acceptable in Polite Society, and heaven help her but she didn't care. There was something particularly delicious about once again being rebellious against all that her peers held dear. She had no inclination to discourage Race from the liberties he wanted, and she had no inhibitions about being in his arms.

Her lips parted again, and when his touched hers, she knew this would not be a gentle kiss. His lips brushed hungrily, greedily over hers, and she matched his fervor. His strong, firm arms wrapped tightly around her back and crushed her to him. It pleased her to hear him swallow small gasps of pleasure as her tongue explored the inside of his warm mouth. Passion, hot and demanding, seared between them.

He kissed his way over her chin, down her neck, and back up to the sensitive spot behind her ears. Susannah's skin pebbled with delicious tingles. He kissed the lobe of her ear, pulling it and the small gold earring she wore into his mouth. Shivers of delight threaded across her breasts, through her abdomen, and settled between her legs. Her lower body strained to get closer to the hardness she felt beneath his breeches. The elating sensations caused her to press her lips to his once again and slide her tongue deep into his mouth with a muffled groan.

Susannah ran her open palms over the width of his strong back. She loved the feel of the expensive wool fabric of his coat beneath her hands. She slid her fingers into the back of his thick, rich hair and gloried in the freedom to touch him as she wished.

He found the hollow at the base of her throat, and his tongue sampled her skin again. "You taste as rich as the finest cream, Susannah."

"You tempt me too much, Race."

"I'll consider that an honor."

Desire soared between them as his hands ran up her back, over her shoulders, and down to her breasts. He cupped them, fondled them as he continued to kiss her lips, her cheeks, and her chest. She moaned her pleasure deep in her throat. Susannah felt as if her insides were twisting into wondrous knots of pleasure, and it was thrilling. She felt more alive than she had felt in years.

She loved the way his lips moved over hers and the taste of his tongue in her mouth. She was eager to enjoy everything she was experiencing, but should she give in to desire for a handsome, charming man as she once had?

Somewhere in the back of her mind, Susannah knew she was playing with fire so, reluctantly, she pushed out of his arms and stepped away from him.

Trying to calm his labored breathing, Race took a deep breath and smoothed down his hair with his hand.

"Susannah," he said.

She turned to him, lifted her chin, squared her shoulders, and without emotion said, "I was eighteen and only three weeks into my first Season when it happened."

Race started toward her, but she held out her hand to stop him from coming closer.

"Susannah, don't. It's not important what happened years ago."

"It is to me. I want you to know everything about my past, and then if you still want me to meet you at a party some evening or go for another ride in the park, I will."

"All right. Tell me anything you want, but know this, nothing you can say will affect what I am feeling for you right now or how I will feel about you after you finish."

She believed him. Susannah turned away from him. He had given her an out. She didn't have to tell him.

So don't.

No, I can't go any further with him unless I do, and my heart tells me to enjoy this man.

Race watched Susannah closely as she turned back to face him, looking strong and confident. She was studying over what he had said. He didn't care a fig about her past, but if it was that important to her, he would listen. It was the present and the future that mattered to him, and he had already decided he wanted her in both. He gave her an understanding smile and nodded once.

"I met him at my first party. He was so confident and handsome. My heart was so young and eager to find the perfect husband before the Season was finished. After our dance that first evening, I knew he was the man I wanted to marry.

"We danced the next night and the next. I flirted with other gentlemen, and I watched him dance with other ladies, but our eyes always found each other across the room. I remember I was so jealous when I saw him dance with ladies I considered prettier than me."

"I can't believe there was anyone lovelier than you, Susannah," Race said.

"There was." She smiled at him. "One of my friends made a match after the first week of the Season to a gentleman she fell madly in love with. I was already into the third week and thinking I was going to be left on the shelf."

He searched her face, wondering if she still loved the man. Race was pleased when he didn't see pining for lost love in her eyes, just an acceptance of what had happened.

"I was worried and eager. Was there another that he loved? Was I going to lose him? When he asked me to join him in the garden one night, I was thrilled and readily agreed. I slipped away from my parents to meet him."

"What happened?"

Her eyes took on that faraway quality that he often saw in Gibby's eyes when he was remembering the past.

"He took my hands and told me how lovely I was and how desperately he loved me. He asked to kiss me, and of course I allowed him to. I saw no harm. I had so many stars in my eyes, I couldn't see anything but him. Besides, he told me he loved me. I thought we were going to be married."

"The beast was lying."

"Yes, but I didn't know that at the time. His kisses

thrilled me. He wanted to touch me, and I wanted him to. Unfortunately, my uncle and two of his friends happened along and caught us with my dress off my shoulders."

Though he really didn't want to know, Race had to ask. "Did you let him make love to you?"

She took a deep breath. "So some would say. I was still a virgin when I married the duke, but alas, I was not untouched according to the strict rules of Society. In fact, my husband was quite surprised I was a virgin."

"And also delighted, I'm sure. Why didn't this other man marry you after he compromised you?"

She gave a mirthless laugh. "We never spoke after that. I suppose the main thing was that he didn't love me. He wanted only to seduce me. After I allowed him to touch me, suddenly I was soiled goods as far as he was concerned. He told my father that if I had let him kiss me and touch me as he had, then I must have allowed others to do the same."

"He spoke like a pig," Race said, his anger rising at this unknown man.

"I blame only myself." She walked over to the window and stared out. "It was my folly. I shamed my parents. My mother took to her sick bed. In fact, I didn't see or hear from her for over a year after my marriage."

Race walked up behind her and laid his open hand on her back, rubbing from one shoulder to the other. "It must have been hard on you to have your mother reject you like that."

"No, I felt it was justified after what I had done. My father told me I would never be welcomed in anyone's house in London again."

"Society's rules can be harsh."

"During that time, my parents seldom let me out of the house, and when I was allowed, I had to hide my face with my parasol. That was all right with me. I didn't really want to see anyone. I was ashamed, not because I had let him kiss me and touch me, but because I was foolish enough to think he loved me. He made me feel like a fool, and that was difficult to accept."

"How did it come about that you married the duke?"

She faced him. "My father heard he was coming to London to look for a suitable wife, so he sent him a letter about me. The duke came to London, and I was presented to him one afternoon. We married three days later. I left London and never came back until I came to find you. So you see, I have a tarnished reputation, and I'm not sure I'll be welcomed at anyone's house."

Race's forehead wrinkled into a frown. "I doubt anyone will recall such a minor event after so many years."

She smiled at him. "It did not seem minor at the time."

"But now you are a duchess—a beautiful, unattached duchess. You will be welcomed by everyone, Susannah, that is why you are already receiving invitations. The day you married the duke, your past was swept clean, and if your parents didn't tell you that, they should have."

Her eyes lingered on his face, and she smiled gently. "So now that you know about my past, do you still want to dance with me?"

Race moved closer to her. "Now more than ever. It does not matter to me that you had a few stolen kisses with a handsome beau when you were so young. Do you mind telling me the man's name?"

"No," she laughed softly. "I have long since lost any feeling I had for Lord Martin Downings. I have no idea if he is still in London or if he is still among the living."

Race's eyebrows rose, and he smiled. "I know of the man and his wife. They attend a few parties, and I can hardly wait for him to see what he gave up twelve years ago."

Race swept Susannah up into his arms and kissed her solidly on the lips. He smiled down at her.

"Get ready to dance, Susannah. I will see to it you receive an invitation to Lord Boatwright's party at the Great Hall on Friday evening. Make your plans to be there."

He turned and strode triumphantly out of her music room.

Nine

My Dearest Grandson Alexander,

While reading through some old letters, I came across this exceptional quote from my dear friend Lord Chesterfield: "Never seek for wit; if it presents itself, well and good; but even in that case, let your judgment interpose, and take care that it be not at the expense of anybody. For wit and judgment ever are at strife, though meant for each other's aid, like man and wife."

Your loving Grandmother,
Lady Elder

SUSANNAH SAT IN THE OUTER OFFICE OF MR. MILES Rexford, waiting for him to see her. The documents she had brought to London with her were tucked safely in a small leather folder and rested in her lap. Mrs. Princeton sat quietly beside her, reading. Susannah knew of no other way to force Race's hand. He had left her no choice but to obtain legal representation in order to get the pearls.

A door opened quickly, and a rather stout, gray-haired man wearing spectacles rushed over to her and bowed. "Your Grace, sorry to keep you waiting."

Susannah rose. "I didn't mind. It gave me time to collect my thoughts."

"Come this way."

Susannah and Mrs. Princeton followed him into his office and took a seat in the chairs he offered.

"Now, tell me, what I can do for you?" Mr. Rexford asked, lowering his bulky body into his large leather chair.

Susannah hesitated only a moment and then handed him the folder. "These documents prove my family is the legal owner of the Talbot pearls. They are currently in the possession of the Marquis of Raceworth, and I want to see them returned to my family."

He peered at her from over the top of his spectacles as he laid his hand on top of the folder. "Hmm. Have you spoken to Lord Raceworth about this?"

"Yes, more than once. He refuses to look at my evidence."

"That's not surprising. If he examined your evidence, he would be forced to make a decision one way or the other as to the validity of your claim."

"I agree, but I have not been able to make him do that. I'm hoping you can."

The man's small, dark eyes appeared eager as he took the folder and opened it.

Susannah remained on the edge of her chair as it seemed to take the man an hour to read through the pages. He grunted every so often and mumbled to himself from time to time, but never took the time to even glance up at her.

Finally he closed the folder and laid it down on his desk. He looked up at Susannah, and in a matter-of-fact tone said, "These documents appear to be legitimate to me. I think you have a strong case that the pearls were stolen from your family. Tell me, have you shown these to the magistrate?"

"No, and at this point, Mr. Rexford, I would rather not. I want this matter to be handled privately if possible. I don't relish the idea of personal business landing in the scandal sheets."

"I understand completely and I will do my utmost to see that doesn't happen, Your Grace."

"My hope is that you can contact Lord Raceworth's solicitor and handle this directly with him and not involve others."

He leaned back in his chair. It squeaked noisily. "All right, I'll see what I can do for you, Your Grace. It might take me a few days to get back to you. First, I'll have to find out who the marquis's solicitor is and make an appointment with him. I'm sure he'll want time to look at this." He patted the folder. "And after we have spoken, I'll be back in touch with you."

Susannah studied over what he said.

"Is there something you don't like? Just tell me."

"Those papers are all I have to substantiate my claim. I would be devastated if anything happened to them."

He held up his hands. "Don't worry, Your Grace. I will not let them out of my sight, and I will not leave them with anyone."

Susannah let out a deep breath of relief and rose. "Thank you, Mr. Rexford, I'll leave this in your capable hands."

———

Later that evening, there was no trepidation in her

movement as Susannah walked up the steps to the Great Hall with Mrs. Princeton by her side. She had been eagerly awaiting the time for them to leave for the ball. The night was almost balmy, which was unusual for the month of May. A golden glow came from the massive double doors that had been thrown wide, and the sounds of lively music drifted on the heavy, damp air.

At the marble landing to the entrance of the building, Susannah stopped in the doorway and looked down into the crowded ballroom. It had been so long since she'd been in the Great Hall, but judging from the swirling throng of people inside, it didn't appear as if any part of it had changed, especially not the impeccably dressed gentlemen and the elaborately gowned ladies filling the open, spacious floor.

The magnificent ballroom was lined down each side with fluted Corinthian columns. Some of the stately pillars formed little alcoves where intimate groups could shield themselves from the masses. The detailed woodwork around the ceiling was touched in gilt, and the walls were decorated with silks, brocades, and ornately painted landscapes. The enormous columns had been draped with vines of bright green ivy, colorful spring flowers, and wispy yards of white and sky-blue satin.

From out of the center of the crowd below, Susannah saw Race striding toward her. She turned to Mrs. Princeton, who was dressed in a dark brown gown with white lace collar and cuffs, and said, "You may feel free to enjoy your evening. I will find you when I am ready to leave."

"Thank you, Your Grace," Mrs. Princeton said and walked away.

Susannah turned back toward Race and smiled as he approached. His expression was tender, and it touched her heart. He looked splendid in his formal evening attire of a black cutaway jacket and slim-legged trousers. His crisp white shirt was covered by a gold-colored, quilted waistcoat.

He stopped in front of her. His gaze skimmed down her face and then back up to her eyes, telling her with his expression that he was happy to see her.

"I've been waiting quite impatiently for you to arrive," he said.

Susannah tilted her head back a little and smiled at him. "I didn't know I needed to be here at any specific time."

He chuckled lightly. "The devil you didn't. I think you were intentionally late just so I would squirm."

"Not so," she argued good-naturedly. "I thought it was still fashionable to be late."

She felt his gaze caress her lips, and somehow she knew he wanted to kiss her. And that made her stomach tingle expectantly.

"You are a beautiful lady, Susannah, and well worth the wait. I'm glad you came."

She looked into his magnificent brownish-green eyes and without delay said, "So am I. I haven't been to a big party like this in many years. I intend to enjoy every moment of it. I want to dance and drink champagne. I want to smile at all the handsome gentlemen and be envious of all the beautiful ladies."

Race's eyebrows rose, questioning her. "I'm not sure I want you smiling at any of the gentlemen, handsome or not, and there is no reason for you to be envious of any of the ladies in attendance." His gaze swept easily down her face and then back up to rest on her eyes. "There is not one lady in London who can compare to your beauty tonight."

Susannah gave him a teasing smile. "You say that only because you are smitten with me. I can assure you other gentlemen will not think as you do."

His eyebrows lifted in mock surprise. "So you think I'm smitten with you, do you?"

"I do."

"Guess what? You're right, and if you keep looking at me that way, I will show you just how smitten I am right here in the doorway."

Susannah shook her head. "That wouldn't be wise, my lord. You kissed me in public the other day and, somehow, fate smiled on me and no one managed to see you. I do not want to tempt fate twice and possibly be ruined once again here on my first night back in the center of Polite Society."

He moved closer and smiled warmly at her. "I don't want that either, because I don't want you to have any reason to say 'no' should I decide to ask you to go riding in the park with me again."

"So there is some doubt as to whether you will invite me again?" she said good-naturedly.

His eyes shimmered with humor. "Of course. A lot depends on whether you step on my toes when we're dancing."

They both laughed.

"What the devil are you two doing standing in the entrance way of the ballroom? Are you trying to make a spectacle of yourselves?"

Susannah spun to see a tall, extremely handsome man, with longish dark-brown hair, walking toward them. Everything about him projected power, privilege, title, and wealth. He had the brightest blue eyes she had ever seen, and his gaze immediately zeroed in on her. Without question, she knew this man had to be one of Race's notorious cousins.

"Morgan," Race said, smiling. "I was hoping you would be here." He turned to Susannah. "May I present my cousin, the Earl of Morgandale. Morgan, may I present the Dowager Duchess of Blooming."

Susannah didn't miss the curious glance Lord Morgandale threw his cousin's way before the earl bowed and kissed her gloved hand. In the way he looked at her with narrowing eyes and a tightness around his mouth, she got the distinct impression that he had reservations concerning her, and she had a feeling it had nothing to do with her ruined reputation twelve years ago.

"It's a pleasure, Duchess," he said, looking straight into her eyes but with enough chill in his voice to belie his words and send icy fingers of disapproval running down her back. "I was wondering when you were going to make your first appearance in Society."

Susannah didn't like feeling as if she had to defend her reluctance to enter Society, but she did understand Race's cousin's curiosity about her.

Keeping a smile on her face, she pleasantly said, "First appearance? Perhaps you didn't know that I was in the park with Lord Raceworth just a few days ago."

Lord Morgandale cleared his throat uncomfortably and then said, "Pardon me, Your Grace. I should have said at a party or ball."

She gave him a knowing smile. "There has been so much to do that it has taken me longer than I expected to get settled into my new home."

"So I understand. I was actually at Race's house for the card party when you arrived there a couple of weeks ago, though we didn't manage to meet that day."

Susannah thought she heard a hint of disdain in his voice, though he kept his face impassive. No doubt he knew that she claimed the Talbot pearls belonged to her family. She couldn't expect Race to keep something as important as that from his cousins. And according to all she had read about them, the three men were quite close.

"I'm sorry we didn't meet at that time. I remember how busy with activity his house was that day, and I'm sure my unexpected arrival only added to it."

He lifted one eyebrow and said, "In ways you'll never know, Duchess."

"Morgan," Race said, "are Blake and Henrietta here?"

"Yes, and Gibby's here, too," Morgan said, turning to Susannah. "Though I believe you have already met our dear friend."

A warm feeling washed over Susannah. Just thinking about the spunky old gentleman made her feel good.

"Indeed, I have met Sir Randolph. I look forward to saying hello to him later in the evening."

"I thought it was you two I saw standing in the doorway when I walked by. What is this? Are the two of you having a meeting without me again?"

Susannah heard a very pleasing and friendly voice, but Race and Lord Morgandale were standing side by side and their wide shoulders blocked her view of the man approaching them.

But when Lord Raceworth and Lord Morgandale turned, it allowed Susannah to see another magnificent man of towering height and broad shoulders striding toward them. He wasn't quite as tall as Race or the earl, but he was equally handsome, and he walked with a stately air befitting a king. Somehow Susannah knew this man was Race's other cousin, the recently married Duke of Blakewell.

Susannah smiled with pleasure and lightly shook her head in awe. How had one woman, the legendary Lady Elder, been blessed with three such masterful and powerful-looking grandsons?

Something Susannah had read just recently in one of Lord Truefitt's columns came back to her as Race made the formal introductions once again.

Everyone in the ton knew that Lady Elder had tried many times by fair and foul means to force her grandsons to marry. After all, she had been married four times. Decades earlier she had successfully married off each of her three daughters to titled gentlemen. And in turn, each daughter had given her a grandson, all in the same year.

The grandsons turned out to be rogues of the highest order, notorious for many reasons, including their titles, handsomeness, and rumored debauchery. But nothing made them more popular than the fact that all three remained bachelors into their thirtieth year. Not even vast fortunes had tempted any of them to propose matrimony to any of the young ladies who fancied them, until the fair Miss Henrietta Tweed made her way to London and captured the heart of the handsome Duke of Blakewell, and she became his duchess.

The duke turned to Susannah and said, "My wife, Henrietta, has been anxious to meet you. She was sorry you declined her invitation to tea."

Though the duke said the word *sorry*, she was quite sure he meant she was *miffed*. Perhaps Susannah had been too hasty in her refusal of the duchess's invitation to tea, but at the time, she was still reluctant to open herself up to too many people, especially those connected to the marquis.

She was momentarily at a loss for words but finally managed to say, "I'm sure no excuse will make up for my being unable to attend that afternoon. Perhaps I can meet her tonight and offer my personal apology."

His Grace remained silent and looked her over as thoroughly as Lord Morgandale had. Susannah's chin lifted ever so slightly, but otherwise she stood perfectly in stature and without shame or guilt and let him assess her for as long as he wanted.

Susannah was pleased with her appearance for the evening. Her amethyst-colored gown had a demure neckline befitting a dowager, though she was far younger than the average widowed duchess. The capped sleeves of her bodice were adorned with plum-colored velvet ribbons that had been tied into perfect bows. The decoration banded her high-waisted gown and trimmed the four flounces of her full skirt. Her maid had swept her hair up and threaded small violet flowers through the curls. At the base of her throat rested a large amethyst circled by diamonds, held around her neck by a velvet ribbon.

Though she felt good about herself, Susannah certainly hadn't impressed either of Race's cousins. But what could she expect? She didn't have much to recommend her. She had been compromised as a young lady, and now in their eyes she was after Race's inheritance from his grandmother. She really couldn't expect to find favor with them. She was content with that.

Her gaze drifted over to the marquis. His sensuous eyes were riveted on her. Even though he had remained quiet and let her assess his cousins, she hadn't lost sight of his nearness. Susannah felt an unexpected rush of joy. It didn't matter what the earl or the duke thought about her; Race found her desirable, and he was the only one she wanted to please.

"That will not be a problem, Blake," Race said, looking completely at ease. "I'll make sure Henrietta meets Susannah before the night is over."

"So it's Susannah," Morgan said, looking from Race to Susannah. "Race wasn't sure what your given name was when I last spoke to him."

"That said, Duchess," the duke said, "may Morgan and I be allowed to call you Susannah?"

Susannah faced the handsome man who had no real friendliness in his tone. The duke knew that, out of respect to her title, they must call her Duchess or Your Grace unless she gave them permission to be so informal and use her Christian name. She had the feeling from both Race's cousins that they would be quite comfortable calling her names that couldn't be used in mixed company.

That thought made her smile.

Because she understood their reluctance to befriend her, she smiled sweetly at first the duke, and then she turned to the earl and said confidently, "You are both free to call me Susannah or anything else you might prefer, including that witch who wants my grandmother's pearls."

Seeing the surprise on their faces, she looked at Race, and they both started laughing.

Race cleared his throat to hide his chuckle. "Now, if you two don't mind, I think it's time Susannah and I had a glass of champagne."

Race and Susannah walked past a shocked earl and stunned duke.

"You are a brave woman, Duchess, to take on my cousins as you just did," Race said as they started down the three steps that led into the grand ballroom.

"I have nothing to fear from them, my lord. Your cousins are predisposed to dislike me, and I understand that. But perhaps now they can at least be comfortable around me, knowing that they don't have to pretend to approve of me, or perhaps I should say approve of the reason I am in London."

His eyes were sparkling with laughter when he said, "I'd say you made that quite clear. It's the first time I've seen both of them totally speechless at the same time. That was worth a handful of gold coins and you gave it to me for free."

"Delighted to be of service," she said as they melted into the mob of revelers in the ballroom.

The first couple of hours at the Great Hall were a blur to Susannah as people were presented to her without a break in the steady flow. Everyone wanted to be able to say they had met the new duchess in Town. She became reacquainted with a couple of ladies she had known years ago, and several of the older women had inquired after her mother. Somehow in the crush of people she and Race had become separated, but every once in a while she would see him watching her from across the crowded room.

If anyone even remotely remembered why she had left London and married the duke so suddenly, no one made mention of it, nor did she feel any hesitancy in the warm greeting she received from everyone she met, except for Race's cousins.

"There you are, Your Grace," Mrs. Princeton said, walking up to Susannah with a tall, slender gentleman she had met a few minutes earlier. Lord Snellingly was a handsome man and easy to remember because not only was his neckcloth and collar so ridiculously high and tight he could hardly move his head, he carried a white lace handkerchief and painted porcelain snuff box in one hand.

The man bowed and then said, "Your Grace, first let me say I have never seen beauty that compares to yours."

"Thank you, Lord Snellingly."

He sniffed and then smiled at her. "Your companion has just told me that you play the pianoforte."

"Yes," Susannah answered, cutting her eyes around to Mrs. Princeton. The woman was positively beaming, and Susannah knew what that meant. Mrs. Princeton thought this man would make Susannah an excellent beau or husband. Even though she had warned Mrs. Princeton not to do any matchmaking, she guessed the woman couldn't help herself.

"I was hoping you might allow me to call on you tomorrow or perhaps another day that would be at your convenience, so that I might listen to you play."

"I'm flattered that you would want to, Lord Snellingly, but I really don't play for anyone but myself, so that won't be possible."

"Oh, but you don't understand," he said, stepping a little closer to her. "I write poetry. Perhaps you've read some of my published works?"

Susannah shook her head and started thinking about how she was going to politely get away from this man.

"No matter." He paused and sniffed. "I'll bring some of my best poems and read them to you. I know if I could sit and admire you while you play that I would be able to write the most inspiring poetry. I can feel it deep in my heart that I could create verse that would make all the ladies in London weep."

"Thank you, Lord Snellingly, but I really couldn't do that." She turned to her companion. Mrs. Princeton was obviously in awe of the man she thought to be a poet and thereby a perfect beau for Susannah, so she would leave Mrs. Princeton to talk to the man.

"Lord Snellingly, Mrs. Princeton. You must excuse me. I see someone I need to speak to." Susannah quickly turned away, not giving either of them the time to respond and delay her.

To escape, she headed for the champagne table and was thrilled to see Race standing there, his back to her. As she approached, he turned around, holding two glasses. He smiled when he saw her and started toward her.

"You are too popular this evening, Duchess," he said, handing a glass to her. "It seems every time I ask you to dance, someone arrives and diverts our attention from dancing to conversations. And the next thing I know you are talking to someone like that fop Lord Snellingly."

"The poet?" she asked.

"That is what he claims, but I've yet to hear of anyone agreeing with him on that account. I wouldn't advise you to encourage him, unless you want him sending you poetry every day."

Susannah thought of the two unpretentious notes she had received from Race. One telling her he wanted to take her for a ride in the park and the other simply indicating he wanted to see her. Both notes had thrilled her immensely. She kept both of them in a secret part of her jewelry chest. She couldn't count the times she had taken them out and read them. They always made her smile.

"No worries there, my lord. I sensed as much from him and slipped away from him as soon as I could, but even with encounters like Lord Snellingly, I am enjoying myself much more than I thought I would."

He bent his head a little closer to hers and said, "Excuse me, but are you by chance admitting that you were wrong about something?"

Her eyes rounded in mock horror. "Surely not. That would go against everything I believe in."

Race laughed and Susannah was amazed by how much she enjoyed just the simplest of conversations with him.

"As soon as the music starts up again, Susannah, we are going to dance."

"Race, Duchess, there you are," Sir Randolph said, walking up to them. "Morgan told me you were here, but there are so many blasted people in here it's difficult to get around to finding anyone."

"I have certainly seen you, Sir Randolph," Susannah said, smiling at the debonair man.

His brown eyes twinkled, and his shoulders lifted. "You have?"

"On the dance floor," Susannah said. "I think you've been out there for most every dance."

Sir Randolph glanced eagerly at Race. "How do I look? Do I seem to be keeping up with the younger ones?"

Race hesitated, so Susannah said, "Most definitely, Sir

Randolph. You appear very fit and agile to me, dancing rings around the much younger gentlemen."

Gibby turned to her, obviously pleased by her comment. "Splendid. That's what I wanted to hear."

"What are you trying to do, Gib?" Race said, looking puzzled. "I've never seen you dance so much."

"Never have. I don't really care much for it. I do it only because it pleases the ladies. Danger Jim said I should dance every night, every dance, to help build up my endurance and help me find my wind."

A deep wrinkle crowded the space between Race's eyebrows. "Your wind? And who the… " Race stopped himself as he threw a glance toward Susannah. She put her champagne glass to her lips to keep from smiling.

Race exhaled deeply and asked, "Gib, who is Danger Jim?"

"He's the bruiser I hired to help me get ready for my fight. He says I have to keep working hard to find my 'bottom.'"

"I can help you with that," Race said in an exasperated voice. "Why don't you try looking at the seat of your breeches? You might find it there."

"Your humor amuses no one, Race," Sir Randolph said with impatience. "Danger Jim said that a man's 'bottom' is where he'll find the depth of his wind, spirit, heart, and courage. Every pugilist has to find that before he will know what he's made of."

"Every man needs to find that whether he ever throws a punch. You know, Gib, there's a reason Lord Chesterfield said, 'There's a fool born every minute.'"

"Nonsense, Race," Susannah said while giving him a stern stare. "I'm certain that Lord Chesterfield said no such thing."

"Well, he should have, because it's a lot truer than most of the blather he wrote to his son."

Susannah scoffed at Race and turned to the older man. "Pay him no heed, Sir Randolph. You don't have to go looking for courage, heart, wind, or anything else. I can see you are brimming with all of them. Just have faith that when you need them most, they will be at your disposal."

"Thank you kindly, Duchess. Race likes to be cantankerous from time to time, so I know not to take what he says to heart."

"You give me reason to be ill-tempered, Gib," Race muttered and then sipped his champagne.

Even though the two men sparred with words, Susannah sensed they had deep respect for each other. There was no hostility, resentment, or jealousy in their tones. She understood Race's concern about the pugilism match. She had never seen one, but she had read a few graphic accounts of the prize-fighting matches, including some of Lord Byron's writings about them. It was not a sport for the fearful or faint-hearted.

"Race, have you seen the posters that went up all over London this afternoon?"

"No." His eyes narrowed again. "What are you talking about?"

"Posters announcing my duel in the park with Prattle."

"It's not a duel, Gib. It's just a fight."

"And I need to come up with a boxer's name. You know all great pugilists have a fighting name."

"Gibby, you are not a boxer, but this is not the place to get into that again. Besides, I just heard someone announce that a dance is starting, and Susannah has promised me a dance."

"I wouldn't talk to you about it anyway. I'm on my way home soon. I can't stay up until the wee hours of the morning anymore. Danger Jim insists I get ten hours of sleep every night. It's already two hours past the time he told me to be in bed."

"Excuse me, Lord Raceworth, Sir Randolph. Good evening to you both."

Susannah looked around to see a tall, tan-skinned man with ink-black hair flowing outrageously long, over his shoulders and down his back. His face was clean-shaven except for a very thin black mustache cresting his upper lip and connecting down to his chin, forming a chin-strap look. His features were sharp and his jaw line angular, giving him an aristocratic appearance.

The man was extremely attractive in an eerie, exotic sort of way. Without being told, she knew this man was the infamous Captain Spyglass.

He wore impeccable formal evening attire, but what made him stand out were the small gold loops he wore in each ear. On the middle finger of his left hand was a shockingly large pearl ring that was surrounded by rubies. Hanging below his intricately tied neckcloth was a Maltese cross fashioned with pearls. Perhaps what she had heard about his pearl obsession was true. The only other man

Susannah had ever seen adorned with so many jewels was the king, the one time she had been presented to him.

"Captain Spyglass," both Race and Sir Randolph said with no friendliness in their voices.

He looked at Susannah with appreciation in his eyes and bowed courteously.

Susannah felt Race stiffen beside her. It was clear Race did not like this man and he did not want to have to introduce them, but after a long pause Race relented and made the proper introductions.

Captain Spyglass kissed her hand and said, "Your Grace, as your humble servant, may I tell you how lovely you are tonight? That amethyst you are wearing is magnificent."

"Thank you," Susannah said.

Race moved closer to Susannah and said, "You must excuse us, but we were heading to the dance floor."

"But there is no music as of now," he said with a smile.

"There will be," Race said, keeping a steady gaze on the man.

The Captain nodded and said, "A moment before you go, please, my lord. I would very much like to visit you again to talk about the pearl necklace you have that I wish to purchase from you. Perhaps I could stop by tomorrow if you would tell me a time that would be convenient."

"There is no time. I'm not interested in discussing anything with you."

Susannah hadn't expected Race to be so rude.

The Captain smiled again and bowed. "Pardon me for disturbing you, my lord. Duchess, Sir Randolph," Captain Spyglass said and turned and walked away.

"I don't trust that man," Sir Randolph said.

"Susannah aptly called him a pirate."

"I agree with her on that," Sir Randolph said.

"But looking at him, I can see why he is on everyone's guest list," Susannah said. "He's quite an impressive man."

Race cocked his head and stared at her. "Impressive, Susannah? And I suppose you also think Lord Snellingly is a handsome man?"

"As a matter of fact, I do think he is quite handsome."

"Which reminds me," Sir Randolph said, "I need to come up with a fighting name."

"You have one," Race said irritably. "It's Gibby, or Gib if you prefer."

"No, I mean for my fight. I need a name like the Iron Man, the Widow Maker, or the Heavy Hammer. A really good prize-fighter needs a name."

"Oh, I know, how about Gib the Pipit?" Susannah said hopefully.

Sir Randolph frowned. "Is a pipit a bird?" Gib asked.

"Yes," she answered. "A small, beautiful bird that resembles a lark."

"Thank you kindly, Your Grace, but I was thinking of something stronger than a bird."

"Then how about Jack-a-lent, Jackanapes, or maybe just the Jackal?" Race asked him.

Sir Randolph threw his shoulders back and puffed out his chest. "If you were using all the Jack names, why did you leave out Jackass? Don't tell me you were trying to spare my feelings?"

"All right, I won't."

Susannah marveled at how easily the two men sparred words with each other yet she neither heard nor sensed true anger in either man.

"I know something that will work," Susannah said, stepping in between the two sparring friends. "How about Gib the Gray Wolf or Gib the Growling Bear? Those are stronger."

Sir Randolph gave her a placating smile. "Something close to that is what I'm looking for. You keep working on it, Duchess." He turned to Race and grinned. "The fight is on."

Susannah sighed as the gray-haired man walked away. "I don't think he liked my suggestions any better than he liked yours."

Race chuckled. "Too bad. I thought Gib the Pipit sounded just like Gibby." He paused. "Is that music I hear?"

She handed him her glass. "Indeed it is."

Race placed the glasses on the table and said, "Let's head for the dance floor."

They turned to leave, and Susannah saw the Duke of Blakewell coming toward them with a beautiful blonde lady walking beside him.

"I think the dance will have to wait a little longer," Race muttered under his breath. "You are about to meet Blake's wife, Henrietta."

"Good," she said. "I've wanted to meet her. This will be my opportunity to make amends."

With the ease that comes only from the peerage, the introductions of a duchess meeting a duchess were dispensed with quickly, and Susannah found herself looking into the friendly eyes of a young lady perhaps ten years younger than she. Unlike the wariness she saw in Race's two cousins' eyes, the Duchess of Blakewell's demeanor was friendly and sincere. Susannah liked her immediately.

"Before we go further, Your Grace," she told the younger lady, "I must apologize again for being unable to have tea with you. It was gracious of you to ask."

The duchess smiled at her. "My heavens, no need to apologize again. I understood perfectly that the timing wasn't good for you. I know I was rushing you, but I was so happy to hear that another duchess was in Town, and one more my age, that I let my eagerness to meet you overshadow my good judgment. I'm the one who must apologize for not giving you more time to get settled before contacting you."

"Perhaps we can arrange another afternoon soon," Susannah offered.

"I would like that. I was about to go to the retiring room. Would you like to join me?"

Susannah turned toward Race. He gave her a slight nod of approval. Their hope for a dance had been thwarted once again.

"All right," Susannah said to the lovely duchess. "Lead the way, and I will follow."

As the two ladies walked away, the Duchess of Blakewell said, "Your outing in the park with Race is the talk of London's drawing rooms right now. I think perhaps I should give a dinner party in your honor and invite a few people over so they can get to know you better."

Susannah's stomach tightened. "Please don't do that,

Your Grace. I don't think that would be a wise idea right now. I don't know how long I will be here."

Her Grace stopped and looked into Susannah's eyes. "What does it matter how long you will be in London? If there's one thing I've learned in my short time, it is if you are a duchess everyone wants to meet you and get to know you."

Susannah stared at her charming face and knew this woman would be a wonderful friend, but the first thing she had to do was be truthful with her. "Your Grace, perhaps your husband hasn't told you, but I'm in Town to lay claim to something his cousin, Lord Raceworth, has in his possession and believes to be his. I don't think His Grace would want you to have a dinner party in my honor."

The duchess turned back to look at her husband. He and Race were deep in conversation. Giving her attention back to Susannah, she said, "But you and Race seem so...so..."

Susannah smiled gratefully. "We are on excellent terms, but I fear his cousins think I have bewitched him."

The Duchess of Blakewell laughed lightly. "Well, Your Grace, it just so happens that I have had some experience with being bewitched and it doesn't bother me at all. I always seem to be in a hurry to get things done, but I will wait a little longer before I suggest a dinner party." Her eyes softened. "How does that sound?"

"Perfect," Susannah answered, and the two ladies walked away laughing.

Ten

My Dearest Grandson Alexander,

No doubt you will agree with this sage quote from Lord Chesterfield: "We must not suppose that, because a man is a rational animal, he will therefore always act rationally; or because he has such a predominant passion, that he will act invariably and consequentially in the pursuit of it. No, we are complicated machines, and though we have one mainspring that gives motion to the whole, we have an infinity of little wheels, which, in their turns, retard, precipitate, and sometimes stop that motion."

Your loving Grandmother,
Lady Elder

LIGHTS FROM THE GREAT HALL FADED FROM VIEW AS Susannah, Race, and Mrs. Princeton walked to where her carriage waited. The coolness of the early morning air was refreshing after the crowded heat of the ballroom. Susannah didn't know how it had happened, except for the fact there were so many people to meet, talk to, and reminisce with, that she and Race were among the last people to leave the ball. The street was almost deserted.

When they reached her carriage, Race looked at her,

and instead of saying good night as she expected, he said, "Susannah, you have lost an earring."

"Oh," she said, both hands going to her ears to check which one. "You are right. I must have lost it somewhere inside."

"Maybe by the champagne table or elsewhere. Perhaps Mrs. Princeton wouldn't mind going back inside and checking for you to see if someone might have turned it over to our hosts. Would you, Mrs. Princeton?" he questioned with a charming smile on his face.

Susannah knew exactly what Race was up to, and so did Mrs. Princeton by the firm set of her thin lips and the glare shooting from her eyes. Though Mrs. Princeton very much wanted Susannah to have a beau, even marry, she would move heaven and earth to protect Susannah's reputation and keep it spotless. Her companion didn't want to leave the two of them with just Benson, her footman, but there was no way Mrs. Princeton was going to say no to the marquis.

"It would be lovely if you would do that for me," Susannah said to her companion.

"Of course," Mrs. Princeton said stiffly and hurried away.

When she was a safe distance from them, Race asked, "Does that woman ever bend the rules for anything?"

"Not much. I'm afraid she's become very protective of me in the ten years we've been together."

"Then I'm lucky to have outsmarted her."

Susannah felt strength and confidence in his hand as he helped her into the carriage. The muggy air of earlier had given way to an early morning chill and she wrapped her cape tightly about her as she sat down and turned back to tell him good night, but he held up his hand to silence her. He gave a quick glance all around, and before she could say anything, he jumped into the carriage beside her and quickly shut the door.

"Race, what are you doing?"

"I suppose I'm tempting fate once again, but I had to get rid of Mrs. Princeton so I could say good night to you without her nosy eyes watching."

She gasped. "You didn't!"

He shrugged but said, "Of course I did." He scooted onto the seat beside her and picked up her gloved hand and placed her earring into her palm.

"You are a devilish rogue," she said and quickly slipped the earring into her reticule.

"And don't forget it," he teased. "I've worked hard for years to earn that title and I intend to keep it."

"With what you did tonight, I don't think you will have any problem doing that. How did you take my earring off without my knowing?"

Race grinned roguishly. "Practice. Where there's a will, there is a way."

"More of Lord Chesterfield's quotes, I presume?"

He laughed. "I hope not. I can't believe we stayed at that blasted party for over four hours and never had one dance."

Susannah looked at his somber face in the dim light of the carriage. She nestled into the soft cushions and sighed. "I fear that is my fault. It's been so long since I've been to such a lavish affair I didn't want the evening to end. The Hall was so glamorous and festive, I'm afraid I was caught up in the magic of the evening. There were so many people to meet and talk to, and it was impossible to get away from some of them."

"Like Lord Snellingly?"

"Ah, no." She laughed. "He was an easy gentleman to run from, but truly the time seemed to fly by."

He edged closer to her and wrapped his arm comfortably around her. She rested her head on his shoulder. The solid warmth of his body dispelled the chilly air in the carriage. He first kissed the back of her hand and then turned it over and kissed the center of her palm. The warmth of his breath penetrated her cotton glove and heated her skin.

"I know. I shouldn't complain. It was your first party in years, and you were indeed the diamond of the ball tonight."

She glanced up at him with disbelief. "You jest. The diamond of the ball is reserved for an innocent young lady and we both know I do not fit into that category."

"But you were, just the same. Everyone wanted to make sure the proper introductions were made so they could put you on their invitation lists. I counted at least nine eligible bachelors who tried to monopolize your time."

She gave him a teasing smile. "That many? Then you must enlighten me as to who they were because I only recognized three of them."

"As Lord Chesterfield used to say: 'The day I do that, it will be a cold day in hell.'"

Susannah laughed freely. "I don't know all of Lord

Chesterfield's sayings, but you and I both know the man never said that in his letters to his son or anyone else."

"Probably not, but since he is dead and won't know it, we can attribute it to him with a clean conscience."

"You are too hard on your grandmother's dear friend. But I was just thinking that there is one good thing about not dancing tonight."

"I can't think of what that might be, Susannah," he said dryly as he rubbed her palm with his thumb.

"Perhaps there will be a next time."

Race let go of her hand and let his fingers drift along her cheek to her chin and he turned her face to his. "I'll make sure there is."

As his tender gaze stayed on hers, his hand slid around to the back of her neck, the heel of his palm resting on her collarbone, his thumb at the hollow of her throat. He bent down and kissed her tenderly, briefly, as if he were shy, and she knew that was not the case. His lips were warm, soft, intriguing, promising more to come. Susannah's breath came in little gasps.

The kiss deepened. A breathless fluttering filled her stomach. When he broke the kiss, Susannah wiped her lips with her tongue. His lips touched hers again, the same as before, brief, non-threatening, but very satisfying. She didn't know how or why such innocent kisses should send deep thrills of desire spiraling through her, but she welcomed them and the way Race made her feel.

She had fallen victim to his charm the first time she saw him, and every time since then, when she was with him, her attraction to him grew stronger.

Susannah lifted her lips to his and whispered, "We don't have much time before Mrs. Princeton returns, Race. Kiss me again."

He needed no more urging. His lips covered hers quickly with hard and hungry pressure as his other arm snaked around her and pulled her tightly against his strong chest. She opened her mouth to him. Their breaths mingled, and their tongues played together as they devoured the heated moment of passion that flared between them.

With one hand he held her close, while the other slipped beneath her cape and found her breast. He caressed her with such skill, she wanted to cry out from the sheer pleasure and excitement his touch created inside her. His movements were exhilarating. As her body reeled from his sensuous assault, she clung to his shoulders, feeling desperate to get closer to him.

His mouth ravaged hers in a savoring kiss that was meant to seduce her and be victorious. His tongue probed her mouth with intensity, and she gave back as much as she took in. His hand expertly kneaded her breast before gliding down her ribs, past her waist, and over her hip, and then slowly moving back up to cup and lightly fondle her breast again.

Susannah sighed with contented pleasure, wanting to give her body over to his exquisite touch. Her arms circled his powerful back. She gloried in the feel of him beneath her hands.

Slowly Race stopped the kiss and moved away from her to the far corner of the seat. His breaths were short and shallow.

Stunned from his withdrawal from her, Susannah asked, "Did I do something wrong?"

"No, no, not you, me," he said huskily. "You tempt me too much, Susannah. I have very little control where you are concerned."

Still reeling from exquisite passion, Susannah swallowed hard and said, "I find myself in the same position as you."

"Yes," he whispered. "But you are a duchess and deserving of more respect than to be taken in a carriage on the street."

That certainly put the situation in perspective for her as to what he was thinking, but his answer did little to satisfy her craving. She was still savoring the way he was able to make her feel. Yes, she was a duchess, but she was also a woman who wanted the touch of this man. Was it wrong for her to want him when he thrilled her in a way she had never experienced before? She appreciated his chivalry and expected nothing less from him, but...

"You are right. I am not a lady of the evening. I am a thirty-year-old widow who has found a man who makes me feel things I have never felt before. I don't want to deny myself this opportunity for I fear I will never have it again." Susannah paused and then said, "Race, will you come to my bed tonight?"

His eyes rounded. He blinked slowly, as if giving himself time to let her words sink in and believe what he had heard. He shifted in the seat and said, "I—of course, if you are sure."

She reflected for a moment on what she had asked of him. She did not regret it. "You seem stunned that I've asked you."

He settled back into the plush cushions once again. He looked at her from hooded eyes. "All right, I am. It's not every day that I have the lady of my dreams invite me to her bed."

A little embarrassed, Susannah smiled to cover her feelings. "I have to admit I'm a little stunned myself that I have asked you. Does my forwardness displease you?"

"Never," he said in a hushed but fervent voice, continuing to keep his distance from her.

"Yet you are still reluctant."

"No, Susannah, I'm having a hard time believing my good fortune."

In the darkened carriage, she couldn't see his eyes too well, but she could see enough to know she had truly shocked him. "You are the first man in a very long time that I have wanted to kiss. No, it's more than that. I long for your touch."

"You make a very strong case, Susannah."

"I would never pressure you to come to me."

"Susannah, please, I feel no pressure except the heaviness in my trousers. I am desperate to have you beneath me, have no worry about that."

"And I have no innocence to protect. I have no young maidens looking to me as an example for behavior. I have lived an exemplary life for twelve years. And now after meeting you, even with the unsettled issue we have between us, I want to be with you the way a woman wants to be with a man she desires."

His eyes were inquisitive as he asked, "Have you had no lovers since your husband?"

"There's been no one." Her gaze fluttered down his face. "I have never wanted one until now, until I met you."

"I will come, but what will you do about your maid and Mrs. Princeton? That woman watches you like a hawk."

Susannah laughed lightly. "She does take her job too seriously, sometimes to my detriment. My bedchamber is on the first floor. They sleep on the second floor, the opposite side of the house, and they are both sound sleepers. If we are careful, no one should know of your presence. There are stairs on the east side of the house that lead to a door on the first floor."

Race opened the carriage door and then looked back at her. "I saw the stairs when I was there the other day."

"Once inside, take the door on the left. It will lead you to a hallway. My room is the first door on the right."

"Make sure the door is unlocked, Duchess. I will be there."

Race stepped out of the carriage and shut the door.

Susannah's heartbeat danced with expectancy, warming her as she tucked her cape tighter about her shoulders. Her decision to invite him to her bed was rash, and perhaps she shouldn't have asked him until she understood her feelings for him. But when she was with him, she simply didn't want to deny herself his attention. The instinctive reaction Race aroused in her was the response of a woman wanting a man's touch. She knew he wanted to be with her as much as she wanted to be with him.

She had never desired her husband's touch, though he was a good and kind man and she was an obedient and faithful wife. She had accepted his attentions whenever he came to her bedchamber, but she had never been pleasured by him.

In her youth, she had wanted Lord Martin Downings's touch; but now, unlike with Lord Martin so many years ago, she was experienced enough to know Race wasn't promising love, marriage, or even tomorrow. He simply wanted to enjoy her tonight, and she intended to enjoy him.

———

Susannah had said good night to Mrs. Princeton and dismissed her maid as soon as her dress and undergarments were unfastened. She had no fear that either of them would wake during the night.

After unlocking the outside door so Race could enter, Susannah was filled with wonder and anticipation. She went to her room and lit a candle on her dressing table and one by her bed. There would be no need for the brighter lamplight tonight. She was nervous yet excited; she was calm yet eager. And she had never felt saner in her life. Race had captivated her like no other man ever had. She believed with all her heart that what she was doing was the right thing for her to do.

With trembling hands, she stripped to her white cotton chemise that fell in length to just above her knees, and then she sat down at her dressing table. She was taking the pins and ribbons out of her hair when she heard a soft, brief knock.

From the mirror, she watched the doorknob turn and the door ease open. Race stepped inside and slowly closed the door. She heard the lock click behind him. He was still handsomely dressed in his evening clothes. She turned on the stool and then rose to face him.

"That didn't take long," she said.

"Fear that you might change your mind, and my eagerness to be here with you, made me hasten."

Susannah smiled and opened her arms to him. Race rushed to her and picked her up in his arms and buried his face in the warmth of her neck.

"Hmm, you smell so damn good," he said, breathing in deeply as he crushed her to him.

"I'm glad you didn't wait. Dawn will be here before we know it."

He set her feet on the floor. She reached up and untied his neckcloth while he shrugged out of his jacket. She took off his collar as he unbuttoned his waistcoat and threw it aside. He yanked his shirt from his waistband and pulled it over his head. Her hands roved up the warm, firm skin of his back and shoulders. She loved the feel of the solid wall of muscles. Her hands moved around his sleek, wide chest and Race unbuttoned his trousers.

Susannah touched her cool lips to the crook of his hot neck, and he groaned. She smiled when she felt him shiver at her touch. How wonderful that she could do that to him by simply placing her lips against his skin.

"Susannah," he whispered huskily. His hands cupped her small waist for a moment and then moved lower to mold his palms over her shapely hips to draw her more snugly against the hardness beneath his open trousers.

He bent his head, and his mouth sought hers in a kiss so tender it was heavenly. He then lifted his head just enough so he could look into her eyes. Though he didn't say a word, she could see that he was giving her one more chance to change her mind, to throw him out of her room, to say she had made a mistake. But Susannah had no such feelings. She had never been more sure of anything in her life. She placed her fingertips to his masculine lips and slowly moved them gently over his chin, down his throat and chest, past his flat stomach, to the bulge beneath his clothing. She let her hand mold and then close firmly around him.

Race shut his eyes and inhaled deeply, as if her touch were exquisite torture.

He exhaled a shaky breath. "You obviously don't know my boundaries, Susannah. I am not that strong."

He lifted the hem of her chemise and in one fluid motion had it off her body and tossed aside. When she stood before him naked in the dim candlelight, she suddenly felt shy and insecure. He could have any young lady in London; what had made her think he would want her? Her breasts weren't as firm as they used to be. She was thin, her shoulders, ribs, and torso not as voluptuous as in her younger years. The changes in her body had never bothered her until now, when more than anything she wanted to please the man standing before her.

As if sensing her apprehension, he smiled sweetly and whispered, "You are beautiful."

Susannah lowered her lashes. "I am old," she refuted.

"Then I am, too, for we are the same age, are we not?" For a brief moment, Susannah felt tears well in her eyes. Even though her body was not as young as it once was, she saw desire for her in his eyes, and at that moment she knew that she had fallen deeply and madly in love with Race.

With tenderness, he reached up and covered her breasts with his hands, lifting their weight.

Susannah gasped with pleasure at his warm touch.

Race rubbed the nipple gently with his thumb and forefinger. Lowering his head, he kissed the rosy tip of first one breast and then the other.

He looked back into her eyes as he licked his lips and then said, "Hmm, you don't taste old." He gently kneaded her breasts as his twinkling gaze stayed on hers. "You don't feel old." He bent his head again and nuzzled the soft, warm spot behind her ear and breathed in deeply as he whispered, "You don't smell old. You taste, feel, and smell heavenly to me, Susannah."

Susannah's spirits soared, and she laughed lightly. "You are much too charming, Race."

"Good. You feel womanly to me, Susannah, very soft, very firmly womanly."

His warm breath floated across her skin with each word he spoke. Filled with emotion, she threw her arms around him and hugged him tightly, hoping he would know, that he would sense the love she was feeling for him at that moment.

"Get beneath the covers while I take off my shoes and trousers. I don't want you to catch a chill."

Susannah climbed onto the bed her maid had turned down and slipped under the cool, crisp sheet and watched as Race stepped out of his slippers, stockings, and trousers. He was a magnificent man, with wide shoulders, slim hips, and powerful-looking legs.

Without hesitating, Race crawled onto the bed and lay down beside her. He enveloped her in his arms, entwining her legs with his, pulling her smaller, slender body against his. He held her close while his lips roved over hers, his hands explored her breasts, her waist, and the smooth plane of her hip and inside her thigh. He touched her as if she were a fine piece of silk, too delicate to be treated harshly.

His warmth was comforting, and Susannah felt as if her body was unfurling and opening to him, to a man, for the first time. She overflowed with love for him and wished she could tell him, but knew it was best to remain silent and keep her feelings to herself.

Susannah feathered her hands over his shoulders, down his ribs to his flat stomach, and then lower to his manhood. Her hand closed around him. She smiled beneath his generous kiss as he gasped in pleasure.

Lowering his head, he found her nipple and gently sucked it into his mouth, letting his tongue stroke her over and over again. The muscles in her thighs clenched tightly, and she moaned softly as pleasure built inside her.

"I never knew I could feel so good," she whispered.

"This is only the beginning, Susannah," he murmured.

Race moved his lips back up to hers with a hungry kiss. His tongue filled her mouth, exploring its depths. His hand skipped down to the downy thatch between her legs, and he caressed her center, filling her deeply, forcing her to silently moan for more. As passion continued to build inside Susannah, her body moved with his fingers. She felt ready to fall off the edge of something but she didn't know what.

As if sensing her demand for more of him, Race rolled on top of her, settling his weight on her. She felt his hardness between her legs, and she opened for him.

Race lifted himself on his arms and looked deeply into her eyes as he coupled himself fully to her. Susannah lifted her hips to meet him.

For a moment he remained motionless, as if savoring something so special that if he moved, he'd lose it. Susannah glanced down to where their bodies joined, and she was filled, overwhelmed with the luscious sensation of being part of Race. Warmth scattered through her. The words of love she wanted to say remained silent and throbbed in her throat.

Race softly placed his lips on hers as he sank deeper into her.

His body moved smoothly with each long thrust. She caught his rhythm and joined him without reserve.

"Susannah, oh, God, you feel so good," he mumbled against her lips.

Gulping in her breath, she managed to say, "I—I've never felt this way. I think I might scream from the wonder of it."

"Don't do that," he said and completely covered her lips with his as her hips arched to meet him in a final thrust that toppled her over the edge of desire and into that sweet heaven called ecstasy.

A moment later, while still trying to calm her breathing, Susannah felt Race's body shudder, and a broken gasp tore from him. He slowly lowered his chest to hers. Susannah's heart pumped erratically, and she turned her face into the hot, damp crook of his neck. Now, she finally knew what had been missing in her life for so many years, and she couldn't help but wonder how she was going to live without it.

"Susannah, tell me I'm not dreaming. Tell me I'm here in your bed making love to you."

Her hands played in the hair at his nape. "Have you dreamed of being here with me like this, too?"

"More than once. Often, since the first time I saw you in my music room I knew I wanted to be right here with you beneath me."

She ran her hands over his smooth, strong back and smiled at him. "Being with you was better than in my dreams. Your touch was so much more than I expected."

He rose on his elbows and chuckled as his gaze drifted down her face. "I'm glad to hear I exceeded your expectations and won your approval."

His eyes were glowing with joy, and she didn't know when she had ever felt this good, this complete, this satisfied.

"Immensely so."

"Since you are so pleased with my, ah—shall we say

performance—so far, I think I should dig into my bag of tricks and show you a few more things, don't you?"

Susannah laughed and hugged him to her.

And so he did.

"Race," Susannah whispered much later as she kissed his cheek. "It is dawn. You must go before the servants start stirring about in my house and yours."

He looked up and saw her leaning over him. He smiled. "Susannah, my servants have seen me come home at every hour of the day and night, admittedly sometimes not properly dressed."

"However," she countered, "we must be circumspect concerning my servants. My life has not been as varied or as colorful as yours, and I can assure you my servants have never seen me improperly dressed, and I think they would faint if they ever saw a man in my bed."

He let the backs of his fingers trickle down her cheek, her throat, to the valley between her breasts, while his gaze held steadily on hers. "I understand, but I do hate to leave you. The air has just enough chill to make your body impossibly warm."

He kissed her shoulder, the crook of her neck, and let his lips travel to the tip of her breast. "Hmm, I think I might decline to leave and stay a little longer."

Susannah rolled away from him. "I think you will not. But if you behave and leave now, I might invite you to return another night."

Race rose on one elbow. He looked so roguishly

handsome with his hair tousled, his eyes shining with laughter, and his broad chest gleaming in the early light of dawn.

"Susannah, after what we shared, you could not keep me away."

Eleven

"MY LORD, ARE YOU AWAKE?"

Race's lashes lifted to the bright light of day. He rolled over to see his valet standing over him. The short, thin man's eyes were rounded in fear. His hands were held in tight fists at his sides, and his moustache quivered. Race's gaze darted around his bedchamber. No other person was present in the room, and nothing seemed out of place. He had no idea what was wrong with the servant.

A quick glance at the clock on the mantel told Race it

was just past nine o'clock. An ungodly hour to be awakened, especially after spending the night as he had in the bed of the most desirable woman he'd ever met. His lids gently lowered as his thoughts quickly took him back to Susannah's bed.

"My lord, are you awake?"

"Yes, what is it, Jenkins?" Race muttered, keeping his eyes closed, not wanting to be distracted from the pathway his thoughts were leading him.

"You should come downstairs immediately."

Something in the man's tone seeped through Race's sleep-clouded mind. He rose up on one elbow and squinted against the harsh light.

"What is it? Is something wrong with Gibby or one of my cousins?"

The man shook his head. "Not that I know of, my lord."

"Then just tell me what the devil is going on, and be quick about it. I'll decide if I need to disturb my slumber to go downstairs."

"You've been robbed."

"Robbed?" Race bolted up in bed and threw the sheet aside. He was wearing only his trousers from the evening before. He'd been too tired from his blissful night with Susannah to step out of them and pull on his nightshirt. "Damnation, Jenkins, what do you mean by robbed?"

"Mrs. Frost went into your book room to dust just minutes ago and found your safe door standing open and empty."

"Empty!" His grandmother's pearls were in that safe.

Race jumped off the bed and headed for his book room, bare-chested and barefoot. He hurried down the stairs, refusing to let his mind go wild with possibilities. He had first to see for himself what had happened, and then he could think.

When he rushed into the library, Mrs. Frost stood sniffling in a corner, twisting the hem of her apron in trembling hands. His safe was located behind a row of books on the fifth shelf of the bookcase. The volumes had been removed, and the safe door stood open. He felt deep into the recesses of the hole. The safe was as empty as a dry river bed.

"Whoever stole the contents of your safe, my lord, took the time to neatly stack the books on your desk," Jenkins said in a shaky voice. "Mrs. Frost said she hasn't touched a thing since she came in here."

"That's right, my lord," Mrs. Frost said in a squeaky voice. "When I saw your safe open, I immediately ran to find Jenkins so he could wake you. I knew something was wrong. The safe wasn't like that last night. When I came in and turned the lamp out, all was well."

"The odd thing is that I don't know how the man got in and out of the house," Jenkins said, looking bewildered. "I checked all the doors and windows before I went to wake you. They are all bolted from the inside."

"Then who the devil could have gotten in?" Race mumbled more to himself than to seek an answer from his servants.

"We don't know. I've called all the staff into the kitchen so you can question them," Mrs. Frost said. "Jenkins and I don't have a clue as to who might have done this. Everyone has been with you for years, and we can't believe any of them would ever steal anything from you."

"I know how loyal my employees are to me, Mrs. Frost."

"But who else could it be but a servant, if all the doors are locked? Unless maybe it was a ghost that entered and took your valuables," Mrs. Frost said, looking horrified at that thought.

Clearly not believing that possibility, Jenkins said, "Perhaps there is some explanation as to how he got in. The gardener told me a few days ago that he found a large hole cut in the hedge at the back of your garden. He said it would take months for it to grow back. I didn't think that much about it at the time, but now I'm wondering if someone was watching the house, waiting for a time they could slip in unnoticed and make off with whatever was in your safe. He must have gotten in and out before we locked up for the night."

A chill rippled down Race's spine. Not all of the doors in his house had been locked all night. He had left the back door unlocked when he slipped out to Susannah's house and relocked it when he came back in. If someone had been watching his house, they would have seen him leave last night.

A sick feeling hit Race's stomach.

Susannah?

Could she possibly have planned this theft with some-one? A knot of denial clogged his throat. No, she couldn't have known he would leave the door unlocked. And he couldn't have been deceived that badly by her, could he? She had wanted him in her bed. She had wanted him. She had thrilled to his touch. She had not faked her enjoyment, of that he was convinced.

But who else could have known that his back door might be unlocked last night? Was she, as he had first thought, working with someone in order to steal the pearls, or did someone as yet unknown to him create this mischief?

"Did you have much money in there, my lord?" Jenkins asked.

Money? He didn't care a damn that the money was gone or the other documents he had in there. His grandmother's necklace was gone.

His mind whirled with thoughts. Was Susannah in cahoots with Captain Spyglass? Was that why the man was nosing around the Great Hall last night? They acted as if they had never met, but was that just a ruse? It was ridiculous the way the man was decked out with pearls dripping all over him.

But Prinny's man, Harold Winston, was there, too. Race had caught a glimpse of the sly little man sometime during the evening. Had Susannah conspired with him? Race didn't trust that man an inch, either. And the one-armed man, Smith, was still being seen all over Town, acquiring jewels for his antiques shop.

Bloody hell, it could have been any of them. It could have been all of them, but the one thing he knew for sure was that Susannah was the only one who could have known there was the possibility his door would be unlocked. She knew he would not decline her invitation and pass up the chance to be with her.

"Susannah," he growled.

Had she deliberately enticed him into her bed so that she would have an alibi and he wouldn't think it possible that she was in on the burglary? Had she sent someone prowling his grounds, knowing there was a hole in the yew, knowing his house might be vulnerable?

She had been so receptive to him, so responsive, so aroused by his every touch. Susannah had set his soul on fire and made him forget all other women he had ever touched. Had he been so blind to what her real motives were?

He didn't have the answers to his questions but he was going to find out, and he was going to start by having a conversation with the duchess.

Without comment to his servants, Race strode out of the book room, down the corridor and through the kitchen to the back door, which he jerked open and then hurried down the steps. His arms swung limply at his sides, his soul felt empty, and a raging storm was blowing in his heart.

"My lord, where are you going?" Jenkins asked, hurrying behind him.

"To see my neighbor," he offered so calmly it frightened him.

"But my lord, you don't have on a shirt, you don't have on shoes. You are not properly dressed to pay a visit to anyone."

Race didn't slow down. "Obviously not, Jenkins, but nevertheless I am going."

The day was gray and heavy with mist. The pathway stones beneath his feet were wet from recent rain. The damp air chilled his bare chest but did little to cool the heat inside him.

"Wh-what are you doing? There is no way you can get through that hedge. The yew is too thick and the hole is too small."

"Watch me."

Race bent down on his hands and knees and, just as he had twice last evening, he crawled through the opening he'd cut a few days ago. A sharp twig slashed across his chest, and he winced. Several more broken shoots scratched his back, but he didn't let it slow him down as he came out on the other side and into Susannah's garden.

"My lord, should I follow you?" his servant called from the other side of the yew wall.

"No, Jenkins. I don't need you."

Susannah's slate path was overgrown with weeds and not as easy to walk on as his well-manicured pathways; still he stalked ahead. He stepped on a pebble and hissed an oath under his breath, but kept following the path he'd walked just hours before, until he reached the side of the house where the stairs led up to Susannah's room.

He stopped for a moment at the bottom and inhaled a bitter breath. He was shoeless and shirtless, but hell, he didn't care. If Susannah had duped him, he couldn't let her get away with that.

Race climbed the steps two at a time. Luckily, the outside door was still unlocked, so he entered and went straight to Susannah's bedchamber door and threw it open.

She stood in front of her dressing mirror, combing out the longest, most beautiful hair he'd ever seen. She wore a simple, sleeveless, white cotton shift.

She spun and gasped.

Bloody hell! He still wanted her, knowing she might have played him for a fool as no other person ever had. He still wanted her, and that tore him up inside.

"Race," she said and threw down her brush and rushed toward him.

He held up his hand, stopping her, hating himself for his lack of control where she was concerned. "Stay where you are, Duchess."

Her wide eyes searched his face as if she had no idea why he was there.

"But you're bleeding," she said.

He looked down and saw several scratches on his chest. One had a long, thin line of blood running down his ribcage.

"What's wrong?" she whispered. "What happened to you?"

"You are what happened to me, Duchess. I think you drew me to your bed with the pretense of wanting my favors, and all the while you had planned with someone to steal my grandmother's pearls." He extended his hand out, palm up. "Hand them over."

She gasped again. "What?" Her eyes narrowed, and she took a hesitant step toward him, her mouth gaping. "What do you mean, hand over the pearls?" she questioned anxiously. "Don't tell me you don't have them."

"And don't pretend to me that you don't know I no

longer have them," he said, louder than he intended, but the feeling that she could have betrayed him in such a manner had hit him like nothing else ever had and his anger burned hot. "Innocence is not looking very good on you right now."

"Please keep your voice down before someone hears you, and tell me what is wrong. Are the pearls missing?"

A grim chuckle passed his lips. "Not simply missing, Susannah, stolen. I'm finding it hard to believe right now that you don't know the pearls were taken last night while you had me all wrapped up in your arms and in your bed."

He was amazed at how easily she managed to look horrified.

"Who took them?"

His eyes locked on hers as he took stock of her shocked attitude. "You tell me. You were the one who invited me to your bed. You must have known I'd hurry over here and leave the door unlocked. Is that why you were so eager for my touch? You knew you would soon have possession of the pearls."

"You think I had someone take them?" she snapped, anger replacing surprise on her face. "That's preposterous! Why didn't you have them under lock and key?"

"I did. Someone picked the lock and took everything in the safe."

"I can't believe you think I had anything to do with that," she said, looking stunned.

Race heard footsteps running down the corridor, and Mrs. Princeton bounded through the open doorway, dressed in a black robe with a white nightcap covering her hair. She gasped and jumped back at seeing him standing in her mistress's bedchamber with both of them only partially clothed. The air between the three of them crackled with raw tension.

"I heard voices," Mrs. Princeton said breathlessly, her rounded eyes darting fitfully from Race to Susannah. "Your Grace, what is wrong? What is the marquis doing here? How did he get in?"

Susannah lifted her chin, and after taking in a deep, solid breath she calmly said, "I'm not sure yet, but it appears the marquis rushed through the bramble bushes to get over here this morning because he failed to keep my grandmother's pearls protected and someone has stolen them from him and of course he believes that thief to be me."

Mrs. Princeton gasped in outrage again. "How dare you, my lord. The duchess is no thief. I insist you leave Her Grace's room immediately. You are not properly dressed, and neither is she. You have violated her sensibilities."

Race didn't bother to look at Mrs. Princeton but instead kept his gaze firmly fixed on Susannah as he said, "I assure you, Mrs. Princeton, that neither your mistress's sensibilities nor any other part of her have been violated."

"I can vouch for the fact the duchess was in her bed all night after she arrived home."

"Why does that not surprise me?" A rueful chuckle rumbled past his lips. "But quite frankly, woman, I have no more faith in your assertions than I do hers. Now, where are the pearls, Susannah?"

"I do not have them," she stated again, his rage provoking an equal measure of anger from her.

He eyed her skeptically once more and curtly said, "But you know who has them and where they are."

"I do not know," she countered fiercely.

Mrs. Princeton marched between Race and Susannah and faced him like a general before his troops. "My lord, leave this bedchamber immediately. Your being here is highly improper, and you are endangering Her Grace's reputation."

"I will handle the marquis, Mrs. Princeton," Susannah said. "You may go."

"But Your Grace," she countered as she swung to face Susannah.

"I understand why the marquis is so upset about the theft that he stormed out of his house like a madman and rushed over here without thought to his appearance. If I had had the pearls in my possession and learned they were stolen from me, I might run out of the house half dressed as well."

"But he has compromised you," she said in exasperation.

"If that be the case, nothing can be done about it now. But I believe I'm not fully compromised unless someone other than the three of us learns of this. I would like for you to go below stairs and keep the other servants off this floor until the marquis leaves. Hopefully, what little reputation I have left can remain intact. Failing that, I survived ruin once before and I'm much stronger now than I was twelve years ago."

Mrs. Princeton didn't move. She stood rigid with her nose in the air, breathing so heavily her bony chest heaved.

"Do it now, Mrs. Princeton. Blast the saints in heaven, I have been married and I know what a man's chest looks like, and so do you. The marquis and I have seen each other now, so how long he stays here does not matter at this point. I assure you, contrary to what you might think about him he will not harm me, and the only danger I am in at present is if the servants see him here in my room with us dressed like this. They will spread it to all the gossipmongers in Town. Your job is to keep that from happening, so I suggest you hop to it."

"Yes, Your Grace."

Susannah's companion walked out the door with a huff and so stiff that Race was sure she would have snapped in two if anyone had tried to bend her.

Race took in a deep, raspy breath, feeling calmer than when he arrived. He hated himself for his lack of control where Susannah was concerned, but last night she had moved him like no other woman ever had. After his time in her bed, he was thinking about words like love, forever, and marriage, but today all those words had been stripped away.

It had been so good between them. No, better than good, it had been the best ever. It had been right. For the first time in his life, he thought he'd actually made love to a woman and not just had sex. He'd thought she trusted him to come to her, to satisfy her, and now he was thinking that all the time he was only a means to get what she had really wanted. The Talbot pearls.

The hell of it was he still wanted her. He still had those desperate, unexplained feelings for her, even more than before if that were possible.

"You may say anything you want to me, my lord, but please keep your voice low."

Race noticed the tilt of her head, the rigid set to her shoulders, and unspent tears brimming in her eyes. Suddenly he felt as if a fist had landed in his stomach. Even if she had duped him, he didn't want her reputation ruined.

He walked closer to her and quietly said, "You could easily have arranged the theft with Spyglass, Winston, or someone else."

She held her ground and didn't flinch as he neared her. "I do not have the pearls, but I do find it rather fitting that the man who had stolen pearls in his possession now has had them stolen from him. Leave my room, leave my house, and never come back. You are not welcome here."

She seemed so resolute, it stunned him. Was he being unreasonable to accuse her? "All right, for now I will. But know this, Duchess, if I find out you do have them, I will follow you to Chapel Gate, or the gates of hell, to get what is mine."

Without saying another word, Race turned and left her room. He had to sort through his jangle of emotions, and he couldn't do it in her presence. What little evidence he had pointed to Susannah as being an accomplice, but she had done a good job pleading her innocence.

A heavy knot of anger and confusion radiated throughout Race's chest and he uttered an oath as he hurried down the steps. He stomped back through the untended garden to the tall hedge. He added fresh scratches to his chest and back as he once again crawled through the man-made hole in the yew, but Race didn't wince.

If Susannah was involved in the theft, she had wounded him much deeper than the shrub.

Twelve

My Dearest Alexander,

My dear friend Lord Chesterfield always was ahead of his time. This quote proves it. "It is most certain, that the reputation of chastity is not so necessary for a woman as that of veracity is for a man, and with reason; for it is possible for a woman to be virtuous, though not strictly chaste, but it is not possible for a man to be virtuous without strict veracity."

Your loving Grandmother,
Lady Elder

SUSANNAH FELT SHATTERED AS SHE WATCHED RACE walk out of her bedchamber, leaving the door open. She couldn't move. If she did, she would break into a million pieces. How could he believe she would betray him in such a fashion or that she would betray him at all?

She needed to think about what she should do now, but her mind was blank. Her body was incapable of feeling, or moving, so she continued to stand in the middle of her room and simply stare into the empty hallway, willing herself not to fall apart.

She didn't know how much time had passed before her shoulders sagged, her chin lowered, and her chest heaved with a deep, painful breath.

After her compromising affair with Lord Martin all those years ago, she should have seen this end with Race coming. It seemed as if fate had once again dealt harshly with her concerning men. But how could she have had any idea of what loomed when just this morning she had been so caught up in the rapture of their lovemaking that she felt as if she had finally stepped out of the darkness of the past and into the sunshine of the future?

Even now, after the angry accusations, she still had an overwhelming feeling that they belonged together.

But why?

What made the Marquis of Raceworth so compelling that she still felt love for him in her heart?

Somehow, she had lost her perspective once again and had been fooled by a handsome gentleman. She hadn't intended to fall in love with Race, but unfortunately that was exactly what she had done.

With her eyes shut, memories of their shared passion spun wildly in her mind, and she had no desire to resist or temper them as she relived every breath, every kiss, and every whisper. She would never forget the strength of his embrace, the thrill of his touch, or the weight of his body on hers. It was the most magical night she had ever experienced.

She now knew that Race had felt none of the loving emotions that had filled and consumed her, lifted her to heights of joy she could never have imagined and would never feel again. To him, she had simply been a woman willing to share her bed with him, therefore proving he was nothing but a rake. But no matter what he thought of her now, she would never be sorry for their night together. He taught her how truly blissful intimacy could be between a man and a woman who desired each other.

She would not beg Race to believe she had nothing to do with the disappearance of the pearls. Susannah had begged only once in her life, even though doing so had gone against every fiber of her being. She had been beside herself with grief over Lord Martin's rejection after he compromised her. But not even that had compared to the desperation she felt when she learned it had been arranged for her to marry the Duke of Blooming. She had begged her father not to force her to marry the fifty-six-year-old stranger. But her father and the duke came to the conclusion that marriage between Susannah and the duke would be a good match. What she wanted no longer mattered. At that time, Susannah had vowed never again to beg for anything.

Now that she was thinking more clearly, she could see why Race thought every finger on his hand pointed in her direction as being the thief. She had stated plainly she wanted the pearls, and she had asked him to come to her bedchamber the very night they were stolen from him. When she thought about it like that, Race was right; she looked guilty.

Susannah had two choices. She could fall apart, pine for Race, and deride herself for falling victim once again to a charming man unworthy of her love. But she had been down that road before, and that choice would lead her to nothing but greater misery. On the other hand, she could pull herself up for a time and forget what had happened between her and Race last night and accomplish what she had come to London to do in the first place. Get the pearls.

That was definitely the better of the two choices.

As Susannah continued to focus on what had happened, she realized she was wasting precious time. She needed to dress and get busy, as she had a lot to accomplish. She walked over to her wardrobe and pulled out a royal-blue carriage dress, chemise, and drawers. She then went to the washbasin and poured fresh water into the bowl. As the cool, wet cloth touched her heated skin, she realized she understood why Race came to the conclusion she was the thief, but she was still deeply hurt by his anger.

She supposed there was some justification for his belief she had duped him by inviting him into her bed. And perhaps if she had been in his position, she might have concluded the same scenario Race had. Once he had time to think things through, she hoped he would see the improbabilities of her having arranged for the necklace to be stolen on the slight chance his door would be left unlocked.

Susannah pressed her face into the cloth. She mustn't allow Race to occupy her thoughts any longer. The only important thing was to find the thief. Race was only a distraction to her real purpose in London. Thankfully, he would now be locked away in her heart to be dealt with when she returned to Chapel Gate and presented the pearls to her mother.

At that time, Susannah would logically look at what had happened between her and the marquis, settle it in her mind, and move on. So she had given her heart to and trusted another man who disappointed her. She would live through it, and perhaps in time the heartache in her chest would heal and her extraordinary feelings for Race would fade.

She must discover who had the pearls before they skipped London. But where should she look first: for the pirate, the prince's representative, or the antiquities dealer? She didn't know anything about the men, how or where to find them. But she had an idea who might be able to help her, and she had no time to waste.

The pearls had been stolen from her family, and now they had been stolen from Race. It seemed if she wanted them, she was going to have to find them and steal them herself.

The thought of being a thief should be more distasteful to her than it was, but she couldn't worry about that.

As soon as she finished dressing, Susannah hurried below stairs. From the doorway of the drawing room, she saw Mrs. Princeton sitting at the desk with several pieces of paper in front of her.

"Mrs. Princeton," Susannah said, walking into the room.

The woman rose quickly and faced Susannah. Her cheeks were pale, her brown eyes uncommonly red and irritated. Her bottom lip shone bright pink as if she'd been biting it.

"Yes, Your Grace."

Susannah winced inside. Perhaps she had been too hard on the woman earlier that morning. Susannah knew Mrs. Princeton had been quite upset that she had been forced to leave the bedchamber without the marquis accompanying her, but Susannah couldn't deal with an irate lover and an irate companion at the same time. She didn't want or need Mrs. Princeton's opinion of Race, and she hadn't wanted her in the middle of their argument.

"I'm sorry you had to witness the uncomfortable confrontation in my room this morning," Susannah said, moving farther into the room.

Mrs. Princeton blinked rapidly. "Please, Your Grace. I must be the one to apologize to you. I failed you miserably, and I'm so very sorry I was unable to do more."

Susannah's throat tightened. "So you were unable to keep the rest of the staff from knowing that the marquis stormed into my bedchamber this morning."

Mrs. Princeton's eyes widened. "No, I did that. I immediately sent your maid and the cook out for fresh vegetables and meat for dinner. They've just returned, neither of them the wiser. I told Benson to leave at once and go to the stables and prepare your carriage for an outing. I'm certain he didn't hear anything, either."

Relief flooded through Susannah. Mrs. Princeton's efficiency was impressive. "Good. Thank you. I appreciate your quick thinking in accomplishing that. But how did you know I wanted my carriage this morning?"

"I didn't. But I thought it was worth the few coins to get Benson away from the house quickly."

Susannah took a deep breath, feeling better that the other servants were not aware of Race's appearance in her room. There was hope that this scandal would not be spread to every house in London.

"Thank you, Mrs. Princeton. That was clever of you. Your quick thinking may have saved me from ruin. I do appreciate that, and you acted most appropriately."

Her thin lips quivered, and she held her arms stiffly at her sides. "Yes, Your Grace, but I'm sorry I failed to take proper care of you. I feel I should resign my post so you can hire someone more capable than I."

Susannah's heart softened. She'd had no idea that the woman was so distressed over what happened. "Mrs. Princeton, it is not your job to take care of me. You are my companion, not my chaperone."

"I know that, Your Grace, and I will understand if you feel you can no longer employ me because I was unsuccessful in my attempt to help you."

"Leave my employ?" Susannah said impatiently. "What on earth are you talking about? You have been with me for ten years. I don't want you to leave. Mrs. Princeton, I know you were unhappy I dismissed you from my room and allowed the marquis to stay so that I could plead my innocence. I had to do that, even at the risk of my ruin. But you did help me. You did exactly as I had instructed and kept the other servants from overhearing Lord Raceworth. You did not fail me. You saved me. Why would I want you to leave my employ?"

"So you're not angry with me?"

"Certainly not," Susannah admonished. "You know me. Your opinion is always welcome, but after I hear it, I must make the decision whether to act on your recommendations or my own. London is an entirely different place from Chapel Gate or even Chapel Glade, and I fear

I may have to do other things of which you might disapprove. But I don't want you to leave."

The woman gave her a quivering smile. "Thank you. I do not want to leave you, Your Grace. I only felt helpless this morning."

"I have valued your companionship all these years and I do depend on you for many important tasks. I need you now more than I ever have. I don't want to hear any more talk of your leaving me."

Mrs. Princeton smoothed the side of her hair with a trembling hand and took in a deep breath. She slowly walked over to the window and looked out. Susannah remained silent, sensing her companion had more to say and not wanting to rush her.

"You know, Your Grace, I have never wanted for you the kind of life I've had." She quickly turned shimmering eyes to Susannah. "Not that you would ever be a paid companion to someone, of course."

"I understood what you meant," Susannah said.

"I've not wanted you to have the emptiness that is inside me. I've always wanted you to remarry and have children. And it's not that I've been so terribly lonely these years—just empty, lacking. Sometimes when I see children, I know that I have missed holding a baby in my arms, kissing soft pink cheeks and having the thrill of little arms around my neck." Her eyes glazed with tears as she turned back to the window and looked out. "But there's more that I've missed. After thirty years, I can still remember my husband's touch and how my body would tremble with expectancy when he came into our bedchamber. You are much too young to live with only memories."

Mrs. Princeton's words stabbed Susannah's heart. She had felt the same way when Race came into her room last night. She trembled with expectancy. With Race, she thought she had found a man who would be in her future, but this morning that dream was shattered. How would she ever be able to find a man who made her feel the way Race had?

Susannah remained silent, knowing she had nothing to counter Mrs. Princeton's words and sensing the woman wasn't looking for sympathy.

Mrs. Princeton inhaled deeply and wiped her eyes with the back of her hand. She looked directly at Susannah and said, "Should you ever decide to relinquish your title as duchess and marry, it would be your duty to marry well. The marquis would certainly be a suitable gentleman for you. He may behave rashly on occasion, as evidenced by this morning, but I believe that is because he is a man of great passion. I have heard talk about him at the parties. I don't believe he is a fortune hunter, a gambler, or a wastrel. You could do much worse."

Mrs. Princeton's emotional flare-up faded as quickly as it had appeared, and she returned to her composed, rigid self. She was letting Susannah know that she was aware that the marquis had spent the night in Susannah's bed.

"I don't know that I will ever remarry, Mrs. Princeton. Fate has not been kind to me concerning men. However, I will take your kind words to heart and think on them."

Mrs. Princeton nodded. "I am available to aid you however you need me."

Susannah smiled gratefully. "Good. Now tell me, what is it that you were looking at when I came in?"

Mrs. Princeton walked over to the desk and picked up several cards and held them out to Susannah. "All these are invitations. Most of these are requests for you to attend parties, balls, and teas. You've had fifteen invitations arrive just this morning."

"That many?"

"There are always a lot of parties near the end of the Season. And it seems most everyone wants you in attendance. It makes them feel quite popular to have a duchess honor them with an appearance."

"I suppose you are right. Tell me, did I receive a letter from my mother?" Susannah asked hopefully.

"No, Your Grace."

Susannah cleared her throat. "Well, maybe tomorrow. Are there any invitations for tonight?"

"Three."

"Marvelous. While I wait for the carriage to arrive, I'll look at them and decide which one I want to attend."

"Do you mind if I ask where we are going this morning?"

Susannah folded her arms across her chest. "I'm going quite improperly to see a gentleman. You will of course go with me, but I must speak to the man alone."

"I understand. I'll get our capes, gloves, and bonnets

while you look over the invitations, so we'll be ready when the carriage arrives."

"Thank you, Mrs. Princeton, for everything."

The older woman smiled shyly and hurried away.

Thirteen

My Dearest Grandson Alexander,
Think on these true words from Lord Chesterfield: "To be heard with success, you must be heard with pleasure."
Your loving Grandmother,
Lady Elder

AN HOUR LATER, SUSANNAH AND MRS. PRINCETON stood in front of Sir Randolph Gibson's door.

A well-dressed butler answered. "Yes?" he questioned with his nose so high in the air he had to look down on Susannah, though he wasn't any taller than she.

"I am the Dowager Duchess of Blooming, and I'm here to see Sir Randolph. If he is at home, I would be pleased if he could give me a few minutes of his time."

The butler snapped to attention and blinked rapidly. It was almost comical at how instantly his attitude changed when he heard she was a duchess.

He swept a low bow and said, "Forgive me, Your Grace. Please come in. Sir Randolph is at home, and I'll check at once to see if he might be available."

"Thank you."

"I'm sure Sir Randolph would want me to offer you tea or chocolate while you wait," the butler said as they walked into the exotically furnished drawing room.

"None for me, thank you, but would you mind showing my companion a place where she might have refreshment while she waits for me?"

"At once, Your Grace," he said and bowed again.

Mrs. Princeton followed him out, and Susannah looked around the room. It was spacious and surprisingly filled with fancy, dark-wood furniture that was covered in embroidered silk fabrics of astoundingly vibrant colors and patterns in shades so rich and striking she decided they could have only come from the Orient.

Life-size statues of Venus and Athena held up the marble mantel that graced the ornate fireplace, and the gold-framed mirror over it was shaped like a large pagoda. The only window in the room was framed with a strikingly odd shade of red velvet draperies. Each panel was held back with large, gold velvet tassels, exposing intricate lace panels covering the panes. Gray skies allowed little light to filter into the room, but lit lamps on either side of the settee gave the room a golden, warm glow.

Susannah sat down on a chair that had an embroidered dragon on the cushion's fabric, and within minutes of her arrival, Sir Randolph came striding into the room with a curious expression on his face.

Susannah rose. The dapper old gentleman bowed and kissed her hand.

"Your Grace, this is an unexpected but nonetheless pleasant surprise. To what do I owe the honor of this visit?"

She smiled at him. "I have come with questions I hope you can answer, but, Sir Randolph, I see your hands are quite swollen. I know you are preparing for your fight. Are you sure you are taking proper care of yourself?"

Sir Randolph held up his hands and looked at them. It seemed he could barely move his thick fingers. They were not only swollen but red and chafed, as well.

"Thank you for your concern, Duchess. This is merely part of my training. I'm toughening and conditioning my hands. In the meantime, they are not a pretty sight."

"I see. You know I wish you all good luck with that, and I hope your hands don't pain you too much."

"Not at all. There is no need for you to worry about me. I'm hearing that Prattle isn't doing anything to ready himself for the fight, but that doesn't matter to me. I think I'm going to win, in any case," he finished confidently.

Susannah smiled at him again. He was so debonair and so sure of himself, it lifted her spirits just looking at him. "I believe you will."

"Sit down, Duchess, and tell me what I can do for you this morning."

"Thank you." She took a seat on the red and gold striped settee, and Sir Randolph eased into the brightly printed chair in front of her. "I know that I don't know you well, but I need to ask you for a favor."

Surprise sparkled in his brown eyes. "It's been a long time since anyone asked a favor of me. It doesn't matter that we haven't known each other long. What do you need?"

She inhaled slowly before saying, "I need to meet Mr. Harold Winston and Mr. Albert Smith. I've heard that the Earl and Countess of Kendrickson usually give a large party, so I'm assuming there is a good possibility one or both gentlemen will be at their home tomorrow night. I was wondering if you might be planning to attend, and if so, would you make the introductions for me?"

His curious eyes searched her face. "I usually go to Lord Kendrickson's party, Duchess." He paused. "First, let me say that Mr. Smith is not of the ilk to be welcomed into any home in Polite Society, so there is no chance he will be there."

"Oh, I see. Not knowing the man, I wasn't aware of that."

Sir Randolph continued to look at her with a quizzical expression. "And as for Mr. Winston, even though he's accepted among the ton and he's throwing Prinny's name around like a bouncing ball, he's not exactly in your social standing either, Duchess."

Susannah understood exactly what Sir Randolph was saying. Social standing meant everything to the members of the ton. "Nevertheless, I would be grateful if you would consent to make the introductions."

"He will probably be there, and I'm happy to do it for you, but what about Race?"

An ache filled Susannah's chest, and emotion clogged in her throat. If Sir Randolph had not heard that the pearls had been stolen from Race last night, she did not want to be the one to tell him. That was Race's call to make, not hers.

"Have you talked to Race today?" she asked.

"No." Sir Randolph kept his wary gaze on her face. "Have you?"

"Yes, and I assume you are wondering why I am asking you this question when I could have easily asked Lord Raceworth."

Sir Randolph leaned back in his chair, clearly undecided on what to say. "No, I'm thinking you didn't ask him because you knew he wouldn't do it."

"That is probably true, but there is another reason as well." She moved to the edge of her seat. "I will only say that Lord Raceworth is not happy with me right now, and he is not a possibility for helping me with anything. That said, I realize he is your dear friend, and you may not want to help me for that reason alone. If that be the case, I will understand and not bother you further."

He seemed to study over his answer before smiling and saying, "Would you like to know how many times I've done things that Race didn't approve of?"

Hope surged inside her. "Judging from your long friendship with him and your fierce independence, I would say too many to count."

"And you'd be right. I do hate to disappoint a lovely lady, so I will honor your request. If Mr. Winston is at Lord Kendrickson's party tomorrow evening, I'll make sure to present him to you."

"Thank you. And if you don't mind, I have one more question."

"Why stop now? Go ahead."

"Do you know how I could go about finding Mr. Smith?"

Sir Randolph rubbed his enlarged hands together and thought for a moment. "His antiques shop is on Watford

Lane. But, Duchess, I don't think he is the kind of man you should be pursuing, no matter how good your reasons."

"I understand your concerns, Sir Randolph."

"You have me very curious, Duchess. I know Race well. I can't believe that he would want you making plans to see these men."

The heaviness returned to Susannah's chest. "Believe me, Race does not care what I do or whom I see. I don't think he would tell me the time of day if I asked him." She rose. "I won't take up any more of your time."

Sir Randolph stood up, too. "There's one other thing you should know before you go."

She swallowed hard. "Yes?"

"I will tell Race about your visit and what I'm doing for you."

She nodded. "I'm perfectly all right with that. He cannot think worse of me than he already does."

Sir Randolph's forehead wrinkled into a frown. "What happened between you two?"

Susannah struggled to renew her inner strength. "I will let the marquis tell you."

Sir Randolph hesitated but finally said, "Fair enough. Is there anything else I can do for you?"

"No, but I'm grateful you have been so kind and helpful."

"I just hope I don't end up regretting this."

"I'll do my best to see you don't."

"Then I'll see you at Lord Kendrickson's tomorrow evening?"

She smiled. "Yes. Thank you, Sir Randolph. You have helped me greatly."

"I don't know that I have, Duchess. Only time will tell."

She looked at him curiously as he walked with her to the door.

———

Half an hour later, a bell jangled as Mrs. Princeton opened the door of Smith's Antiquities Shop at 139 Watford Street. Susannah stepped inside, and the first thing she noticed was the overpowering yet pleasant smell of citrus incense. The room was crowded with furniture but well lighted. At a quick glance, she counted four lamps burning brightly.

Obviously, Mr. Smith didn't want anyone to have trouble seeing his wares, and by the fleeting glimpse she gave the place, she'd say most of his collection was more bizarre than traditional. The stuffed head of what looked like a wild boar stared directly at her from the front wall, two matching stone gargoyles with bright red eyes watched her from her right, and a life-size brass suit of armor stood on her left.

"Good afternoon, ladies," a short, slim-built man said, appearing from behind a Japanese silk screen painted with gray swallows, colorful blossoms, and white cranes.

Susannah knew at once he had to be Mr. Albert Smith because Race had said that the man had only one arm. The empty sleeve of his black wool coat had been neatly folded and pinned at his shoulder. He wore an affable expression on his face, along with a pair of spectacles that rode low on the bridge of his nose. From behind the screen, another man stepped into her view. He was younger, taller, and more robust.

"Sir, I am the Dowager Duchess of Blooming."

His light blue eyes widened with eager surprise. "Forgive me, Your Grace," he said and immediately bowed. "Thank you for coming into my humble shop. I am Mr. Smith, and this is my associate Mr. Helms. How may I assist you?"

Susannah didn't want to appear anxious, and she hoped her own nervousness didn't show. "I would like to browse through your shop, if you don't mind. I see you have many extraordinary pieces that have already caught my eye."

He smiled impatiently. "Yes, yes, by all means. Please take your time, and let me know if I can help you."

"Thank you," she said.

Susannah took her time and slowly walked around the shop, Mrs. Princeton following her every move like a dutiful companion. Occasionally, Susannah would pick up a fine china figurine and examine it closely, or touch the rough fabric of an old tapestry, or stop and admire a painting on the wall. But she was always cognizant that Mr. Smith and his colleague were pretending not to watch her every move.

"I don't think this is the kind of place you should be in, Your Grace," Mrs. Princeton whispered when they were quite a distance from the two men.

"Perhaps not," Susannah whispered, "but nonetheless we stay here until my business is concluded."

On a side table, beside a miniature statue of Athena, she saw several old music scores on torn and tattered pieces of aged parchment.

She carefully picked them up. Looking at the notes, she could see the melody was intricate and complicated. She tried to sound the notes in her mind. Learning new music was always a challenge, and she desperately needed something to take her mind off Race. She had not come to shop, but there was no way she could pass up the music. Playing the pianoforte always calmed her, and finding these old, rare copies gave her a new confidence to finish the task at hand.

Susannah handed the scores to Mrs. Princeton to hold, and then she headed over to the magnificent desk where Mr. Smith stood looking at an account book.

"Yes, Your Grace," he said with a wide smile. "I see you found something of interest."

"I do have a penchant for music played on the pianoforte."

"Excellent. How else may I be of service?"

As casually as she could, Susannah said, "I noticed on your shop window that it says you deal in jewelry, but I don't see any here in your shop."

He lifted the spectacles from his nose and laid them on his desk. He smiled cunningly and said, "Oh, my, yes, Duchess, I have some exceptional gems and gold pieces. I acquire precious stones from all over the world, but of course because of their value I must keep them in the safe in my office. I'm happy to bring them out here one at a time and show you what I have, or if it's more comfortable for you, you and your companion can join me in my office where it will be more private and you can look over all that I have for as long as you want. Mr. Helms will watch the shop for me."

Susannah's stomach jumped at the thought that he might actually have the pearls, yet she had an innate reluctance to go to the back of this man's shop. Instinct told her this was not a man to trifle with. She had to calm herself. Finding the pearls could not be as easy as simply having this man present them to her, but oh, how she would love it if it turned out to be so.

Swallowing her hesitation, she said, "Of course, we'll follow you to your office. I would very much like to see all that you have."

"Certainly."

Mr. Smith picked up his spectacles as he nodded to Mr. Helms. He then turned back to Susannah and said, "This way."

Susannah and Mrs. Princeton followed Mr. Smith down a dimly lit corridor to a small, damp room that held an oak desk with baroque, trumpet-shaped legs. It was littered with papers and books. Mr. Smith walked over to a skirted round table that stood against a far wall. He pushed the lamp and a small statue of David to one side and lifted the hem of the brown brocade cloth and bunched it up on the table. Susannah briefly saw what appeared to be a large iron safe with two key holes in it, one underneath the other, before Mr. Smith knelt in front of it.

Her gaze darted to Mrs. Princeton, who was standing near the doorway, stiff with apprehension, holding the music to her chest as if it might somehow protect her from whatever it was she feared. Looking back at Mr. Smith, Susannah watched him pull a ring with several keys on it from his coat pocket and unlock the top lock.

He rose and said, "Excuse me. I have to get the other key from another room." He went back out the door. Susannah glanced at Mrs. Princeton and raised her eyebrows in a hopeful gesture.

"There, that didn't take long," Mr. Smith said, hurrying back into the office. "For safety purposes, I have to keep one of the keys hidden, you understand."

"I can see the wisdom of that," Susannah said calmly, even though she felt as if all her insides were quaking. And she didn't exactly know why. It wasn't as if Mr. Smith or his associate had said or done anything to make her fearful of them.

When she first walked into the shop, the scent of the citrus incense was pleasant, but now, with the pressure of what she was doing, it was beginning to give her a headache. Knowing that there was the slightest possibility she could find the pearls kept Susannah's mind occupied and her hands calm.

Mr. Smith quickly cleaned off an area of his desk and slid an oil lamp over. He pulled a camel-back chair around and said, "Please, Your Grace, sit here where you can be comfortable and see well. I'll bring everything to you."

She accepted the chair and stared as he knelt in front of the safe again and put the key in the bottom lock and twisted the handle. The heavy door swung open. With his hand, he pulled out several velvet boxes and two trays filled with an assortment of jewels and carefully put them all on the desk in front of her. She was amazed at how he managed to do so much with just one arm and hand.

Susannah took her time and calmly looked at everything Mr. Smith spread before her. He showed her elaborate gold and jeweled crowns, large diamond necklaces, and loose rubies, emeralds, and sapphires. She complimented exceptional pieces and asked questions about others until her head began to pound. When she felt she couldn't look at another gem, she said to him, "I haven't seen any pearls, Mr. Smith. Do you have any?"

His brow wrinkled, and he pursed his lips. "I did, but not now."

Susannah tensed but hoped it didn't show on her face. "What do you mean?"

Disappointment flashed in his eyes, as if he could see a sale slipping through his fingers. "I had some of the most beautiful pearls in the world a couple of weeks ago, but a gentleman came in and purchased them all."

"A gentleman bought them all?"

"Every one," Mr. Smith said, clearly disappointed he had no pearls to show her. "I don't talk about anyone who visits my shop, as I keep my client list private, but this, this man, he was a very strange person. He bought every pearl and wanted more. He asked if I knew where he might find others. I told him I was happy to check with my sources and see what I could do for him. I called on a well-known man in Town. A marquis," he said as his eyes sparkled. "I thought he might be willing to part with some very rare pearls he has, for a handsome sum of course, but he was not interested." Mr. Smith shrugged. "But I can speak to him again. He might be more willing if he knows my client is a beautiful duchess."

Putting two and two together quickly, Susannah came up with the scenario that Captain Spyglass was probably the gentleman who had bought all of Mr. Smith's pearls and that Race had to be the well-known marquis he spoke with about the Talbot pearls.

Susannah smiled. "No, that's not necessary. I'm not that eager. I just found it odd that among all these extraordinary gems there were no pearls."

If what Mr. Smith told her was true, and there was nothing in his features to indicate he was hiding the truth from her, she didn't think he had stolen the Talbot pearls from Race. He was much too free with his information to be hiding a theft.

Still, to be sure, she said, "Do you mind if I ask, was the man who bought the pearls Captain Spyglass?"

Mr. Smith's eyes rounded, and he pushed his spectacles up closer to his eyes. "Yes, how did you know? Forgive me, Your Grace, for speaking so much about him. I don't usually talk about my clients."

She gave the man a reassuring smile. "You have told me nothing about the man I didn't already know. In fact, it's well known throughout London that Captain Spyglass has been buying pearls from all over the world. And when I met him, he was dripping in pearls." Susannah kept going. "And might I conclude that the gentleman you spoke of who has the rare pearls is the Marquis of Raceworth?"

"I—I've said far too much, Your Grace."

"Nonsense, Mr. Smith. It was written in Lord Truefitt's column that Lord Raceworth received the Talbot pearls from his grandmother."

Relief washed down Mr. Smith's face. "Yes, that is how I knew he had them. I mentioned the gentlemen only because I wanted you to know the reason I have no pearls to show you. I would be pleased to notify you when I can obtain more pearls. I would consider it an honor to have something you wanted."

She rose. "That would be lovely. Thank you, Mr. Smith."

He swept his hand across all the jewels that lay on the desk in front of her and questioned, "Did you not find anything to your liking? I have more."

Mr. Smith went back to the safe. It was clear he didn't like the idea of a possible sale slipping away. "Oh, but I did find something I wanted," she said with a smile. "I am delighted that I found the old music scores. My companion will pay you for them. She will leave you my card so you can send me a note should you get more music or pearls."

The man beamed and bowed graciously, knowing he'd made the only sale he was going to get from her today but pleased he might have other opportunities in the future.

"Most assuredly. I am always available to be at your service, Your Grace."

Susannah nodded and started threading her way back to the front door. She wanted to get away from the intense citrus scent and clear her thoughts and pounding head.

She hoped she wasn't being gullible but she believed everything Mr. Smith had told her. She had watched him closely and concentrated on his eyes and his mannerisms, not how well he could do things with only one arm. She was almost positive he didn't have the Talbot pearls. His story about Captain Spyglass and Race rang true. His recounting matched with what Race had told her the first day they met. She remembered Race saying the antiquities dealer wanted to buy the pearls for a client.

For now, at least, she felt confident in marking Mr. Smith off the list of possible suspects. She had no doubts that if he'd had the necklace, he would have shown it to her. So that left Mr. Harold Winston and Captain Spyglass for her to deal with. And she had to factor in that there was always the possibility of someone else who hadn't revealed himself to Race the way she, Captain Spyglass, and Mr. Winston had.

Susannah nodded to Mr. Helms as she walked past him. The bell on the door jangled as Susannah stepped onto the boardwalk that ran along the street, leaving Mrs. Princeton to deal with Mr. Smith and the scores. She closed her eyes and breathed in deeply, hoping the damp air would clear the heavy smell of incense from her mind and clear her head, if not her clothing.

"Susannah?"

Her eyes popped open, and she found herself staring into Race's troubled eyes. After their angry parting earlier that morning, it stunned her that her heart still fluttered uncontrollably at the sight of him.

She took a step away from him. A light breeze

feathered his hair across his forehead, making him amazingly attractive, and she winced from the emptiness in the pit of her stomach.

A deep frown creased his forehead and around his eyes. "Why am I not surprised to see you here?" he asked.

She took in another deep breath to fortify herself. "Probably for the same reason I am not surprised to see you here. I do not take kindly to your following me, my lord."

He raised his eyebrows. "Following you? Is that what you think? I wasn't, but I can see that I should have. I came here to see if Smith had closed his shop and escaped London with my grandmother's pearls. What excuse do you have for being here?"

She had to admit that once again the circumstances made her appear guilty. "Perhaps it was your grandmother's dear friend Lord Chesterfield who said, 'Looks can be deceiving.'"

Concern edged his features, and he said, "Susannah, the man inside that shop deals with criminals. If you had nothing to do with the theft of the pearls, you should have no dealings with that man."

"If?" she exclaimed. She held out her empty hands, unable to keep from defending herself yet again. "Do I look like I have any pearls on my person? I have no pockets on this cape and none on my dress. I don't even have a reticule with me today." She untied the satin ribbon that held her cape together and flung it off her shoulders and draped it over her arm. "And as you can see, I have no pearls around my neck."

"Then what are you doing here?"

"Do you really not know, my lord?" she asked incredulously. "I am here because I know I do not have the pearls, and the only way I can prove I don't have them, or that I don't know who has them, is to find them myself, which is what I intend to do. If you suspected Mr. Smith might have the pearls, reason should tell you that I would suspect the same thing."

Race's gaze pierced hers. "This is a dangerous game you are playing."

She whipped her cape around and fitted it onto her shoulders again.

"But play it I must." She remained firm and collected. "And have no doubts that I am playing for keeps. I intend to find that necklace, and when I do, mark my words, my lord, I will keep it."

"Did you tell him the pearls had been stolen?"

She blinked rapidly. "Of course not. I merely asked to see what jewels he had, and he has no pearls because Captain Spyglass bought them all."

Race stepped closer to her, his gaze fixed tightly on hers. In a low voice he said, "I will not let you put yourself at risk over this."

Anger rose up inside her. Anger for the way he had made her feel last night. Anger because he was now pretending to care about her well-being. Anger because she had an aching sense of despair because she would never feel his touch again.

Susannah suddenly jerked her head so close to Race's face he flinched. "How dare you think you have any control over me. *You* cannot stop me from doing anything I choose to do. I am mistress over my own life, and I can take care of myself. I will thank you to stay away from me."

Susannah heard the door jingle behind her and knew Mrs. Princeton had come out of the shop. She glanced over her shoulder to her companion. "Come along, Mrs. Princeton. The day is getting late, and we have a party to get ready for."

Fourteen

My Dearest Grandson Alexander,

I found these words in an old letter Lord Chesterfield once wrote: "I am now privileged by my age to taste and think for myself and not to care what other people think of me in those respects, an advantage which youth, among its many advantages, hath not."

Your loving Grandmother,
Lady Elder

RACE SAT IN THE FAR CORNER AT THE TAPROOM OF the Rusty Nail, feeling a loneliness he had never experienced before. He felt cold and empty inside, and he hadn't been able to shake the fact that no matter how he tried to convince himself differently, he had behaved like a first-class bastard to Susannah earlier that morning and not any better when he'd seen her coming out of Smith's Antiques Shop just a few hours ago.

It was late afternoon and raining. The damp air held a chill, and he was mindlessly watching a servant stoking the fire he'd just built in the fireplace, and listening to raucous laughter and balls pinging together in the billiards room nearby. Race was still trying to swallow the bad taste his encounter with Susannah left in his mouth, but not even his drink was helping.

Perhaps he hadn't had enough wine.

Yet.

No doubt as the evening wore on that would change. Perhaps it had been a justifiable reaction at first that he had considered her an accomplice to the theft, but why hadn't he simply believed her when she'd denied it? He should have. Perhaps it was the fact that the evidence pointed to her as being the most likely suspect.

But now he was rethinking that, and the guilt he felt for accusing her so fiercely bore down on him like a heavy weight.

After he left her house that morning and returned home to dress, he'd found himself stopping whatever task he was doing, be it buttoning his riding breeches or tying his neckcloth, and he would start thinking about his night in Susannah's arms. It staggered him that on the one hand, his body felt immensely satisfied from their lovemaking, and on the other, he desired her once again with an all-consuming fire that defied his being able to explain it. He couldn't get the memory of their night together off his mind.

Somehow, she had bewitched him.

He swirled the dark red wine around in his glass. Race shook his head, cleared his throat, and took another sip of his wine. It was past time for him to compose himself and to deal with Susannah and the theft rationally. For some reason, uncharacteristically, he hadn't yet put all the facts into perspective.

Susannah had truly looked shocked when he accused her of stealing the pearls. She was definitely angry he had stormed into her bedchamber without thought for her reputation. She had been right when she told him the theft was his fault. And later that morning, she was convincing when she said she would find the pearls and she would keep them.

Now he was beginning to see what he had been unable to see earlier. Susannah was not part of the theft, and she was willing to put herself in danger to find the pearls.

Her desire was not news to him. She had freely told him she wanted the necklace. What made him think she wanted it badly enough to steal, when she had been trying to get him to look at the documents she had brought to prove the pearls had been stolen from her family? Documents he'd never looked at.

Was it because of what he was feeling for her that the mere thought she might have betrayed him turned him into a madman? He didn't know why he had jumped to the wrong conclusions based on flimsy evidence.

He hadn't told her he would leave his door unlocked, and she certainly wouldn't have arranged an elaborate plan to steal the pearls just on the assumption that he'd be so eager to get in her bed he wouldn't remember to lock the door. He knew all that now, but now it might be too late.

He picked up his wine and drank again. Over the rim of the glass, he saw his cousins sauntering into the taproom together, impeccably dressed and both looking like the proud, titled gentlemen they were.

They pulled out chairs and sat down as he placed his wine on the table. Race motioned for the server to bring over two glasses.

"What has Gibby done now?" Blake asked, folding his arms across his chest and tilting his chair on its back legs.

"Gibby?" Race questioned.

"Isn't he the reason you summoned us here?" Morgan asked.

For a brief moment, Race had forgotten they didn't know why he sent word for them to meet him here in this quiet and exclusive gentlemen's club not far from White's. He supposed he would have to tell Gib about the stolen pearls too, though he dreaded it. Gibby had always idolized their grandmother and he didn't like anyone saying or doing anything to disturb her memory.

Race brushed an imaginary crumb from the table and then sat back in his chair. Issuing an audible sigh, he said, "No, Gib is not the reason I wanted to see you."

"What else could have you looking so glum?" Blake asked as the server put two glasses on the table in front of them and poured wine into both.

"Leave the bottle," Race said.

Morgan grinned. "This must be serious. You look like you've lost your two best and only friends, and we know that can't be true because here we sit right in front of you."

"I didn't lose my friends," Race said flatly. "I lost something else. My safe was robbed last night."

"What?" his cousins said in unison as the front legs of Blake's chair hit the floor with a thud.

"The contents of my safe were cleaned out last night, including Grandmother's pearls."

"Damnation," Blake said.

"Bloody hell," Morgan whispered. "What the devil happened? Did no one in the house hear the thief breaking in?"

"Was it one of your servants?"

"I don't think so," Race said quietly, looking from one cousin to the other. "No one had to break in. The back door was left unlocked."

"I hope you turned off the bloody servant who was careless enough to do that," Blake said.

"Unfortunately, I'm the one who left the door unlocked."

"You?" Morgan questioned.

Race nodded.

Blake shrugged. "Locking up is one of the reasons we have servants. I know they are all careless at times. That's just the way of it. It's not your fault. Don't be too hard on yourself. We expect our homes to be sacrosanct."

"The thief must be a servant," Morgan argued. "There can't be that many people who know where your safe is located or how to get into it. I'd venture to say that most of your servants know."

"All the servants had already been dismissed for the night when I went out the back door and left it unlocked."

"And someone just happened to know you left the door unlocked?" Blake questioned.

Morgan rubbed his temple and studied over that comment. "I agree. That seems a bit far-fetched to me, unless someone has been watching your house, just waiting for it to be vulnerable."

"Wait. Something's not right," Blake said, drumming

his fingers on the table. "Why do I get the feeling there is something more to this story than you are telling us?"

"Like who knew you would be going out and leaving it unlocked?" Morgan asked.

"A woman?" Blake said, catching on to Morgan's line of thinking.

"Maybe Susannah?" Morgan offered.

Blake's forehead wrinkled. "The duchess? How?"

Race remained quiet.

Morgan took a sip of his drink and then looked at Blake and responded, "Easy. She lives in the house directly behind him, and something tells me she knew he would be with her."

The corners of Blake's lips lifted in a knowing grin. "As in all night?"

"Most of it, anyway," Morgan offered.

"You two can be such bloody blackguards," Race mumbled.

Blake landed a fist on the table with a thump. "So she lured you into her bed, and then she had someone sneak into your house and pilfer what she came to Town for. She got the pearls."

"I thought so at first, but not anymore. There are other, more likely suspects," Race countered, not wanting his cousins to condemn Susannah as he had.

"But if not Susannah, who?" Blake queried.

"I don't know the answer to that yet."

"But we do know whom she was in bed with," Morgan remarked slyly. "Did she give you that little scratch under your eye?"

Race reached up and touched the scrape he'd received on his cheek while crawling through the hedge after he'd left Susannah's house that morning. That cut was minor compared to some of the ones on his chest and back. He looked like he'd been in a fight with a cat and lost.

Race didn't want to discuss Susannah with his cousins. He had to tell them the necklace had been stolen but he didn't have to tell them anything else about Susannah.

Blake picked up his wine glass and took a sip. "Have you been to see the magistrate?"

"Not yet and may not for a time. I will be having some things done that he wouldn't approve of. I spent most of the afternoon with a man on Bow Street named Mr. Walter Bickerman."

"I've heard of him," Blake said. "He has one of the best reputations of all the runners."

Race nodded. "He immediately dispatched men to watch Spyglass's and Winston's residences, Smith's shop, and Spyglass's ship, the *Golden Pearl*, which as of a short time ago was still in the harbor. They will be followed wherever they go, even if they leave Town. That way we'll know where they are at all times."

"I think I'm missing something." Morgan paused and rubbed the area between his eyes with his thumb. "How is following them going to get the pearls back?"

Blake rested his forearm on the table. "It stands to reason that if Spyglass is the thief, he will now prepare to leave Town, since obtaining the pearls seems to be the only reason he came to London."

"I would think all of them are smart enough not to

run the minute they got their hands on the pearls," Morgan offered. "That would be like waving a flag and saying they were guilty."

"Bickerman and I discussed that. But we thought it was better to have the houses, shop, and ship watched anyway, to be safe. He is going to hire a man who can go in and search for safes and hiding places and try to find the pearls."

"Now that sounds like the right thing to do," Morgan said.

"And the reason the magistrate doesn't need to know about this."

Race swallowed wine past a tight throat. "Yes. I wanted to go in and check the safes myself, but Bickerman reminded me of a very important point. I wouldn't know how to open their safes even if I found where they were hidden."

Blake tilted his chair back again. "Yes, our grandmother saw that we were taught how to ride, play cards, and shoot, but not how to open a safe. How thoughtless."

"I don't think our grandmother intended for us to rob anyone," Race countered dryly. "The good thing is that Bickerman knows of a man who can do just that and he's going to employ him for me."

"Someone who knows how to break into a house and open safes?" Morgan asked. "Who is he?"

Race chuckled ruefully. "He wouldn't tell me, of course. People who can do that sort of thing don't want too many people knowing they can do it. It's against the law, you know. Bickerman knows how badly I want the pearls back, and he wants the money I've promised when he finds them."

"So, I suppose the possibility that the duchess might be in on this will end your affair with her," Blake said.

Morgan picked up the wine bottle and topped off their glasses. "I'm sure it will. Remember Lord Chesterfield said that 'Love ceases to be a pleasure when it ceases to be a secret.' We know about his liaison with her, so what fun could it be for him now?"

Blake agreed with a nod and said, "But I was just remembering one of Chesterfield's other quotes. 'Hatred is by far the longest pleasure; men love in haste, but they detest at leisure.'"

"Damn both of you," Race muttered. "You know good and well Chesterfield never said either of those things. You're both making them up just to get me riled, as if I wasn't already."

"Actually," Morgan said, "I believe it was a long-dead woman writer named Aphra Behn who first wrote what I quoted, and I do believe it to be true." Morgan chuckled. "But I think I prefer what Blake quoted."

Blake smiled at Morgan. "I do too, and I'll tell Lord Byron you said so the next time I see him. I think he is given credit for the quote about hatred and love, not that I know whether he was actually the first one to say it."

"Who was it who said 'There are two things a man will wait forever for: love and revenge'?" Morgan asked.

"That's enough," Race growled. By the stunned looks on their faces, he'd spoken roughly, but he was ready to put an end to their madness. "I need help from you two ninnies, not mindless quotes that mean nothing and that I care nothing about."

"Well, why didn't you just say you wanted help?" Blake argued. "In that case, I will talk to Susannah. Since I'm a duke and she a duchess, we should be able to have a respectful conversation. I'll let her know in no uncertain terms that the pearls will be returned immediately or she will face dire consequences."

The last thing Race wanted was either of his cousins talking to Susannah. No one could ever be as hard on her as he had been.

"That's not necessary, Blake."

"I think it's a good idea," Morgan argued.

"If you must know, I've already talked to her."

"What did she say?"

"What do you expect she said, Morgan? She denies having any knowledge of the theft, and I believe her. For now, I know it is best for me to leave it to Bickerman's man to look for the pearls, as much as I wanted to ransack their houses myself."

Blake drummed his fingers on the table once again. "Why are you so certain that Susannah is not an accomplice?"

Morgan's eyebrows lifted. "He's protecting her."

"Call it what you like," Race said in a warning voice.

As if sensing the conversation between Morgan and Race was heating, Blake changed the subject by saying, "What else was stolen?"

"Oddly, nothing of great importance: a small amount of money, some legal documents, but nothing I can't live without."

"All right, so what's next?"

"Bickerman will watch Spyglass, Winston, and Smith like a hawk with his eye on his prey, until we find out which one is the thief," Race said.

Both his cousins nodded.

"There's one other thing. Keep this to yourselves. I don't want anyone else to know, except of course Gibby, who I see is making his way toward us."

"You do plan to bring charges once the thief is caught, don't you?" Morgan asked.

"Of course," Race said without hesitation.

"What are you three guardian fools doing huddled together here in the corner, looking as if you are plotting to kidnap Prinny?"

While Blake rose and pulled over a chair for Gibby, Race motioned for the server to bring over another glass.

Gibby made fists and threw two or three light punches on Morgan's upper arm. "Did that hurt? Did you see how fast I boxed?"

Morgan grinned at him. "Yes. You're fast and strong for an old man."

"Good." Gibby smiled, and all four of them laughed.

"What are you doing here?" Blake asked.

"I came to find Race," Gibby said, sitting in the chair Blake handed him. "I've looked everywhere for him today, and some places, like this one, twice."

"What do you have going on, Gib?"

"I'm sure it's not a crisis, but I wanted to tell Race that the duchess came to see me today."

Race went rigid, and his two cousins leaned intently

toward Gibby. The old man's eyes darted from one to the other.

"Susannah came to see you?" Race asked.

"What did she want?" Blake added.

"What did she say?" Morgan asked.

Race sighed heavily. "Would you two please let me ask the questions, since this conversation concerns me and not you?"

Blake and Morgan leaned back in their chairs and nodded to Race with conciliatory expressions on their faces.

"Susannah?" Gibby said. "Is that her name?"

"Yes, but never mind that, Gib," Race asked impatiently. "What did she want?"

"She asked me if I would introduce her to Winston and Smith, the men who tried to buy the pearls from you."

"What the devil for?" Morgan asked.

"I have no idea. That's why I came to find him," Gibby said, pointing his thumb toward Race. "I told her where Smith's shop was located and agreed to introduce her to Winston."

Race remained quiet, but his mind started working. Susannah had already been to Smith's shop to talk to him. Did she think she would go to Spyglass's and Winston's homes and question them? Or worse, search their houses for the pearls? Fear for Susannah's safety tightened inside him. She was treading in dangerous waters, and it was his fault for suspecting her in the first place.

Gibby continued, "She told me she had seen you this

morning but wouldn't tell me why. She said you would tell me. By the way she was talking, I knew something must have happened between you two but she wouldn't say what."

Race's cousins looked at each other and then at Race.

Gibby rested his hands on his knees. "What are you three trying to keep from me?"

"Should I tell him?" Morgan asked.

"No," Race said. "Our grandmother's pearls were stolen from me last night."

Gib looked from one cousin to the other and then back to Race.

"You told me the pearls were safe," Gibby said with no accusation in his voice.

"They were," Morgan said. "They aren't now."

"Do you have any idea who took them?" Gibby asked.

"Three men and one lady readily come to mind," Blake said ruefully.

Gibby's eyes widened, and he spread his swollen hands on the table. "Are you telling me you think Her Grace had something to do with stealing the pearls?"

"No," Race said firmly.

"All we really know is that she's one of the four who wanted them," Blake added.

"That doesn't mean anything," Gib argued. "Who wouldn't want them? Probably everyone wants them."

Morgan added, "She wanted them badly enough to interrupt Race's card party a couple of weeks ago, not to mention his slumber last night."

"Morgan, you are about to hit the floor," Race muttered.

Morgan held up his hands in surrender and tilted his chair away from Race.

"At this point, anyone could have stolen them," Blake offered.

"What are you going to do?" Gibby asked.

Race took another sip from his wine and briefly told Gibby about his meeting with Bickerman and what the runners would be doing to find the pearls.

"So the only thing to do now is to wait and see what turns up when the houses are searched."

Gibby leaned back heavily in his chair and sighed. "Why would Susannah want to be in contact with Spyglass, Winston, or Smith if she was in on the theft?"

"Only one thing I can think of," Morgan said. "She wants Race to think she's innocent. She knew you would tell him of her visit."

Gibby rubbed the back of his neck and shook his head. "No, that doesn't feel right."

Blake picked up the wine bottle and added another splash to the three glasses on the table. "Race, don't let this get to you or change any of the plans you already have in place. There is the possibility that Susannah is doing this to make it look like she's not involved. Just let Bickerman handle this."

Race didn't want Susannah to even think about contacting those men. He knew he was not going to be any good at waiting. Already he wanted to see Susannah again. He wanted to tell her once again to stay away from those men. The thought of her being alone with any of them made the hair on the back of his neck stand up.

"Just in case you want to talk to her about any of this, she'll be at the Kendricksons' party tomorrow night," Gibby offered.

"In that case, I think we'll all be there," Blake said.

"Race, while you are deciding what to do about the pearls, Susannah, and the men," Morgan said, "I suggest that since we are all together, we talk to Gibby about this fight with Prattle."

Race was in no mood to talk about Prattle, but he didn't say anything because he was happy to get them off the subject of Susannah.

"What do you want to say to me?"

"It's no secret that we don't want you going through with this fight," Morgan said. "Race was supposed to talk to you about the possibility of paying Prattle off. It could very well be that money is what he was after in the first place."

"If he wants money," Gibby said, "he'd better bet against himself and put a wager on me, because that's the only way he's going to get any blunt out of this fight."

"I heard just today that Prattle made rumblings that he may not go through with the fight," Blake said, "and now he has men offering him money to go through with it, win or lose. I don't think he's going to back out."

"Look at your hands, Gib," Morgan said. "You're too old to fight."

Gibby looked at his enlarged hands and said, "I have people coming up to me on the street just to wish me luck. Why would I want to give that up?"

"Because you are not a young man anymore," Morgan offered.

"Fiddlesticks. Lord Chesterfield always said 'You are as young as you feel.'"

"Gib." Blake laughed. "You know Chesterfield never said that."

"He could have said it," Gibby argued. "You don't know he didn't."

"Yes, we do. Remember, our grandmother drilled his best quotes into us. That's not pompous enough for him to have said."

The server put a glass of milk down in front of Gibby. Morgan and Blake looked at Gibby.

"What is this about?" Blake asked.

"Don't ask," Race said.

"It all has to do with getting my body strong for the fight."

Gib stood up and threw three or four punches into the air as he shuffled his feet back and forth.

"How's that? Am I getting quicker?" he asked, throwing more jabs into the air.

"No," Morgan said with a grin. "You look old and tired."

And with that, Gibby threw a hard punch that landed on Morgan's chin and knocked him out of his chair onto the floor.

Race and Blake shook their heads and laughed as Morgan got up, rubbing his chin.

"You bloody bruiser, you really hit me," Morgan said as his eyes widened.

"Of course I did. Sorry about that." Gibby grinned. "I guess I forgot for a moment that I was old and tired."

Morgan straightened his coat and sat back down in his chair. "If you were twenty years younger, old man, you'd be lying flat on the floor right now."

Gibby made fists once again and struck a fighting pose. "Prove it to me. I can take it. Come on, I'm ready. It's all in courage and skill, not age. Danger Jim said I need a practice round. Which of you guardian fools is up for it?"

They all shook their heads and slid their chairs away from the table as they mumbled, "Not me."

"That's what I thought."

Gibby smiled, picked up his glass of milk, and drained it.

Fifteen

My Dearest Grandson Alexander,

What do you think of these words from Lord Chesterfield? "There is a certain dignity of manners absolutely necessary to make even the most valuable character either respected or respectable. A joker is near akin to a buffoon, and neither of them is the least related to wit. There are many avenues to every man, and when you cannot get at him through the great one, try the serpentine ones, and you will arrive at last."

Your loving Grandmother,
Lady Elder

THE NIGHT WAS UNSEASONABLY WARM AND THE velvet night sky was filled with twinkling stars as Susannah and Mrs. Princeton walked toward the front door of Lord Kendrickson's home. Susannah was eager for the night to begin. She had many things she wanted to accomplish.

Now that she had, for the time being at least, marked Mr. Smith off her list of possible suspects, Susannah's main objective at the party was to meet Mr. Harold Winston and gain an opinion of him, and to see Captain Spyglass again. She wanted to talk to them both, and in some context mention pearls. She wanted to watch each man closely and see if either man acted nervous, wary, guilty, or in any other way suspect.

She knew that sometimes a person could find out what they wanted to know just by observing how someone reacted to whatever was said. As far as she knew, neither man knew that she wanted the necklace too, or that it was now missing—unless of course one of them had it.

One of the other things she intended to do tonight was to stay away from the Marquis of Raceworth should he be in attendance at the party. She had received another maddening note from him earlier in the day that simply said:

You owe me a dance.

Race

How dare he think she owed him anything after the way he had treated her? He thought her capable of conspiring with someone to steal from him. Still, her heartbeat quickened and her breath shortened just thinking about him. Her head told her to crumple the note and throw it in the fire, but her heart wouldn't let her. She had quickly folded it and tucked it in the secret part of her jewelry chest with the other two notes from him.

Their night together in her bed still filled her thoughts during the day and haunted her dreams at night. But he had treated her abominably, and she was determined to have nothing to do with him, no matter how heavy it made her heart.

After Susannah and Mrs. Princeton greeted their host and hostess for the evening, they left their outerwear with the servants and followed the sound of the music and loud chatter coming from a room nearby.

Susannah wore a wide-strapped, high-waisted forest green under-dress with a heart-shaped neckline cut lower than most of her modest gowns. Over the green sheath, she wore a scooped-neck, long-sleeved, ivory tulle gossamer-thin gown that flowed like a gentle breeze every time she moved. Around her neck, threaded on a piece of ivory satin ribbon, lay an emerald large enough to cover the hollow of her throat. She wore no earrings or any other jewelry. The emerald spoke for itself.

"Your Grace." Lord Snellingly bowed. "I've been watching the door, hoping you might be here tonight." He stepped back and admired her from head to toe with a dreamy gaze. "You look absolutely exquisite tonight."

"Thank you, and good evening, Lord Snellingly."

"After I met you the other night, I was inspired to write a poem for you." He sniffed and pulled a piece of paper from his coat pocket. "I'd be honored if you would allow me to read it to you."

Susannah glanced over at Mrs. Princeton as if to say "you did this to me" before smiling at the man. "Perhaps another time would be better, my lord. I just arrived, and there's someone I must see right away. Please excuse me." Susannah quickly turned away, not wanting to give the man time to persist.

"Would you like me to stay by your side tonight?" Mrs. Princeton asked as they hurried away.

"Of course not. Don't be silly. I'm quite capable of fending off unwanted advances from men. I would very much like for you to find someone to converse with and enjoy yourself tonight," Susannah answered. "A party is supposed to be a delightful occasion, even for companions."

Mrs. Princeton gave her an impertinent smile. "I shall enjoy myself as long as I know that you are accomplishing what it is you've come here to do. That is my only objective for the evening."

"You can get entirely too accommodating at times, Mrs. Princeton," Susannah said with a teasing smile on her lips. "Please get yourself something to drink, to eat, or whatever you wish, and do not worry about me. I will find you when I am ready to leave."

Mrs. Princeton nodded and turned away. Susannah looked around the dance floor at the far end of the room and froze. She felt as if her heart had jumped up in her throat. Race was dancing with a stunning young lady in a beautiful ivory-colored gown that made her look like an angel. Her shiny golden-blonde hair sparkled with every twirl under Race's arm. The young lady stared into his eyes as if he had mesmerized her.

And no wonder!

The marquis was heart-meltingly handsome as he swept the lady across the dance floor with the ease of a gentle breeze floating past her cheek. His black evening coat was cut perfectly to fit across his straight shoulders and broad chest. Susannah didn't know how such a tall, powerful-looking man could be so light on his feet. He looked to be a superb dancer, but that was no surprise. He was, after all, Lady Elder's grandson.

Was that jealousy she felt? Surely not. It was tension and anger and envy that he was dancing with someone else when his note had said "You owe me a dance."

As Susannah watched him, unbidden memories flashed through her mind and warmed her. His hand gliding down her naked hip, his lips on her bare breasts, their bodies joined in passion too furious to be controlled. She remembered he had told her she didn't look old, but how could she not when compared to the young lady he was dancing with?

Susannah continued to stare at him and remember their night together, until suddenly she realized that Race was looking back at her. His intense gaze scrutinized her face. Her heart fluttered maddeningly in her chest as their eyes met and held. Her stomach quickened deliciously, her skin tingled, and her body knew that in spite of the gulf of distrust between them, and as much as she hated to admit to herself, they still wanted each other.

She stood perfectly still and watched his gaze skim slowly down her face, over her breasts, which were barely concealed by her gown, before he lifted his gaze to her eyes once more as he followed the steps of the dance. A tingle of awareness settled low in her abdomen.

Was he remembering every touch, every breath, and every taste of their coming together? All of a sudden Race missed a step, and his foot landed on his partner's. The beautiful young lady yelped and almost stumbled. Race caught her, and Susannah could tell he was apologizing, but by the expression on the young lady's face she was not happy with him.

Race glanced back to Susannah. She quickly covered her smile with her hand, spun, and bumped into the Duchess of Blakewell.

"Oh, excuse me, Your Grace."

"Excuse me, Your Grace," Henrietta echoed Susannah's words.

"I'm sorry. I wasn't looking where I was going."

The lovely young duchess smiled at her and said, "Good evening, and no harm done. I saw you from a distance and wanted to come over to say hello to you."

Susannah could only assume by the friendliness of her tone and sincerity of her smile that she had no idea that just yesterday her husband's cousin accused Susannah of stealing his grandmother's pearls.

Pushing away those unwanted thoughts, Susannah smiled with more easy pleasure than she'd felt in a long time. She saw nothing but honesty and friendliness in the lovely lady's face. And Susannah needed a friend with all that she had going on in her life right now.

"I know we haven't known each other long, but would you please call me Susannah?"

"Of course, I would like that, and please call me Henrietta."

Susannah nodded.

"Do you remember meeting Mrs. Constance Pepperfield last night?"

"Good evening, Your Grace," Constance said and curtsied.

Susannah looked at the striking woman who stood beside Henrietta. Susannah guessed Mrs. Pepperfield's age to be about the same as her own. The lady's red hair had been shaped into tight curls on the top of her head. Her wide green eyes were filled with delight as she spoke to Susannah with the confidence of a woman who was in control of her own destiny.

"Yes, of course I remember. How very nice to see you again."

"Somehow, Blake managed to persuade Constance to be my chaperone when I first came to London, and she easily made the change from chaperone to friend after Blake and I married."

"What a nice compliment," Susannah said and suddenly felt another pang of envy. She wished she had a friend she could confide in. It wasn't that she didn't appreciate Mrs. Princeton, but even though Susannah gave her companion wide parameters concerning their relationship, they had never made the leap from employee–employer to friends, as Henrietta and Mrs. Pepperfield had.

"If your schedule permits, perhaps we can go to the park together one day next week," Henrietta said. "I hear there is a traveling troupe performing there with several amazing acts."

"That would be lovely. I've heard about the man who gets into a cage with a tiger. I've wanted to go."

"Perhaps I could check on that for the two of you and plan a date that would work for you both," Constance offered.

"Is that all right with you?" Henrietta asked Susannah.

"Absolutely. Thank you, Mrs. Pepperfield, for offering to do that for us."

Constance smiled. "Leave it to me and I'll take care of everything."

"Good." Henrietta smiled. "Since the weather has been so warm, we'll plan to bring a basket and blanket and make an afternoon of it."

Constance replied to Henrietta's comment, but Susannah didn't hear what she said. Susannah was watching the Duke of Blakewell walk up beside Henrietta. He put his arm protectively around her waist, pulling her close to his side, all the while keeping his gaze on Susannah. Even though Susannah knew the two were newlyweds and subject to be somewhat more affectionate in public than would ordinarily be acceptable, she had the feeling the duke was sending her a message. She sensed he wanted her to know that Henrietta was off-limits to her.

"Good evening, Susannah, Constance. I see you are enjoying the company of my lovely wife this evening."

"Good evening, Blake," Susannah managed to say without a hint of the reservation she was feeling inside.

"You see her enough as it is, Blake," Constance remarked. "Though she loves you dearly, she does enjoy being unattached from your hip once in a while and spending time with her friends."

"You never change, Constance."

"I don't ever intend to," she quipped.

Somehow, Susannah knew instantly that Constance and Blake had a longstanding respectful relationship with each other, and another pang of envy hit her. What was wrong with her? She knew that Race's cousins had been wary of her from the moment they met her. But

then what should she expect? Morgan and Blake knew
she had come to London for no other purpose than to
stake a claim on their grandmother's pearls.

And why should she feel such envy? She hadn't come
to London to make friends or even to attend glamorous
parties given in the finest homes in Mayfair. And she certainly hadn't come for the depth of passion she had experienced with the marquis. The necklace was the reason
she came to London.

"It appears that suddenly you aren't wasting any time
getting to know as many people as possible, Duchess,"
Blake said, looking directly at her.

By the stern expression on his face and the arrogant
tilt of his chin, Susannah decided the duke was letting
her know that even if his wife wasn't aware the pearls had
been stolen last night, he was, and that she might well be
the nimble-fingered thief.

"One can never be acquainted with too many people,
don't you think, Your Grace?" Susannah spoke to Blake
as easily as if she had the same relationship with him as
Constance.

"That depends," he said with what could only be
called a half grin on his lips. "I've found that some people
are not worth knowing."

Her gaze stayed on his, and she smiled easily, confidently at him. "True, but then I'm sure you have also
found that there are some people who are worth everything in the world, are they not?"

He nodded once to let her know that she had hit her
mark.

"There you are, Duchess, Duchess, Duke, and Constance," Sir Randolph said as he walked up with a short, very thin man by his side.

With all the ease of a man who knew his way around the most complicated of formal introductions, Sir Randolph managed to do what Susannah had asked of him. She was standing face-to-face with Mr. Harold Winston, the man who could have stolen her grandmother's pearls from Race.

His eyes were small and such a light shade of blue they were almost eerie. His nose was slightly pointed and turned up. His lips were completely surrounded by a short beard that ended in a point, though his cheeks were clean-shaven. Within moments of the introductions being completed, Henrietta, the duke, and Mrs. Pepperfield excused themselves and melded into the crowd.

Just looking at Mr. Winston, Susannah could easily believe he had stolen the pearls. The man hadn't been able to tear his gaze away from the emerald around her throat for more than a second or two since he had walked up.

After a few moments of polite conversation, Sir Randolph said, "Duchess, would you excuse me? I forgot there was something I needed to ask the duke."

She smiled at Sir Randolph and was pleased to see that the swelling in his hands had subsided. "Of course."

"Perhaps you'll save a dance for me later?" he said with a wink.

"Most certainly, Sir Randolph."

He spoke to Mr. Winston, and then left.

"Your Grace," Mr. Winston said the moment Sir Randolph's back was turned, "forgive me for staring, but the emerald you are wearing tonight may well be the finest and largest I've seen in a private collection."

His eyes sparkled with eagerness to know about the stone. She smiled graciously at him as her hand crept up her chest to fondle the stone at the base of her neck. With her dress cut as low as it was, most men wouldn't even notice she had on a necklace.

"How nice of you to recognize its significance."

With his gaze still firmly latched onto the gem, he added, "I know there aren't many emeralds the size of that one in existence, and it looks flawless. Tell me, has it been in your family for a long time?"

"No. My husband gave it to me on our wedding day. He told me only that he had purchased it on one of his trips abroad, knowing he would remarry one day and it would be the perfect gift for his bride."

"A very thoughtful man."

"Yes, God rest his soul. You seem to have more than a casual interest in gems, Mr. Winston, and certainly more than the typical gentleman."

His shoulders went back a little farther, and he lifted his chin proudly. "With good reason, Your Grace. I am a master jeweler, and I work for the prince. I seek out rare gems and gold pieces and buy them for him."

Susannah raised her eyebrows. This man had given her the perfect invitation to ask about pearls. He couldn't have been more accommodating if she'd planned the entire conversation ahead of time.

"What an important job that must be."

He laughed lightly and then sniffed, obviously pleased with himself. "Yes, quite. It is an honor to serve the prince. He has quite the passion for exquisite gems, and I've been fortunate to add many to his collection."

"I'm intrigued. How would you go about doing something like that?" she asked innocently.

"Mostly from private sales, of course. For instance, someone might have seen this magnificent emerald you are wearing tonight and mentions it to me. I would then approach you and ask to see it." He stopped and moistened his lips. "If I thought it might be something that would catch the prince's attention or something he would desire, then I would ask if you wanted to part with it for a sum of money far greater than its value."

"And what is the usual outcome?"

He shrugged. "Sometimes people will sell and sometimes they won't," the man said, noticeably happy that he could give her so much information about his work. "I know the prince would be pleased to add your emerald to his collection. Tell me, do you have any interest in parting with it?"

"I'm afraid I couldn't possibly, but what an honor for you to work for the prince. Tell me, does the prince ever wear pearls, or only precious stones and gold?"

Mr. Winston didn't blink, hesitate, or do anything suspicious at the mention of pearls. Surprisingly, he gave her a knowing smile and said, "No doubt you've met, or, at least, you have seen the gentleman here tonight who is wearing pearls. If the prince had a collection like that man, he would probably rather see them on a lady than on himself."

Susannah carefully watched every facial expression and mannerism, but Mr. Winston didn't seem to be the least bit nervous that she had mentioned pearls. But that could be because he was so confident in his position as jeweler for the prince, and it didn't necessarily mean he had not stolen the necklace.

"You're talking about Captain Spyglass, are you not?"

"Yes. He's wearing a magnificent pearl cluster ring tonight and the most beautiful rosette brooch I have ever seen. I've heard quite a bit about the man, and after we were introduced I asked him if I might take a look at his collection while he is in London." Mr. Winston stopped and rolled his eyes. "He said 'perhaps,' if you can believe that. Clearly leaving no doubt he's not one of the king's subjects."

Susannah couldn't hide her smile. Mr. Winston didn't appreciate the captain's snub. "Maybe he is afraid you would offer to buy some of his pearls."

"And I might. From all I've heard, the man's fortune is in his pearls and that scandalous ship that sits in the harbor."

Out of the corner of her eye, Susannah saw Race standing not far away, glaring at her with intensity while he talked to a young lady who didn't seem to notice that his gaze was not on her. Susannah's stomach jumped, and she was furious with herself that he could disturb her so pointedly.

Though she wanted nothing more than to run from

Race, she held her ground and spoke with Mr. Winston for a little longer before excusing herself.

Susannah didn't know where the ladies' retiring room was located but decided to find it. She needed a few minutes to collect her thoughts. She wanted some time alone to think about what Mr. Winston had to say. Seeing Race was causing her more pain than she had imagined and she wanted to get him off her mind.

As she turned down a dimly lit corridor, she heard someone call her name. She turned around and looked straight into the dark-blue eyes of Lord Martin Downings, the man who had ruined her twelve years ago.

He was heavier around his middle, and of course older than when she'd last seen him. His once thick chestnut-colored hair was thinning on top and graying at his temples, but he was still a handsome man.

"Forgive me. I should have said Your Grace." He bowed arrogantly.

Staring at her former beau, Susannah realized she felt absolutely nothing for him. She had always wondered what she would feel if she ever saw him again. Would she be filled with the longing of unrequited love, bitterness, or even anger that he had rejected her all those years ago and left her to face alone the repercussions of their tryst? A calming peace washed through her, and she relaxed, knowing she felt none of those things. She had no more emotion for him than if she were meeting a complete stranger for the first time.

Susannah smiled and lifted her gloved hand for him to kiss. "Lord Martin, it's been a long time since I've seen you, but you are looking well."

He smiled and took the tips of her fingers in his and squeezed them a little more firmly than necessary, making her immediately wary. He kept his dark-blue gaze on her face while he kissed the back of her hand, letting his lips press overly long before lifting his head, stepping closer to her, and saying, "I've been in the Cotswolds for a few days and returned last evening to hear you were in Town and attending parties." He moved closer to her, and in a low voice said, "Why didn't you let me know you were coming to London?"

Susannah thought his question presumptuous, but as she pulled her hand from his, said, "Why would I?"

He smiled suggestively. "So that we might get reacquainted, of course." He stepped even closer to her, and Susannah backed up. "Surely you knew I would want to be with you again, privately of course."

Susannah gasped. She was insulted by Lord Martin's forwardness and felt no compunction about not sparing his feelings.

She waited until a server passed them in the hallway and then said, "But I had no desire to see you."

He pouted, lowering his head, showing his double chin, before raising his eyes to look at her face. "How can you say that after all we meant to each other?"

She smiled confidently at him. "Because it is true, Lord Martin. I know I really should be grateful to you, but the truth is I'm not."

His eyes lit up, and he smiled eagerly. "Grateful to me? Really?"

"Yes," she said and waited for another server holding a tray of glasses to pass them before adding, "If you had offered to marry me twelve years ago, I would have accepted, and today I would be living a very dull life. As it is, my life has been exceedingly happy and full."

His smile drooped. "Surely you don't mean that."

"I do. Now, excuse me, I was just on my way to speak to someone."

"Wait!"

She turned away, but Lord Martin grabbed her upper arm so suddenly and firmly that Susannah gasped. "How dare you touch me," she whispered harshly. "Take your hands off me."

"Not until you hear what I have to say. Duchess or not, I must explain my actions of long ago."

She tried to pull free of him. "I will not hear what you have to say. Release me immediately."

"What's going on here?"

Susannah heard Race's voice behind her and turned as his protective hand settled firmly against her back. A deep wrinkle of anger marred his brow, and his gaze shot daggers at Lord Martin.

Lord Martin snatched his arm back as if she'd suddenly burned him, and he stepped away from her.

"Nothing, my lord," Lord Martin said, pulling nervously on the tail of his coat.

"Good," Race said and then glanced down at Susannah. "I believe this dance is mine, and it's starting right now." He looked back at Lord Martin and coldly said, "Touch her again and I will break your hand."

Lord Martin huffed. "How dare you be so offensive, my lord!"

Race reached over and grabbed him by his neckcloth and shoved him aside. The trembling man stumbled back and almost fell.

"You don't know what offensive is yet." Race didn't take his deadly stare off Lord Martin. "Waylay her again and you'll find out."

With his hand confidently on her back, Race started propelling Susannah forward.

"What do you think you are doing?" she asked as she walked beside him toward the dance floor.

"As Lord Chesterfield always used to say, 'I'm saving you from a fate worse than death.'"

"If I wasn't still so angry with you, I would laugh at that. You know good and well Lord Chesterfield never said anything of the kind."

"Really?" he questioned, sweeping her with his hot gaze. "I thought he did. Must have been Gibby."

Susannah inhaled deeply. She was too attracted to Race for her own good. Why did she want to laugh at his silly attempt at humor? Why did she feel like the luckiest woman in the world to be walking by his side? Why did just looking at him thrill her very soul? Why didn't she hate the very sight of him for making passionate love to her one night and tearing her heart out the next morning?

"I watched Lord Martin kiss your hand as if he wanted to eat your entire arm."

That was exactly what his kiss had felt like. She was tempted once again to smile at Race but was able to suppress the urge.

"I can manage Lord Martin without your interference or your brute help," she assured Race.

"Can you?"

"Yes, and I can handle you, as well."

"Handle me, Susannah. Tell me I'm the worst kind of beast and I treated you appallingly and you never want to speak to me again."

Race smiled so genuinely at her that her heart melted into a watery pool.

"You are an impossible man at times. Everything you said was true and more. You are a horrible man."

"I agree. But for the moment, back to Lord Martin. If you can manage him, why did he grab your arm and not let go when you tried to walk away from him?"

Susannah shook her head and kept walking but didn't look over at Race. "He is a harmless oaf. I do not want to discuss Lord Martin or anyone else with you. You are much more a threat to me than he has been, is, or ever will be." She stopped at the edge of the dance floor. "Furthermore, I do not want to dance with you."

He stared down at her with such an engaging smile, Susannah wanted to let all her hurt from his accusations wash out of her, but she couldn't. She was still too raw from his thinking her capable of stealing from him. That had cut her too deeply.

"You owe me a dance," he said, his voice hushed.

For some reason the words excited her as much as his note had, but she had to deny those wonderful feelings.

She jerked her head toward him. "I beg your pardon. I don't owe you anything. You accused me of theft."

His gaze fluttered down her face to her lips. "I might have acted hastily."

She gasped. "You might have?"

"No, you're right, I did. I'm not a perfect man, Susannah." He looked into her eyes and softly said, "We never had our dance."

His heated body on hers as they moved together as one flashed through her mind. She gave him a quizzical look. "Didn't we?"

His passionate gaze held on hers, and she saw in his expression that no matter what he might have thought her capable of, he wanted her.

"You're right," he said, "we did, but not on the dance floor."

The music started. He reached down and picked up her hand. "You do know how to waltz, don't you?"

"Of course," she said as he led her to the center of the floor.

They took their positions, and she gave him a stiff frame. She felt strength and warmth in his touch. On the correct note she stepped back, and the marquis stepped forward. At first she felt rigid in his arms, like she didn't belong, but within seconds she was floating along effortlessly with him.

"I believe I told you yesterday morning that I never wanted to see you again, and now you have accosted me for the second time since then."

"No, you told me never to come to your house again, that I wasn't welcome there."

"Most gentlemen would recognize that means a lady

doesn't want to see the man anywhere, anytime, any place, and she certainly doesn't want to dance with him in front of a hundred people."

"I'll keep that in mind for next time."

"Pray God there won't be a next time," she mumbled as she allowed him to glide her across the floor, never once bumping into any of the other couples crowding the small space.

"You might be interested to know that I received a letter from my solicitor today," Race said.

"Why should that interest me?"

"He wants to discuss with me some documents that a Mr. Rexford has made him aware of and he would like for us to meet concerning that."

Susannah's eyes brightened for a moment, but then she looked away from him and focused on one of the other dancers. "It hardly matters anymore, does it, my lord? You no longer have the pearls."

"Susannah, look at me."

She hesitated for a moment but relented and returned her gaze to his. Sincerity was etched in every feature of his face. "I will get them back. And when I do, I will look at your documents."

Hope soared within her, but she said nothing and looked away again.

"Why were you talking to that man?" Race asked.

"Lord Martin just wanted to know why I was in Town," she fibbed, not wanting Race to know her former beau expected her to pick up with him where they had left off.

"Not Lord Martin. Mr. Harold Winston. Why were you talking to him?"

"I will talk to anyone who I think might have the pearls."

"All right. Why did you ask Gibby's help concerning these men?"

"I don't owe you an explanation for anything I do. I will talk to anyone who I think can help me accomplish my goal."

His eyes turned stormy and his hands tightened on her. "It's my fault the pearls were stolen, Susannah, and it is my responsibility to find them. I don't know what meanness these men might be capable of. You must stay out of this and allow me to handle this."

"I think you have forgotten that I want the pearls as badly as you do. Perhaps more so."

"I haven't forgotten anything about you. We were lovers, Susannah."

She glanced around them to see if any of the other couples on the dance floor might have been close enough to hear what he said. Thankfully no one was, so she whispered, "Don't remind me."

"I don't have to," he offered. "You've been thinking about it all evening, as have I. What you do, whom you see, is important to me. I will not let you play games with these dangerous men."

"You will not let me?" she answered, swift and sharp. "First, you have no proof these men are dangerous. Second, how dare you think you can keep me from doing anything I want to do?"

"When you challenge me like that, Susannah, it only makes me eager to prove you wrong."

"I am not challenging you. I'm simply telling the truth."

Susannah realized the music had stopped and the dancers were leaving; a couple of curious people looked at them.

"Race, we can stop dancing now. The music has finished."

His gaze darted around. He stopped and let go of her but hung back from the other dancers as they left the floor. "What did you find out from talking to Winston?"

"Why would I tell you anything?"

"I have a runner from Bow Street working on finding the pearls, Susannah. He is a professional and knows how to do certain things. There is no need for you to become involved in this intrigue."

Susannah tensed. "You may hire whomever you wish and do whatever you wish, but do not try to tell me what I can and cannot do."

He hesitated before answering, "Susannah, I think you want to drive me to madness, and much as it pains me to admit it to you, you are succeeding."

She felt her eyes grow misty, and that angered her. She did not want this man to reduce her to tears. "I don't care enough about you to drive you mad. I want only to find the pearls and return them to my mother."

She saw by the quick blink of his lashes that her words stung him, but he recovered quickly. "You don't care about me? That's another challenge, Susannah, that begs me to prove you wrong."

"No. I want you to leave me alone." The words were almost a plea.

"I have not been able to get thoughts of you out of my mind. I can't get the taste of you off my lips, I can't…"

"Stop," she whispered.

"I know you have been thinking about me, as well."

"You flatter yourself, Race." Their eyes locked together. "You thought I had the necklace."

Sorrow filled his eyes. "I was wrong about that."

He looked at her as if his gaze was absorbing her, but she couldn't trust him again. "It's too late to apologize."

His gaze swept down her face. "All right. I deserve that. But, Susannah, you must not do anything impulsive in your search."

"Impulsive?" she whispered earnestly. "What is impulsive, Race? Asking you to join me in my bed?"

"No, not that," he confessed on a broken sigh.

"Then perhaps your storming into my bedroom was impulsive?"

"Very."

She stepped closer to him, her gaze piercing his. "Let me make this clear to you, Race. My mother is sick. She wants the pearls returned to her. I was naïve, a fool to think I could get them from you legally. I should have known that with men like you, Mr. Winston, and Captain Spyglass, there would be no possibility of that, but I didn't know. Hear me well on this. I will beg, borrow, or steal the pearls to get them to my mother."

"Steal them, Susannah?" he challenged.

She paused. Had she said that?

Yes.

Had she meant it?

Yes.

Susannah took a deep breath. Her throat felt tight and dry, but she felt confident, strong. "The pearls were stolen from my grandmother, stolen from you. If that is the only way I can get possession of them, so be it. Now, stay out of my way, Race, you are hindering my efforts."

Susannah turned and marched off the dance floor.

Sixteen

My Dearest Grandson Alexander,

Read this and know one of the reasons I was always so fond of Lord Chesterfield. "I will let you into one secret concerning myself. I desired to please, and I neglected none of the means. This, I can assure you, without any false modesty, is the truth. Call it vanity, if you please, and possibly it was so; but my great object was to make every man I met with like me and every woman love me. I often succeeded."

Your loving Grandmother,
Lady Elder

SUSANNAH HAD SEEN RACE AT EVERY PARTY SHE HAD attended for the past week. It wasn't easy watching him dance, laugh, and converse with so many beautiful young ladies each evening when she wanted to be the only one he had eyes for. They had spoken politely to each other on several occasions, but he had not asked her to dance again, nor had he tried to seek her out for a private conversation. He had obviously taken her at her word when she told him she wanted him to leave her alone. She supposed he was doing exactly what she was doing, trying to figure out who had the pearls so he could get them back.

She still had the notes he had sent her in her jewelry

case. Sometimes after staring at his house, she would take the notes out and read them and hold them against her heart before putting them away again. She couldn't explain it, but she felt close to him when she held them.

After dressing for the day and finishing her chocolate and toast, Susannah hurried below stairs. As she expected, Mrs. Princeton was in the drawing room, sitting at the desk, with papers scattered all around her.

"Good morning, Mrs. Princeton. How are you on this lovely morning? You did notice the bright sunshine, didn't you?"

Mrs. Princeton rose. "Indeed, Your Grace. And I am very well. I'm working on the mound of invitations that have arrived since yesterday afternoon. Even though it is nearing the end of the Season, the number of parties each evening has not declined. I have some of them opened and ready for you to look through, but I'm sure this will be the first one you'll want to read." She held out an envelope.

"Race?" Susannah whispered as she reached for it and then could have bitten her tongue for saying his name out loud.

"No, Your Grace," Mrs. Princeton said kindly. "It's from your mother."

"Oh, even better," Susannah said, trying to cover for herself.

Susannah took the envelope from her companion. She walked over to the window and stood in the sunshine, not wanting Mrs. Princeton to witness the flush of embarrassment that heated her cheeks. She was furious with herself for even thinking Race might have sent her one of his outrageous but cleverly informal notes.

She opened up the letter and read:

> *My loving daughter,*
>
> *My one joy throughout the day is when I pick up your letters and reread them. I do miss you, my dearest, but I am tremendously grateful for what you are doing for me. Do not fret over my condition. Just do what you went to London to do, and hurry home to me so that I may have the joy of your company once more.*
>
> *With all my love, I am your*
Mother

Susannah's shoulders sagged; her heart ached. She laid her forehead in the palm of her hand and took in a deep, steadying breath. Susannah didn't know how or why she had wasted so much time in London. How long ago had she first met the marquis and asked him about the pearls? Three weeks or maybe closer to a month, and she was no nearer to getting them. No, she was farther away, in fact, because she no longer knew who had them.

Suddenly a thought crossed Susannah's mind, and her heart started racing.

That's it!

Why hadn't she thought of that idea before now? She knew exactly what she needed to do, and it would be the perfect foil to draw out the person who had the pearls.

She quickly figured how long it would take for a special courier to get a letter to her mother and how long it would take for her mother to respond back to her. If the spring rains hadn't bogged too many roads, a few days, possibly a week at most? Would fate, for once, be kind and give her that much time to work on finding the pearls?

It was a chance she had to take.

She dropped the letter from her mother onto a chair and said, "Mrs. Princeton, I need a quill and vellum. I want to write to my mother immediately."

"What is wrong? Does her letter bring bad news? Is there anything I can do to help you?"

"No, nothing right now. Continue what you are doing, but I will want this letter posted to her today."

It took Susannah several tries and much longer than she had hoped, but she finally had the letter to her mother worded the way she wanted and sealed it. Susannah hoped her mother would not fret or worry about the odd request she was making but simply honor it speedily and without question.

"Your Grace," Mrs. Princeton said, turning to Susannah from where she sat surrounded by invitations. She extended a note to Susannah. "This arrived for you a couple of days ago. Captain Spyglass is giving a party on Saturday night and you received an invitation to it. Should we decline this one?"

"Captain Spyglass?" Susannah drummed her fingers on the desk. "I heard he was having a party, but since I hadn't received an invitation I thought I wasn't invited."

"It's still three days before his party. There is time before you have to make a decision whether to go."

"No, no, of course I want to go. I can't pass on a chance to spend an evening in his home."

As Susannah said the words, an idea formed in her mind. She rose and walked over to the window again and stood in the sunlight while she studied over the plan. She could do it. She was sure of that. All she had to do was persuade Mrs. Princeton to help her.

"Mrs. Princeton," she said, walking back over to the settee. "I need a word with you."

"Yes, Your Grace." She rose to face Susannah.

"Do you remember I told you a few days ago that I might have to do some things you may not approve of or perhaps do something you don't think is in my best interest?"

"Yes." She remained perfectly still, as if bracing for what might come next.

"I hate to ask this of you but I truly have no one else to trust."

Mrs. Princeton relaxed slightly. "You know you can trust me. I am at your service. Whatever you need, I will do."

"Good." Perhaps fate had finally decided to smile on her. "This will be so much easier with your help. When we are at the captain's party Saturday evening, I intend to search his bedchamber for the pearls."

Mrs. Princeton looked at Susannah as if she'd lost her mind and whispered, "You can't do that."

"Of course I can."

"Then let me rephrase what I said. You shouldn't do that."

"Nonsense. The way that man covets pearls, I would think he keeps his collection in his bedroom, guarding them with his life, and that's the first place I'm going to look. If I don't find them there, I'll search his book room."

Mrs. Princeton's eyes were wide. "You simply cannot be caught in that man's bedchamber or anywhere else, Your Grace. It's just not acceptable for you to be there for any reason. Besides, he is a dangerous man. I heard some ladies talking about him when we were at Lord Kendrickson's house last week. They think that man used to be a pirate and that he has acquired most of his wealth by robbing ships at sea."

"Yes, I've heard that story, too. And with all the pearls he has, it could be true. I am not worried about any supposed danger right now."

"I will do it for you."

That startled Susannah. "What? Mrs. Princeton, I cannot let you do that."

"My reputation does not matter, but yours does. I will search his bedchamber for you."

Susannah's heart softened and she smiled gratefully at her devoted companion. "I cannot let you do that, but you can help me by keeping the captain occupied while I search."

"How can I do that? He will have no desire to speak to a gray-haired companion."

"Perhaps you can gain his attention by fainting or pretending you are drunk and making a fool of yourself."

Mrs. Princeton gasped and her back stiffened.

Susannah smiled at her prudish companion. She was willing to break the law for her but not pretend to be drunk!

"If you don't like my suggestions, I will leave it up to you as to how you keep him occupied long enough for me to scour his bedchamber."

Mrs. Princeton's eyes narrowed and concern etched its way across her face. "I don't know if I can do this."

"Mrs. Princeton, my life might very well depend on your acting abilities." Susannah didn't enjoy being so forceful but she truly had no choice if she was going to find the pearls for her mother.

"Yes, Your Grace."

"Thank you. Now, would you please see to it that the letter gets on its way to my mother? I'm going to go practice my music and prepare myself for what I have to do."

———

Race's lids fluttered open to the bright light of day and a banging inside his head. He rolled over and slung the sheet aside, revealing that he'd gone to bed again in his trousers rather than his nightshirt. He rubbed his forehead and then his temples. What happened to him last night? He couldn't remember the last time he'd been so deep in his cups that he woke with a headache.

He'd given up heavy drinking years ago, but after his frustrating meeting with Bickerman yesterday, he failed to watch the amount of wine he consumed throughout the evening. Bickerman's runner had searched Winston's and Spyglass's homes and Smith's shop and house and had not found the pearls.

Bickerman explained to Race that he was working on a plan to search Spyglass's ship, but that would take more time and expertise because the *Golden Pearl* was never left unattended.

Race lay on his back with his forearms covering his eyes. Was that music he heard? Yes, lovely, soothing pianoforte music.

Susannah.

He could wake up to that sweet sound every morning. Suddenly he bolted up in bed and looked at his window. It was open only a little, but everything was so still and quiet in his room that he heard the music drifting in from Susannah's house.

Just the thought of her aroused him.

Why was she playing the pianoforte so early in the morning? He glanced over at the clock on the mantel. It wasn't that early. It was already afternoon.

He rose and went to the window to look out. The bright sun hurt his over-indulged eyes. The sky was cloudless and as blue as any sapphire he'd ever seen. He pushed the window up as far as it would go and inhaled the fresh air. He propped his hands on the windowsill and listened. The melody drifted across the air into his room, pleasing him, soothing his banging temples.

Race stared at the back of Susannah's house and longed to see her, to touch her, to press his body to hers and sink inside her once again.

Race squeezed his eyes shut. After the way he had treated her, he wasn't surprised she hated him and never wanted to be with him again. He had been a rake, a scoundrel, an idiot of the highest order. He knew that. What had made him overreact and assume she had something to do with the theft? Was it because he was trying to counter how she made him feel? And how was he going to make it up to her for the way he had treated her?

That night at Lord Kendrickson's party she had made him painfully aware of two things. One, if she had the pearls she would have already left and taken them to her ill mother. Two, he ached to be in her good graces again. Not only had his night in her bed been the most extraordinary of his life, but he enjoyed talking to her, looking at her, and just being with her. He wanted to walk in the park with her, dance with her, and make love to her again.

The music continued to drift in as he shaved, washed, and dressed. Many times over the past few days he'd thought about going through the hedge to see Susannah and ask her to forgive him but stopped himself every time. She had made it perfectly clear she didn't want to see him, and he didn't blame her, but he was tired of her rules. From now on, he was taking over. He was not without charms and he was going to use them to woo her back into his life and into his arms.

And he knew a good place to start.

He walked over to a small chest and opened the top drawer and took out a sheet of vellum, a quill, and a jar of ink. After dipping the tip of the quill into the ink, he quickly wrote:

I want to see you.

"No," he muttered to himself. He had already written

that to her. He crumpled the paper and threw it to the floor.

He tried again but didn't like the second any better than the first and that sheet of vellum landed on the floor, too. He looked at the blank paper, searched his heart and wrote:

> *I'm sorry.*
>
>   *Race*

———————

When Susannah and Mrs. Princeton arrived at Captain Spyglass's home on Saturday night, Susannah told Benson to stay with their carriage and not leave it for any reason. If by some stroke of luck she managed to find the pearls, she wanted to be able to leave quickly. The chatter coming from the crowd on the first floor was loud and boisterous as they left their wraps with the servants on the ground floor. They quietly made their way above stairs and walked into the crush of elegantly dressed people.

Candlelight threw shadows all around the room as Susannah nodded, smiled, and said good evening to first one person and then another as she moved through the shoulder-to-shoulder throng. Her dutiful companion followed tightly in her footsteps, looking as nervous as a cat facing a hound.

She stopped and spoke with the charming Constance Pepperfield about which day would be good to go with Henrietta to the park. She bumped into the dashing

Sir Randolph Gibson, whose hands looked completely normal for a change. His spirits about his upcoming victory were still buoyant, and all he wanted to talk about was his highly publicized fight.

As the evening wore on, she spent more time than she wanted to with Lord Snellingly, who once again asked if he could read poetry while she played the pianoforte for him. From a distance, she saw Lord Martin and Race's cousin Lord Morgandale, but she hadn't caught sight of Race. She wasn't surprised he had decided not to attend a party given by one of the men he thought might have stolen the pearls. But she had to admit to herself that she had hoped he would be present.

Race was back to writing her short, concise notes, which thrilled her. She eagerly looked forward to them so much that she carried the last one he sent her in the beaded reticule that swung from her wrist. She liked the fact that he was reminding her he was around but he wasn't pushing her to see him.

Susannah didn't let anyone hold her up for long as she continued to walk around the ground and first floors of the house, making a mental note of all the closed doors, until she came face-to-face with her host and prey, Captain Spyglass.

He bowed and kissed her hand. At first glance she didn't think he was wearing any pearls, but then she noticed multiple strands of pearls had been attached like fringe to the ends of his neckcloth. He was a master at creating new ways to wear pearls.

"Your Grace, I am pleased you have honored me with

your presence on this night, when there are so many other wonderful parties to attend."

Susannah smiled at him and realized she felt no guilt about what she had to do. "Nonsense," she said. "I'm delighted to be here. You must know everyone in the ton coveted an invitation to your party."

He beamed. His thin dark mustache and tanned skin made his teeth seem exceptionally white. For all of his exotic appearance, he was a handsome man.

"You are most gracious. Come, let me get you a glass of champagne."

"Thank you," she said easily and walked beside him toward the champagne table. "I've heard you have a vast pearl collection."

He laughed. "Yes, rumors abound about my pearls. I treasure every one, and I probably do have the largest collection in the world. People say to me why pearls? And I say why not pearls?"

"Tell me, do you ever allow anyone to see your collection?"

He chuckled lightly and rubbed his hand over his chin. "Not very often, I'm afraid, but I have been persuaded to on a few occasions. Why? Would you like an invitation to see my collection, Duchess?"

She glanced over at him, not wanting to appear too eager. "I can't imagine any woman would not want to see it."

"Then perhaps one day I will invite you."

"I'll look forward to that," she said with a satisfied smile.

Susannah continued to talk with the Captain for a few more minutes and then excused herself. She felt her best chance of being unobserved was while there were many people in the house. Once the crowd started thinning to go on to the Great Hall or other parties, it would be more likely that she would be noticed in an area of the house where she shouldn't be.

She had no fear for her own safety. At this point, finding the pearls was the only thing that mattered.

In a corridor on the first floor, Susannah stopped a young servant who was carrying a tray of glasses. Her hair, eyes, and skin were as dark as Captain Spyglass's. "Excuse me," Susannah said. "Can you tell me where the ladies' retiring room is located?"

The nervous young woman said, "The first door on the right at the top of the stairs on the second floor."

Susannah smiled pleasantly and said, "Thank you. I wanted to make sure I didn't go into the wrong room. It would have been dreadful if I had accidentally gone into the master of the house's bedchamber."

The young woman smiled again and said, "Oh, you couldn't do that. His room is on the ground floor and he keeps it locked. The Captain has a bad knee and doesn't like to climb the stairs any more than necessary."

Susannah's spirits fell like lead in water.

Locked!

But just as she thought all hope of searching his room had vanished, Susannah caught sight of a key ring peeking out of the edge of the servant's apron pocket. Susannah knew she had to get that key ring.

With no time for further thought, she said, "Thank you, you've been most helpful." She started to walk past the servant but instead pretended to stumble and knocked the tray of glasses out of the young woman's hands. They fell to the floor with a horrible crash, breaking most of them.

Susannah quickly glanced around to see if anyone had heard or seen the commotion. The servant immediately dropped to the floor to pick up the broken glass. The roar of the chatter from the crowd must have muffled the shattering glass because no one came running.

"I'm so sorry," Susannah said, bending down to help the young woman pick up the broken pieces. "That was very clumsy of me."

"Please, don't help me," the servant said.

"But it was my fault. Look, there's a piece of broken glass over there. Don't miss that one."

When the servant turned and reached for the stray glass, Susannah reached for the key ring, slid it out of the apron pocket, and put it directly down the front of her gown.

"If anyone sees you helping me, I will lose my job. Please rise."

Susannah saw the fear in her eyes and immediately stood. "I understand. Thank you once again. You have been a great help to me."

Though she was anything but, Susannah calmly walked away, looking down at the front of her dress to make sure the key ring was not showing. She didn't know how much time she would have before the servant missed her keys, so she had to find Captain Spyglass's bedchamber immediately.

With all the aplomb she could muster considering how fast her heart was beating, Susannah wove her way through the crowd on the first floor and found Mrs. Princeton.

A servant passed by with a tray of champagne, and Susannah took a glass, deciding she needed something to fortify her for what she was about to do. As she lifted the glass to her lips and took her first sip, she saw Race walk through the door. Suddenly, her stomach felt as if it had a hundred butterflies in it and all of them were trying to get out. Just the sight of him filled her with sweet longing.

Her breasts tightened as she remembered how his lips had moved so effortlessly over hers, how gentle his hands had been, and how wonderful she and Race had made each other feel. Though she saw his gaze searching the room, it didn't appear he'd seen her. She quickly turned away from him. She didn't need to have her mind on him. She had allowed him to distract her for the last time.

Susannah gave the glass of champagne to Mrs. Princeton and said, "I'm ready to begin my search. I must go down to the ground floor, but you stay up here and keep your sights on Captain Spyglass."

"Yes, Your Grace."

Mrs. Princeton looked stiff, and her bottom lip quivered. Susannah exhaled heavily. "You don't have to go speak to him. Just watch him, follow him, and if you see him heading below stairs, faint or start screaming."

"That won't be difficult to do, Your Grace."

Susannah gave her a warm smile and patted her upper arm as she walked past her and whispered, "Thank you for your bravery."

As inconspicuously as possible, she made her way to the ground floor, where a servant stood by the front door ready to greet new arrivals or get wraps for those departing. She pretended to be looking at a painting until she saw him turn his back, and then she quickly rounded the corner out of his sight. A runner of fine Turkish carpet muffled Susannah's steps as she tiptoed down the dimly lit corridor on the ground floor. The darkened passageway seemed to stretch forever toward the three doors at the end. One of them had to be the master of the house's bedchamber.

Her heart pumped wildly with fear and with hope. If only fate would smile on her and she could find the pearls in a velvet pouch in the first drawer she opened. A constant roar of near panic filled her ears, but she forced herself to remain calm and collected as she tried the knob on each door. Only two of the doors were locked. The one room that wasn't had been filled floor to ceiling with furniture from the upper rooms.

She pulled the key ring out of her clothing and counted five keys on it.

Taking a deep breath, she decided to try the door in the center first. She put first one and then another key into the keyhole and tried them until only one key was left. She put it in and turned, but it didn't unlock the door either.

Were none of the servant's keys to this door?

As she moved on to the other door, tension and fear had her fingers numb and she began to doubt herself. Why had she agreed to come to London on this ill-fated mission? What had made her think she could get the pearls legally, let alone by theft? She should be in her own home at Chapel Gate, leading her quiet life, playing her music, reading poetry. But if she had never come to London, she would have never met Race. She wouldn't have felt alive for the first time in years. She wouldn't have fallen in love. Unbidden, memories of his kisses, his touch, his… No, she had to push those thoughts aside. He would not distract her again.

Maybe she'd just been in too big a hurry. With shaky hands, she started trying the keys again.

Click.

Was that the lock? She pulled the key out, turned the knob, pushed the door open just a crack, and listened. No sound came from inside the room. She looked behind her again. The corridor was empty. She opened the door a little farther so that she could stick her head inside for a quick peek. Her gaze scanned the handsomely appointed room that appeared to be Captain Spyglass's bedchamber.

Only one light burned in the room, a small oil lamp on a dressing table. A tall, turned-spindle bed stood against the far wall. The draperies and coverlet were the creamy color of aged pearls. They were trimmed with gold cord and bullion fringe. Her gaze darted around the luxurious room. Glowing embers smoldered in the fireplace on the back wall.

"What the devil are you doing?"

Startled, Susannah jumped and dropped the key ring onto the carpeted floor of the corridor with a loud thud that seemed to reverberate through the whole house.

Her cheeks flamed with heat. "Oh, by the saints in heaven, Race, you frightened the life out of me," she whispered.

"Obviously not," he said, bending to pick up the keys. "You seem to still be breathing."

She frowned. "No thanks to you. What are you doing here?"

"Following you." He held up the keys. "How did you get these?"

"By making a poor servant girl spill a tray of glasses, and no, I am not proud of myself for doing that but I am pleased. I've found Captain Spyglass's bedchamber, and now I intend to look for the pearls."

Race reached behind her and pulled the door quietly closed.

"What are you doing?" she asked.

"Once again, I'm saving you from a fate worse than death. Spyglass is not the kind of man you can cross, Susannah. He may look innocent enough, but I assure you if he caught you in his bedchamber you would find out just how dangerous he really is."

"Give me back those keys and go away. I don't need you to help me find the necklace."

His gaze swept over hers. "Why didn't you listen to me? I told you I have an expert who is doing just that. I can't believe you would put yourself in this kind of danger all for a few strands of pearls."

"I am not concerned about myself," she insisted. "Have you never listened to anything I have said?"

His eyes searched her face, and softly he said, "I have heard everything you have said to me. I will find the pearls, Susannah."

"I don't want your help," she said indignantly. "As you can see, I'm making progress on my own. You have said you would look at my documents, but I don't trust you to turn the pearls over to me. If you find them, you will keep them."

Voices sounded from just around the corner behind them. A chill flew up Susannah's spine, and she felt as if her heart jumped into her throat.

Race pulled Susannah to his chest.

"Which key locks the door?"

Susannah looked down at the keys. They all looked alike. "I'm not sure."

"Bloody hell," Race mumbled.

The voices drew nearer.

"Let me do the talking, and you had better kiss me like you mean it."

There was no fear of that not happening as Race's mouth came down on hers in a demand so great it took Susannah's breath. She felt his hand working feverishly, trying keys in the lock as his lips roved over hers. Forgetting that danger was mere seconds away, Susannah surrendered completely to the power Race had over her. Their lips were ravenous, exploring with no thought of parting as their breaths mixed, their bodies pressed.

"See here, what are you doing? Come away from there."

Race broke the kiss, and Susannah heard a click. The door was locked. Race dropped the key ring into his coat pocket.

"Did you hear me? I said move away," the man demanded again.

Susannah and Race jerked apart as a tall, thin man with black hair walked toward them.

Race cleared his throat and pushed Susannah behind him, shielding her as much as possible. He wiped his lips with the back of his hand and pulled on the tail of his coat.

"Sorry, we were just strolling down the corridor. No harm in that, is there?"

As the man advanced, Race moved them away from the three doors at the end of the corridor and continued to protect Susannah as much as possible from the perturbed man's view.

While keeping his eyes on Race and Susannah backing up, he tried the two doors and made sure they were locked.

"Move away from here to have your tryst. This is a private area of the house."

"Thank you," Race said. "That is exactly what we will do."

Race took hold of her elbow and whispered, "Where in the house did you make the maid spill the glasses?"

"What could that possibly matter?"

"I want to put the keys on the floor in that area. When she finds them missing, that will be the first place she goes looking for them, and I intend that she find them."

Susannah told him where she had pilfered the keys.

"Get your wrap. I'll find Mrs. Princeton and send her down to you. Go home."

She gasped. "I will not. How dare you start ordering me around?"

His hand tightened on her elbow. "I do not want you here if there is any fallout from the missing keys. Go home and leave your door unlocked for me. I will come to you tonight."

"No." Her voice remained firm, and her eyes held steady on his. "It will not be unlocked. You will be wasting your time to come to my door."

His brownish-green gaze swept up and down her face. "It's a chance I'm willing to take." He turned and hurried up the stairs.

Seventeen

RACE DOWNED THE LAST OF THE BRANDY IN HIS glass and stared at the back of Susannah's house from his book room window. He had waited and watched for over an hour as all the lights in the house had gone out except the one that came from Susannah's room. She had told him not to come. After their passionate kiss in Captain Spyglass's home, how could he not? He was consumed with yearning, and he wanted to make love to her. He wanted to feel her warm and responsive body beneath him. He craved more of her, and the only thing that separated them was two gardens.

After he had watched Susannah and Mrs. Princeton

leave Spyglass's party, he had hurriedly stashed the maid's keys in a corner of the corridor on the first floor where Susannah had swiped them. He hoped no one would ever be the wiser about what really happened to the keys.

It knotted his stomach to think how close Susannah had come to getting caught in Spyglass's bedchamber by that butler, guard, or whatever the hell he was. Race didn't even want to think about what might have happened to her if he hadn't seen her walking down the stairs and decided to follow her. She was too bold and audacious for her own good.

Race was impressed with her courage and her determination, but she was playing a risky game that involved people far less scrupulous than she could imagine. From all Race had heard, and despite Spyglass being welcomed to parties by people in Polite Society, he would not be forgiving if anyone tried to rob him. Just the thought of her being found snooping in Spyglass's bedchamber sent fear skittering through Race's chest and down his spine.

He untied his neckcloth and threw it on top of his desk and then discarded his collar, too. Had Susannah meant it when she told him not to come to her door? Even though she had looked and sounded like she meant it, she was not indifferent to him. Proof of that lay in how quickly passion flared between them during that brief embrace in the corridor. Just thinking about that aroused him.

Without further thought, Race strode out of the

house and tromped through his garden. He found the hole in the yew he'd cut. He had forgotten how long it had been since he had cut it, and already it was growing back together. Mrs. Frost had told him the gardener had almost collapsed into a fit when he saw what some prankster had done to his perfectly trimmed hedge.

Race bent down and with some difficulty managed to crawl through the hole. He was careful not to scratch his face this time. He wanted no more lewd remarks from Morgan.

The night was bright with a large moon and more stars in the sky than he could remember seeing in a long time. He breathed in the fresh, cool air and thought only of getting to Susannah. He hastened his steps and quietly took the outside stairs two at a time until he reached the landing on the first floor.

The moon was in just the right angle to glisten its beams on the door. Race smiled and reached for the knob in anticipation. He turned it as he pushed on the door with his other hand. The knob didn't move and neither did the door.

Not wanting to believe what seemed to be the obvious, he added more pressure and turned the knob again. The door was bolted from the inside and it wasn't going to budge.

For a moment, Race just stood there and stared at the door. His heart beat erratically. He had been so sure she would unlock the door for him that it momentarily stunned him that she hadn't.

Trying to gather his tattered wits and bruised ego,

Race blew out a disappointed breath and then moistened his lips. Was it possible she hadn't felt all that he had during their one night together? He laughed quietly to himself. No, that he would not believe. She had wanted him as desperately as he had wanted her. She had not been faking her pleasure. He was sure of that.

Perhaps he had destroyed any soft feelings she had for him when he accused her of stealing the pearls. She had been furious with him, and at the time he'd been too blinded to see the truth. He had misjudged her, barged into her house like a wild boar, and worse, he hadn't really apologized to her for either of those things yet. No wonder she kept the door bolted against him. A note scribbled on a piece of foolscap didn't constitute an apology.

Race ran both hands through his hair in frustration at his own loutish behavior. She should have slapped him that morning or thrown her hairbrush at his head. Maybe that would have knocked some sense into him, since he seemed to have taken leave of it.

Thinking on it now, he didn't know how he could possibly have thought she could have betrayed him so soon after she had completely yielded her body to him. What madness had sent him over the edge of reason into insanity?

Love?

No.

Yes.

He raked a palm through his hair once again. Was what he felt for Susannah love? It must be. But how had it snuck up on him?

"Bloody hell and damnation, too!" he whispered softly into the darkness.

If it was love, what was he going to do about it? Falling in love wasn't anything he'd planned for his near future.

He had fallen hard for her the moment he laid eyes on her. He could no longer deny that to himself or anyone else.

He had always expected, had always wanted to one day fall madly in love, but he'd always thought it would be with a young and untouched lady like Blake's wife Henrietta. It had never crossed his mind that he would fall in love with a beautiful, self-assured, and fascinating widow his own age. Susannah was a lady who was more than his equal in intelligence, courage, and title. She had not only turned his world upside down, but she had set his world on fire, too.

He had absolutely no desire for the silly young ladies making their debuts into Society. He wanted Susannah. He didn't understand it but felt as if he'd been waiting for her his entire life.

It was odd, but he didn't care that she had been married or what her husband may or may not have made her feel when she was in his bed. He didn't even care if she'd had other lovers. All that mattered to him was that Susannah be his. And he wanted her with him for the rest of his life.

But had he realized that too late? Had he lost her forever because of his own foolish behavior?

Race squeezed his eyes shut and shook his head for a moment. He took in a deep breath and squared his

ONLY A DUCHESS WOULD DARE

shoulders. He could win her back. He was certain about that. Obviously not tonight. Maybe not tomorrow, but he would woo her back to him. If he had to, he would move heaven and earth to do it.

Set with determination, Race turned away from the door, but before his foot hit the first step down he heard a soft click behind him, and he stopped.

Was that sound the bolt on the door?

He did hear it, didn't he?

Race spun and stared at the door as his heart hammered in his chest. The moon still shone brightly on the knob. It wasn't moving. Was his mind playing tricks on him? Had he only heard night sounds of crickets, frogs, or something else? Was what he heard just the creak of an old house settling on its foundation? His gaze remained frozen on the door, and he listened but heard nothing more.

Race suddenly relaxed and laughed softly to himself again. Could he have wanted her to unbolt the door so desperately that he imagined she had? But then hadn't he imagined himself wrapped in Susannah's glorious arms, in her warm bed, many times over the past few days?

Could he leave her house without trying the knob one more time?

No, he couldn't.

Race quietly retraced his steps to the door and then hesitated. Did he want to feel such heart-wrenching rejection again should his senses be playing tricks on him?

Still…

He took a deep breath and squared his shoulders. Slowly his arm snaked out toward the knob, but his fist remained closed. If the door was still bolted, what would he do?

Break the door down?

No.

He would take his time and woo her.

He was not without charm when he chose to use it. And he would use it. He would make such a romantic assault on her, she would be begging him to come back to her bed.

His hand opened and then closed around the cold knob. He turned his wrist, and the knob moved. He laid his open palm on the door and pushed slowly. The door opened, creaking slightly. His legs went weak. He swallowed a gulping groan, and he fell against the doorjamb, breathing heavily.

She forgave him for his tactless and boorish behavior.

Relief so satisfying that he wanted to throw his fists in the air and yell melted through him. A surge of sweet anticipation started in his chest and moved low in his loins. He was filled with gratitude and uplifted by the knowledge she wouldn't have opened the door had she not forgiven him for the way he had treated her. And she wouldn't have unlocked the door had she not been certain he knew she had nothing to do with the theft.

All he could think right now was that his grandmother's necklace be damned. Susannah was a hell of a lot more priceless to him than a few strands of pearls.

Very quietly, he walked down the corridor to her room. He opened her door, slipped inside, closed the door behind him, and turned the key in the lock. Susannah was sitting up in bed with a book in her hand.

An oil lamp burned on the night table beside her; a low fire glowed in the fireplace.

She looked so inviting dressed in a white sleeveless shift with her glorious brown hair flowing onto the pillows behind her. All the loving emotion he felt for her swelled in his chest. Desire and expectation rippled down his spine and settled into the hardness between his legs.

Their eyes met across the room and held. She looked cautiously at him. She was wary of him and he didn't blame her. He hadn't given her much reason to trust him up to now.

Race shrugged out of his coat as he walked toward her, letting it fall to the floor behind him. He kicked out of his shoes and propped one hip on the edge of the bed beside her. Without speaking, but keeping his gaze locked on hers, he took the book from her, closed it, and laid it on the table beside the lamp. He pulled the tail of his shirt from his trousers, lifted the shirt over his head, and flung it aside.

He then slipped his hand around to the back of her neck, pulled her gently to him as he lowered his head to hers, and brushed her soft, moist lips with his, easing over them with the lightest contact.

Contentment settled sweetly over him.

"I'm sorry I was such a beast," he whispered into her mouth. He lifted his head and stared into her eyes once again. "I can only hope that—"

The pads of her fingers flew to his lips and silenced him. "All is forgiven, Race."

Doubts rose up inside him. That was too easy. He knew how despicable he had been. "When I first got to your door tonight, it was locked. I didn't blame you for not wanting me to come."

Her eyes questioned him. "You waited?"

He nodded. "Not because I knew you would open it eventually, but because I hoped you would."

"I almost didn't."

"What made you change your mind?"

A smile broke across her face, and as she looked at him, her eyes softened. The caution he'd seen moments before was gone, and he saw trust. She had never looked more beautiful to him than she did at that moment. Giving him her trust, her body, her all, made him jubilant like nothing ever had, and he knew in his heart he would never let her down again.

"You. This." Susannah wound her arms around his neck, leaned forward, and kissed his neck, letting her lips skim along his shoulders, down his chest, and across each nipple.

A spiraling heat of desire swirled, searing and deep in his loins, and Race trembled with need at her gentle touch. He suddenly had a great desire for her to know that he loved her.

"Susannah, I—"

"Shh," she said, silencing him with her lips on his. "No more need be said," she whispered into his mouth. "Just make love to me, Race."

"With pleasure," he whispered as he accepted her kiss, her forgiveness, and her lips.

She was wrong, though. There was much more that needed to be said between them, but he would leave it for later. He didn't want to talk right now, either. He just wanted to touch, to taste, and to see her.

He raised his head and smiled down at her as he fingered the lobe of her ear. "Your skin is so soft," he whispered as his hand left her earlobe and traveled down to her jaw and followed the bone around to the other ear.

She arched her head back, giving him freedom to touch her as he pleased. He caressed the tender skin behind her ear with his forefinger while his thumb played in the hollow of her throat.

He bent his head and slanted his lips over hers in a slow, tender kiss. His fingers trickled down her neck to her chest to the firm swell of her breasts, nestled warmly beneath the cool cotton fabric of her night rail. Her breast was full, soft, and her nipple firm beneath the palm of his hand as he caressed her.

"Susannah," he murmured softly as he moved his head low. With his mouth, he found her taut bud hidden beneath the thin material of her shift and gently tugged on it, nipping it with his teeth. Her nipple grew harder under his playful touch. The soft, feminine sounds of enjoyment she made elated him and added to his own satisfaction.

Desire for her grew strong, overpowering every other feeling. He kissed his way back up to her lips. They parted, and she leaned sensually into him, deepening the kiss. His tongue swept inside her mouth, slowly, delicately, so he could enjoy the sweet taste of her.

His arms slid around her back, and he leaned her into

the pillows as his mouth ravished hers. His tongue played with hers, tasting, teasing, giving, and taking.

He heard her soft moan of desire and felt her tremble with yearning, and it gave him immense satisfaction.

Eagerness to possess her tore at him, but he kept it at bay as his lips left hers and his tongue swept down her neck, tasting her, and back up to her mouth again. A whisper of satisfaction eased past his lips and into her mouth as he cupped, lifted, and caressed her breast, feeding his insatiable desire to touch her with all the hunger he was feeling.

He kissed her harshly, madly, and Susannah accepted his roughness and eagerness. That pleased him, aroused him.

Her hand dropped to his thigh and then slipped to the throbbing shaft between his legs. Her unexpected touch sent rushing, delicious warmth sizzling through him, and he lifted his body toward her. His uneven breaths quickened, and so did hers. She caressed his hardness with careful confidence, and he sensed her desire rising to match his.

Race felt her hands working on the buttons of his trousers, and he quickly helped her slide them down and off his legs and feet. He grabbed her night rail and pulled it up and over her head and flung it away, leaving her beautiful nude body for him to devour with his eyes, his lips, and his tongue. He tumbled her off the pillows and stretched his body beside hers on the bed. He wanted to give Susannah all the pleasure she had experienced the last time they were together and more.

He continued to massage her breasts, loving the feel of their full, firm weight in his hands. Occasionally he would stop and tease the nipple with his thumb and finger. He ran the palm of his hands and tips of his fingers over her naked shoulders to her breasts, to her waist, down the slim plane of her hip and inner thigh, and then back up again as he devoured her with his gaze.

"You are beautiful," he whispered.

"So are you," she said with eyes that were heavy with passion.

He chuckled and then grinned. "Men aren't beautiful."

She smiled convincingly at him. "You are. Your body is."

Burning heat surged in his loins, and a longing ached in his heart to completely possess her and make her his. She reached up and let her fingertips glide softly, tantalizingly slowly over his chest, down his midriff, and lower. He trembled with need, loving the fact she had no inhibitions, and allowed her hands to go lower and close around his hardness, feel its thickness and weight. He gulped in a ragged breath. Her feather-light caress teased him and offered no mercy to his burning need.

He kissed her lips tenderly and enjoyed the unrestrained freedom with which she touched him. Race threw his head back in measured pleasure as his muscles contracted in sweet pain.

When he could take no more of the exquisite torture, he lifted his taut body on top of hers and softly groaned from the satisfaction of having her beneath him once again. His body throbbed to complete their union, but he wanted to hold off a little longer and make sure she was ready for him.

He bent his head and kissed that warm, soft spot behind her ear. He inhaled the womanly scent of freshly washed hair and lightly perfumed skin. With tenderness, he slowly kissed his way down her face, moving as if they had all the time in the world.

With a gentle hand, he once again raked his fingers down her breast, to the curve of her waist, and then over her slim hip and to her shapely inner thigh.

Race moved his hand back up and caressed the warm skin of her abdomen before inching his hand lower until he found her softness. He rubbed the center of her desire with his thumb in a gentle circular motion as he lovingly kissed her lips. He heard the uneven tempo of her breathing, and he felt the urgent pressure of his manhood wedged against her hip.

She moaned in pleasure and trembled beneath his touch. Race smiled against her lips. There was immense satisfaction in the way she responded to him.

He didn't want her excitement to end too soon so he stopped the stroking of her center and in one fluid motion he entered her with all the love he was feeling for her. Her body tightened around him like a leather glove, and Race almost lost control.

A low groan of pleasure rushed past his lips, and he sucked in a hard, ragged breath.

Her arms completely circled his back as she kissed his chin, his neck, and back up to his lips once more. He moved slowly, pushing in and out with long, easy strokes.

He moved inside her, and her lower body quickened in response, her hips lifting to meet him with a desperate eagerness, as if to take more of him into her.

Within moments, Race felt her body shudder, and he knew it was time. He slid his hands under her back and cupped her tightly to his chest, making her one with him as they reached the climax of their pleasure at the same time, and he emptied into her.

With uneven breaths, Race gently lowered his weight on top of her. She stroked his back, down his buttocks, and up to his shoulders again with loving hands while he rested his face in the crook of her warm neck. He inhaled deeply, drinking in her warm womanly scent.

Lying with her, he realized he didn't give a damn about the pearls for himself—not one damn if it meant he couldn't have Susannah. She was the woman he wanted in his life. The only one he wanted for now and for always.

Susannah was right for him. And that was all that mattered.

It was important to him that she know he wanted her. No other woman but her. But how did a man go about telling a woman he loved her? He had never done that before. And with all that had happened between them, would she believe him?

He rolled off her onto his side. She turned and snuggled tightly, fitting her body perfectly against his, with her head nestled on his arm.

Race lifted her chin with the tips of his fingers,

looked into her eyes, and said, "Susannah, I know you're going to find this difficult to believe, but I'm in love with you."

Eighteen

My Dearest Grandson Alexander,

 Here are more strong words from Lord Chesterfield:
"In the mass of mankind, I fear, there is too great a
majority of fools and knaves, who, singly from their
number, must to a certain degree be respected, though
they are by no means respectable."

       Your loving Grandmother,
       Lady Elder

SUSANNAH'S EYES POPPED WIDE OPEN, AND FOR A moment she was too stunned to move, but slowly, as his words sank in, she smiled and then softly chuckled.

Race's eyebrows rose in concern. "What's wrong?" he said, propping on his elbow.

"You, again."

"Me again?" His eyes turned guarded. "I have to admit that laughing, no matter how nice it is to hear, is not the reaction I expected when I bared my soul to you."

She moistened her lips. "Race, I'm not a young inno-cent who needs to be coddled with phrases about love that you don't mean."

The instant the words finished tumbling from her lips, she saw pain in his eyes, as if he'd been sucker-punched in the stomach, and she instantly regretted her flippant attitude. But how should she react to such a bold statement after the way he had treated her when the pearls were stolen?

A deep frown wrinkled his brow. "You think that's what I'm doing? Just trying to make you feel good about having shared your bed with me?"

Her expression softened, and she cupped his cheek with her hand. "Aren't you? Aren't you confusing me with some of your younger conquests?"

He grabbed her hand and kissed the inside of her palm, never letting his gaze leave hers. "No, Duchess, I am not trying to flatter you, and I am not trying to deceive you. I do understand your feelings. I'm perfectly willing to wait for you to fall in love with me. But hear me well, Your Grace, I have never told another woman that I loved her, because I have never been in love before. I know I haven't given you any reason to believe anything I've said. That was an error on my part, but know this, I will give you time to see how determined I am to make amends for my past and then make you mine forever."

Susannah felt her heart melt, and for some reason she couldn't understand, tears pricked her eyes. Was he telling the truth? Did he really want her to be his forever?

"I want to believe you, but I'm troubled by all—"

He touched her lips with the tips of his fingers as his eyes searched her face. "Say no more for now. I've told you before that I am a patient man. I'm willing to wait for you to accept my love and return your love to me."

Race softly placed his lips on hers, drawing her closer

to his chest with his strong arms. He kissed her reverently for what seemed like hours before his kisses turned impatient and physical. His tongue played over hers inside her mouth as his hands moved over her breasts, down her curves, around her hips, until his finger found the dampness between her legs.

Susannah welcomed his hot, eager touch as she felt his rising desire pulsating on her abdomen. Further words weren't necessary, because somehow she knew he wanted to prove to her what he thought she didn't know, that she loved him, and that he was very much in love with her.

"Tell me I don't have to love you, now, Susannah," he whispered against her ear. "Tell me you don't long for this, and I will believe you. Tell me."

Her pleasure was so intense she wasn't sure she could speak, but she managed a breathy "I can't."

Race chuckled into her mouth. His fingers continued to pleasure her until she thought she would scream from wanting, before he finally pushed inside her, merging their bodies into one. With his thighs wedged between hers, they moved together until all too quickly they were once again engulfed in the exquisite, luxuriant sensation of feeding love to each other.

With gulping breaths, Race relaxed on top of her for a moment before rolling onto his side. He pulled her close to his chest once again, and she snuggled. To her surprise, she felt his body shake and realized that now he was the one laughing.

Having no idea what he was thinking, she tensed.

Looking up into his face, she saw that his eyes were closed. "What is so humorous?"

"You, making me prove my love."

"Making you? I believe you are the one who felt you needed to do that."

He kissed the tip of her nose and then closed his eyes again. "Give me a few minutes to rest, and I will prove to you once more that I love you, Susannah, or twice more if you are still not convinced."

She looked down at his face in the soft glow of the lamp, and her heart felt so full she thought it might burst. Maybe he really did love her. And if he did, why wouldn't he let her answer him back? She felt his body grow still, his breaths evened out, and she knew that he slept.

Susannah snuggled closer to him. She had never felt such contentment. Yes, she believed he loved her, and she loved him, but there was something devilishly exciting about his thinking she wasn't ready to admit she loved him yet. But she would tell him.

Soon.

Susannah kissed his forehead, smiled, and closed her eyes.

Sometime later, something caused Susannah's lashes to flutter up. She knew immediately Race was still beside her. She turned her head and saw he was lying on his back, looking out the window as the first fingers of dawn showed in the sky.

He looked thoughtful and as if his mind was a thousand miles away. Was he already regretting telling her he loved her? Was he wondering why she never told him she loved him?

She rolled onto her side, propped her chin in her hand, and stared down at him. She caressed his chest with the pads of her fingers.

"Race, why do you look so somber? Have I made you unhappy?"

He smiled, picked up her hand, and kissed every finger as he caressed her face with his gaze. "No, of course not. I was just doing some deep thinking."

"Deep thinking? That sounds ominous. Should I ask why, or assume that what I don't know can't hurt me?"

He smiled and brushed her long hair over her shoulder to her back. "I was thinking about you and Gibby."

"Oh?" she questioned.

"You are both strong-willed, capable people, yet you are both putting yourselves in danger, and I've not been very good at helping either of you."

She gave him a playful smile. "It seems to me that I remember letting you help me with quite a few things tonight."

He reached over and caressed the full swell of her breast. "I'm not talking about what we shared in this bed. I'm talking about things like your going to see Smith at his antiques shop, talking with Winston at parties, and trying to sneak into Spyglass's bedchamber."

"I have never tried to hide from you that I wanted the pearls and that I don't intend to stop looking for them."

His hand drew a line from the base of her throat, down between her breasts, to the hollow of her stomach. "I'm thinking that it is time we stopped working alone and started working together. We should pool our meager resources of evidence about who might have the pearls and see if we can find out who has them and how to get them back."

Her eyebrows lifted in mock horror. "Now I know why you wanted to get back in my bed. You want information from me. You want to know what I've discovered from the suspects so you can find the necklace first."

His hand slid to the back of her neck as he rose and kissed her soundly on the lips. "That is not the reason I came to your bed, and I'm fully prepared to prove that to you once again."

She smiled, letting her fingertips trip across his collarbone. "I would take you up on that if not for the fact that it is dawn and it's time for you to go."

"I am serious about this, Susannah. You will be safer working with me, and we'll be more successful working together than alone."

She sank her teeth into her bottom lip and studied his proposition for a moment, and then said, "Now that you no longer believe I have the pearls, I would very much like your help in finding them."

"Good."

"We can plan a time to get together later and share our information, but for now, you need to leave. Everyone in the house will be awake soon."

He nodded while his hand caressed her shoulder and upper arm. "But first, do you mind if I ask you something about what happened twelve years ago?"

She gave him an understanding smile. "No. I have nothing to hide and nothing to fear about that time in my life."

"If you could have changed what happened after you were caught in the garden with Lord Martin, how would you have changed it?"

Her eyebrows drew together. "If you are asking me if I wish I'd married Lord Martin, I don't. In fact, after I saw him again, I'm very happy I didn't marry him."

"No, that's not exactly what I'm asking. You told me you begged your father not to make you marry the duke. But what did you want to do?"

Susannah shrugged. "Race, I was eighteen. I'm not sure what I wanted."

"But if instead of making you marry him, if your parents had gone to you and said, 'Lord Martin will not marry you. What is the best thing we can do for you?' What do you think you would have said to them?"

Susannah turned serious and thought for a few moments. No one had ever asked her what she would have liked to have happened. Every decision had been made for her without her consultation or argument.

"I probably would have asked them if we could live in another place where no one knew me, so I could start over with a whole new life without the feeling of condemning eyes watching me. Why do you ask this of me?"

"I was thinking about Prattle's sister and wondering what she must be feeling about what her brother announced to everyone in the park, about the fight, and about her reputation among her friends now."

"She is probably wishing her brother had handled the matter privately."

"That's what I was thinking. I'm certain Gibby is innocent of her charges. He is too much of a gentleman and always has been. All his life, his honor has meant more to him than his life. This whole thing could have been handled quietly if only Prattle hadn't made his accusations public that day."

"You think he did that for a reason?"

"Yes. Perhaps he was too deep in his wine, or maybe he was hoping Gibby would just pay them off. But what he didn't know is that Gibby is much too honorable for that."

"Sir Randolph is certainly enjoying the attention the fight has brought to him."

"Yes, it's one of his weaknesses. He adores being the focus of anyone's attention. I fear the aging Miss Prattle has become a pawn in her brother's scheme to get money from Gibby. What I don't know is whether she's a willing or reluctant participant."

"Are you thinking that, either way, since her brother smeared her name all over London, she might be wishing she could move to another place and start over?"

Race nodded. His hand slipped under Susannah's hair to cup her neck and he gently pulled her to him and kissed her softly. "Did I ever tell you that I think you are a wonderful lady?"

"No, and unfortunately, right now you don't have time to tell me. You need to dress and go to your own house before the day begins."

He kissed her again. "I don't want to leave you, but I agree I must." Suddenly his eyes turned serious again and he said, "Susannah, I am sorry I was such a brute to you about the theft."

She reached over and kissed his eyes, his nose, and each side of his mouth and then smiled at him. "No more apologies."

He grinned and crawled off the bed and picked up his trousers. "I'll come back this afternoon, and we can talk more about what you've discovered from your conversations with Winston, Spyglass, and Smith."

She pulled the sheet up to her waist. "And you can share what you've found out as well."

"Of course." He grinned at her as he pulled his shirt over his head. "I've ruled out Smith."

"So have I, but you cannot come over this afternoon," she said.

"What? Why?"

She smiled mischievously. "I already have plans, my lord."

He stopped tucking his shirt in the waistband of his trousers and frowned. "What kind of plans? No, don't tell me, just change them."

She lay back on the pillow and stretched her arms over her head. "I'm afraid that won't be possible."

"Susannah, do not tempt me with thoughts of your being with another man, or I will crawl back in that bed with you and once again show you why I am the only man for you," he said, shrugging into his coat.

Susannah laughed. She absolutely loved the fact

that he thought he had to win her love. "All right, if you must know, I'm going to the park with Henrietta and Constance."

His eyes widened as he stepped into his shoes. "Really?" he said, not bothering to fasten the buckle on his shoes. "I'm glad you two are getting acquainted."

She lowered her arms. "Yes, but I'm afraid Henrietta's husband still thinks I'm a troublemaker of the highest order and that somehow my errant ways will rub off on his sweet, innocent wife."

Race laughed and walked over to the bed. "I think it is positively splendid that Blake thinks you're a troublemaker. Damnation, but that makes me feel good! You must not ever let him know any different."

Race bent down and kissed her quickly and then asked, "What party are you attending tonight?"

"Mrs. Princeton arranges my schedule, so I'm not sure. Why?"

"Send me a note when you decide which one and let me know. I will attend the same party," he said and headed for the door.

She raised her eyebrows. "Wait. Do you not trust me to stay away from Captain Spyglass and Mr. Winston?"

He quietly unlocked the door and turned and threw her another grin. "Not an inch."

―――――

Later that day, Race waited in the private card room of the Rusty Nail with a bottle of wine and two glasses sitting on the table in front of him. He had chosen this place to meet Prattle, knowing he could trust the proprietor of the club to keep this meeting quiet.

Race wanted to get the matter of the fight and the pearls settled so he could concentrate on Susannah. He closed his eyes and breathed in deeply, and he could smell her womanly scent. He could taste her on his lips and hear her soft breaths.

Race heard the door open and glanced up to see Prattle standing just inside the room, looking like a rat staring at a roomful of hungry cats.

"Come in and close the door," Race told him.

Prattle obeyed and shuffled toward the table. The man wasn't very tall, but he was round as a barrel and looked solid as a rock.

He stopped in front of Race, nervously twisting his hat in his hand. "My lord?" he said, with sweat beading on his upper lip and shining on the top of his balding head.

"There's no reason to be nervous, Prattle. I only want to talk to you. Sit down."

"Yes, my lord."

Race poured him a glass of the dark red wine and slid it toward him. The man looked at the glass as if it might contain poison, so Race picked up his glass and took a sip before saying, "I'm hearing about Town that you don't really want to fight Sir Randolph. Any truth to that?"

Prattle placed his hat on the table and picked up the glass and took a long drink, downing more than half of what Race had put in the glass. He wiped his mouth with the back of his hand and then said, "I'm not a fighting man."

But he obviously was a drinking man. Race looked at the man's large shoulders and barrel chest and found it odd that such a stout man didn't have the stomach for fighting. But maybe that was a good thing. With his build, if Prattle knew how to fight, Race wasn't sure there'd be a man who could beat him.

Race kept all that to himself and simply said, "Neither is Sir Randolph a fighter. Yet you challenged him to a duel and he accepted."

"I-I know now that I shouldn't have done that. I'd had a bit of ale the night before and I was jug-bitten when I talked to Penelope that morning. I didn't really want to harm anyone."

"I wish you had thought of that before you made your pronouncement in the park with more than thirty witnesses."

Prattle's round eyes twitched, and his heavy cheeks trembled. "I-I don't know what happened. Some kind of madness overtook me and I wasn't thinking clearly. We went to see Sir Randolph later and apologized. We asked him not to—"

"Wait a minute," Race said, leaning over the table. "Are you telling me that you and your sister went to see Sir Randolph?"

"Yes, of course. Penelope apologized and told him she was sorry for what she told me and hadn't meant to cause so much trouble when she asked him to kiss her. She knew him to be a gentleman and was hoping if she accused him of compromising her, he might simply agree to marry her."

"Didn't she realize what she was doing to Sir Randolph's honor and her own reputation by accusing him of something that wasn't true?"

"Not at the time. She was dreadfully sorry, my lord. She thought if she accused him of wrongdoing, he might agree to marry her to keep scandal away from his good name. She told him she had always fancied him. She asked him what she could do to make it up to him."

Race was going to strangle Gibby. That devilish whipster should have told him about this. "What did Sir Randolph say?"

"He said the only thing we could do was go on with the fight. That I'd already ruined my sister by challenging him in the park, and if we didn't fight our reputations would be ruined too."

Gibby was probably right about that. The entire city was in a heated fervor over the fight. Race picked up his glass and sipped his wine.

"How is your sister now?"

The man breathed deeply. He had such a sad look on his face. "She won't come out of the house. She knows this is her fault, and she says she's never going out in public again."

"There's enough blame for both of you to carry, but there might be something I can do."

"I know I don't deserve a portion, but if there's anything you can do to stop the fight, I'd be obliged."

"I'm talking about helping your sister, Prattle, not you. Unfortunately, at this point, I agree with Gibby. The fight must go on. The men who have put down their wagers deserve their fight. If you didn't show for the mob that will gather in the park, they would probably come and find you both and make you fight. And quite frankly, you both would deserve it. However, your sister started this by her error in judgment."

The man cast his eyes downward.

"This is what I'm prepared to do. You and Gibby will fight, and you will make it a good fight. You must hit him because he will hit you. But after a reasonable amount of time, let him knock you to the ground and stay down. And if you do that, I will see to it that your sister gets enough money to move to a new place where she can start her life over, away from this scandal. Whether or not she wants you to go with her, I'll leave to her."

Prattle's eyelids shot up and his eyes bulged. "You would do that for us?"

"For her, Prattle, not you. Also I insist that neither of you speak of this incident again."

The man picked up his wine glass and took another long drink. He wiped his mouth with the back of his beefy hand.

"I'm glad she confessed to Sir Randolph. That was the right thing for her to do, and that is why I'm willing to do this for her. Now, do we have an agreement?"

The man looked calmer. "Yes, my lord. I know exactly what I must do."

"Good." Race slid a card toward Prattle. "This is the name of my solicitor. The day after the fight, you are to take your sister to his office and he will have everything ready for her."

The man's heavy cheeks trembled again. "I don't know what to say except thank you kindly, my lord."

"Nothing else need be said, Prattle. Feel free to finish your wine before you go, and from now on take better care of your sister."

Race rose and walked out the door.

Nineteen

TENSION COILED TIGHTLY IN RACE, BUT HE HAD NEVER seen a more beautiful day in Hyde Park. There wasn't a cloud in the azure sky. The sun beat warmly on his neck while a cool breeze stirred the midday air. A boxing match always drew crowds, especially if it was free, and this one had brought out thousands from every walk of life.

Race had never seen so many people in the park. There was chatter and laughter all around him. In the distance he heard someone playing a lively tune on a flute, and he smelled the harsh scent of burned wood from campfires. Carriages of every size and description, from gigs and curricles to fancy coaches, had been brought in close to the ring with men, women, and children standing on the seats, sitting on the rooftops, and hanging off the sides of them, hoping to get even a glimpse of the fight. More than half of the crowd that had gathered wouldn't be able to see any of the much-touted pugilists' match between Gibby and Prattle, even though Gibby had picked the highest mound in the grassy park to set up the prize ring. It was highly unlikely that more than a couple of hundred would be able to see any of it, but thousands would be able to say they had attended.

Pugilism had long been one of the most fashionable of amusements in London, even though it was usually brutal, ending only after one of the bruisers was unable to come to the scratch, which was the center of the ring, and continue the fight.

Race groaned silently at that thought. He didn't know if he could trust Prattle to keep his end of their bargain and not do irreparable damage to Gibby, but Race had resigned himself to the fact that he'd done all he could to ensure that Gibby wouldn't be hurt too badly. And to ensure that Gibby wouldn't ever find out what he had done to help him.

Race looked over at Susannah, who sat beside him, and smiled to himself. He loved her more than he would have thought possible. It made him feel good just sitting beside her. He had crawled through the hedge in the dark of night to see her three times this past week, and each time it became harder and harder to leave her.

Falling in love had been the last thing on his mind when Susannah had first arrived at his door. Now, he couldn't imagine her not being a part of his life. He wanted to marry her and make her completely his, but he wanted to give her more time to realize she loved him. He knew it was asking a lot of her to give up her prestigious and coveted title of duchess, but he wasn't planning on her giving it up until he convinced her he would never make her sorry she had.

Race let his gaze stray over to Mrs. Princeton, who sat on the other side of Susannah. She was giving him a less than friendly look, so Race leaned back in his chair and turned toward Blake, who was to his left. No doubt the woman had figured out by now that he was slipping into Susannah's bedchamber, judging by the evil eye she was giving him. Blake's wife Henrietta was seated beside him, with Morgan on the other side of her. They all had front-row seats for an event Race had wanted never to happen.

When they had first arrived at the park, the group of them had to wade through a sea of gorgeously gowned women wearing wide-brimmed hats and faultlessly dressed gentlemen to get to their seats in the dignitary section circling the ring. All the others were at liberty to find their own places to stand or sit, be it their carriages, their horses, or nearby trees.

Race and his cousins had wanted to ride with Gibby in his carriage to the park for this event, but he had insisted he didn't need them for anything other than as spectators. Gibby wanted only Danger Jim, who had been teaching him to box, and his assistant to be at his side during the fight.

The day before, Gibby had allowed Race and his cousins to be with him in the park as he spent an enormous amount of time making sure the ring was the right size and that chairs for the dignitaries were a safe distance from the rope.

There was talk in all the clubs that the prince himself, an ardent admirer of boxing, might appear for the match. Race had seen the Lord Mayor, the Duke of Norfolk, and several Members of Parliament, but so far he hadn't seen anything to suggest that the prince would be in attendance.

With all the advance advertisements that had been plastered all over London by Gibby and others, Race didn't think anyone remembered or even cared why Prattle and Gibby were going to box. The crowd just wanted to see a free fight.

"I can tell you are nervous for him," Susannah said in a quiet voice.

He turned to her and sighed. "I was hoping it wouldn't show, but yes, I'm worried about the old man. It's difficult to bear the thought that he might get half his teeth knocked out, his jaw broken, or worse."

Susannah's face wrinkled in quiet concern. "You did what you could to stop him. He is well capable of making his own decisions. He decided he wanted to do it. Don't blame yourself for any of this."

He gave her a grateful smile and nodded. He wanted to reach over and touch her soft cheek, hold her hand and lean in close to her, but knew those things were forbidden, so he refrained and promised himself she would soon be his.

"I know you told me you have never seen a boxing match, but look across the ring and directly in front of you on the first row of seats to the robust man wearing the solid red waistcoat. He is England's current boxing champion, Daniel Mendoza."

Susannah eyed the man before saying, "Ah, I had already noticed him because even from here I can see how misshapen his nose is."

"I'm told his jaw doesn't work too well, either. There are several other well-known pugilists here. At the end of the row to the left is John Jackson. He owns a fighting club. He spent a couple of days with Gibby, teaching him how to protect himself as well as how to box, before turning Gibby over to Danger Jim for more lessons. There are also several members of the Pugilistic Society here. It surprises me that they have come."

Susannah smiled at him. "Perhaps they want to make sure they have no new up-and-coming competition."

"Gibby and Prattle?" Race chuckled. "This is such an amateur fight, I doubt the bruisers are worried about two men well past their prime taking the shine off their accomplishments. The boxers probably came so they could have a good laugh."

"Tell me, did Sir Randolph ever come up with a fighting name for himself?"

Race grinned. "I think you cured him from wanting another name when you suggested he should be called a bird that looked like a lark."

Suddenly from a distance, Race heard the sound of bugles trumpeting, and everyone who was seated rose and looked behind them. Even as tall as Race was, there were so many people he couldn't see what was going on.

Morgan stood on his chair, looked around, and then

glanced down at Race and Blake with a rueful grin and said, "I don't believe this. It is Gibby's coach, being pulled by six white horses. It's decorated with red and white ribbons. There's a bugler sitting with the driver. They are both dressed in white."

Race looked at Susannah and shook his head. "I should have known Gibby would have to make a grand entrance. He is all about getting attention."

The crowd started clapping and cheering as the people parted to allow Gibby's coach to come in close to the ring. When it stopped not far from them, the footman jumped down and opened the door. Gibby stepped out, dressed in a buff-colored satin jacket with gold buttons down the front and epaulets on his shoulders.

Loud cheers and chanting of his name erupted to the point it was deafening. Gibby waved and smiled at the huge gathering. His trainer, Danger Jim, and two other bruisers stepped out of the carriage behind Gibby and flanked him as he walked to the rope, ducked under it, and entered the prize ring.

Race had no idea where Prattle came from, but all of a sudden he entered the ring from the other side, with only one lone man standing beside him. The short, thick man was wearing a simple black shirt, breeches, and stockings. There was such trepidation in Prattle's expression, he looked like a hen staring at a fox.

Gibby taunted Prattle with a wave and a smile, and the crowd roared its approval once again. Gibby then made a production of taking off his jacket and handing it to one of the men standing beside him. Most pugilists fought bare-chested, but Gibby wore a collarless, buff-colored shirt, breeches, and stockings. He looked much thinner than Prattle, and more fit and muscular than Race would have thought possible, given his age.

Race shook his head and chuckled to himself. Under any other circumstances, Sir Randolph Gibson would never appear before anyone half dressed. Even seeing it with his own eyes, Race had trouble believing Gibby was going through with this fight.

A middle-aged man dressed in a collarless white shirt and black breeches stepped into the ring, and within seconds the crowd quieted down. The referee called Gibby and Prattle to the center and talked to them for less than a minute before blowing a whistle and stepping aside.

Race tensed. He hoped Prattle kept to his part of the bargain as the two men lifted their bare knuckles into the air and began to circle each other. Race had tried to make it clear to Prattle this had to be a real fight, but he didn't want Gibby hurt. Gibby would know if Prattle just gave up and didn't try to win.

Gibby, the taller of the two men by at least a head, wasted no time advancing on Prattle, delivering several jabs to his head and a couple of punches to his stomach. From what Race could see, only one fist had actually made contact with Prattle's midsection. The crowd roared its approval of Gibby's aggressiveness with his rapid punches and dancing feet. Even though Prattle was stocky, he was quick on his feet, and he was bobbing and weaving to avoid Gibby's fast fists.

It was clear neither man really knew the art of boxing

for sport, or about timing and judgment of throwing their punches to insure accuracy, but both men were giving it a valiant effort. Suddenly one of Gibby's bare, tight-knuckled fists made contact with Prattle's chin, snapping his head back, by what seemed to be an accident to Race. The expression on Prattle's face instantly changed from fear to anger. Race moved to the edge of his seat, and so did every one else on the row chairs.

Suddenly, Prattle was the one advancing on Gibby, but the old man didn't seem bothered by it. He was quick on his feet, and by sidestepping and dancing around, he was able to avoid all of Prattle's jabs, but at the same time he wasn't able to land any of his own, either. Race's hands clenched into fists, and he flinched as one of Prattle's fists landed against Gibby's forehead. Race wanted to stop the fight before Gibby got hurt but knew he couldn't.

It seemed like hours instead of mere minutes before the whistle blew, and the two amateur bruisers went to their corners for a moment of rest and water.

When the whistle blew again, Gibby and Prattle moved back to scratch and once again started circling each other, occasionally throwing a long punch or a short jab in the other's direction, sometimes making contact and sometimes missing completely. The crowd started yelling for blood, and that sent a chill up Race's spine.

In the blink of an eye, Prattle unleashed a powerful left hook to the liver, and the blow staggered Gibby. Prattle took advantage of Gibby's weakness and went at him again, with another quick left-right combination, which sent Gibby slumping to the ground.

Race and everyone else in the dignitary seats jumped to their feet. The crowd yelled for Gibby to get up.

The referee quickly held Prattle at bay with his arm. Race felt Susannah's comforting hand touch his, and he briefly squeezed her fingertips.

Gibby scrambled to his feet and shook his head as if to clear his vision and then started his fancy footwork again. The whistle blew before he and Prattle could resume the fight, and they each retreated to their corners again.

"Shouldn't we stop this madness?" Morgan asked in an angry voice as they retook their seats and the crowd quieted down. "Haven't we let this go on long enough now?"

"No," Race said reluctantly. "This is Gibby's wish. Not ours. We have to let him fight it out."

"Much as I hate it," Blake said, "I agree with Race. We can't intervene."

"But that man looks like a bull, and Gib looks like a plucked ostrich. I'm afraid the man's going to kill him."

"It's still Gibby's fight," Blake said.

Race remained quiet and satisfied that he hadn't told his cousins about his talk with Prattle. From the way the fight was going, it didn't look like the man was going to keep his end of their bargain, anyway.

The whistle blew and the boxers returned to the center of the ring and started their wary dance. Prattle was sweating profusely and sucking short, shallow breaths, appearing completely winded. After only a few jabs, Race could see the bigger man was giving out fast. Gibby hadn't let his knockdown dampen his spirit or aggressiveness. He advanced on Prattle again, looking as composed and unruffled as he had when he exited his coach. Race had to hand it to the old man. He had grit. And he had certainly found his bottom where his courage was stored.

The two men circled each other and soon started throwing short jabs and long punches, neither of them very good at hitting their mark. It wasn't long before the whistle blew, and they retreated to their corners for rest, for water, and for a pep talk from the men waiting for them ringside.

The fourth round started, and it seemed as if Gibby and Prattle were evenly matched in the amount of punches thrown by each of them. Prattle had an eye that was almost swollen shut, and Gibby had blood at the side of his mouth. All of a sudden, Prattle connected with a strong, fast right to Gibby's stomach, and he doubled over, clearly in pain. Race watched as if in slow motion as Prattle moved in close with his right arm cocked, ready to wallop Gibby and finish him off.

Race, Susannah, and the rest of the entourage sprang to their feet and yelled, "Gibby!"

Sir Randolph Gibson must have heard them, because he straightened and as he came up he landed a stunning right uppercut to Prattle's double chin.

Spittle flew from his mouth, sweat flung from his body as Prattle's head snapped back. His eyes rolled back in his head, and he landed on the grassy mound with a heavy thud.

Gibby froze.

The crowd fell silent.

The referee bent over Prattle and tried to rouse him.

Race's heart hammered like a stick on a drum. He looked at the man sprawled motionless on the ground. Was Prattle faking the knockout? If so, he was doing a damned good job of it. Race had seen enough fights to know that it looked as if Gibby had somehow literally knocked the man cold.

The official rose and yelled, "He's out!"

The crowd went wild with loud cheers and thunderous clapping.

Gibby held both fists into the air and gave a victory shout as the two men who stood with him wrapped his jacket around his shoulders.

Race felt limp with relief. He didn't know why he had ever worried about Gibby. The man lived a charmed life and was obviously more than able to take care of himself.

Not caring at the moment who in the crowd might see or what they might say, Race reached down and hugged Susannah to him briefly. She would be his wife soon enough. Somehow, he was going to make sure of that.

Twenty

THE LARGE DOORS OF THE GREAT HALL WERE OPEN wide so the evening's cooling breeze could flow through the stuffy ballroom. Music, laughter, and chatter hummed excitedly throughout the room. Hundreds of candles glittered and sparkled off the walls, making the hall bright and cheerful as Susannah danced across the floor with the handsome Lord Westford, who was doing his best to impress her with his charming smile.

Facing Lord Westford in the quadrille, Susannah twirled under his arm, sidestepped, and clapped her hands. She curtsied and smiled at him in all the right places, but her mind wasn't on the earl. She had thoughts for no one but Lord Raceworth. Her gaze kept straying to the entrance of the ballroom as she waited for him to appear.

Lord Westford seemed very fit and quite intelligent. He would be a suitable catch for any lady, but Susannah felt no spark of romantic interest when she looked at him. Race had already captured her heart. She didn't know why she hadn't told him so these past few days. Perhaps she was just waiting for him to recognize, himself, that he had her heart safely in his care.

Immediately after Sir Randolph's victory, Susannah had insisted Race go with his cousins to follow Sir Randolph to his house. Even though Race was elated the dashing fellow had won, she could see concern for him in Race's eyes. She knew he wanted to make sure his friend of long standing was going to be all right and have no lasting ill effects from the hard blows he took from Mr. Prattle.

Susannah and Race had quickly agreed to attend the party at the Great Hall before he left with Blake and Morgan.

Finally, the dance ended, and Lord Westford politely escorted her back to where Mrs. Princeton sat chatting with some aging dowagers, but before Susannah could catch her breath Captain Spyglass walked up to her and bowed.

"Good evening, Duchess. Might I say that you are a vision of beauty tonight?"

Susannah smiled cautiously and said, "Thank you, Captain Spyglass. And how are you on this fine evening?"

Susannah still considered him the primary suspect for stealing the Talbot pearls. Once again, he was wearing more pearls than she had ever seen any woman wear.

Tonight, he wore only one earring that consisted of three rather small pearls that fell from a gold stud. Clusters of pearls took the place of buttons on his waistcoat.

"I'm very well, Duchess, but busy. I wanted to make sure I spoke to you this evening, for this may be the last party I'm able to attend. I'll be leaving London soon."

Susannah's heart started pounding. Trying to sound normal, she said, "But the Season is not over. Why would you leave before the last party?"

"I never stay too long in one place. My heart is full of wandering. I have made many friends here and will not hesitate to return to London one day, but for now, I'm ready to set sail for warmer climates. I've decided England is too wet for springtime."

"So, will you be sailing for the South of France, or perhaps Italy?"

He laughed. "No, I won't be that close by. I will be sailing to much warmer climates than that. I will probably find an island in the Caribbean, though which one I haven't decided on. Please excuse me, Duchess." He bowed again. "I see our host for the evening and I must go speak to him."

"Of course," she said. "I wish you Godspeed wherever your journeys take you."

As the captain turned away, so did Susannah. Where was Race? She had been at the party for at least two hours, and there had been no sign of him or Sir Randolph. She was beginning to worry that something was wrong with Race or the winner of the fight.

She was anxious to tell Race about Captain Spyglass's

plans to leave. Even though Race had runners watching the Captain's every move, he would still want to know the man intended to exit London soon.

"Your Grace, how wonderful to see you this evening. Your eyes are so bright they could light the night sky."

Susannah forced a smile and said, "Thank you, Lord Snellingly. How are you?"

"Never better now that I'm looking at your fair face," he said, holding a piece of paper as well as a handkerchief in his hand. "It just so happens I have a poem here that I wrote for you a few days ago. It's not long. Only four lines. May I please?"

Maybe if she let him read the poem, he would stop pressing her about it. "All right, Lord Snellingly, please do."

He cleared his throat and sniffed as he looked down at the paper and read:

> "Mere words are inadequate
> When candlelight graces your face
> I long to tell you of my love, dear one
> With a fierceness that clutches my
> heart like a summer wind."

Susannah stared at him, speechless, searching for something nice to say about his dreadful poem, when suddenly a man's hand slid in front of her and gave her a glass of champagne. Susannah turned and saw Race standing so close to her she could feel the warmth of his body.

He smiled, and her heart fluttered excitedly. All her earlier frustrations melted away.

"Excuse us, Snellingly," Race said and ushered Susannah away from the poet.

"Thank you for rescuing me. He was reading me a poem that was positively dreadful."

"I've heard his poetry and I agree. But it seems you have been busy tonight. You were talking with Spyglass."

She gave him a teasing smile. "Well, you know better than I what Lord Chesterfield said about 'while the cat is away.'"

Race moved closer to her, and in a low voice said, "The mice will play. And yes, thanks to my grandmother, I know Lord Chesterfield's poppycock better than I know the back of my hand, and that saying did not come from him, but I do think it fits you perfectly right now."

"It's so easy to attribute everything to him, don't you think?"

"Yes, whether he said it or not." Race took a sip of his champagne. "Now, tell me, what did Spyglass have to say?"

"As it happens, the captain told me something very interesting. He said this would probably be his last party as he will be leaving London soon."

The humor left Race's face, and his eyes narrowed. "That could mean he is already preparing the *Golden Pearl* to set sail."

"My thoughts exactly. Mr. Bickerman is going to have to make haste with his plans if the pearls are on his ship, as we suspect."

"I'll talk to Bickerman later tonight and tell him about this, if he doesn't already know about Spyglass's plans. He's keeping a tight watch on the ship. But don't worry, Susannah, I'll see to it that Captain Spyglass's ship doesn't leave port until it has been thoroughly searched, even if I have to get the Thames Police to detain it. Now, I don't want you worrying about any of this. Bickerman will take care of everything. Understood?"

"Race, I trust you completely."

His gaze swept lovingly across her face. "That's what I wanted to hear."

For reasons she didn't understand, Susannah suddenly felt shy. "I was watching the entrance for you. I didn't see you come in."

"I came in one of the side doors with Gibby and my cousins. We knew if we came in the front doors, Gib would immediately be swamped with people wanting to congratulate him."

"How is Sir Randolph?"

"You mean other than the fact he has a cut lip, a black eye, and very swollen knuckles?"

"Ouch!" she said with a grimace.

Race chuckled. "No, really, he's doing exceptionally well for an old man who went four rounds in the prize ring."

"I'd like to see him and offer my congratulations on his victory."

"Let's go and do it now, as I'm desperate to have some time alone with you."

They started toward the ballroom. "I don't think that will be possible tonight."

His brows drew together as they made their way through the crush of people. "Duchess, that is not what I want to hear from you."

"You must speak to Mr. Bickerman about Captain Spyglass's ship."

"Never fear. That will be done first. But then I'm coming to see you, and I will continue until you come to your senses and agree to marry me."

Susannah gasped and looked around. "Race, you shouldn't say that so loud. Someone might hear you."

He smiled. "So be it. I am not afraid to let people know that I love you and I want to marry you."

Susannah's heart lifted; her hands trembled with expectancy. She stopped in the middle of the room. "Are you really asking me to marry you?"

Suddenly a hand clapped Race on the back, and Blake, Henrietta, Morgan, and Sir Randolph gathered around them. Susannah smiled as greetings were exchanged among the group. There would be time later to talk to Race about love and marriage. But for now, she was so happy he wanted to marry her, she felt as if she were walking on air.

She knew she was not Race's cousins' favorite person, but at least they tolerated her in good humor. She liked the fact that it didn't bother Race, but instead he reveled in it. Sir Randolph's face was horrifying. Both his eyes were swollen as well as one side of his mouth, and there was a cut above one eye.

"Sir Randolph," Susannah said, "how wonderful to see you looking so well. Congratulations on your victory."

The dapper gentleman bowed. "Duchess, thank you kindly. There was one time this afternoon I was beginning to have doubts as to whether I would win."

"I never lost faith in you," she said with encouragement.

"I want everyone to know that Gibby promised us," Race said, pointing to his two cousins, "that he would never do anything as foolish as this fight ever again. We intend to hold him to that."

"I gave my word," Sir Randolph added.

"And we all know what your word means to you, don't we?" Henrietta said.

"Indeed we do," Susannah agreed. "I believe he once said something to the fact that if a man loses his wealth, he's lost nothing. If he loses his good health, he's lost something, but if he loses his honor, he's lost everything."

"That is exactly what Lord Chesterfield said, and I believe it and live by every word of it," Sir Randolph agreed.

Morgan chuckled. "I think one or both of you have added words or taken words from Chesterfield's actual quote, but you are probably close enough."

Susannah noticed, as they continued to chat, that the noise in the room slowly got quieter. Suddenly, she saw the people in front of them stepping aside, parting as if to let someone pass. Gasps and soft whispers rumbled throughout the room.

Race gave Susannah a questioning glance. "I wonder what's going on."

"I have no idea."

"Maybe the prince came in to offer his congratulations to Sir Randolph," Henrietta offered.

"Can't be," Gibby said. "He's already sent me a congratulatory note. Besides that, the prince always has someone announce him. But I don't know of anyone else who would bring about this kind of hush in such a large crowd."

"Damnation," Morgan said and then looked at Race. "It's not the prince, but who the hell is she?"

Morgan pointed to the entrance to the ballroom where on the landing stood a regal older lady dressed completely in black except for five strands of pearls that circled her neck and fell to her waist.

Race's chest tightened as he stared at the pale woman surveying the faces in the ballroom.

"Who is she?" Blake whispered.

"I have no idea," Race murmured. "I've never seen her before, but I have seen those pearls around our grandmother's neck many times."

Susannah swallowed a lump of fear that lodged in her throat and took her breath. Slowly she stepped forward. "I know her. She is my mother, Mrs. Madeline Parker."

Race whipped his head around to Susannah and she groaned. She saw doubt and distrust in his eyes once again. What was her mother doing walking into the ballroom wearing the pearls?

"Race, let me explain," she whispered.

His eyes were wide with disbelief. "You took the pearls and gave them to your mother?"

His accusation stung. "Race, no."

"You told me you didn't steal the pearls and I believed you."

"I didn't," Susannah insisted.

His gaze held fast to hers, as if he searched for answers. She couldn't believe this was happening after their relationship had just begun to heal.

"Are you telling me your mother stole them?"

Susannah gasped in shock. "Of course not. I asked her to send them, not bring them and wear them. Let me explain."

"There's no time for that, Duchess," Morgan said. "Spyglass and Winston are descending on your mother right now, and she looks like she's about to faint."

"With those pearls around her neck, she could be in danger," Blake added. "I don't trust either one of them. They might try to grab the pearls and run. We've got to get her out of here."

"Morgan is right. You can explain at your house, Susannah," Race said. "Right now, we have to get your mother home. I'll go with you and ride up front in the carriage with your driver."

"You are not leaving without us," Blake said to Race. "Morgan and I will be right behind you in my carriage, just in case Spyglass or Winston decides to follow and cause trouble. Henrietta, you ride with Gibby, and I'll see you at Susannah's house."

"Let's go," Race said. "They've reached her."

Like horses heading for the barn at feeding time, Race, Susannah, Morgan, Blake, Henrietta, and Gibby all waded through the crowd toward the entrance of the ballroom.

By the time they arrived, Spyglass and Winston were

standing in front of Susannah's mother, admiring her and the pearls. She was backing away from them, her eyes sweeping from one to the other in fear.

Susannah rushed up to her and the words started tumbling past her lips. "Mother, how did you get here? What are you doing here? You don't look well."

"I don't feel well either, Susannah. Thank God you are here." Her voice trembled and her eyes darted fitfully from side to side. She grabbed hold of Susannah's arm and held tightly.

"How did you find me here?"

"Your maid told me where you were, but I was beginning to doubt her information."

"This lovely lady is your mother?" Spyglass asked Susannah.

"Yes, I can see the resemblance now," Winston added. "We were just welcoming her to the ball."

Captain Spyglass stepped in closer. "And, Madame, may I be so bold as to ask about the exquisite pearls you are wearing?"

Susannah's mother lifted her chin disdainfully and turned her pale face away from Spyglass in contempt. "No, sir, you may not."

The Captain turned to Race. "Lord Raceworth, I know you have the Talbot pearls, so these must be Bess of Hardwick's pearls. I'm told the two collars were similar in length and rarity."

Before Race could speak, Susannah's mother clutched the pearls to her chest and said, "These are not Bess's pearls, sir. Susannah, who are these gentlemen? Is this the sort you have been cavorting with while in London? I'm astonished and can see I have arrived not a moment too soon."

Mrs. Princeton appeared as if from out of nowhere and stood close to Susannah's side, watching every man around her charge as if she was a vulture and they were her dinner. "Mother, I was preparing to leave. I need you to accompany me."

"I'll call for your carriage," Race said, throwing a quick glance at Susannah. "You get your wrap."

"Excuse us, gentlemen," Susannah said and slid her arm around her mother's arm.

"Madame, before you go," Captain Spyglass said, "I would very much like to call on you and talk to you about the pearls you are wearing. I collect pearls."

"And I buy jewels for the prince," Mr. Winston said, elbowing in front of the pirate. "I know Prinny would be interested in your exquisite necklace."

Race stepped between Susannah's mother and the men. "Take your mother to your carriage."

Susannah immediately started walking toward the door with Mrs. Princeton on one side and her mother on the other. Morgan and Blake followed her.

"I have always wanted to see the Talbot pearls," Captain Spyglass said to Race with a smoldering glow in his eyes. "I don't suppose you would agree to let me have just a glimpse of them before I leave London, would you, my lord?"

Race looked at the man with contempt in his eyes. "Not a chance in hell, Captain." Race cut his eyes around to Winston. "That goes for you, too. Stay away from the duchess's house or I'll see to it that both your bodies are found at the bottom of the Thames."

Winston gasped.

Spyglass laughed.

Race strode out of the ballroom and into the night air, his mind whirling with possibilities. Was the reason Susannah hadn't told him she loved him because she knew all along where his grandmother's pearls were? She must have known her mother had them. But she looked as shocked as he was to see her mother. If Susannah didn't steal them, who did and how did Mrs. Parker get them?

No matter what the true answer was, he was certain that right now Susannah was wondering how she was going to explain it to him. Whatever the answer, he was not going to turn his back on Susannah again. He loved her, and he intended to marry her.

It was a wet ride to Susannah's house, but they made it inside without incident. Susannah had one of her servants stoke the fire in her sitting room to take the chill off the dampness, and then pass a glass of sherry to everyone except Henrietta and Sir Randolph who had not yet arrived. Susannah had made her mother comfortable on the settee with a blanket tucked around her legs. Her face was ashen, and Race noticed she cupped her glass with both hands to hold it steady enough to take a sip. It was obvious to him that the woman was not well.

After proper introductions were made, Susannah turned to Race with somber eyes and said, "May I explain?"

"Please do, Duchess," Morgan answered for Race. "Because right now someone in this room is looking guilty of theft."

"Enough, Morgan," Race told him.

Susannah walked over and stood in front of Race. "More than a week ago, I wrote to my mother and asked her to send the fake pearls she is wearing to me."

"Wait a minute," Race interrupted. "Those aren't real?"

"Fearing I must be in some kind of trouble, she decided to leave her sick bed and bring them to me."

"Let me tell him, dearest," her mother said in a soft voice as she lifted the strands in her hands. "Yes, my lord, these are nothing but glass beads expertly made to look like pearls." With shaky hands, she held them up for his close inspection. "As best I understand it, the Talbot pearls were pawned by one of Lord Talbot's daughters after his death. They ended up in the hands of a wealthy merchant. My father bought them from that merchant for my mother at a great cost. My mother had such fear they would be stolen that she had a jeweler make a copy to look as much like the real ones as possible. These." She fingered the pearls as her mind seemed to drift back in time.

"Go on, Mrs. Parker," Race said.

"Unfortunately, the real ones were eventually stolen from my mother anyway by a trusted servant who knew the difference between the fake and the genuine. The servant was never seen or heard from again. No doubt he sold them to whoever bought them for your grandmother or, who knows, they could have changed hands several times before Lady Elder obtained them."

Race turned confused eyes to Susannah. "Why didn't you tell me about this?"

Susannah's stomach was jumpy. She would rather have been alone with Race to explain all this to him, but she couldn't very well ask his cousins to leave.

Taking a deep breath, she said, "At first there was no reason to tell you. We were not on the best of terms with each other when I asked her to send them to me. And later when we, ah, well…" she said, stumbling over her words.

"When our relationship mended," Race said.

Susannah gave him a grateful smile. "Yes. I hadn't heard from my mother and didn't know if she would send them. I thought it best not to tell you about the fake pearls until I could show them to you. My plan was to do exactly what my mother did tonight. I would wear them with the hope of drawing out the real thief and make him wonder if he had the real pearls or the glass beads. It never dawned on me that anyone would think they were Bess of Hardwick's pearls."

Susannah's mother reached up and touched her arm affectionately. "Though Susannah worded her letters carefully, I sensed she needed my help. I decided to come to London without her knowledge. I had to stop often to rest, so it took me longer to get here than I had hoped. When I arrived tonight, she had already left for the evening. I asked her maid where she had gone and then dressed and followed her."

Morgan threw up his hands. "All of this is well and good, but we still don't know where the real pearls are."

"No, but this was a clever idea," Race said. "Mrs. Parker told Spyglass they were not Bess's pearls. So perhaps whichever man has the real pearls will be looking for an expert to examine them first thing tomorrow morning to make sure they have the Talbot pearls, and Bickerman's runners will be there to capture them."

"Your Grace?"

Susannah turned to her companion. "Yes, Mrs. Princeton?"

"Sir Randolph and the Duchess of Blakewell are here to see you."

"Show them in."

Sir Randolph and Henrietta walked in, and Susannah noticed at once that Sir Randolph was carrying a small satchel.

Introductions were made, and Race took time to briefly tell them about the fake pearls.

"I knew that," Sir Randolph said.

He reached into the satchel he carried and pulled out a black velvet drawstring bag. Susannah's mother and Race gasped as they recognized the black bag. From inside, Sir Randolph drew out five long strands of pearls.

"Those are the real pearls," her mother said, reaching for them. "I would know them anywhere."

"Gibby?" Race questioned with denial etched in his face. "How did you get those?"

"I stole them from you. I am the thief," he answered.

"Why? How? How did you get into my safe?"

"As to how, I might be old but I still have a few tricks up my sleeve. I was in the King's army for several years. I learned a few things during that time."

Sir Randolph walked over to Race. "I meant only to take the pearls, but figured if I did that, you might know it was me, so I took everything else that was in your safe. It's all in there," he said placing the satchel on a chair. "As to why I had to take the pearls, they belonged to your grandmother. I had to protect them for her. When the fourth person came knocking on your door wanting them, I knew it was only a matter of time before someone tried to steal them from you so I decided to do it before anyone else had the chance."

"Why didn't you tell me?" Race asked.

Sir Randolph's smile was misshapen from swelling. "Now why would I have done something like that? You would have made me give them back to you."

"Gibby, do you know what I have been through trying to find out who took those pearls?"

"Maybe."

"Maybe?" Race said angrily as he advanced on the battered man. "You know that I accused Susannah of taking them."

Gibby looked at Susannah. "I'm sorry about that, but there was nothing I could do."

"I should wring your neck and finish what Prattle—"

"Race," Blake said and stepped in front of him.

"It doesn't matter now," Morgan added. "The pearls are back in your possession. That's all that matters."

"I'm afraid not," Susannah's mother said in a quiet

voice from the settee. "There's the matter that they rightfully belong to me. Susannah has documents proving my
grandfather bought the Talbot pearls and where they
were reported stolen. The pearls belong to me."

"I'm keeping the pearls, Mrs. Parker," Race said without hesitating.

Susannah's mother's eyes widened and she looked to
Susannah for help.

It had always been Susannah's fear that if Race found
the necklace he would keep it. "Mother, the marquis has
promised me that he will look at our evidence, and I'm
sure that once he does he will have a change of heart as to
who they belong to."

"No, I won't," Race said as he walked over to stand
by Susannah. "They belong to the Raceworth family." He
looked over at Mrs. Parker and said, "With your permission, I'd like to marry your daughter."

Susannah gasped and felt her heart rising up to her
throat. Race looked at her with loving eyes before gazing
back at her mother.

"The Talbot pearls will no longer be yours or mine. I
will give them to Susannah on our wedding day, and then
they will be hers."

Race took Susannah's hand and kissed it. "I know
I'm asking a lot of you to give up your title as duchess to
marry me, but I promise to love you forever and never
make you sorry you agreed."

Susannah was too astonished, too euphoric to speak
at first because he had asked her in front of everyone.
"You want me to marry you?"

He smiled. "As soon as I can make it happen."

"Yes," she said without hesitation as she looked up into his glowing eyes. "I love you, Race, and I will gladly give up my title to marry you."

The room erupted into cheers and clapping from everyone, including Susannah's mother.

Race bent down and whispered into Susannah's ear, "Leave your door unlocked. I will be coming through the yew again tonight."

"You can't. My mother is here," she whispered back to him.

"Then I suggest you put her on the second floor with Mrs. Princeton. I will not be denied your bed tonight."

Race turned to Susannah's mother and with a smile said, "Hide your eyes if you so desire, Mrs. Parker, because I'm about to kiss your daughter."

Without further warning, Race pulled Susannah into his arms and kissed her soundly on the lips.

Susannah thrilled to his touch.

THE END

Don't miss the first book in The Rogues' Dynasty series
from *New York Times* bestselling author Amelia Grey

A Duke
TO DIE FOR

Available now from Sourcebooks Casablanca

My Dearest Grandson Lucien,

You would do well in life to heed Lord Chesterfield's wise words: "Never put off till tomorrow what you can do today."

Your loving Grandmother,
Lady Elder

LUCIEN TRENT, THE FIFTH DUKE OF BLAKEWELL, strode through the front door of his town house, taking off his riding gloves.

"Your Grace, I'm glad you're home."

"Not now, Ashby," Blake said, tossing his gloves, hat, and cloak into the butler's hands without breaking his stride. "I don't have time." He'd stayed too long at the shooting match, and now he was running late.

One of his cousins was racing a new horse in Hyde Park at four o'clock, and the other had a high-stakes card game starting at six. Blake didn't plan on missing either event. But in order to make both, he had to finish reviewing at least one account book for his solicitor. The poor fellow had been begging for them for over a month.

From the corridor, Blake walked into his book room. Piled high on his desk was the stack of ledgers, numerous miscellaneous correspondence, and invitations he'd left unopened for weeks.

He shrugged out of his coat, loosened his neckcloth, and sat down at his desk with an impatient sigh. There were times when being a duke was downright hellish.

Grudgingly, he opened the top book, determined to make a dent in the work he had to do.

"I'm sorry to disturb you, Your Grace," Ashby said from the doorway.

Blake didn't bother to glance up from the ledger he was thumbing through, trying to find where he'd left off the last time he looked at it…which was too many days ago to remember. He still hadn't become completely used to hearing himself called "Your Grace," even though his father had been dead almost two years.

It was a time-consuming task, keeping up-to-date with all his holdings and property, not to mention the details of the various businesses in which his father had invested over the years. His solicitor constantly sent documents for him to sign or account books to check. And, last year when his grandmother had passed on, her estate had added more responsibilities to his already full desk of unattended paperwork.

His new role in life had certainly curtailed his once

daily and quite enjoyable activities of riding, fencing, and late afternoon games of billiards and cards at White's or one of the other gentlemen's clubs he belonged to. He was not accustomed to being on anyone's schedule but his own.

The butler cleared his throat.

"Yes, Ashby, what is it?" Blake finally said when it was apparent the man wasn't going to leave him alone until he had his say.

"There's a young lady here to see you, sir."

That got Blake's attention. He glanced up at the tall, thin, and immaculately dressed butler, who wore his long graying hair held neatly away from his sharp face in a queue.

"A young lady, you say?"

"Yes, Your Grace."

"Who is she?"

"Miss Henrietta Tweed."

"Tweed," Blake said aloud as he thought about the name for a moment. He couldn't place it. "Who is with her?"

"Just her maid."

"No other chaperone?"

"None that I saw."

That was odd.

It was unusual for a young lady, or any gentleman, to call on him without making prior arrangements—and altogether inappropriate for a lady to do so without a suitable chaperone. Blake shrugged. On another afternoon he might have been intrigued by this strange request to see him, but not today. He didn't have time to entertain anyone.

"Just take her card and send her away."

Blake picked up his quill, dipped it in the ink jar he'd just opened, and returned his attention to the numbers in front of him.

"I tried that, Your Grace. She says she doesn't have a card."

The quill stilled in his hand. That was most curious, too. A woman without an appropriate chaperone and without a proper calling card. For half a second he wondered if one of the ladies he'd met earlier in the day at Hyde Park had followed him home. And there were other possibilities. It was rare, but he knew that sometimes a lady of the evening would be bold enough to seek out a titled man in hopes of bettering her station in life by earning a few coins or becoming his latest mistress.

Blake's interest was piqued once again, though he had to admit almost anything could take his mind off accounts and ledgers.

He glanced back up at the butler. "What does she look like?" he asked, thinking that would help him determine if she warranted interrupting his work.

Ashby's chin lifted and his eyebrows rose slightly. "Like a young lady."

Sometimes Blake wished he hadn't kept his father's annoying butler. The old man could be downright impudent at times. But Ashby kept the household and the sizable staff running in near-perfect order. The butler's work was testimony to the care with which his father had trained the man. That, and that alone, was what kept the aging servant at his job.

"Did she say why she wanted to see me?"

"Not exactly, Your Grace."

In exasperation, Blake laid down the quill he had just picked up. "Ashby, what the hell did she say?"

Unflustered, the butler replied, "She said you were expecting her."

"Was I?" Blake asked. Since Blake had turned off his father's secretary a few months earlier, the butler had tried to help him keep up with his social calendar, but so far neither one of them was doing a good job.

"Not that I'm aware of, Your Grace. She also said that her trunks were on the front steps."

Blake made a noise in his throat that sounded like a mixture of a grunt and a laugh. He must have been in too big a hurry to notice her luggage when he came through the front door.

"What the devil?" Blake said. "I'm expecting no one, especially a young woman with baggage and no proper chaperone. She obviously has the wrong house." He rose from his chair. "Did you question her about who she is looking for?"

"Yes, Your Grace. She said the Duke of Blakewell was expecting her."

"That's not bloody likely when I have no recollection of knowing anyone by the name of Tweed."

"She also suggested that I should speak to you at once so that you could clear up what she called my obvious confusion."

That sounded rather impertinent coming from someone who was apparently befuddled herself. No doubt the quickest way to handle this situation was for him to take a moment or two to speak with her.

Blake looked down at his paper-cluttered desk. His eyes centered on the open book in front of him, and he swore softly to himself. Reviewing the latest entries would have to wait again.

"Show her to the front parlor and say I'll be in to see her."

"Right away, Your Grace." Ashby turned stiffly and walked out.

Blake marked his place in the ledger with a dry quill. He hastily retied his neckcloth and reached for his coat. No doubt the woman had him mixed up with someone else. The sooner he dealt with the waif and sent her on her way, the faster he could get back to checking the balances in the accounts book so he wouldn't miss the race or the card game. For the most part he got along quite well with his cousins, but they would be unforgiving if they felt he'd slighted them.

When Blake approached the doorway to the drawing room, he saw a short, rotund lady with her back to him warming herself in front of the low-burning fireplace. It took only a glance at the fabric of her cloak and bonnet to know that she was not a lady of means.

What was Ashby thinking to allow her entrance into the house?

"Miss Tweed," he said, striding into the room, determined to set her straight and then have a word with his errant butler.

The chit turned to face him and he immediately realized she had on a maid's frock. At the same time, from the corner of his eye, he saw a rather tall, slender young lady rise from a side chair in the far corner and come toward him. When he looked at her, Blake felt his stomach do a slow roll. She moved with exquisite grace and an inner confidence lacking in most of the young ladies in Society.

Big, almond-shaped eyes—bluer than a midsummer sky and fringed with long black lashes—pierced him with a wary look of impatience. Her lips were full, beautifully sculpted, and the shade of spring's first rose. The color of her skin was a sheer, pale ivory, and her complexion was flawless.

She was the loveliest creature he'd ever seen.

She wore an expensively tailored black cape that parted down the front as she walked, showing a blush-colored traveling dress. Her wide-brimmed bonnet with tightly woven trim matched her cape and gloves. He couldn't help but wonder what color of hair was hidden beneath her headpiece.

For some reason he found it exceedingly seductive the way the satin ribbon of her bonnet had been tied into a perfect bow under her chin. He had a sudden urge to reach up, pull on the end of the black ribbon, and untie it…despite the fact that every inch of her said "lady."

"Yes, I'm Henrietta Tweed." She inclined her head a little as if pondering whether to say more. "I'm waiting for the Duke of Blakewell."

Blake bowed and then said, "At your service, Miss Tweed. I am he."

Her eyes narrowed slightly. That was the only outward sign that she was confused for a moment. Quickly, she regained her air of confidence. She lowered her lashes as she curtsied in front of him.

"I apologize, Your Grace. I didn't recognize you."

A prickle of desire rushed through him and settled low in his groin as he watched her dutifully acknowledge his title. He found everything about her tremendously seductive.

"No harm done," he said.

Blake's gaze swept over her face once again. She appeared to be a self-assured, capable young lady who wasn't the least bit intimidated by his title. He also noticed she wasn't indifferent to his appearance as her gaze slowly swept down to his riding boots and then innocently crawled back up to his face. Her close observation of him sent a rush of heat like he hadn't felt in years searing through his loins.

Ashby cleared his throat. "Should I have Cook prepare tea, Your Grace?"

Despite all the work he had to do, not to mention contending with a cheeky butler, Blake found himself agreeing. Quite frankly, how could he say no to this intriguing lady?

"Yes, Ashby, and take the young lady's wrap. Have tea served in here after you show Miss Tweed's maid to the kitchen for refreshments."

"Yes, Your Grace."

Blake watched as his unexpected guest took off her gloves and then untied the bow beneath her chin. Her hands were lovely and without jewels. He'd never realized just how stimulating it could be to watch a lady take off her bonnet until he found himself experiencing another twinge of desire as the soft, fluttering ribbons slid along her shoulders.

She had lush, golden blond hair arranged neatly on

top of her head, and Blake had no doubt that it would be gorgeous hanging down her back. She handed her bonnet, cape, and gloves to her maid and softly told the woman she would be fine alone and to follow the butler to the kitchen.

Blake waited to speak until the maid and Ashby left the room. "I'm afraid I don't know of you, Miss Tweed. Who is your father?"

With ease and more self-confidence than anyone her age should have, she walked closer to him, keeping her gaze pinned on his. He liked the way her carriage was straight but not stiff. He liked the way she looked directly at him and didn't try to impress him with batting lashes, false smiles, or the unnatural soft voice some ladies used when talking to him.

Blake also liked the way she looked in her simple, high-waisted traveling dress. It was long-sleeved and quite modest for the current fashion. The fabric was of a fine quality, though not the best available. The neckline was high and trimmed in dainty pink lace that made her look absolutely fetching.

He was more curious than ever to know who she was.

"My father was Sir William Tweed. Considering your age, you probably never met him. I must assume your father knew him."

"And what makes you say that?"

"Because the Duke of Blakewell is the last name on my father's list."

What in the hell was she talking about? He became more intrigued with each word she spoke.

"What list is that, Miss Tweed?"

She clasped her lovely hands together in front of her, and once again she looked straight into his eyes. "If you don't know what I'm talking about, Your Grace, we have a problem."

"At last we agree on something. Those are the truest words you have spoken thus far."

A wrinkle of concern settled between her eyes, but it in no way detracted from her beauty.

"You were supposed to receive a letter and some rather important documents from a solicitor named Mr. Conrad Milton that would announce my arrival and explain everything about me."

Blake immediately thought of his desk. Not only was the blasted thing covered in account books that hadn't been reviewed, along with papers and documents that hadn't been signed, it was littered with all kinds of correspondence that hadn't been opened.

For the first time since becoming a duke, Blake wished he had taken his responsibilities as the Duke of Blakewell a little more seriously.

"I've been behind on mail recently. Just tell me why you are here."

"All right." She unclasped her hands and calmly let her arms fall comfortably to her sides. "I am your ward and your house is supposed to be my new home."

Blake couldn't have been more shocked if she'd thrown cold water in his face.

"What? No. This is ridiculous." A strained chuckle caught briefly on his breath. "I can assure you that you are not my ward, Miss Tweed."

She took a deep breath but otherwise remained composed.

"If only that were true, Your Grace, but I'm afraid it isn't. I don't know what happened to the letter or the documents you were to receive, but rest assured there are papers that prove the Duke of Blakewell is next in line to be my legal guardian and the sole trustee of my inheritance."

"Guardian? How old are you?"

"Nineteen."

"But you carry yourself like…"

"Someone older?"

She was not only beautiful, she was perceptive, too. Why was he finding everything about her appealing? She was obviously laying out some elaborate scheme and expecting him to swallow it, yet still he found her fascinating.

"Yes," he said.

"I assure you I've had to grow up quickly."

For a moment Blake thought he saw a hint of wistfulness in her bright blue eyes, but it was so fleeting he wasn't positive. And nothing else in her manner had caused him to think she was in the least unsure of herself, which was remarkable concerning her situation, if the tale she told was true.

"Regardless of your age, I can't be your guardian. Don't you know who I am?"

A knowing smile gently lifted the corners of her attractive lips. Blake's lower body responded once again.

"Your reputation stretches much farther than all

of London, Your Grace. In the scandal sheets, you are referred to as the Devilish Duke."

Far from being insulted that she brought up that nickname Society had placed on him some years ago, he threw up his hands and said, "My point exactly. Who in their right mind would expect me to be the protector of a young lady's reputation? I'm the kind of man fathers safeguard their daughters against. There has been a mistake."

She didn't appear perturbed in the least. "I agree. I can only assume your father was the Duke of Blakewell who agreed to be my guardian, should anything happen to Lord Palmer."

"Who is Lord Palmer? I thought you said your father was Sir William Tweed."

Another smile played at the corners of her lips, irritating the hell out of him even though he found it extremely provocative. There was nothing humorous in this debacle if, by some cruel twist of fate, she had truly been left to his care.

"Lord Palmer was my guardian for the past year and a half. Before him there was Lord Brembly, and before him, Viscount Westhavener."

Blake stared in disbelief. "How many guardians have you had?"

Very sensibly she said, "Far too many, I assure you, Your Grace."

"I'm trying hard not to be frustrated, Miss Tweed, but I'm not making much progress because I'm not seeing a connection between you and me, or my father."

She remained so calm it was maddening. It annoyed

the hell out of him and challenged him at the same time. This lady was very confident of her place in life, though he couldn't imagine why, considering the convoluted story coming out of her.

She lifted her slightly arched brows. "I'm afraid the explanation is rather lengthy."

Blake glanced up at the clock on the mantel. It was past three o'clock already, and he hadn't even started on the accounting ledger. No doubt he wouldn't make it to see Morgan's horse compete at Rotten Row—and he wouldn't make Race's card game either if he didn't get Miss Tweed settled right away. The work for his solicitor would just have to wait until tomorrow.

"As soon as I find or receive the correspondence you've mentioned, I'll have my solicitor look it over and straighten this out. In the meantime, tell me where you need to go tonight, and I'll see that you get there."

Her shoulders stiffened, though just barely. "I have nowhere to go, Your Grace, but here."

Those simple but unflinching words took the starch out of him. Either she had come up with the grandest scheme imaginable to get in his good graces, or she was serious.

Blake turned away from her for a moment and silently cursed under his breath. What the bloody hell was he going to do with her?

He turned back to face her and said, "Perhaps you have a relative or a friend who will take you in."

"None that I know of."

"You have no relatives at all?"

His question brought a long moment of silence from

her. There was an uncertain quality to her eyes as they searched his face.

"Surely if there were anyone, my father would have put their name on the list before that of a stranger."

That she had no one was hard for him to believe. Sometimes Blake felt as if he were in some way related to half the people in London, and because of his grandmother's four marriages, he probably was.

"I've had a very long day, Your Grace. May I sit down?" she asked.

He couldn't very well say no. "Yes, of course."

If he'd been thinking clearly, he would have asked her to take a seat earlier, but nothing had gone as it should have from the moment he walked through his front door. Ashby had even had to prompt him to do the proper thing and offer tea.

She sat on the dark-green brocade settee with surprising assuredness for a nineteen-year-old with no place to stay. Blake was in no mood to sit still, but he took a side chair opposite her anyway.

Mrs. Ellsworth, his housekeeper, brought in a tray with tea and placed it on the table that stood between him and his guest. Blake waited impatiently while tea was poured, though he declined a cup.

He watched Miss Tweed sip her tea from the dainty china and noticed her hands again. He liked the feminine look of them. Her fingers appeared smooth and nimble, nails neatly trimmed. He had the sudden thought of those hands feather-soft on his chest, trailing seductively over his body.

Blake mentally shook himself and said, "It looks as if I'm going to need that lengthy explanation after all, Miss Tweed. Where exactly did you say you come from?"

"Originally?" That wistful look came into her eyes, but again only for a moment. She took a deep breath, and he had the feeling she was calling on some inner strength to sustain her.

Blake realized that she wasn't one to feel sorry for herself, and he liked that about her. He rarely noticed so many things about any young lady. Over years of attending the Season, he'd come to think that there was little difference among them, but Miss Tweed could have him rethinking that.

"I was born in Dover, but I haven't lived there for quite some time. My parents were killed in a carriage accident when I was seven. I went to live with my only relative, my father's half brother, Lord Phillip Bennett, and his lady. Unfortunately, Lord Phillip met with an untimely death at sea a couple of years later. Viscount and Viscountess Westhavener were next on the list. They were wonderful to me. They hired a governess who taught me to read, write, and add numbers as well as all the things a young lady is supposed to learn to adequately manage a large household. I was with them for four and a half years."

"Then what happened?"

"Viscount Westhavener was struck by lightning late one afternoon as he walked in his garden. The viscountess asked that I be allowed to stay with her, but unfortunately it couldn't be allowed. My guardianship had already been decided by my father's long and able list.

"I had to go live with Lord Brembly and his lady in Dorset. When he died by falling off the roof, I was uprooted once again and sent to Mr. Henry Pippin's home in Essex. He was thrown from his horse and killed shortly after I arrived, so I was moved yet again to Lord Palmer's home. Regrettably, he succumbed to consumption only a few weeks ago."

"Bloody hell, that's way too many guardians to have had in twelve years!"

"Yes, it's been most unfortunate. And now I find myself at the door of the last man on the list."

"Mine. The Duke of Blakewell."

"Yes."

Damnation. If all she said was true, and it was too bizarre not to be, what was he going to do about her? He was having a devil of a time just keeping up with his duties as a duke. And now he was being pressured by some political hogs to take his father's place in Parliament. But all that aside, there was no way he could take on the responsibility of a young lady. He didn't have a thought in hell about what to do with her.

"Miss Tweed, if my father and mother were here, I'm sure they would be honored to abide by your father's wishes and take care of you. But as you can understand, I can't be your guardian."

He wasn't sure what he expected from her, but it wasn't the spark of triumph that flashed in her bright eyes. She looked pleased, as if he'd said exactly what she wanted to hear.

"I understand perfectly, Your Grace, if you feel you

can't be my guardian. I'm going to be twenty at the end of summer, and I truly don't need anyone to look after me. I'm more than qualified to take care of myself. All you need to do is draw up a document and sign it, giving me power to be mistress over my inheritance."

Blake gazed at her lovely face. He could see in the expression on her face and in her blue eyes that she believed what she was saying. She thought she could handle her affairs and take care of herself as proficiently as a man. He almost laughed. He, of all people, knew how difficult it was to keep up with account books.

She had the countenance of an innocent, not the guise of a woman of the world. Looking at her then, he knew a guardian was exactly what she needed, because he was thinking how kissable her lips looked, how soft her skin appeared, how he would love to feel her shapely body pressed solidly against his.

He cleared his throat and tamped down his wayward thoughts. She was not trying to be seductive in any manner, yet he found her immensely so.

"I'm still not totally convinced I'm in charge of you, but I'm certainly not about to sign anything at this point."

She placed her empty cup on the tray. "Once you are convinced that what I say is true, I hope you will reconsider allowing me to be mistress of my inheritance. Besides, it's in your own best interest. I don't want to see anything happen to you."

That was an odd statement. "What are you talking about?"

"The inevitable, Your Grace. All five of my previous

guardians have died. There is a curse on the list of names my father made all those years ago. If you take on the responsibility of being my guardian, I'm afraid you will die, too."

A quick smile parted his lips, and then he laughed with ease. She was so refreshingly direct that he was absolutely taken with her.

"You must be trying to amuse me, Miss Tweed. Congratulations. It's working. But I'm afraid your mind is playing tricks with you. There is no such thing as a curse."

She gave him an indulgent smile but said, "I beg to differ. Everyone who has ever been responsible for me and my considerable inheritance has died an untimely death."

Blake had no intention of dying any time soon.

He gave her a roguish smile and said, "Bad luck, Miss Tweed. It's all just bad luck."

She sat back in the settee and folded her hands in her lap. "Then perhaps you need to think long and hard about that, Your Grace, because all that bad luck just landed at your door."

About the Author

New York Times and *USA Today* bestselling author Amelia Grey's awards include the Booksellers Best, Aspen Gold, and the Golden Quill. Writing as Gloria Dale Skinner, she won the coveted Romantic Times Award for Love and Laughter and the prestigious Maggie Award. Her books have sold to many countries in Europe, Indonesia, Russia, and most recently to Japan. Several of her books have also been featured in Doubleday and Rhapsody Book Clubs.

Amelia read her first romance book when she was thirteen and has been a devoted reader of love stories ever since. She is the author of over twenty-five books. Happily married to her high school sweetheart for over thirty-five years, Amelia lives in Northwest Florida.

A DUKE TO DIE FOR

Stunning Regency romance from *New York Times* and *USA Today* bestselling author Amelia Grey

Miss Henrietta Tweed is convinced that she carries a curse—one that's responsible for killing her previous guardians. So when she's sent to Lucien Trent, the fifth Duke of Blakewell and the last man her father trusted to care for her, she knows the only way to save the duke is to persuade him to sign over her inheritance and set her free. Lucien doesn't believe there's a curse, but he is certainly more enchanted by Henrietta than he ever expected to be…

"Intriguing danger, sharp humor, and plenty of simmering sexual chemistry."

—*Booklist*

For more info about Sourcebooks's books and authors, visit:

sourcebooks.com

AN INCONVENIENT DUKE

When the duke starts searching for
answers...no one's secrets are safe

Marcus Braddock, former general and newly appointed Duke
of Hampton, is back from war. Now, not only is he surrounded
by the utterly unbearable ton, but he's mourning the death of
his beloved sister, Elise. Marcus believes his sister's death was
no accident and he's determined to learn the truth—starting
with Danielle, his sister's beautiful best friend.

**"As steamy as it is sweet as it is luscious.
My favorite kind of historical!"**

—Grace Burrowes, *New York Times* bestselling author,
for *Dukes Are Forever*

For more info about Sourcebooks's
books and authors, visit:

sourcebooks.com

AN UNEXPECTED EARL

The Earl is playing a deep game...
and he's got everything to lose

Brandon Pearce, former brigadier and now the Earl West, is determined to help the girl he once loved save her property and the charity she's been struggling to build. But he'll have to deceive her first...

Sexy Regency featuring a second-chance romance between a stubborn ex-soldier facing a new kind of enemy, and a strong-headed heroine who will fight tooth and nail for those she loves.

"Enchanting...Harrington combines suspenseful mystery and charming romance in this compulsively readable treat."

—*Publishers Weekly* for *An Inconvenient Duke*

LESSONS IN FRENCH

Poignant and delightful Regency romance from
beloved, bestselling author Laura Kinsale

Trevelyan de Monceaux and Lady Callista Taillefaire were
childhood sweethearts with a taste for adventure, until the fate-
ful day Callista's father discovered them embracing and drove
Trevelyan away in disgrace. Nine years later, Trev is back, and
as they get embroiled in all manner of mischief, Callie discovers
Trev can still make her blood race and fill her life with excitement. But the secret he's hiding means he can't give her what
she wants most—himself.

**"Kinsale creates magic... I wish for every
romance reader...to experience the singular and
extraordinary pleasures of a Laura Kinsale novel."**

—Lisa Kleypas, *New York Times* bestselling author

EARL'S WELL THAT ENDS WELL

A lonely Earl finds love where he least expects it...

Arthur Shelton, Earl of Macklin, has helped four young noblemen recover from grief and find love, but he's learned to live his own life as a widower. Then he encounters Teresa Alvarez de Granada, a charming Spanish noblewoman, and is immediately entranced...

"A daringly different kind of Regency...a charmingly rendered romance."

—*Booklist* for *A Duke Too Far*

For more info about Sourcebooks's books and authors, visit:

sourcebooks.com

A DUKE TOO FAR

Secrets to reveal, legends to unravel,
and a love to fight for...

Peter Rathbone, Duke of Compton, is struggling to handle the
responsibilities of his family home and his grief over his sister
Delia's death when he's astonished by the arrival of Miss Ada
Grandison, who bears a mysterious letter that she claims holds
the secret to saving his ancestral home. Peter's life is about to
get even more complicated...

**"All the sparkling wit and flirtatious
banter of a Georgette Heyer novel."**

—*Publishers Weekly*

For more info about Sourcebooks's
books and authors, visit:

sourcebooks.com

A FAVOR FOR THE PRINCE

The prequel to Jane Ashford's beloved The Duke's Sons series, featuring the Duke's youngest son

Lord Alan Gresham is a bit embarrassed when the Prince Regent demands that he abandon his science experiments to work on an extremely important project—getting rid of a ghost. Alan is determined to debunk this obvious hoax as quickly as possible—until he meets a maddeningly forthright beauty.

Ariel Harding is also on a mission to discover the source behind the hauntings. Working together will get them the answers they seek. But only if they can keep their hands off each other...

"Jane Ashford absolutely delights."

—*Night Owl Reviews* TOP PICK for *Nothing Like a Duke*

THE HEIR

A *Publishers Weekly* Best Book of the Year

An earl who can't be bribed. A lady
who can't be protected...

Gayle Windham, Earl of Westhaven, is the dutiful heir of the
Duke of Moreland. Tired of his father's unrelenting pressure to
marry, he escapes to his London townhouse for the summer,
where he finds himself intrigued by the secretive ways of his
beautiful housekeeper. Anna Seaton is a talented, educated
woman...so what is she doing here?

**"Luminous and graceful...a refreshing
and captivating love story."**

—*Publishers Weekly* Starred Review

For more info about Sourcebooks's
books and authors, visit:

sourcebooks.com

THE SOLDIER

New York Times bestseller

A weary soldier home from war. A beautiful
neighbor who could be his salvation...

Even in the quiet countryside, Devlin St. Just, the oldest but
illegitimate son of the Duke of Moreland, can find no peace.
His idyllic estate is falling down from neglect, and nightmares of war give him no rest. Then Devlin meets his new
neighbor...

**"A delicious, sensual historical romance
capturing the spirit of the time."**

—*Booklist*

THE WINDHAMS: THE DUKE'S DAUGHTERS

From breathtaking ballrooms to the picturesque countryside, *New York Times* and *USA Today* bestselling author Grace Burrowes takes you to a Regency England you won't want to leave...

Lady Sophie's Christmas Wish

Expected to join her family for Christmas in Kent, Lady Sophie Windham finds herself trapped in London by a snowstorm, with an abandoned baby and only the assistance of a kind, handsome stranger standing between her and complete disaster...

Lady Maggie's Secret Scandal

Lady Maggie Windham has secrets...and she's been perfectly capable of keeping them—until now. When a blackmailer threatens to expose Maggie's parentage, she turns to investigator Benjamin Hazlit to keep catastrophe at bay.

Lady Louisa's Christmas Knight

No one would guess that Lady Louisa Windham hides a scandalous secret—except perhaps family friend Sir Joseph Carrington, a man with secrets of his own.

Lady Eve's Indiscretion

Lady Eve Windham needed a plan. What she found was a marquis. When Evie suggests to Lucas Denning that they could be each other's decoy to ward off their matchmaking families, it seems like a perfect plan....

"With stunning sensuality between realistic characters, the simple truth is that Grace Burrowes always delivers a delectable story."

—*The Romance Reviews*

For more info about Sourcebooks's books and authors, visit:

sourcebooks.com

Also by Amelia Grey